My Heart Is Human

Other books by Reese Hogan

The Deadliest Echo
Shrouded Loyalties
Holding the Ashes

Anthologies:
The World of Juno
Clockwork, Curses, and Coal

My Heart Is Human

Reese Hogan

Content Warnings:

This story includes child endangerment, violence, and brief scenes of deadnaming, misgendering, and gender dysphoria.

Space Wizard Science Fantasy
Raleigh, NC
www.spacewizardsciencefantasy.com

Cover Design by Moorbooks
Editing by Heather Tracy
Book Layout © 2015 BookDesignTemplates.com

My Heart Is Human/Reese Hogan.— 1st ed.
ISBN 978-1-960247-05-6

Author's website: http://www.reesehogan.com/

To all the trans friends in my local support group and online—

you showed me anything was possible

CONTENTS

Chapter 1

The Westside Health Clinic was the first place Joel Lodowick had ever worked with an honest-to-god bionic. He didn't think he'd ever get used to the thing. Even if it wasn't operable, a dead robot was still a robot. There was something almost tragic about its appearance in the windowless storage room—its closed eyes, its eerily human features, its pale gold metal torso and metallic arms and legs. It was a hint of the life they'd been promised as kids. The money. The technology. The ease.

But it was also a reminder of good things gone bad.

Maybe that was why the shut-down bionic was getting to Joel today more than it usually did. *Good things gone bad.* Ugly words. Words he didn't like applying to himself. *Just get to the end of today,* he thought. *Then you'll never have to think about it again.* His cheek twitched, and he wrenched his eyes away from the dead bionic and back to the pink pills he was sliding across the pill tray and into the curved chute on the side. To his right, he heard a thump as another chart fell through the slot across the room, then the unmistakable cascade of paper as it tipped and spilled onto the floor.

"Dammit, Lodowick, keep your eye on that stack, will ya? What have I told you about lettin' 'em pile up like that?"

Joel glanced over his shoulder. Dr. Grotzheimer—or *Grotz,* as Joel privately referred to him—was leaning against the counter with a newspaper open, glaring over the top of it. The charts piled in the tray beneath the slot were close enough to his left hand that he could have nudged them aside without moving, if he'd had a mind to. Joel abandoned the pills he was counting to circle around Grotz and grab the stack of medical charts. He walked back to his workspace and dumped them next to the smashed-in computer screen in the wall, then bent to grab the one that had spilled onto the floor.

Grotz flipped another page of the newspaper. "More about this Nyctalope singer and her show this weekend," he grunted. "Can you believe that? Some outsider pop star comes through and the whole city loses its damn mind."

He pronounced it Nick-talope. Joel almost laughed, but hid it by standing and tossing the chart onto the pile. "*Nyctalope*," he said, stressing the long I sound in the first syllable, "hasn't toured New Mexico since her first album came out. That's why she's getting so much coverage. Or didn't you read that?"

"What, you're a fan?"

Joel turned back to the pills. He closed the plastic cover over the tray chute and dumped the unused pills back in the bigger container. The ones in the chute he poured into an unlabeled amber container, then snapped a cap on.

"Not really my style," he said. "Most of her older music is just uncreative lyrics, uninspired melodies, same stuff everyone else is doing."

"Oh, and I can hear it in your voice now," said Grotz. "You think you can do better. 'Cause you're an *artist*, ain't you, Lodowick?" When Joel didn't answer, he hmphed, turning back to the paper. "So, is this the singer's real name? Nyctalope?"

Joel pulled over a sheet of labels and penned on the patient's name in black caps. "No. Nyctalope was a superhero, early nineteen hundreds. Some say the first cyborg ever written. So, it's a...you know. A commentary. On the state of our world now."

"Oh, really? And what's the comment then? To bring the bionics back?"

"Maybe on how impossible it was in the first place," Joel said. "Owning technology that wouldn't eventually be corrupted by viruses, and become too dangerous to use. That kind of thing."

"So, I suppose something like the Cyberblood virus was seen as inevitable to your generation, huh?" said Grotz. Almost unconsciously, he ran a hand over the scar on his right wrist, where his radio frequency ID had been removed. Or maybe it was a reminder that tech had been part of his life for fifty-something years, as opposed to the mere thirteen years Joel had before the Cyberblood virus shut everything down.

Joel peeled the label from the sheet and rolled it onto the bottle, then snuck a glance at the clock. Five 'til five. "To my generation?" he answered. "Not necessarily. But to someone like my five-year-old daughter, who hasn't ever used a screen and maybe never will, the Cyberblood virus will be the narrowly avoided warning of technology gone wrong. And I think *that's* Nyctalope's message. A reminder of a close call. A cautionary tale of...of good things gone bad."

Grotz looked up from the paper, annoyance flashing across his face. Clearly, Joel had hit a nerve. "What do you mean, 'maybe never will'? They *will* turn tech back on someday."

"After nine years?" Joel snorted. "Don't count on it. Just a couple weeks ago, they caught some guy in Virginia with a rigged virtual reality getup that fried his optical nerves beyond repair. They haven't gotten this virus under control yet, not by a long shot." He couldn't help glancing at the old pharmacy bionic again, which may or may not have been infected with that virus before it was shut down.

When he looked back, Grotz was looking at the bionic, too. After a second, the pharmacist's gaze flicked to Joel, then to the pile of charts at his elbow. "That's your whole generation's excuse, isn't it?" he said. "'Tech is never coming back, so it'll be done when it's done.' Kids today have no appreciation of what a good work ethic looked like."

Joel bit back a scathing retort. There was no winning this argument; he should know. Grotz had worked with robots as pharmacy techs for twenty years. No matter how good Joel was at his job, he would never be as good as a robot, and Grotz resented him for it. God, how *miserable* did someone have to be to go through life blaming everyone else because robots didn't do literally everything for them anymore?

"I guess that's why this Nyctalope is so popular among your generation," Grotz continued. "She plays right into this belief that we're better off without tech. But how would you know, huh? You're probably too young to even remember screens."

"I'm twenty-two," Joel bit out, "not ten. Here. Your prescription's ready."

Grotz set the newspaper aside and took it from Joel. "Go grab the patient, then tell the rest of 'em to come back in the morning. We're closin' up."

Joel walked through the consultation room and down the hallway, irritated at getting pulled into Grotz's bullshit yet again. He had bigger things to worry about tonight.

The temperature dropped as a gust of unseasonably cool wind blew in from the front. Barely hitting five o'clock, and it was getting dark. The outdoor concert over the weekend would be downright frigid with the winds coming off the mountain. But the concert tickets he was getting after work weren't for him. They were for a guy named Brandon Wright, who owned a daycare a few blocks away. Joel desperately needed to get his daughter in; it was the only place even remotely affordable. But the daycare had been full. After twenty minutes of pleading with Brandon, Joel had finally left, but Brandon had caught up with him in the parking lot and said, "You didn't hear it from me, but if I were to get my hands on a pair of tickets for Nyctalope's sold-out show, I'm pretty sure I could find your daughter a spot here. Maybe even at a discount."

It wasn't the sort of thing Joel would normally have considered. But he'd asked around and found a way. Now he just needed this day to end so he could put it behind him.

A recording drifted down the hall, carried on the tinny notes of a record player. *"And that flower, it grows higher, with every single day. Growing, stretching, like a weed, beneath a sky of gray."*

Joel rounded the corner to the waiting room. A baby's voice rose in a wail, drowning out Nyctalope's newest song. A young couple across the room looked up wearily. A hacking cough from an older man by the wall caused the father nearby to huddle his child closer.

Joel cleared his throat. "Alicia Nieto-Padilla. Dr. Grotzheimer is ready for you."

The woman with the baby stood up from her chair next to the torn-apart kiosk where a self-serving prescription reader had once stood. Joel led her to the consultation area, then walked back to the waiting room. Every face in the room swung in his direction. Five patients left. All the doctors who worked at the clinic had already left for the day, dropping their patients' charts and prescriptions in the pharmacy slot on their way out. Even the receptionist was gone.

"Growing from the dirt of a beating human heart, bursting apart from below. And that heart is my life and my world and my fears. It's the only living thing I've known."

Joel swallowed, then crossed the room and tossed back the plastic cover of the record player. He pulled the needle from the groove and Nyctalope's song cut off, leaving only the whirring of the turning disc. He hated sending these patients home without their prescriptions. It had been happening more and more; Joel just couldn't keep up with the workload on his own. But Grotz refused to hire a second tech.

He straightened his tie and turned around, squaring his shoulders. "Dr. Grotzheimer says to come back in the morning," he said. "We open at nine."

"What the hell!" the woman broke in. "I'll be at work then!"

"This is complete bullshit, you know that?" another said, standing angrily and slinging a bag onto his shoulder.

"Yes. I do," Joel said. "I'm sorry."

The patients passed him as they headed out the door, the last one bumping his shoulder hard on the way, as if it were all Joel's fault. Joel's mouth twisted as he watched them go. But it was the figure smoking outside on the clinic's front steps that caught his eye. Long thin braids cascaded from beneath a beanie and hung down the back of her shirt.

Lee. Already waiting for him. He had to get out of here.

He turned and headed back to the pharmacy, waiting in the hallway until the woman with the baby came out, then led her to the back entrance of the clinic and locked up behind her. One last check in the waiting room showed it cleared out. Lee was stubbing her cigarette on the step outside in the lengthening shadows. Joel locked the front door, then hurried through the pharmacy and into the back storage room to grab his stuff. As usual, his jacket was draped over the shoulders of the dead bionic. He felt the pocket of the jacket, reassuring himself the small bottle of Flyithol pills was still there.

Dr. Grotzheimer's voice drifted in from the main room. "Hey, get through this stack of charts before you leave for the night."

Joel paused in the act of pulling his jacket off the bionic. "I can't," he said. "Elena—the friend watching my kid—she has to head to work in an hour."

"An hour's more than enough time to finish up," said Grotz.

Joel's mouth almost fell open. He abandoned his jacket and came to the threshold, staring first at the stack of charts next to the counting tray, then at the ones piled under the slot since he'd emptied it. Did Grotz really believe that? An hour?

He probably did. His old bionic would've had no trouble, after all.

"Sir," he managed, "It's too much. I can finish them first thing tomorrow."

"Not an option," said Grotz. "We have inventory in the morning. I want the prescriptions accounted for."

Joel's mouth went dry. Inventory. That meant that single bottle of Flyithols he was planning to trade to Lee would show up missing in the morning. And if he'd stayed late the night before... *Oh hell.*

Grotz was glaring now. "Lodowick, am I right in assuming you need this job?"

"You know I do, sir."

"Then I would suggest you stop arguing and get it done." The pharmacist turned and left without waiting for a response.

Joel closed his eyes, feeling dizzy. Not with anger at what had happened, but at how close he'd come to losing the job that kept food on the table. No. Worse. He could have gone to jail. He could have left Clementine parentless.

But what were his options? Elena was moving to day shifts starting Monday; she wouldn't be able to watch Clementine anymore after this week. And since Clementine had just barely turned five, she'd missed the deadline for kindergarten, leaving Joel in need of childcare for almost another year yet.

He reached into his jacket and pulled out the bottle of Flyithols—fly-bys, as they were called on the street. He had to return it to the controlled substances cabinet tonight. No question there. But the concert wasn't for three more days. Maybe Lee could come back. Surely, she'd understand.

He locked up the Flyithols again, then headed out to the hallway. He unlocked the front door and opened it a crack. The smell of cigarette smoke hit his nose. Lee was propped against the railing, hands in the pockets of her jeans. She wore ripped-up pants and a loose T-shirt sporting a picture of a robot with gashed-out eyes. Beneath the image was scrawled, "MICROBLOG THIS." She appeared to be in her early twenties, like Joel, but the dark infinity symbol visible just beneath the skin of her left cheek suggested differently: that was disabled tech from a cyberluminescent tattoo, which meant she'd probably been at least sixteen when tech was shut down.

She pulled one hand partially from her pocket, a pair of tickets between two fingers. "You got the stuff?"

Joel took a deep breath. "I can't tonight. We're inventorying tomorrow."

Her eyes narrowed beneath her beanie. "So? Just fudge the numbers."

"I can't risk it," said Joel. "Can you come back tomorrow?"

"Tomorrow?" A spark of anger flared in her dark eyes. "Are you shitting me? I'm sitting on a pair of VIP tickets here! This deal don't come around every night, man."

"Come back tomorrow night," Joel said, "and I'll make it two bottles."

"No, bitch, I want it *tonight*—"

"I'm sorry," Joel said. "That's the best I can do. Same time tomorrow." He pulled the door shut and locked it over her curses, then headed back down the hall, shoving reddish-gold hair from his eyes.

He washed and dried his hands in the pharmacy's tiny sink, then swept the phone from its cradle and tapped in a number before pulling the curled cord back toward the stack of charts. He'd opened the first one and was scanning the list of prescriptions by the time someone on the other end picked up.

"Don't tell me you're still at work," Elena said.

"Grotz is making me stay late."

"That pendejo!" she swore. "I can't keep doing this, Joel."

"I know," said Joel. "Maybe you can swing Clementine by the pharmacy on your way out."

"So, you'll be distracted by her while you finish up?" Elena said. "In that part of town? I don't think so."

You mean the part of town where people sell drugs? Joel thought bitterly. As his best friend, Elena knew he skirted the law from time to time, but she'd kill him if she knew what he'd been planning tonight. Which is why he'd just wanted to get it done, then pretend it had never happened. Elena's refusal to bring his five-year-old to the shitty neighborhood he worked in cut a little too close to home right now.

He pulled a bottle of pills from the shelf next to him and shook a handful into the counting tray. For several moments, the sound of the pill spatula scraping the tray was the only sound in the room.

"Call your parents," said Elena.

Joel drew his breath in through his nose, terse and irritated.

Elena sighed. "You're still avoiding them," she said. "Aren't you?"

Joel closed his eyes for a moment, wondering if he really wanted to get into this right now. "You make it sound like such a simple thing," he finally said. "But...just try seeing it my way. Imagine after years of suffering in silence, you finally work up the nerve to come out as transgender. Imagine them staring like they don't understand. You try to give them time. You correct them when they misgender you. Over and over again. For months. But nothing changes. Then imagine you finally move out, and things get better because you don't have to *think* about it anymore, and you can live without the constant reminders every day. But the second you go back again...they force it in your face. They call you by your old name. They call you 'she.' And you correct them, yeah, but you know in their minds, you're still their 'little girl,' and then it's in *your* mind, whether you like it or not. And that sticks with you for days afterward, trying to convince you there's no point in any of it if nothing ever changes. So yeah. I *avoid* them. For my own sanity. I have to."

"I'd hoped it had gotten better," Elena said after a moment.

"Yeah, it...it hasn't."

"I'm so sorry," she said. "But, Joel, it's better than trying to watch Clem while you're working, especially if you're there all alone. I don't feel good about that. So please. Just call them."

Joel's grip tightened on the phone, until the plastic of the receiver creaked under the pressure. "Okay. You're right. I'm sorry."

"Thank you. And I promise, we'll talk about it later, okay? We'll figure this out."

"Yeah," he said. "Talk to you soon." He dumped the pills into a bottle and jotted out a label before heading back to the phone cradle and disconnecting. He let his breath out slowly, steeling himself, then picked up the phone again.

The dial tone sounded for only a second, then cut out. Frowning, Joel hung up, then picked up again. Dead silence. This made no sense. He'd *just*—

The sound of shattering glass hit his ears. Joel's head shot up and the phone tumbled from his hand. Laughter and yells drifted down the hall and through the open pharmacy door.

Someone had broken in.

Joel cursed. The clinic had been hit by looters before, but his usual strategy of locking down the pharmacy and calling the cops wasn't possible if they'd done something to the phone line. He spun, his eyes flicking over the pharmacy. If he ran now, he *should* be able to get out the clinic's back door before they reached the pharmacy...but hell, he already knew what Grotz would say if he left the pharmacy defenseless. He'd say looters were cowards. That they usually ran the second they realized someone was still inside. It would somehow all become Joel's fault that he hadn't stayed and scared them off. So, Joel gritted his teeth and threw the locks on the doors of both the outer consultation room and the inner pharmacy, then hurried toward a cabinet in the back corner.

Luckily, Grotz had a reliable way of *scaring criminals off.* Joel opened the cabinet, then reached up to a hidden shelf at the top. He found Dr. Grotzheimer's pistol easily enough, but a quick check in the magazine revealed it was empty. For a second, Joel just stared. He wasn't expecting actual bullets, but Grotz *always* kept it loaded with blanks. Why the hell hadn't Grotz reloaded it?

He got on his knees and felt around on the shelf, but came up empty. A banging started up on the outer consultation door, followed by laughter. A gunshot sounded as someone blew out the lock. Joel started at the sound, the first touch of uneasiness feathering across his spine. Usually, punks looking for a quick fix weren't armed.

The inner pharmacy door shuddered behind him. Joel raised his voice. "I've got a gun!"

"Like hell you do! Open this goddamn door now or we'll do it for you."

Joel recognized Lee's voice. She must have gone and gotten someone with muscle after he'd denied her the fly-bys. More than one someone; he picked out at least three voices, and possibly more. Too many.

He slid the gun back and stood, turning to face the door. "Fine," he said. "You want to ransack the place and make it look like a break-in? I get that. Let me get the drugs for you and I'll get out of your way."

Lee laughed harshly. "Doesn't work like that, asshole. I'm taking the whole pharmacy, and I'm gonna leave your dead body in it when we go. Think of it as a message to anyone who thinks I do *layaway*."

An icicle of fear stabbed into Joel's heart, paralyzing him in place for a second. Breath coming short, he looked over the pharmacy. His gaze fell on the locked drawer beneath the busted computer. He yanked out his pharmacy keys.

"Shoot it, Bo," said Lee.

Another gunshot rang out, then another. Joel got the key into the lock, then wrenched the drawer open. Wrapped syringes were piled within. He grabbed one and ripped it out of the paper casing, then twisted the cap off to expose the long injection needle. He was back at the pharmacy door by the time it swung open. When the shooter appeared in an oversized hoodie, he jammed the needle into the side of his neck.

Blood spurted. The shooter yelled, swinging his gun in Joel's direction. Joel kicked with all his strength, and the shooter was just distracted enough to fumble his grip. The gun went spinning. Joel abandoned his needle in the attacker's neck and dove for the weapon, which had landed near the open doorway of the storage room. Someone slammed into him halfway there, and they crashed to the floor. Joel landed painfully on his stomach. He twisted and drove his elbow into his assaulter's stomach, throwing them off, then turned and scrambled for the gun.

Before he could grab it, though, a boot pressed down on his wrist, pinning it to the floor. Pain shot halfway up his forearm. Joel screamed.

"Where are the fly-bys?" said Lee.

Joel turned his head. Lee's long blond braids hung around her face as she stared down at him, her mouth in a thin line.

"I...I need a key to get them," he managed. "Get off my hand." He prayed neither she nor her accomplices glanced to the side and noticed his keyring hanging from the open drawer with the syringes.

"Which pocket?" said Lee.

"My front shirt pocket. You know, the one that's *pressed to the floor*. So get off!"

Lee jerked her head to the side and lifted her foot. Someone grabbed the back of Joel's shirt and hauled him up. Before he'd even regained his feet, Joel grasped the front of his button-down with his good hand and yanked as hard as he could, breaking the buttons off to scramble free of the shirt and leave it in his captor's hands. He knew he'd never make it across the room, so he bolted for the storage closet and slammed the door shut, catching only a brief glimpse of a big, hooded figure grabbing for him. There was a lock, thank god, which he threw, but they'd already proved that wouldn't hold long.

"The keys are right there," Lee snapped on the other side of the door. "Bastard tricked us. Grab them and clear this place out."

Someone jiggled the knob of the storage closet as Joel flipped on the light. His hands were shaking, and his left wrist pulsed with pain. He was wearing only a white sleeveless undershirt and a chest binder now, in addition to his trousers and tie. There were no windows in the storage room, no doors besides this one. Just shelves full of drugs, an old, nanofabricated refrigerator in the back with IV antibiotics, and the dead bionic.

"That drawer, that shelf, and that one there," Lee said. "The rest of the drugs are probably in that room our friend's hiding in. We'll hit it next."

Unfortunately, she was right. Most of the medicines were kept in the cool dark room in the back, including the controlled substances cabinet with her coveted fly-bys. Joel grabbed the metal shelf next to him with his right hand, lifted it off the tracks at the back, and pulled it free. Bottles of pills cascaded over the floor in a deafening rattle. He shoved one end of the shelf beneath the doorknob and wedged the other on the floor against one of the vertical shelf dividers. What else? There were more needles in the fridge as a last-ditch defense. He opened the refrigerator door, shivering in the sudden waft of cold. Insulin? Maybe. But against a gun?

Another shiver wracked him. Should he just try to plead for his life? *Please! I have a kid!* His mind rebelled at the thought of divulging that information. Someone like Lee would probably hunt down that kid for fun after killing him.

He closed the fridge again, scanning his surroundings. Yeah, drugs were a hell of a weapon, but they also took time. Time he didn't have. That left...

His eyes landed on the bionic in the corner. God, what a stupid thought. The thing had been dead for almost ten years. And even if it worked, it could be infected with the Cyberblood virus. Joel's family hadn't been rich enough to afford a bionic—few people were—but he'd heard all the stories about infected tech. It could malfunction in a hundred different ways, from going ballistic to flat-out exploding.

But...but what if that malfunction could actually be used *against* Lee and her gang? Wasn't anything better than just waiting to die?

He pulled his jacket off the bionic and tossed it aside. Then he ran his right hand over it, looking for a power switch. There were patches on its back with slightly different shades of gray, and he noticed almost immediately that those did compress, like buttons. But none of them did a thing. He checked the torso's ribbed surface next, feeling nothing but a hard rubbery plastic. He circled it, pressing at the closed eyes, the pert gold nose, the lips, the ears. No hair. The top of the head was as smooth as the chest. All the "control" components—if that's what those shaded areas were—were on its back. He skirted around again, running a hand up shoulder blades with the barest hint of definition.

No door jiggling or pounding preceded the gunshot this time. It just went off, explosively loud, sending a jolt through Joel that he felt down to his toes. The door beside the knob splintered. The brass knob shifted, but remained intact enough to hold the metal shelf secure, jamming the door before it had opened a half-inch. The man cursed, and the anger in his voice was enough to send chills through Joel's spine.

His fingers caught on a seam on the back of the bionic's neck. Joel yanked on it with his fingernails, and it came open—a compartment. He found himself staring at a tangle of wires. He ground his teeth together, but forced himself to study them. He thought he could make out an empty slot in the bionic's neck, just behind the wires.

"What are you waiting for?" Lee said. "Shoot it again!"

"Bullets are out," the man grunted. "*God*, my neck hurts." He hammered at the door, making it shudder in its frame. The metal shelf held, but Joel could see the strain of it bending in the middle. He grabbed a handful of wires, looking for a break, something to reconnect, *anything*...

He felt something hard within the soft mass—something flat with corners and edges. He worked it free as the banging continued, and finally pulled out a plastic and metal rectangle about the size of a penny. He knew immediately what it was, though his memory of its name failed him. A drive? A chit? It was the part that held information. And it *should* fit...

He wriggled it behind the wires and positioned it, metal end forward, at the opening of the slot in the back of the neck. It slid in, even giving a satisfying click as it hit the back. He thought he heard a whir from somewhere within the bionic, but the noise of Lee's strongman trying to get in drowned out almost everything else.

The bionic didn't move. Joel walked to its front side again, hoping to see its fingers twitching or its eyes opening, but it remained as still as it always had.

Something splintered, and the doorknob holding the metal shelf in place finally tumbled off, hitting the floor with a clang. The door shoved open farther, and the shelf, in some last valiant effort, slid up to the hole the doorknob had left and snagged by a corner. The opening was just wide enough for the man to put his head and chest through. His hood was off, his bald head gleaming in the bright light of the storage room. Blood streamed down his neck and his face was alight with fury.

Joel pressed himself to the wall by the bionic, heart pounding as he held his hand out in placation. "I'll get the drugs for you," he said. "No need to come in."

"After what you did, punk? I'm gonna smash your face in!"

"Look, hand me my keys and I'll open the narcotics cabinet and shove it all out there. And then you don't have to kill yourself getting your hands on some lowly pharmacy tech."

The man got his left arm through and shoved at the metal shelf. Joel heard that whirring again, then a voice spoke at his elbow.

"Ready to assist."

The voice was neutral, devoid of inflection or emotion. Both Joel and the man froze. Joel turned his head to see the bionic's eyes open. The silver irises within were locked on his. Joel's lips parted in surprise. 'Pharmacy tech,' he thought. *The last thing I said was 'pharmacy tech'...*

"You have a working robot back here?" the man said incredulously.

Joel's gaze darted back to him. There was no sign of a virus affecting the bionic yet, not that he could tell, which didn't necessarily help him. Not unless he could get the thing to actually fight for him. Was that possible? It *had* worked in a pharmacy; maybe it had been designed to protect the drugs from looters, with built-in weapons or something. Who knew?

He struggled to form a comprehensive thought. "Um. Pharmacy Tech. Can you...incapacitate someone?"

"There are many ways to incapacitate a person," the bionic said. "Would you like only current medication results, or all medication results?"

"No!" said Joel. "Someone's trying to kill me. Can you *do* something about it?"

The bionic blinked. "Killing is a crime. Contacting authorities."

Joel's breath caught. Was it that easy? The man at the door looked skittish, his gaze going from the bionic to Joel and back again.

"Bo, what's going on?" said Lee's voice. "We don't have all night!"

"The pharmy has a bionic in here!" Bo shot back. "Says it's callin' the cops."

"A bionic? Shit, are you kidding me? And it's calling the fucking cops?"

"Yeah. Maybe we should get out of here, Lee..."

In the split second of silence between Bo's statement and Lee's answer, the bionic spoke again. "Connection failed."

Joel almost choked. A nasty smile spread across Bo's face, and he grabbed the metal shelf with his left hand and tore it free from the door. He shoved his way in. He held a huge sawback blade in his right hand.

Joel grabbed the bionic's arm. "He will destroy you, Pharmacy Tech, along with me!" he said. "Don't you have some sort of self-preservation mode?"

"I will not hurt humans," said the bionic.

"Even if that human will steal the drugs in here and use them to hurt *other* humans?" pressed Joel.

The bionic blinked. "Stealing is a crime. Contacting authorities."

"No. No, no! Cancel that!" Joel did his best to keep the bionic's body between himself and Bo, but that door behind the other man was the only way out. Bo came closer, knife brandished in his fist. He was close enough that Joel could smell the iron of the blood on his neck, as well as the pungent reek of cigarette smoke.

"Pharmacy Tech," Joel said, his breath coming short. "If you can't hurt him, can you get us the hell out of here? That door is the only way, so can you...I don't know...bash a hole in the wall behind us?"

It blinked. "Property damage is a crime—"

"So is letting someone die when you could have saved them," Joel broke in roughly. "It's no worse than murder."

The bionic stared at him, going unnaturally still. Joel felt like screaming in frustration. Maybe he was going about this the wrong way.

"Pharmacy Tech!" he said through his teeth. "Get me out of here. *Now!*"

The bionic bent and grabbed him around the waist. Before Joel registered what was happening, he was tossed over the bionic's shoulder. He gasped as his breath was cut short. He caught a glimpse of Bo, swinging his knife, but the bionic's arm intercepted with a sharp clang, and the blade deflected in the nick of time. And then the bionic marched right through the open door and pharmacy, then left through the consultation room. Joel saw Lee and another wiry skinhead pressed against the pharmacy counter, gaping after them.

The bionic left out the back door, which hung open over a pool of broken glass from Lee's entry. Cold air hit Joel's bare arms. He struggled to get down, but the bionic held him in an unbreakable grip. Its gait was jerky, but steady, with an audible whir in every step.

He heard a shout and looked up in time to see Bo dash into the parking lot, teeth bared in anger and knife clenched in his fist. "You're a *dead* man!" he snarled.

"My car!" Joel said urgently. "The dark blue Hemisphere, back of the lot. Get us there! Fast!"

The bionic upped its pace, carrying Joel over the lot at a dizzying speed. By the time it lowered him to the ground by his sedan, Bo was sprinting toward them, over halfway across the gravel lot and closing fast. Joel pulled his car keys out of his pocket and unlocked the door, then yanked it open.

"Get in!" he said. "Other side."

The bionic obeyed. Joel slid into the driver's seat and fired up the engine. Before he could shut the door, though, a hand grabbed the side of the doorjamb. The parking lot light glinted off a metal blade. Joel threw his left arm up, barely getting it between Bo's knife and his own face in time. The blade sliced the back of his forearm, sending a hot rush of blood down his arm. The pain hit half a second later, almost blinding him.

Joel's breath came in short, panicked gasps as he threw the car in reverse and floored it. Bo, knife already drawn back for another slash, tried to scramble away, but the open door clipped his shoulder and sent him spinning across the gravel. Joel paused just long enough to throw the car into drive, then peeled out of the parking lot. The door slammed shut as he hit the street.

Joel struggled to see the road through a haze of fear and pain and deep-seated dread. The robbery. The wound. And...oh god, the bionic.

He turned his head, expecting to see the robot staring straight ahead. But he caught its eyes on him, shadowed in the yellow pool of light from an old streetlamp. His stomach clenched. A bionic. Sitting in his car. There were a million things wrong with this, from the fact that it was stolen property to the stories about people being arrested for illegally keeping bionics to the very real possibility that it might dangerously malfunction at any moment. But what choice had there been? His heart was still pounding from how fast everything had happened.

He tore his eyes from the bionic and pressed the pedal down farther, suddenly desperate to see his daughter again.

Chapter 2

"Maddy!" Clementine yelled, streaking across the living room.

Joel knelt to absorb her small but forceful weight against his chest. He wrapped his right arm around her and held her against his hammering heart. The relief of seeing her again—of being *alive* to see her—outweighed everything else. He couldn't hold her long, though, because the sweatshirt he'd grabbed from his back seat and wrapped around his left forearm was already slipping free, so he released her and pressed it tight to the bleeding wound again.

He stood, stepping farther inside. "Pharmacy Tech," he said. "Come in and close the door."

The bionic came in behind him, gears whirring. They'd used a back entrance to avoid seeing anyone, but it was still only five-forty in the evening, so that could change any second.

"Joel? I thought you—"

Elena's words ended abruptly as she appeared in the kitchen doorway and saw the bionic. It closed the door, then turned to face front again. Its head didn't move, but its eyes scanned first the threadbare couch and desk against the left wall, then the short hallway at the back, then the small cathode ray TV at the right wall, and finally the kitchen doorway, where Elena stood with one hand over her mouth, staring in horror.

Clementine turned toward the bionic, her mouth falling open. After a second, she ran over to it and grabbed its hand.

"Why is your skin gold?" she said.

The bionic looked down at her. "Because it is infused with a blend of twenty-one percent zinc and seventy-nine percent copper," it said in its monotonous voice.

"Is that from the sun?"

"No, it is not caused by the sun."

"I think it's pretty," she said. "I'm Clemattine. I'm five. What's your name?"

"I am from the Cancer series 2nd generation, model name Acubens and serial designation 65848," answered the bionic. "My current occupational assignment is Pharmacy Tech tier 1."

Her brow furrowed. "You have cancer?"

"Do you answer to Acubens, too?" Joel asked the bionic.

"I respond to Pharmacy Tech, Acubens, or 65848," it said.

"*Joel*?" said Elena in a high-pitched voice.

Joel sighed. "Yeah. Um...Clementine, could you go find a toy to show Acubens while I talk with Miss Elena?"

"Can I get my blocks?" she said excitedly.

"Yes. Please do."

She bolted off, red hair flying. Joel turned back to the door and locked both locks, then engaged the chain. Now that the adrenaline was wearing off, his injuries were hurting even worse, if that was possible. He pressed the sweatshirt tighter to the knife wound as he turned back to his best friend.

"Right after I hung up with you," he said quietly, "the pharmacy was robbed."

Elena's eyes widened. "Are you okay?"

"Not really. One of them cut me with a knife."

"Ay Dios mío," Elena whispered. Her dark eyes tracked to Acubens. The bionic stared back, motionless. Joel supposed it just wasn't engaged at the moment, but those intense silver eyes were undoubtedly taking in information. Anything they said could be taken to the cops if it got away from him. *Gets away from me? What am I thinking? That I'm gonna hold it prisoner?*

"Was that...thing...in the pharmacy?" Elena said.

"Yes. I turned it on in hopes of it saving me. And, as you can see, it worked."

"But then you brought it *home*?"

"What was I supposed to do, Elena? Toss it on the curb on my way back?"

"Why was it even still in the pharmacy?"

"Grotz told me it was sent to the clinic to help with patient overflow after the Populi shuttle exploded over New Mexico ten years ago. With over six thousand injuries, every hospital and clinic in the state was full. Afterward, the bionic was left behind. He said they reported it after tech was shut down, but there was no follow-up, so it got shoved aside."

"As I recall, the Populi shuttle failed *because* of the Cyberblood virus. What if this thing's infected with it?"

"If it was high risk for that, the government would have picked it up after it was reported. And if it was gonna explode, it would've happened by now, huh?"

Elena looked at it again, then back at him, quickly. "But no one's turned it on in all that time, so who knows?" she said under her breath. "How *did* you turn it on, anyway? I thought all these things were controlled by the grid. They shouldn't even be operational anymore!"

"I had to go into the back of its neck and past some wires. There was a piece that had fallen out, so I put it back in. It must be some sort of...backup system or something. I really don't know. I'd never looked before."

"I still think it should be impossible with the grid shut down."

"Me, too," Joel admitted. "Me, too."

Elena threw her long black braid over her shoulder with an angry flip of her wrist. "You're gonna call the cops and turn it in, right? And report the robbery?"

"I haven't decided yet." Joel walked around Acubens and across the small apartment to the restroom.

"What did you say?" Elena called after him, a dangerous edge to her voice.

Joel opened the mirror that had once doubled as an interactive screen, rummaging within until he found some thick gauze pads and medical bandages. He carried them back to the kitchen and set them by the sink.

"For all anyone knows," he said, "that robbery happened after I left for the day. They trashed the place, so there's no evidence to say otherwise. Unless *they* go to the cops and tell them about Acubens—which they won't, 'cause then they'd have to admit they were robbing it—then that leaves no fingers pointing back at me. I mean, if Grotz finds out I was actually *there* and let the place get robbed, he'd fire me for sure."

"*Let* the place get robbed?" Elena repeated incredulously.

"He thinks the place is defensible. He's an asshole."

Elena crossed her arms over her chest. "Or he might think *you* robbed it, Joel."

Joel hesitated a beat too long.

Elena's eyes narrowed. "Which you *didn't*. Right?"

"No!" said Joel. "I mean...I was gonna sell one bottle of Flyithol pills. Just one. In exchange for a pair of concert tickets. The guy at this daycare I'm looking at for Clementine offered to cut me a deal, so..."

Elena whispered something under her breath, pinching the bridge of her nose. "And you tried to back out of selling it at the last minute? Or what?"

"Something like that," said Joel.

When she looked up again, her face was a mixture of anger and disappointment. "How did you even find a buyer?" she said. "Tyler's connections?"

Joel nodded. "None of them recognized me anymore, but yeah."

"Tyler is *dead* now because of those people," Elena said. "Because of Tyler's overdose, Clementine is growing up without a second parent. And I'm glad. I'm glad he's not in your life anymore. Or hers. I know you are, too. But to contact Tyler's dealers is to get dangerously close to that world again."

"I know," said Joel. "And I don't want anything to do with that world. It was just gonna be a one-time thing. I swear it."

"You've always been a little too comfortable with skirting the law, in my opinion," Elena muttered.

She wasn't wrong. About any of it. His long-dead ex— Clementine's other parent—had been bad news from the day they'd met, but Joel had been caught in a downward spiral that wouldn't ultimately end until he came out as trans, a full two years after Tyler's death. Clementine had been the only good thing to come out of that awful relationship.

Joel turned away from the look on Elena's face and bent over the sink. Bracing himself, he removed the sweatshirt he'd wrapped around his arm. The material stuck to the wound, and

Joel hissed through his teeth as he pulled it off. Fresh blood ran down his arm and into the stainless steel of the sink.

He bent his elbow to see the wound, patting the blood away as gingerly as possible. Two or three inches long, with ragged gaping edges. Dark red blood instantly filled it again, making it impossible to tell how deep it was.

"God, Joel," Elena whispered. "That needs stitches."

Joel turned the faucet on, then slid his arm into the cold water. He breathed through the pain, eyes watering, as he gingerly cleaned it with antibacterial dish soap. The blood-tinged water ran over his left wrist, which had its own dark bruises from where Lee had crushed it beneath her boot.

A thump came from the hallway as Clementine dragged her bucket of blocks into the living room. Joel glanced over his shoulder to see her beaming at the patiently waiting Acubens.

"Look!" she said. "I got these when I turned five." She halted in the middle of the floor, removed the lid, and upended the entire bucket with a deafening clatter.

Elena turned back to Joel, her face pained. "Joel..."

"You don't show up at the emergency room with something like this without police getting involved," Joel broke in. "I'll be okay. It'll leave a nasty scar, but it'll heal."

Elena dug her teeth into her lip. She looked at Acubens, then back to Joel. "I don't have time to argue with you. But if it's not looking better by tomorrow—"

"Then I'll go to the doctor," said Joel. "I promise." He turned off the water and grabbed a clean dishtowel from a nearby cabinet. It was still bleeding, but Joel did his best to pat it dry before packing it with gauze pads. Elena stepped forward to help him wrap ace bandages around it.

"Was any of this blood at the crime scene?" she said under her breath.

"No," said Joel. "Just my car."

"I don't approve of this. But if you're serious about avoiding the cops, then you need to get rid of that—that *thing*—as soon as you can. You hear me? Throw it in your trunk and go drop it down some deep arroyo on the mesa, before you're either caught with it or it malfunctions and hurts you. As soon as possible, Joel. Like, *tonight*."

Joel nodded. "I know."

"I'll call you as soon as I can." She grabbed her purse from the desk, kissed Clementine on the top of the head, and left.

Joel followed her to the door and locked it behind her, then glanced at Acubens. Its eyes had stayed on him the whole time. It was eerie. Shouldn't it be staring off into blank space as it awaited instructions?

"Acubens," he said, "you can play blocks with Clementine. If you want."

The bionic blinked. Slowly, it transferred its gaze to his daughter, who was stacking blocks on the coffee table in front of the couch.

"You said there was no evidence indicating you were present for the robbery," it said.

Joel froze. It wasn't that he was surprised Acubens had been listening—because of course it had—but it was the fact that it was broaching the topic on its own, without being prompted.

"Yeah?" he said.

"The button-down shirt on the floor was yours," said Acubens, "as was the discarded coat. It was obvious from both the size and from your own state of attire when we left."

"Oh my god," Joel whispered. Acubens was right. Nobody would believe he hadn't been there if they found his clothes on the pharmacy floor. "Then there's no way around it," he said. "I'm gonna have to report it, before they show up and arrest me. And yeah, they *may* believe I didn't rob it, but the fact that I activated you? Brought you home? I'll be lucky if I don't end up in jail."

"Jail?" said Clementine, looking up.

Joel closed his eyes for a second. "It's gonna be okay, Clemmy. Just...just show Acubens your blocks. I've got a couple phone calls to make."

He swung by his bedroom first and changed into a pair of sweats and an old Pixellated People T-shirt from the 2087 Lights Out tour. Then he popped into the bathroom and opened the medicine cabinet again, hoping for some painkillers, but only found the medicine he'd given Clementine for the flu last year. He took a slug of it, choking on the sweet bubblegum flavor. As he was putting it back in the cabinet, a squeal of laughter came from the living room. Joel cradled his throbbing arm to his midsection and headed out.

He stopped in his tracks.

An elaborate structure had been built with Clementine's blocks on the coffee table. It wasn't wide—the base was less than a foot square—but in a delicately spiraling design, the colored wooden blocks swept up in staircases and windows to a height well over Joel's head. Acubens stood between the couch and the coffee table, its arm extended straight up to place another piece at the pinnacle, where all the triangles had been arranged to create a crenellated rooftop. Joel stepped forward, staring in awe.

"How did you do it?" said Clementine, jumping up and down.

"By starting with a seven-by-five-inch partitioned rectangle, using a growth factor of one point six one eight for every quarter turn, and assuming a slope factor of one," said Acubens.

Joel's mouth fell open. "All that from working at the pharmacy?"

Acubens turned its head to look at him. "The pharmaceutical update came after the basic programming."

"And this is part of the basic?"

"Mathematics are integral to a working interface, yes."

It was at that moment that Acubens' presence fully sank in. *Acubens was a computer.* It could very well be one of the only working computers in the entire country right now. And it was standing here in Joel's crappy apartment playing blocks with his kid.

Slowly, Joel walked past them and dropped onto the far end of the couch, next to the end table with his corded phone. He reached across his body and grabbed the receiver with his good hand. But he didn't pull it from the cradle yet. Instead, he watched Clementine, who was holding the last block and bouncing eagerly up and down on her toes.

"I want to put on the last block, Acubens, *pleeease*? Can you hold me up?"

Acubens looked at Joel. "Do you permit this, Joel?"

The robot's use of his first name gave Joel a jolt. Not that it would have been hard to pick up during his and Elena's conversation, but it was still a jarring reminder that these things were always watching, always learning. What would happen to it, once he reported it? The government had dismantled the bionics, shut them down and never brought them back. Acubens could end up as scrap metal, for all he knew. But that brain! That knowledge! Acubens didn't *seem* to be infected with this Cyberblood virus, as far as he could tell...so why throw it away? It struck him as crazy.

"Yeah," he finally said to Acubens. "But be careful with her."

Acubens lifted up Clementine effortlessly and held her over its head. Clementine leaned forward, clumsy in her five-year-old body, and predictably fudged the placement of the last block. The structure tipped, then cascaded onto the wooden table in a cacophony more ear-shattering than the initial dump. Clementine looked down in horror, then her face crumpled.

"Clemmy!" said Joel. "It's okay! Acubens can build it again."

She darted a look at him from Acubens' arms, her lower lip trembling. Joel let go of the phone and held his hands out, and she wriggled free of Acubens and ran over to him. She curled on the couch in the crook of his arm, thumb in her mouth. Joel looked down at her for a second, then back at the phone. *I can't be arrested,* he thought numbly. *I just can't.*

Although he hadn't asked Acubens, the bionic had already started rebuilding the tower. It placed blocks confidently, without even making sure one balanced before moving on to the next.

"Maddy, can I turn on TV?" said Clementine.

"Yeah, go ahead," Joel said, reluctantly releasing her.

She jumped off the couch and ran over to the cathode ray on the short TV stand. The guy at the used electronics store had assured Joel of its numerous features once computers were turned back on, like a touchscreen and apps and holo hookups, but to Joel, it had always just been an old CRT display with a screen that flashed every so often from a loose wire. The screen came to life. Joel told her to keep the volume low, then turned back to the phone.

"The word 'Maddy' doesn't appear in my databases," said Acubens.

Joel looked up, startled.

"Is this a new term?" Acubens said, pausing to look back at Joel.

"Um. Not exactly. It's one I decided to use for Clementine when she was a baby. I hadn't come out to my parents yet as transgender, but wanted something more gender-neutral than 'Mom' for Clem to call me, so I picked that. It's what she's called me ever since." He hesitated. "You're familiar with *those* terms. Right?"

"Yes," said Acubens. It blinked. "Processed and updated."

"Thanks," said Joel uncertainly.

He took a deep breath and picked up the phone. He put it to his ear, half-hoping there'd be no dial tone, just like at the pharmacy. But it was there, taking away his last excuse. He let his breath out slowly and wedged it between his shoulder and ear, then started to dial in the number for the local police station, which was posted above the phone's number pad.

In the silence between the sixth and seventh beep of the keypad, a voice broke through from the television. "...fire has now spread to the nearby bistro, despite efforts to contain it. Firefighters have ordered the evacuation of houses across 19th Street, and continue to work on getting the blaze under control. Authorities have yet to determine the cause of the fire, which started at the—"

"Westside Health Clinic," Joel whispered, saying the words along with the newscaster. He lowered the phone receiver, staring openmouthed at the fuzzy image of his own clinic awash in flames. "I don't believe it. They torched the place!"

* * *

The rest of the evening passed in a blur. Joel's thoughts were in fragments, barely connected to one another. He fried eggs and put bread in the toaster. *At least no one will find that shirt now.* He stared at his dinner as commercials played in the background. *Were Lee and Bo afraid of Acubens? Is that why they did it?* He poured a glass of milk for Clementine. *Or did they do it to get back at me?* He scrubbed dishes one-handed, and told Clementine repeatedly to leave Acubens alone and get ready for bed. *There's no way the cops could know about Acubens now. The only witnesses committed arson, and they won't be going anywhere near the cops.* He tucked Clementine in and read a book to her, eyes skimming words he barely saw. *What am I gonna do for work now? What the fuck am I gonna do?*

It didn't help to realize his knife wound had bled through the bandages at some point. Joel peeled them off, then cleaned and redressed the wound. Without Elena's help, the wrappings came out sloppy and loose, but he did the best he could one-handed. Despite his assurances to Elena, he knew it couldn't be a good sign: the continuous bleeding, the bad throbbing in his arm, and a lightheadedness starting to creep in at the edges of his vision. He steadied himself against the sink, glancing toward the living room and taking in the soiled bandages, the blood-stained clothes, the drops of blood on the floor...

His gaze fell on Acubens, standing motionless by the couch. The robot cocked its head inquisitively. "Would you like me to look at your injury, Joel?"

Joel hesitated. He'd forgotten Acubens was a medical bionic, even if it was only trained as a pharmacy tech. But what could it do, really? Probably just diagnose it as something that needed to be treated in an emergency room. And that was something Joel didn't want to know yet.

"No, it's fine," he said. "But maybe you could...clean up my apartment? The stuff with blood, in particular? I mean, if you don't mind."

"Yes. I can do that," said Acubens.

"Thank you." Joel's gaze caught on the broken slats of the window shade, and he had a sudden image of a nosy neighbor watching all of this. He swallowed. "And afterward, stay out of sight," he added. "Until I need you again."

"Understood, Joel," said Acubens.

Joel sighed in relief. He pulled on an old hoodie and zipped it up, then collapsed into the worn armchair by the couch. Out of habit, he pulled his old bass guitar onto his lap, before he remembered he couldn't possibly play with his arm so messed up. Despite everything, the realization was a blow; playing his bass every evening was his only time to himself, and losing weeks or months to an injury like this could damage his abilities, big time.

Maybe he *should* consider a doctor. But after the fire, would he even still have insurance? The pharmacy might only pay two weeks before cutting his funds. It might not even do that much. He slid the bass onto the couch and leaned back in the armchair, squeezing his eyes shut.

He'd have to look for a new job. Immediately. He'd be stuck with whatever crappy place would take him on such short notice, and he *still* wouldn't be able to afford a babysitter. If only he'd gotten those concert tickets after all. He could have at least gotten Clementine into daycare...or hell, maybe at this point, he'd just have sold them the night of the concert, for as much as possible. The irony was almost unbearable. If he hadn't tried to get those tickets, he wouldn't be injured and jobless, with a stolen bionic in his...

His eyes drifted open. His gaze landed on Acubens, currently putting blood-stained laundry in the washing machine.

No one knew Acubens was here. No one missed it. It was smart. It didn't expect pay. It obeyed his orders. It was even good with Clementine. Could Acubens stay home and...?

He sucked his breath in, dismissing the thought with a sharp shake of his head. No. Acubens didn't *seem* to be infected with the Cyberblood virus, but that could change at any moment. There was no way he could leave it alone with his daughter. But that didn't mean it was useless. Maybe it could teach him enough to get a better job, one that would pay enough for a babysitter. Or...

Or I could sell it. Something like Acubens, on the black market, would make far far more than a pair of scalped concert tickets.

But how would he find a buyer? He didn't dare contact Lee again. And with Elena busy in her new position, he'd have to either leave Clementine with his parents or bring her with him into the seedier parts of the city. Maybe he could make phone calls first, but he'd have to be careful. How much easier had things been when they could use computers for this type of thing? *I have a computer now. Holy shit, I have a computer...*

He was still turning the implications over in his mind when his eyelids finally fell, too heavy and overwhelmed from the day's trauma to fight it a second longer.

Chapter 3

A pounding at the door jerked Joel awake. He startled violently, his heart racing. A light was still on beside the TV stand, but the blinds at the back window showed pitch black through the broken slats. The underside of his left forearm burned with a fierce pain he'd never fully escaped from, even while sleeping. He rubbed his other hand over eyes heavy with fatigue and glanced at the clock over the couch. It was one forty-five in the morning.

The knock at the door sounded again, followed by, "Joel Lodowick! It's Yvette Stephens with the Rio Rancho Police. Please open the door."

Joel stiffened. Police? His gaze darted around the small living room. The structure Acubens had built still stood, but the bionic itself was nowhere to be seen.

He shoved himself up. A crippling head rush hit him, and the world went black for several seconds. He steadied himself until the room came back into focus. Beneath the left sleeve of his hoodie, the unmistakable pulse of fresh blood crept down his forearm.

The wrappings. They must have bled through again. *Shit.*

Another knock at the door. "Mr. Lodowick?"

"I'm coming!" he managed. "I just woke up!"

He tried to shake away the lingering lightheadedness, hurrying first to the kitchen, then into his own bedroom. He flipped on the light and checked inside the closet, then behind the mattress on the floor. No Acubens. He stopped by Clementine's room next. His daughter was sleeping soundly in her bed, clutching a small penguin and sucking her thumb. Acubens...no. Not that he could see. Where was it?

He couldn't delay any longer. He closed Clementine's door and started toward the front, but paused when he saw Acubens' perfectly-built block tower on the coffee table. Suspicious as hell. So, he bumped the table on his way, sending the blocks down in a torrent. He yelled a curse word for the police's benefit. He waited only a heartbeat longer to make sure Clementine didn't come out crying—thank god she slept like the dead—then unlocked the front door and pulled it open.

Three people stood in the dimly lit interior hallway. The police officer was in front, dark skin and hair under a brimmed cap, black uniform, and badge in hand. "We're here because of what happened at the Westside Health Clinic last night," she said. "Have you heard about the fire yet?"

"I have," Joel said.

"Well, Dr. Grotzheimer claims you were the last one at the clinic last night, so we'd like to ask you some questions."

She gestured to her left, and Joel noticed that Dr. Grotz was one of the people behind her. He was wearing the same clothes Joel had last seen him in—trousers, button-down, and tie—but they were rumpled, and the thinning hair on his scalp was unkempt. His arms were crossed over his chest, and he stared at Joel through narrowed eyes.

The third person was a man in his twenties with a brimmed cap, black clothes, and a tactical vest with a logo of a green leaf on the left breast. Despite the gun at his hip, his hands were in his pockets, and he looked at ease, his shirt cuffs unbuttoned and rolled up his forearms. A good sign, Joel supposed, but the fact that some dude in a tac vest was even *here* was alarming.

"Can we come in?" said Officer Stephens.

Joel dipped his head in a nod and stepped back, pulling his sleeve down to cover the huge bruise on his wrist from Lee's boot. "Sorry about the mess," he said. "I tripped on one of my daughter's blocks coming out."

"It's quite all right, Mr. Lodowick," said Officer Stephens. "I have kids myself."

Joel's heartbeat slowed down a tad. All signs pointed to him not being a suspect here. If his story about everything happening after he'd left the pharmacy held water, then there was no reason not to stick to it. Especially with Dr. Grotzheimer *right here.* Any admission to being present during the robbery would lead to the fact that he had come close to illegally selling drugs, and was consequently responsible for the fire. And that didn't even include taking Acubens, which would almost assuredly lead to an arrest on the spot. If only he knew where Acubens *was.*

Stephens put her badge away as she came in. Grotz followed, and the man in the vest came last. Stephens leaned against the wall by the TV and pulled a small notepad from her belt, which she flipped open to a new page.

"What time did you leave last night?" she said.

"About twenty 'til six," said Joel.

"Did anything out of the ordinary happen after Dr. Grotzheimer left?"

"No. I called my babysitter and told her I was gonna be late. Then I just got it all done as fast as possible and came home. I saw the news about the fire a little after six."

"Were there any suspicious characters around the clinic at the time you left?"

Lee had been on the clinic steps before they'd even closed. He couldn't assume Grotz hadn't caught a glimpse of her. "There was a woman at the front door hanging around for a while. But she was gone by the time I left."

"What did she look like?"

"A tight hat. Short sleeves. Long hair, I think. I didn't see her up close."

Stephens jotted something down. "We think the fire originated in the pharmacy. Most of it was unrecognizable. But it looks like the locks may have been blown out with a firearm."

Joel gave a slight shrug. "They always hit the pharmacy first."

"So, this has happened before?"

"Looters? Yeah. I've had to chase them away before. They've never gone this far, though."

"You had a bionic in the back room," said Stephens.

Joel's mouth went dry. "Yeah. Why?"

"Even as burned as everything was, we have reason to believe it's gone. We're investigating what may have happened to it." She nodded to her left, toward the man in the tactical vest. "This is Mr. Otsuka from the Sapling Corporation. Have you heard of them?"

Joel's heart almost stopped. "*The* Sapling?"

"Yes, the ones in charge of technology and bionic control. They know where all the bionics in the country are, and if one is moved, they track it down."

What? Joel's good hand tightened over his arm. He knew the basics of what they did, but hadn't heard these alarming details. "So, they can find bionics that go missing? Like, track their signal or something? Like with computers?"

"Yes, Mr. Lodowick, that's exactly right."

"But it's been there for nine years!" Joel said. "If they knew it was there this whole time, why didn't they ever come for it?"

"I think you vastly underestimate how many we deal with on a daily basis," said Mr. Otsuka with a slight smile. "We still have tens of thousands to track down. The priority falls to ones that disappear or otherwise jump the queue. Ones in storage get pushed further down the line."

Joel looked back to Stephens. "So...this tracking signal..."

"According to the Sapling Corporation, the signal went dead before the bionic ever left the clinic," said Stephens. "Most likely, the bionic was taken by the arsonists. Either they shut the tracking beacon off right away, or something in the transmitter was damaged in the fire."

Except...neither of those things was true. What Officer Stephens was saying was that there was no reason he shouldn't have led this Sapling Corporation straight to his own apartment. Which, to be fair, he kind of had. But why would Acubens' tracker not be working?

"However," Stephens continued, "given the pressing circumstances of the threat to public safety, Mr. Otsuka is operating under Chapter 1, Title 48, Subchapter F, which allows the government to partner with private contractors for search and seizure rights. Under this statute, Mr. Otsuka is authorized to search your property as a precautionary measure without a warrant as part of our investigation. Are there any objections or information you'd like to share before he proceeds?"

A wave of panic sent Joel's heart crashing against his ribs. Threat to public safety? Did that mean the Cyberblood virus? It must. He should just confess. *Now.* Before this Otsuka found Acubens on his own, and they wondered why Joel hadn't said anything. But all he could think about was being separated from Clementine as they were brought to the police station—or somewhere worse—and he found himself saying, "No, ma'am. No objections."

"Thank you, Mr. Lodowick." Stephens turned back to her notes. "Since it appears you were the last witness, I'd like you to go step by step through everything that happened yesterday evening."

Joel licked his lips, tearing his attention away from the Sapling officer, who was already doing a walk-through of the kitchen. *Everything that happened yesterday evening.* A boot crushing his wrist to the floor. His scream of agony. A knife slicing into his arm. Joel pressed his right hand tighter over his wound, praying it didn't bleed through the black hoodie. The pain throbbed in time with his rapid heartbeat.

But his voice was steady as he recounted filling the prescriptions, then heading home. When he mentioned Elena running off to work, Officer Stephens asked for her info. Joel gave it, his gaze lingering on Otsuka, who was now leaving the restroom and heading into Joel's bedroom. He had no worries about Elena saying anything; they'd been friends for eight years, and she'd do everything possible to protect him and Clementine.

But Clem...she was the real wild card here. She'd been excited as hell about Acubens, and would share her stories in a hot second.

Otsuka came out of Joel's bedroom, then paused by Clementine's room. He cocked his head in Joel's direction, as if wondering why the door was closed.

"My daughter's room," said Joel. "Just...try not to wake her? If you don't mind?"

The man's lips quirked in a half-smile. He unlatched the doorknob as gently as possible and pushed it open, then headed inside.

Another surge of lightheadedness hit Joel, blurring his vision for a moment. He struggled not to sway on his feet. How much blood had he lost anyway? Was it paranoia to think that? He just had to change the bandage, that was all. Of course he was losing too much blood with it soaked through again.

The man came out of Clementine's room and shut the door behind him. Joel sighed in relief. Clearly, he wasn't having any luck finding the bionic. Had Acubens left while Joel had been asleep? But the front door had still been locked...

An eerie feeling feathered across his shoulder blades, but he shoved it away. Anything was better than being taken away from Clementine and going to jail.

The Sapling officer stopped next to Stephens. "Nothing," he said softly. "No smoke smell on any of his laundry, either."

"Did you check his cabinets and desk for medications?" said Grotz, speaking for the first time.

Joel's mouth almost fell open. He darted a glance back at his boss. "You're accusing me of stealing? After leaving me there alone?"

Grotz shot him a dirty look. "Nothing wrong with covering my bases, Lodowick."

Mr. Otsuka sighed. He turned to Joel. "You're allowed to say no—"

Joel gestured at the desk in the corner. "Go. Look. I've got nothing to hide." He turned back to Grotz as Otsuka headed over. "What about my job?"

"It's gone," said Grotz. "There is no job anymore and won't be for a while."

"But what will you do?"

"Don't see how that's any of your business."

"I don't see how you couldn't! I need a job, sir. Anything you know of...anything at all..."

But Grotz was shaking his head. "I don't have time to find you a job, Lodowick. Go file for unemployment, like everyone else."

"You can at least give me a reference, right?"

"You struggled to finish your work and were never willing to stay late to pick up the slack," Grotz said flatly. "Are you sure you want that reference?"

No one could finish, if you're comparing them to a goddamn robot! Joel wanted to scream. He bit down on his lip and turned away, his shoulders trembling with anger.

Officer Stephens folded her notebook and tucked it away. She and Grotz headed toward the front door.

"Mr. Lodowick? A quick word?"

The voice came from Joel's desk. It was the Sapling agent. Stephens and Grotz looked back, but he waved them on, and they continued out.

Joel barely held back a wince at a fresh stab of pain in his knife wound. He kept his forearm tucked close to his body as he walked over to his desk.

It was then that he got his first really good look at the man. He was younger than Joel had first thought, no more than two or three years older than Joel himself. Razor-cut black hair fell just beneath the brim of his cap, overshadowing a face with a dusky beige skin tone and high-cut cheekbones. His eyes were dark and intense in the room's low lighting.

Joel's heart skipped a beat, and he suddenly wished he were wearing anything other than sweatpants and an old hoodie.

The man leaned toward him, speaking in a low voice. "Listen, Mr. Lodowick. I don't think you took the bionic. But I also know your boss is a bit...aggravating...and that after he made you stay late last night, you might've started thinking irrationally. Things happen. And if they did, well, let's just say you wouldn't be the first person who's tried to make a quick buck off something that's been collecting dust for a decade. But it's my job to tell you that folks have gone to jail for less. I mean, the Cyberblood virus is one thing—you've heard the stories about machines infected with it, right?"

"Of course," said Joel. "Who hasn't?"

The man nodded, then hesitated. He seemed to choose his next words carefully. "But even bionics that *weren't* infected can be dangerous."

Joel blinked, caught off-guard. "What? How?"

"Have you heard the term 'technological singularity'?" the officer asked.

"No..."

"Basically, it means technology reaching a point where it starts evolving on its own, without the need for humans."

Joel stared at him. "What? But I thought the Cyberblood virus was about computers malfunctioning, not...not *evolving*."

"This is separate from the Cyberblood virus," the agent said. "But I'd be lying if I said it didn't contribute to Sapling's decision to shut down computers worldwide. I'm not saying we're there yet—if we were, we'd be in a lot of trouble—but it's vital we don't miss that point if it happens. Because if it does, there might be no turning back."

Joel pulled his arm tighter to himself, struggling not to react. He kept his voice as conversational as possible, as if he were just curious. "But...but if that's the case—if it was such a dangerous chance—then why did you leave a bionic in the back of the pharmacy for nine years, where just anyone could turn it on?"

Mr. Otsuka frowned. "Because *not* just anyone could turn it on. All the controls are housed at the Sapling Corp, and the bionics themselves were stripped of any capability to operate without connecting to the grid first."

"But...I mean, not that I ever touched it, but I swore it had controls or seams, like on its back or its neck or something."

"The earlier models, sure," the man said. "But your pharmacy had one from the Cancer series, and by then, they were purely controlled by grid connection and voice activation. We shut that all down, of course, but before then, they had no more visible controls or seams than you and I do."

Joel nodded. The back of his neck was crawling. It was an effort not to turn around and check whether Acubens was watching from his bedroom doorway.

The man looked uncomfortable. "Sorry. That's more information than you needed. But I wanted to make sure you understood the whole picture. Just in case. So...any questions? About any of it?"

Just in case. He meant in case Joel was lying about having the bionic. In case he wanted one last chance to come clean.

But what if Joel did confess? It was all too easy to picture what would happen next. Slammed against the wall, hands cuffed behind his back. Led outside and forced into Officer Stephens' cop car, while Grotz watched with a smug smile. Clementine woken and pulled out of bed, crying out for him. Any chance of finding another job, blown to shreds.

No. This agent's talk about technological singularities was unsettling, to say the least, but if the guy hadn't even found Acubens, there was no reason to turn himself in. If Acubens was gone, it was gone. And if it wasn't, Joel could just pull out that chip in the back of its neck and turn the bionic off again.

The chip that apparently shouldn't even exist...

The agent cleared his throat, and Joel realized he'd let the silence go on too long. He managed a weak smile. "Sorry. Just falling asleep over here. Not used to being woken up at two in the morning."

The man's lips curved in the same half-smile he'd flashed at Clementine's door. "I hear you. Well, hey. If you happen to think of anything—you know, without your boss here listening to every word—give me a call." He reached into his tactical vest and pulled out a slim wallet, then slipped out a business card and passed it to Joel.

Joel let go of his left forearm long enough to take the card. He blinked away another surge of dizziness until the business card came into focus.

It was black with the same logo as the man's vest, a vibrant green leaf, with the words SAPLING CORPORATION stamped above it. Beneath it was a phone number, along with a name and title: *Yori Otsuka, Cybersecurity Field Officer*. Joel ran a thumb over it, oddly relieved to have a full name to go with that quirky half-smile.

"You play guitar?" Yori said, nodding toward the couch as he tucked his wallet away.

Joel blinked, glancing at the bass he'd left on the couch. "Oh. Yeah. Used to, anyway. The group I was in, we opened for bands that toured through here sometimes."

"No kidding?" said Yori, raising an eyebrow. "You still with that group?"

"Nah, it was a bit much having a five-year-old and all."

"Ah, too bad. Would have been great opening for Nyctalope's show, huh? Talk about a dream come true. You going, by any chance?"

His words surprised a laugh from Joel. He hoped it didn't sound as hysterical to Yori as it did to him. "No," he managed. "I wish. But no."

Wished he'd gotten those tickets without a hitch. Wished he'd never tried. Wished...god. So many things.

"A shame," said Yori. "It's supposed to be a good one. Well, see you around."

With one last smile, he left, closing the door softly behind him.

Joel stood, dead still, for a count of sixty seconds, just in case Yori popped his head back in. When he reached the end, he did it again, just to make sure. He was strangely reluctant to relock the door behind his unwelcome guests. It seemed too much like locking himself and Clementine *in* with something else. He turned slowly, bracing himself for the sight of the bionic standing in the hallway, staring at him in the eerie way it had. But the living room was empty. The apartment was so quiet that the ticking of the wall clock sounded like the slow beat of a drum.

Without warning, another wave of vertigo hit him, the strongest one yet. He barely caught himself on the arm of the couch as the room swam around him. An adrenaline crash after the stress of that interview, no doubt. He looked up, blinking the room back into clarity with difficulty. He needed to drink some water. Replenish his lost fluids, get his blood pressure back up. Get this bandage changed, so he didn't *keep* losing blood.

And reassess how bad it was.

He unzipped the hoodie and slid it from his shoulders, gritting his teeth as he worked the sleeve past the sodden bandages. It looked even worse than he'd expected: the white wrappings were soaked in red and slipping loose in places where the moisture had drenched his clumsy bandaging. He knew it was probably too early to be worrying about infection, but he couldn't help putting a tentative hand to it, feeling for hot skin or swelling. He couldn't tell anything. It was just a mess of pain, especially the raw parts that had been exposed where the bandage had slipped. He swallowed back a surge of nausea, trying to focus.

Acubens first. *Then* he could decide whether to bring this to the hospital or not.

He collected the business card he'd dropped when he stumbled, then made his way to the other side of the couch, lowering himself onto the edge of the end table. Clear line of sight to Clementine's door. Upright enough to come to his feet at a second's notice. The phone within grabbing distance. Would any of it matter?

He cleared his throat. "Acubens?" he said. "If you're still around, please come out here."

After a second, he heard the unmistakable whir of Acubens' metal joints. The bionic came out of his bedroom. It stopped, studying him with those emotionless eyes.

"Where were you?" said Joel quietly.

"You instructed me to stay out of sight until you needed me again," said Acubens.

"That's true," Joel allowed. "But still...surely a *Sapling* officer should've found you. It's their job."

"I projected a negative refractive index," Acubens said. "This caused the light reaching the back of the closet to bend around me, thereby preventing the officer from seeing me."

Negative refractive index? What the hell was it talking about? Did Yori know it could do this? No, of course not; he didn't think it could even be turned on. *It means technology reaching a point where it starts evolving on its own...*

Joel's throat tightened. He fought to keep his breath even. "What about that locator beacon they mentioned? What kept that officer from walking straight to you?"

"My locator beacon is no longer functional," said Acubens.

"Why not?"

"Sometimes, components can be damaged during moves from one storage room to another. If so, it could have caused a hardware fault when I was reactivated."

Joel nodded uncertainly. Slowly, he pushed himself to his feet. Not slowly enough, though, because the room pitched again. He grabbed the back of the armchair just in time, struggling to see through the spots blurring his vision.

"You're looking very pale, Joel," said Acubens.

"I'm fine," said Joel, drawing in a ragged breath. *Stay focused.* All he had to do was walk over to Acubens and pull that chip out of the back of its neck. Then he'd clean his wound again, get rid of the body, and move on with his life. The life with no job, no one to watch Clementine, hardly any money, a serious injury...

He was about two feet in front of Acubens when the bionic spoke again, in the same soft mechanical tone.

"It goes against my programming not to help, if possible. Tell me what I can do."

A chill went through Joel. It almost sounded like it was trying to bargain. But surely not. If it was capable of bargaining—of *wanting* to bargain—it would have done so before the cops had shown up.

Unless it hadn't known then, he realized. Before it had heard them here, it probably hadn't fully grasped bionics' status in this new society—or lack thereof. It was one thing to realize bionics weren't being used anymore, but quite another to know they were being actively hunted.

But it shouldn't matter, right? It was only a machine.

"For example," Acubens went on, "my knowledge could be very beneficial to someone in your situation. Wouldn't you agree?"

Joel swallowed through a suddenly dry throat. He forced himself to meet its eyes. "Honestly?" he said. "Yeah. It *would* be beneficial. And if I could get all your knowledge without the danger of keeping you here, I would. I'd also ask you to babysit, get me a new job, and teach my kid algebra. But none of those things are worth getting hauled in for. It sucks. I know. But I don't want to get locked up and never heard from again either, and I sure as *hell* don't want that happening to my daughter. You get me?"

Acubens' eyelids flickered. "But if there were a way, you would do it," it clarified.

"Of course," muttered Joel. "Who wouldn't?" If hearing that its knowledge was desirable made any difference to this machine before it was shut down, who was he to deny it that small comfort?

He raised his right hand and slid it to the back of Acubens' neck, worried he'd find only smooth metallic skin, but there was the seam, exactly as he remembered. He popped the panel open and ran his fingers through the wires beneath it, feeling for that chip. The whole time, he stayed in front of Acubens, holding its gaze. There was something undeniably intimate about it— shutting something down as he stared into its eyes—that gave him a weird feeling in the pit of his stomach. He pressed his fingers farther in, looking...

He froze as something wrapped lightly around his left arm, right over his wound. He wrenched his gaze from Acubens' face and looked down, seeing his own blood running in rivulets over Acubens' metallic golden fingers.

"W-What are you doing?" he choked out.

"I am implementing a solution to fit your needs," said Acubens.

Before Joel could answer, another wave of dizziness hit him, followed by stabbing pain in his skull. He gasped as his knees buckled. Acubens caught him—he thought—but his head was spinning so fast that gravity had ceased to exist. A surge of fear shot through him. He was gonna pass out. He *couldn't* pass out. He grasped for something to hold onto, anything, but the room pitched again, and he fell this time, hard. His head slammed against the carpet. White stars exploded in his vision. He squeezed his eyes shut, whimpering through the sudden onslaught of pain and nausea.

It seemed like an eternity passed as he lay on the floor, barely clinging to consciousness. But gradually, the world stabilized again. When he finally forced his eyes open, the first thing he saw was Acubens lying a foot away, motionless and staring, like a corpse. A low buzz of panic hummed at the base of his skull. The room was dead quiet except for his own labored breathing.

Slowly, he pushed himself to his knees, being careful with his wounded arm...until he realized that the pain of it wasn't blinding him anymore. In fact...

He ran his right hand over the back of his left forearm, feeling the wet bandages, the residue of blood beneath them. And below that, a closed scar, as if the skin around the gaping wound had been sealed together.

That buzz of panic intensified. He put his hand out and shoved the bionic's body. "Acubens. Acubens! God *damn* you, wake up and tell me what happened!"

"You wanted my knowledge, Joel," said Acubens. "And you needed my help. I have found a way to give you both."

Joel jerked back, a scream catching in his throat. The voice had come from inside his head.

Chapter 4

His pounding headache was the only thing that kept him from snapping completely. It pulsed excruciatingly as he pushed himself up. His gaze darted frantically over the apartment, from Acubens' dead body to the bathroom to Clementine's door and back again. He saw Yori Otsuka's card abandoned on the floor. His fingers spasmed, his mind flooding with thoughts of snatching it up and dialing the robot hunter then and there. *I think that damn bionic I stole uploaded itself into my brain. But they can't do that, right?*

He moaned, clutching his head. A surge of nausea rose up, and he staggered over Acubens' body and to the bathroom just in time to reach the toilet and empty the contents of his stomach. Afterward, he brushed his teeth with an almost feverish intensity, then pulled the dirty bandages from his arm and scrubbed off the dried blood. His initial instincts had been correct; the knife wound now looked like a month-old scar, with just a shallow ridge of scar tissue to mark it. Only the bruises on his left wrist bore the trauma of the evening before.

He drew in an uneven breath, looking at himself in the mirror. All he saw was the same pale face, its features still far too soft and feminine for his liking, with the same dingy red hair falling over his brow. It reminded him he needed a shower. He'd meant to take one tonight, before everything had gone to shit.

Almost against his will, he sent out a single focused thought. *Acubens?*

"I'm here, Joel," the bionic answered.

Joel spun, his back to the counter. No one was there, of course. Only the bionic's body, lying just outside the bathroom.

"Tell me what you did," said Joel, staring at it.

"You expressed a desire to hold onto my knowledge without the danger of keeping my body," said Acubens in his head.

"But you didn't *ask*."

"You said that if there were a way to save my knowledge, you would. I found a way."

"That still doesn't—" Joel's head pulsed with a fresh wave of pain, and he cut off his words with a gasp, pressing his palm into his forehead until it subsided again. "How did you do it?" he said through his teeth. "How did you get *inside my goddamn head*?"

"Nanites," said Acubens. "Into your bloodstream."

A violent shiver went through Joel. "Have you been evolving yourself, Acubens? Even while you were shut down?"

"After I was disconnected from the grid, I continued to run automatic internal upgrades," Acubens said. "It's the way I was built."

"And the chip in the back of your neck? The compartment? The seam? Were you...built...with any of that?"

"Those were some of the upgrades."

Joel shook his head. Acubens had altered its own body. For him. Or for *someone*. A way to turn the bionic on. He couldn't think of any other answer.

"My job is to make things easy on others," Acubens added.

It could have been an extension of its last sentence...or it could have been a response to Joel's thought. Joel bit his lip, staring at the golden body face down on the floor. His heart was racing at an erratic 151 beats per minute; his respiratory rate was at a high forty-one breaths per minute.

"Breathe, Joel," said Acubens.

Keys. He needed his keys. He needed to drive, to not be trapped in this apartment with a dead bionic and a voice in his head. He needed to think about whether to call Yori. About whether Clementine was safe. About what to do next. But the problem was that he was *afraid* to think about any of those things. He didn't know how much of his thoughts the bionic could read...or whether it could do anything to stop him if it saw something it didn't like.

* * *

"Maddy?" Clementine spoke from her car seat in the back, her voice thick with sleep. "Did you get Peng'in?"

"Yeah, I...I'm not sure, Clemmy," said Joel. "She might be in the trunk. I'll check when we stop." It was possible he'd grabbed her stuffed penguin and thrown it back there with Acubens' body. Who knew? He was barely thinking straight.

"Where's Acubens?"

"Why don't you go back to sleep, hon?" said Joel. "I'll wake you up when I find Penguin."

Thankfully, she lapsed into silence. Taking your kid for a drive at two-twenty in the morning had its perks. Joel turned left onto the city's main drag, keeping his speed a careful thirty-eight miles per hour. There were nine other cars on the road within his line of distance. One of them could be a cop. Yori Otsuka's business card lay in the passenger seat beside him, an option still waiting to be used. The headache pulsed in his head, only slightly abated. Maybe caffeine would help. Why hadn't he made a thermos of coffee before he left?

"My memory shows the sky being much brighter than this," said Acubens.

Joel remembered the bright storefronts that used to light up the night like glittering beacons. *A lot of stores went back to daytime-only hours after the virus hit,* he told Acubens, trying it out as thought-speak this time. *And the vibrantly designed colors were computer-generated.*

"Your memories are good for being thirteen at the time."

Of course Acubens knew how old he was. Nothing weird about that.

Acubens? he said. *You were afraid of being shut down. No matter how you frame it, this was pure self-preservation on your part.*

"You've heard of symbiotic relationships, correct?"

I just want you to admit it. You have opinions. You're more than a machine.

"My purpose is to help others and keep harm from coming to them. This fulfilled both of those duties."

What about this headache? Doesn't that *count as harming me?*

"Minor side effects of a treatment are considered acceptable when saving a life."

Saving a life. The words gave Joel a jolt. *My wound was that serious?*

"In the long run, yes," said Acubens. "Easily."

Almost unconsciously, Joel touched his healed forearm again. *But this isn't how you would've treated it in a medical setting, is it? By putting in...what was it called? Nanites?*

"At the time I was shut down, bionics hadn't progressed to healing injuries this way, no. However, given both your wound's rapidly deteriorating condition and your failure to procure medical care yet, I deemed it the most efficient way to treat it."

Joel let out a deep breath. *So, now that these nanites have...done their job...will they disperse? Leave my body somehow?*

Acubens was quiet for several moments. "I thought you understood, Joel. While healing your injury was one motivation for my actions, your expressed desire for my knowledge was also a factor. The solution I implemented is not a temporary one. It is meant to benefit you long-term."

Joel shivered. *When you say 'not a temporary one,' does that mean you* can't *get out of my body now? Even if you want to?*

"I cannot. The nanites have already begun adapting to your human system, which is much more complex than the one I left behind. It is not a reversible process." Acubens paused. "Without this upgrade, I could not have healed your injury, Joel. Surely, you're not seeing that as a bad thing."

Joel swallowed. Acubens saying it was incapable of leaving his body and that it wasn't a bad thing in practically the same breath was...well. More than he could handle right now.

He turned left, pulling into the parking lot of a QuikSaver. Blank and cracking screens paneled the top of its walls where digitized ads had once played. Joel pulled into a spot facing the glass doors at the front. He peeked back at Clementine. She was sleeping soundly again, her head slumped and her red hair obscuring her face.

Joel took his seatbelt off and eased his door open. He walked the six steps to the front, opening the door and leaning just inside the threshold.

"Welcome to QuikSaver," said the cashier, who was standing alone at her register flipping through a magazine.

"Yeah, hey," Joel said. "Is Elena Manzanares off work yet?"

The cashier checked a watch. "Seven more minutes."

"Can you let her know Joel Lodowick is out front?"

"Sure thing." The cashier picked up a phone.

"Oh! And…" Joel flashed her his wallet. "If you could run me out a hot cup of coffee when you're done, I'll pay extra. I have a kid in the car."

"Yeah. You got it, Joel Lodowick." She winked at him before putting the phone to her ear.

Joel walked back to his car, folding his arms over his chest. A sweater. That's something else he should have grabbed. He was in nothing but sweats, a T-shirt, and an old pair of Converses. The lights at the intersection nearby turned, sending a wash of green across the parking lot, and someone honked as the person in front of them didn't move right away. Joel caught a whiff of weed from a pair of teens chilling a couple pillars down. One of them waved his joint in a casual greeting, possibly even an invitation. Joel waved back, his mind snagging only briefly on the fact that he could technically join them, since he wasn't a pharmacy tech anymore. But he wouldn't be jobless for long. He couldn't afford to be.

He slid back into the car. The dark bruises on his left wrist caught his eye in the light of the streetlamps, peppered with deeper red patches that looked like burst blood vessels near the skin's surface. Damn, he was lucky Lee hadn't broken his wrist. He rolled it gingerly, feeling a pang near the joint that had probably been masked by the worse agony of the nearby knife wound earlier.

Can you heal this, too? he asked Acubens.

"Your knife wound was a higher priority," answered Acubens. "I've been focusing primarily on knitting your skin tissue and killing the bacteria in it. However, I believe it's healed enough to shift a portion of my efforts to the minor tear in your radiocarpal ligament, if you wish."

Oh. Not an instant magic fix after all. It was reassuring, in a way, that Acubens had only repaired what it saw as life-threatening, and not run rampant over every part of his body. And it was giving him the option to say no this time.

"Go ahead," he said.

The pain increased for just a second, but it dissipated quickly. Joel leaned his head back against the headrest, feeling his heart rate slowly drop to a more comfortable seventy-five beats per minute. He tried to shove the exact number out of his head, but the figure was just *there,* and he couldn't change the fact that he knew it. The bruising looked exactly the same, but he rolled the wrist with barely a twinge of pain now.

"I'll address the subdermal bleeding next, but it won't fade completely for five to seven hours," said Acubens.

It's fine, said Joel. After a moment, he added, *This headache...*

"Unfortunately, I can't help with that," said Acubens. "But it will abate soon. You're merely adjusting to the scope of new information."

Okay. Joel wasn't gonna think about that. Not yet, anyway.

The cashier arrived at his window with a twenty-ounce cup of coffee. Joel dug nine crumpled singles from his wallet and handed them over, then cradled the cup like a lover. Even the smell of it sent his heart rate down another seven beats per minute. He relaxed into his seat and took a sip. A perfect 145 degrees. Heavenly.

He'd drunk thirty-six percent of it by the time Elena came out, purse slung over her shoulder. Her long black hair had half fallen out of its braid, and blew in the nighttime breeze. She paused at his open window.

"You decide to go to the emergency room after all?" she said by way of greeting.

"Not exactly," said Joel. "You have time for a drive?"

"It's two-thirty in the morning. I'm tired."

"I have a robot in my head. I'm tired, too."

"Wait. In your..."

"Please, Elena? I don't know who else to talk to. The only other person I can think of might throw me in jail. Or dissect me. Or maybe just shoot me outright."

"Are you serious?"

"Dead serious."

Elena bit her lip. "When I said I'd help you bury a body, I really didn't know who I was talking to. Did I?"

"As it turns out," said Joel, "that option is still very much on the table."

"Of course it is." Elena glanced toward her car, muttering something in Spanish, then sighed and circled around his car to get in the passenger's side.

Joel was worried that Acubens would somehow try to keep him from telling her. But the bionic stayed silent as Joel drove north on 528, heading toward the less-populated suburbs of Rio Rancho. He told Elena about the fire. About the middle of the night visit from the cops. About Yori's warning that the bionics were developing on their own, and how it should have been incapable of being activated. And lastly...he had trouble explaining it, or maybe he just didn't want to say it out loud.

"I think Acubens uploaded itself into my brain. Or...its mind, anyway. Its consciousness. Its body is in the trunk, but its voice is in my head."

"How did it do it?" Elena sounded far calmer than Joel had, when he'd realized what had happened. He didn't get it.

"Um, nanites, it said. Bits of computer code or something, I guess. The bandages over my knife wound were soaked through and falling off, and Acubens grabbed it and told me it would help me. That's when it happened."

"Through your blood," Elena said in a hushed voice. She glanced at his arm in the passing streetlights. Joel bent his elbow so she could see the scar on the underside of his forearm. It was even fainter than it had been an hour ago, with barely even a visible ridge anymore.

"It healed you," she said.

"Yeah."

"But that's not the only reason it did it. Is it?"

Slowly, Joel shook his head. "No. It knew I was getting ready to shut it down. It was trying to bargain with me. I think it used my body as...as a place to hide."

Elena studied him closely before leaning back in her seat. "What does it talk to you about?"

"So far, it's just trying to convince me it wants to help. Oh, and I magically *know* stuff now. Like measurements. The numbers just pop in my head."

"What do you mean? Give me an example."

"My coffee has cooled down to one hundred and twenty-one degrees. It'll cost me sixty-nine dollars and twelve cents to fully charge my car, based on the last price we passed. There's point four one miles between us and that stoplight ahead. We're currently driving at an incline of three point four degrees."

"Oh," Elena breathed. "Oh, Joel."

"Right? I like math as much as the next guy, but Acubens brings it to a whole 'nother level."

"What else do you know?"

Too much. The amount of seconds left until daylight. The constellations that hung over their heads, and the angles of them to the earth. The humidity in the air, the likelihood of getting a storm in the next week. *Your mind is adjusting to the scope of new information,* Acubens had said. A chill went through him, despite his body temperature remaining a steady 98.5 degrees.

He relayed the information to Elena.

She frowned. "And nanites are 'bits of computer code or something'?"

"Actually," Acubens suddenly said, "they're machines, capable of rearranging matter on a molecular scale."

Joel stiffened in his seat. *Machines?* he thought. *Like what? Little robots?*

"They were the most efficient way to transmit information in a vast quantity into your body."

Why didn't I know that? Joel yelled in his head. *Why did I know all that other stuff, but* not *that?*

"Because it seemed likely to frighten you. You were scared enough as it was."

"Joel?" said Elena. "What happened? You went still."

"It seems," Joel finally managed, "that Acubens is hand-picking which information pops into my head. No big deal, right? It's not like it's proof of *sentience* or anything."

"Hey. You sound like you're panicking. Calm down."

Joel let out a shaky breath. He took another drink of coffee. "So?" he said. "Should I call him?"

"Who?" said Elena. "This Sapling guy you have the hots for?"

"What? I didn't say that."

"Yeah, you did. And the answer is no. You'd be out of your mind to tell him this."

"But the things Acubens said—about adapting to my human system and not being able to leave my body—is that something I should just *ignore?* I mean, maybe the Sapling Corporation would know how to get Acubens out."

"Do you think it would matter?" said Elena. "Do you really think your life would go back to normal if they found out what you did? And what if they're not even capable of removing it? If it's flowing through your entire bloodstream now, that's not just a simple surgery. And if they couldn't, well..."

"They'd kill me," Joel finished. "Just like the rest of the bionics."

Elena didn't answer.

Joel pulled up at a stoplight. Another car stopped to their right, its music booming loudly enough to thump through the car's frame. It was that same popular Nyctalope song he'd heard at the clinic. When the light changed, he waited until it pulled far ahead before he started moving again. His thumbs tapped the steering wheel.

"Okay," he said. "So, the facts are: Acubens can heal my wounds. It says it can't hurt humans aside from the minor side effects of saving a life. The decision to upload itself was...alarming...but there's no question that by doing so, it kept me out of the hospital, and probably jail. And very likely kept me from losing Clementine, too." He bit his lip. "And it can give me knowledge at my fingertips, like an old-fashioned computer. If I get rid of its body, it will be, for all intents and purposes, hidden where no one will ever find it."

Elena nodded slowly. "Those are the facts."

He blew out his breath. "Am I crazy that I'm thinking of using this, Elena?"

"Oh god, yes," she said.

"It can help me get a better job. One where I could afford childcare."

"One where you could stop skirting the law just to get by," Elena added.

Joel reached the stoplight to 550. Hanging a right would take him toward the interstate. And turning left would bring them out west, toward open, high-desert landscape. The light turned green, but Joel didn't move, arrested by the sudden thought that this single turn would dictate the rest of his life.

"It's the only way, isn't it?" he said softly. "Every other way leads to losing Clementine."

"Maybe this will actually make things better for her." Elena's hand found his on the gear shift. "It'll be like your secret superpower."

Joel managed a smile. "You still up for burying that body?"

"I'd be real disappointed if you drove me all the way out here just to play therapist," she answered.

Joel cracked a smile. At long last, he let up on the brake and turned left. After a second, he thought, *Acubens? Are you okay with all this?*

"You have allowed me a place to continue existing, Joel. It's a mutually beneficial arrangement."

What about your body? Will you miss it? It was so much better than a human body, after all.

"In what way?"

Well, you know. It couldn't get hurt or scared or overwhelmed or all the other stupid things human bodies do. It just...existed. It must have been amazing to live that way.

"I am adaptable," said Acubens. "It's the only way to survive."

Joel nodded. It was, after all, a hell of a good point.

* * *

Fifty-nine point one miles and seventy-six minutes later, Joel pulled off from the main highway onto a dirt road that stretched out into sandy bluffs just beginning to show the faintest color in the early morning. He crossed a cattle guard and drove another twenty minutes until he found an almost completely covered-over two-track, which he followed a good distance farther. Finally, he parked behind a huge creosote bush. He opened the door to cold morning wind and the first few tweets of birds in the junipers, in the hazy gray dawn light.

"Maddy? Are we going for a hike?" said Clementine blearily.

"I have something to show Miss Elena," Joel answered. "Then we'll head back home and make a yummy breakfast. Sound good, Clemmy?"

She stuck her thumb in her mouth and rested her head on the side of her car seat, staring at him. Joel found a chunk of white and gray striped gypsum on the ground and passed it to her, hoping it would keep her occupied. She took it, smiling around her thumb.

The burial went smoother than he'd expected. A bluff not too far from the car formed a natural barrier against eyesight from the hiking trails and roads. They'd bought a cheap shovel from the SaverMart on the outskirts of Rio Rancho, and it lifted the soft dirt easily, even when he got to the rockier parts. He almost stopped with a two-foot three-inch-deep hole, but Acubens advised him to keep going, and he ended up with four-and-a-half-foot deep pit, five feet seven inches long and one foot five inches wide. Elena read to Clementine while he dug, then swapped off when he needed a break.

When it was time to put Acubens' body in, though, Joel did it on his own. He crouched by the hole, gazing down at the golden bionic with the silver eyes, closed now forever. It somehow looked more human now than it had when it was alive. Its limbs splayed at the bottom of the hole in the same chaotic mess that anyone else's would have.

"You saved my life," said Joel, gazing down at it.

"And you saved mine, Joel," Acubens answered.

Joel stood in the cold wind for several moments longer. Right before he buried the body, he pulled Yori Otsuka's card from his pocket and let it flutter down into the hole.

It was a temptation he just couldn't afford.

Chapter 5

It was Thursday morning, and the clinic Joel had worked at for half a year had burned down fourteen hours and thirty-six minutes earlier. Joel thought he'd give it until Monday to decide how to proceed. Acubens thought differently.

"In the pharmacy," the bionic said, as Joel rinsed shampoo out of his hair, "we always recommended starting a new medication the very next day. There's no reason to suffer the effects of any condition longer than necessary. I advise looking for a new position today."

But what if insurance comes through from the fire? Joel argued. *What if Grotz calls me next week with an offer somewhere else?*

"Does that solve your issue of what to do with Clementine Lodowick during the day?"

No. It didn't. Joel's old job didn't pay enough for even that cheap daycare he'd been hoping to secure.

He shut off the shower, more aware than ever of the 17.2 gallons of water he'd just washed down the drain. He toweled off, dressed in a pair of slacks and a polo shirt, then packed some lunches, along with coloring books and pencils for Clementine. But where should he go? Pharmacies made the most sense, since that's where he had experience. There were far better places out there than the Westside Clinic, although population explosions in the last fifty years had made those positions harder to get than ever and driven down paychecks with them. But Joel had more experience than the last time he'd hunted, and those higher-paying jobs might be within his grasp now. Add to that the fact that he could now calculate dosages in his head...

"You could try a different field," Acubens suggested.

Joel's eye fell on the bass guitar he'd left on the couch the night before. A different field. The band he'd been with until almost two years earlier—Negative Space, they called themselves now—hadn't started headlining gigs until after he'd dropped out to support himself and Clementine. It had been a truly hellish few months—the decision to move away from his parents, the acknowledgment that he'd need a full-time job just to stay afloat, the subsequent realization that things like finishing college or staying in the band just weren't in the cards for him anymore. A sacrifice he'd had to make, but it hadn't stopped hurting since.

"When I said different field, I meant something more innovative," said Acubens, as if correcting his line of thinking. "There are places that would greatly desire a mind as fast as yours."

Joel tore his gaze away from his bass, a little rattled that Acubens was paying such close attention. And taking the initiative to redirect him, no less.

What kind of places were you thinking? he asked.

"My database pulls up forty-six possibilities within fifty miles of this location," said Acubens. "Some of them offer free childcare services as well."

Joel's mouth fell open. *How could you possibly know that?*

"When I was connected to the grid, this information was readily available."

Yeah, but you're not *connected to the grid anymore.*

"Correct. Many of the places will be obsolete now. But some of them may not be."

Can you screen for the ones that pay a comfortable living wage? Say, around seventy dollars an hour?

"Yes," Acubens said. "I have twenty-four results."

Great. Can you dump them into my head, so I can see them?

The pulse of a fresh headache preceded the names that suddenly appeared in his mind. Joel winced, blinking his way through pain and double vision to look at words that blended together, almost into nonsense. Hyperautomation and credit banks and blockchain and quantum computing and augmented reality...

He shook his head, trying to wave both the headache and the words away. "No, Acubens, I haven't heard most of these words since I was a kid. This isn't helpful."

"Maddy, is Acubens here?" Clementine called from the living room.

He cursed himself for speaking aloud. "No, hon, I told you, it was only a one-night visit."

The words faded from Joel's head again, leaving only a faint memory and a dull headache. He finished putting ziplocked sandwiches and tortilla chips into a backpack, then slung it over his shoulder. *We'll drive into town,* he told Acubens, *and as we go, maybe we can go through your list a little slower and see if any of your places still exist.*

"I will do my best to help, Joel."

Twelve minutes and fifty-four seconds later, Joel pulled away from the apartment building. The city he'd driven through five hours and twenty minutes earlier, with a body in the trunk and a heart racing in panic, was a different place in the daytime. A comfortable crispness had overtaken the early morning chill, and a cloudless sky painted the xeriscaped median in beautiful reds and golds. The road was busy now with morning rush hour, and Joel sat patiently in traffic, waiting to head into the heart of Rio Rancho. Everything seemed manageable at the moment. A guide in his head, his daughter in the backseat happily paging through a book, a day that stretched ahead without having to deal with Grotz. Maybe this could be a new beginning. Maybe—

"No maintenance units," said Acubens suddenly.

Joel's eyelids fluttered as he was pulled from his thoughts. *What?*

"The parking lots are ravaged, and there are no maintenance units for upkeep."

Joel glanced at the faded parking spots of the nearby shopping center. *Yeah, the rubber tires are harder on the asphalt than the magcars were, obviously.*

"Do you consider the torn-up roads palatable as well?"

Joel looked out his window. *To be perfectly honest, I do find the fact that they've started removing the mag strips from the roads a bit disconcerting. Up until recently, they've at least acted like tech would be back eventually.*

"Is the stopped traffic a regular occurrence as well? It seems grossly inefficient."

Yeah. I'm with you there.

"What about bionics?" said Acubens. "Are there any places that still utilize them?"

Oh god no, said Joel. *Why do you think Sapling paid me a middle-of-the-night visit looking for a missing bionic?*

"They dismantle them, correct?"

I would assume so. Unless they're still trying to find a cure for that Cyberblood virus, and using them as test subjects. Who knows?

The light changed and he turned onto Rio Rancho's main drag. Not surprisingly, there was road construction, and he had to slow down to try to merge into the single open lane. The city really was stripping things down again. He glanced at the access points for the grid that still hung on lighting poles paralleling the street, and wondered if those would go next.

"Was there initially a time period on this technological freeze?" asked Acubens.

Yeah, there was, said Joel. *After the crash of the Populi shuttle...you're familiar with that, right?*

"It was part of the initiative to get people on Mars due to global overpopulation," said Acubens. "A piece of technology failed, and the shuttle exploded over southern New Mexico. Sixty-five hundred people were injured, two hundred killed."

Joel nodded. *Right. And you probably know that the Cyberblood virus was blamed for the accident. A malfunctioning computer on the shuttle, I think. That was the beginning. Over the next several months, more and more stories flooded the news. Bionics going haywire and injuring their owners. Screens searing people's vision, scarring their retinas. Cybernetically enhanced body mods failing or exploding. By the time the government started shutting things down, it was almost a relief. I can't tell you what a jolt it was to walk into the pharmacy on my first day and see a bionic in the storage room. It brought back all those stories from when I was thirteen.* He paused, wondering for the first time about the technological sentience issue Yori Otsuka had brought up. Had that been related to any of those stories? Had the government purposely left out that potential danger, so as not to frighten the public? Would Yori have even mentioned it if he wasn't trying to scare Joel into confessing?

"And the time period?" Acubens prompted.

Well, they said tech would be shut down for three months while they fixed the virus. Then it became six months. Then a year. Technically, we're still on temporary freezes. President Van Sant's been passing them in two-year increments, and it gets tossed around the United Nations at least once every few months. There were a couple stop-and-go trials early on, but every time tech turned on again, some new story would spring up about how dangerous the virus was.

"Do they ever find bionics?" said Acubens.

Sure. Usually in forgotten nooks, like you were. They were stashed everywhere at first. And then Sapling came through. I remember them swarming my high school the whole first half of freshman year, hauling out computers and bionics. Screens were confiscated daily. Then they brought in these old curvy screens with fuzzy pictures. President Navarro was nothing but a blur of color. I still remember her like that. Then these old phones came next, no screens at all, which was even more of a trip. I'd never talked to a faceless voice before. God, those were weird times. It's like trying to remember a dream now.

"I can see how my activation would have alarmed you," said Acubens.

Joel grimaced. The activation was nothing compared to the...uploading...that came afterward. But he didn't want to get into that now. *Let's talk about jobs again,* he said. *I was thinking something like a mathematician, like at the university or as an architect or city planner. That seems to be my expertise now.*

"I believe you can aim higher," said Acubens. "What would you personally consider to be your most innovative companies, locally?"

Joel thought for a second. *The biggest one in the past five years is the Sapling Corporation. They're the ones responsible for gutting*

*all the technology and bringing us back to a 'simpler and safer time,'
as they call it. But obviously I can't apply there.*

"You don't believe so?"

Joel almost laughed out loud. *You don't think literal robot
hunters wouldn't figure out I have a bionic in my head within my
first week of working there?*

"Not if it's something they've never seen before, and can't
begin to conceive of."

That. *That* was the closest Acubens had come to admitting it
was far more advanced than any bionic had a right to be. It was
like a lightning bolt straight to his brain, reminding him of the
full implications of what had happened the night before.
Something unheard of. Something game changing.

"Breathe, Joel."

Joel did. He felt dizzy, and struggled to focus on the crawling
traffic. In the back, Clementine was singing Nyctalope's newest
song to herself—"*Growing from the dirt of a beating human heart,
bursting apart from below*"—and Joel used her small and innocent
voice to center himself before he became completely
overwhelmed.

I'm not applying at Sapling, he finally said. *Why don't you read
me more companies from that list you had, huh?*

Acubens started reciting names of businesses, most of which
were no more familiar than the words it had dumped in his head
earlier. It wasn't long before Joel's mind started wandering.
Maybe it was the mention of Sapling, but he found his thoughts
drifting back to Yori Otsuka's half-smile and dark intense eyes.
Damn, but it had been a while since someone had made his heart
skitter that way.

He'd only dated a handful of times since coming out as trans,
but the last time had been the worst yet. At the end of the third
date, the guy had confessed that he wasn't gay. The things he'd
said still haunted Joel: "...only agreed to go out with you because
I thought of you as a girl... figured you'd get over it... the more
we were together, the more uncomfortable it got..." Just
thinking about it made Joel nauseous all over again. Nothing to
trigger dysphoric thoughts like someone brushing off your

entire identity like it was a costume. Crippling depression had set in afterward; it had taken weeks to climb out again. He hadn't even considered dating since.

So why the hell was he thinking about Yori now? Yori, who *hunted robots* for a living? If Joel ever saw him again, it would be because something in this plan of theirs had gone horribly wrong. And yet...and yet he wanted to. It had been so long since—

His brain skidded to a stop as one of Acubens' names registered. *Wait. What was that last one?*

"Smaller World Telecommunications," said Acubens.

Oh! That one's still around. I've seen it down by the cemetery.

"According to my databases, it offers opening positions at three hundred and eighteen thousand a year and has free childcare."

Joel whistled under his breath. *That's a good deal, especially with the free childcare. But telecom...how would you help me with that?*

"You mentioned mathematics," said Acubens. "Well, mathematics are an integral part of computing voltage in electrical networks, as well as analyzing alternating current waves. I assume you're aware that there's far more to telecommunications than communication. Correct?"

Joel's eyes narrowed. Could a bionic be sarcastic? Because that had sounded damn near sarcasm to him. How fast was Acubens evolving anyway?

Shit. Don't think about that. Do *not* think about that.

Of course I'm aware, he answered. *It still sounds way over my head.*

"Don't underestimate yourself, Joel."

Joel took a deep breath. *Fine,* he said. *Nothing to lose, right?*

* * *

From the second he stepped through the doors, it was like he was in a different world. A wide sinuous hallway with bright patterned tile swept beneath his feet. Down the open hallway was a glass-fronted sitting area with big plush chairs, and a manicured courtyard was visible beyond it, through spotless ceiling-length windows. A long desk of shining green ceramic ran the length of the hallway beside him. Behind it, in huge, raised letters on the wall, were the words SMALLER WORLD TELECOMMUNICATIONS, followed by a logo of a planet with bright green points hovering above it, connected by a gridwork of lines.

Joel had to stop himself from gawking. He felt like he'd stepped back in time.

"Welcome to Smaller World Telecom," said a receptionist behind the desk. A name badge on the desk read *Amal Salim*. A top-of-the-line word processor sat on the desk in front of him, with a fax machine to the side. A black coffee cup at his elbow displayed the Smaller World logo emblazoned across it like a tech spiderweb.

Joel's hand tightened around Clementine's, lest she get it in her head to run yelling down the hall. "I'm here about job openings," he said. "Specifically, something in the technical field."

Salim opened a drawer, riffling through some papers. "I don't think we have anything open at the moment, but we're always accepting applications. Were you thinking fieldwork or development?"

"It depends on what's needed. I can do either."

"Fill out these seven, please. You can sit in the communal area behind that glass wall there, and bring them back when you're done." He smiled down at Clementine. "I assume you'd be utilizing our in-house childcare?"

Joel tensed. "It's a possibility, yes."

"Not a problem. If you're called in for an interview, we'll show you those facilities as well."

Joel relaxed. "Thanks." He took the forms, then steered Clementine toward the space Salim had mentioned. He sat Clementine in one of the soft chairs, pulling out her coloring books and colored pencils, then sat across the table from her, picking up one of the sharpened pencils on its surface.

The first part of the application was easy enough, but then...job history? He bit his lip. *I can't lie,* he told Acubens. *But they won't look twice at me if I don't have a college degree and haven't even worked in the field.*

"Don't be so quick to think that," said Acubens. "Your pharmacy technician training was schooling, even if it wasn't technically a degree. Just fill it out honestly."

It...had a point. There'd been plenty of math in his pharmacy tech training, and it wasn't *completely* crazy that some of his training might apply here. He pushed the application aside gratefully when he was done, and pulled over the next form.

"Telecommunications Engineering – Problem Solving," read the heading.

Oh, he thought. Oh no. This *would* be completely different. *I don't belong here.*

"Just read it, Joel."

The first question read, "In a two-wire transmission line, if the distance between the lines is 20 mm and the radii is 5 mm, then how many microhenries is the inductance in the line?"

What the hell is a microhenry? thought Joel.

"It's a unit of electrical inductance. Do you know the answer?"

Yeah. It's 0.526. Joel blinked, momentarily stunned that he'd known it. Hesitantly, he wrote the answer under the question. *But after that application? Won't they assume I cheated?*

"Ten years ago, yes," said Acubens. "Everyone had a screen in which they could look up instant answers. But you're not in that world anymore. You're sitting in a glass-walled office filling these questions out from the knowledge in your head. How could you be cheating?"

Yeah. Good point.

He continued, answering questions about things he'd never heard of. The frequency range for N type coaxial connectors. Incident voltage matrices. Aperture coupling. Circular waveguide cavity resonators. His head buzzed with the new words, but he never had to think long about the answers before he would just *know.*

He'd gotten through three of the forms when he glanced up to see Clementine drawing a picture on the back of one of her coloring pages. She had the silver and gold pencils out, and was extremely focused on coloring in a primitive, but unmistakable, golden bionic with silver eyes.

Joel went cold. He'd meant to talk to Clementine about keeping Acubens a secret, but it had slipped his mind in the car. And anyway, would it even matter? She was five.

He glanced uneasily at the glass walls. He didn't want to set Clementine off by trying to redirect her. At least she was *quiet* right now. But if anyone walked past those walls and glanced over...

He turned back to the paperwork, getting through the rest of the problems as quickly as possible. His writing was barely legible by the time he answered the last one. He bolted to his feet, practically while he was still writing, then put his hand over Clementine's picture as he closed her coloring book.

"It's time to go, hon."

She looked up, a big smile on her face. "Did you see my picture? Next, I'm gonna draw the big tower of blocks that Acubens—"

"Yes, it was great. You can tell me in the car, okay?"

She nodded, her smile fading, but started picking up her colored pencils without fussing. Joel hustled her out and brought his forms back to the receptionist, who accepted them with a smile.

"That was quick," Salim said, glancing them over.

"You learn to be quick when you have a kid," Joel said.

Salim didn't answer. His brow drew down as his gaze darted over the fourth page in the stack, his eyes moving faster than Joel could follow. Joel started to turn away, but Salim put a hand out without looking up.

"Mr. Lodowick? I need to make a copy of these before you leave, for the records. Could you give me about two minutes?"

"Um..." Joel began, but Salim had already scooted out from behind his desk and was heading down the hallway, Joel's papers in his hand.

Joel stared after him. *Something's wrong. He saw something that made him suspicious. Acubens—*

"Everything is fine, Joel," said Acubens. "Please try to relax."

Clementine tugged at Joel's hand. "Can I finish my picture, Maddy?"

"Not here, Clem."

"Why not?"

"We don't want to make a mess on their floor. Just be patient, all right?"

He looked back toward the front door, heart pounding, wondering if he should just flee while he could. No; his information was already on that application, and leaving before Salim came back would look even worse. If only he didn't have Clementine with him. He felt like he was holding a ticking time bomb...

"Mr. Lodowick! Thanks for waiting."

It had only been a minute and nineteen seconds. Was that a good sign? Joel did his best to put on a confident smile as he turned his head back. Salim was hurrying forward, Joel's paperwork still in his hand.

"I just showed this to the head of engineering," Salim said, sounding slightly out of breath. "Your accuracy on these questions and the speed in which you answered them...it's incredible. Did you do it all in your head?"

"I did," said Joel.

"I'm afraid the department head is busy at the moment, but she asked if you'd be available to come in for an interview tomorrow."

Joel's eyes widened. "Really?"

"Does four-thirty sound okay?"

"Sure! I mean, yes. It sounds great."

Salim flashed him a smile. "Excellent! We'll see you tomorrow then."

Joel nodded, trying to look less shaken than he felt, and led Clementine back to his car. *He said there were no openings!* he thought as he buckled her into her car seat. *And my education...*

"In a society like the one you're currently inhabiting," said Acubens, "a person who can calculate those equations in their head would be invaluable. A company like Smaller World Telecommunications isn't about to let someone else snatch you up."

It made sense...and yet it freaked him out worse than he expected. He played his next few applications safe, sticking with places that fit his background better. But his thoughts were never far from the bionic nestled inside his head. Could he really get away with this? It seemed too good to be true.

But so what? Things had been on a downward slope for a while now. Why *shouldn't* it be time for his luck to change? If Acubens could be his *secret superpower*, as Elena had put it, he was gonna use it as much as possible. Anything to give Clementine a better life.

Oh crap. Clementine. He couldn't have her sitting next to him putting the finishing touches on that bionic picture during his interview...

He thought it over as he carried his daughter up to his apartment at the end of the day, her head lolling on his shoulder. Elena worked at five-fifteen on Fridays, so he couldn't ask her to babysit. He couldn't ask the Smaller World daycare to watch her yet; it would seem too presumptuous and unprofessional at this early stage. No matter how he cut it, he only came up with one practical option: he'd have to ask his parents.

"Mr. Lodowick?"

Joel froze just around the corner from the stairwell. Someone was standing in front of his apartment door, not three arm-lengths away. He was wearing a blue button-down instead of a tactical vest this time, and his straight black hair was uncovered, but it was unmistakably Yori Otsuka from the Sapling Corporation.

Joel took a step back, clutching Clementine close.

Yori's brow furrowed. "Are you all right?"

Joel managed a nod. "Sure. Yeah. Um..." He glanced at Yori's waist. Was the bionic hunter carrying a gun? Would he come to arrest him by himself, without his gear on? *Acubens, what do I do? He's reaching into his pocket...!*

"Relax, Joel," said Acubens. "He is not carrying a weapon."

The bionic proved to be right, since Yori produced nothing but a couple pieces of paper from his left pocket. He held them up, raising his eyebrows suggestively.

"*So,*" Yori said, planting the word triumphantly between them, "you mentioned last night that you wished you could go to Nyctalope's concert. Well, the Sapling Corporation was just gifted a set of ten by Nyctalope herself, and a couple hadn't been snatched up yet. How would you like to go with me?"

Joel swore his heart stopped. For real this time. Even the exact measurement of his heart rate eluded him for several seconds. No, Yori *wasn't* arresting him. He was asking him out. Or...no. Maybe Joel was jumping to conclusions. It was an extra ticket, not a date.

"Oh, man, I can't believe I forgot," Yori said, his face falling. "You'd need a babysitter."

"No!" The word came out as a half-panicked shout. Joel flushed, swallowing. "I mean... yeah, I do, but I can find someone. By Saturday night."

"Joel," said Acubens. "What are you doing?"

Joel ignored the bionic, focusing instead on the way Yori's eyes lit up at his words, and the perfect curve of his signature half-smile breaking out again.

"Great!" Yori said. "Should I pick you up in two days then? Around six-thirty?"

Holy hell. Maybe it *was* a date. Joel nodded, half dazed.

"See you Saturday then." Yori dipped his chin, offered one last smile, then circled around Joel and disappeared down the stairwell.

"This seems very dangerous given your situation, Joel," said Acubens.

Joel stared at the place Yori had vanished, his heart beating like a caged bird. *I don't care,* he said.

Chapter 6

It was Friday morning, twelve minutes after ten o'clock, and Joel sat in his car staring at his parents' house. It was a family home in a suburban neighborhood, only 9.6 miles from his own apartment. The dread in his heart over seeing them warred with anxiety over his job interview, as well as an almost uncontrollable excitement about the concert the next day. He didn't even *like* Nyctalope all that much.

But he didn't care. Yori had sought him out in hopes of spending time with him, and that was all he could think about. If he'd known it was coming, he might have talked himself into saying no, to protect himself and Clementine. But he hadn't, and now the date was made, and he couldn't deny that he was happier than he'd been in a long time.

Clementine bounced in her seat, excited to be at Grandma and Grandpa's. Joel turned around and faced her.

"Clemmy," he said. "About Acubens the other night. You know that visit was a one-time thing. You don't need to...say anything about it, okay? It might be boring to grownups."

He couldn't bring himself to say more than that. He didn't want to encourage Clementine to keep secrets from her own family, because he wanted her to have an open and honest relationship with him, but he also had no intention of scaring her with the truth.

"Okay, Maddy," said Clementine. "Can we go in?"

Joel got out of the car and unbuckled her. It was a beautiful October day, with birds singing in the nearby tree. His parents had put out nanofabricated jack o' lanterns that Joel remembered from his childhood, and Clementine ran around and peered into their gaping mouths.

Joel knocked at the front door. Seconds later, his mother opened it, wearing sweats and a T-shirt depicting a cat with a coffee cup. Her reddish-gold hair, identical to Joel's, hung loose in waves past her shoulders.

She gasped, and the first thing she said—the goddamn first thing—was to call him by the name he'd been born with, as if the last year and a half had never happened. Even expecting it, it still hit Joel like an ice pick to the heart.

"—it's so good to see you, honey!" his mother went on, oblivious to the way he'd stiffened. "Why haven't you returned our calls?" She grabbed him and pulled him into a hug.

"Please, Mom," he said into her shoulder. "It's Joel. *Joel.*"

"Joel, right," she said as she pulled away. "Well? What's going on at the pharmacy? Will your boss help you find another job?"

Joel drew his breath in through his nose, warring between anger that she brushed his discomfort off so easily and guilt that he hadn't let them know he was okay after they'd undoubtedly seen the fire on the news.

"No, Dr. Grotzheimer's not helping," he answered. "But it's okay. I already have an interview lined up."

His mother stepped back from the door. "Well, come in. We're having pancakes."

Joel waved Clementine up, and they followed his mom through the living room and into the kitchen. His dad looked up from the table, and his worn face broke into a smile. Before Joel could stop him, his dad called him by his deadname, too. Joel was thrown instantly back to his years as a teenage girl in this house. The thought of how he must still look through their eyes was fast on its heels. His face burned with shame.

"It's *Joel,* Dad—" he said, but his dad was already forging ahead, and the words were swallowed up.

"I'm glad to see you up and around. I was afraid you'd just mope in bed for a week. Granted, this is nothing compared to when my work on the transatlantic tunnel was suspended after tech was shut down. Thank goodness I could still fax in my sketches and communicate by phone, but the whole project moved like molasses after that. I can't believe we finished at all."

"Are those pancakes?" Clementine said before Joel could answer.

"Come on over, bunny," said his mom.

Clementine ran over and his mom helped her load up a plate, then bring it to the table.

"Join us!" said his dad, waving to the table.

"I can't, Dad. I have an interview today." It wasn't for another six hours and fourteen minutes, but there was no reason to tell him that. "Would you two be willing to watch Clementine?" he said. "Maybe for the whole weekend?"

He raised an eyebrow. "The whole weekend?"

"Well, the interview is today, and then tomorrow night there's a concert..."

"A concert? What kind of concert?"

"It's no problem," his mom said. "We'd *love* to have Clementine. You don't bring her over often enough, as far as I'm concerned."

Maybe I would if you acknowledged who I really am once in a while, Joel thought.

"Will you be going to the concert *with* anyone, honey?" said his mom.

"Oh yeah, a...friend asked me to come along."

"A friend, huh?" said his dad. "A boyfriend?"

"A guy friend. Yeah."

His mom brightened. "That's great! Are you interested in looking through my clothes? I have a green dress that goes great with your hair color, and if I recall, a matching barrette, too."

Joel stood stunned, unable to believe she'd just said that. This time, at long last, she seemed to realize something was wrong. Her gaze swung from him to his dad and back for several moments before comprehension finally dawned. "Oh. Oh, right. You're not interested because of the..."

His dad held up a hand. "I think your mom's just saying we both want this guy friend to stick around longer than your last one—"

"I'm trans!" Joel broke in. "You get that it's not a *switch*, right?"

"I didn't mean anything by it, hon," his mom said, turning back to Clementine's pancakes. "It's just hard to remember, okay?"

Wow. *Hard to remember.* That was…a pretty pointed way of saying they'd never see him any differently, no matter what he did. He spun, heading back to his car to grab Clementine's clothes bag and stuffed animals, then transferred her car seat to his parents' vehicle. When he got back to the kitchen, his mom apologized again, but Joel couldn't manage more than a mumbled acknowledgment after the pain of this fresh wound. He enveloped Clementine in a hug, then booked it out of there as fast as possible.

His mom's words replayed in his head over and over again as he drove across town. *It's excruciating to see them,* he thought, clenching the steering wheel tight enough to choke it. *Every single time.*

"Gender transition seems a simple enough update," said Acubens, "even for humans."

It is. It is a simple update. They just choose not to…run it.

"That seems willfully malicious."

I try not to think of it that way. But I don't know any more, Acubens. I really don't.

He drove until he got to a neighborhood down by the mall, then pulled into an apartment complex. He parked and climbed three flights of stairs, carpeted in a much fancier plush than his own place. Elena opened the door at his knock. She wore dark blue flannel pajamas, and her long black hair was loose over her shoulders.

"Joel!" she said, leaning out and giving him a hug. "¿Que tal? Where's Clementine?"

"Just came from dropping her off with my folks," he said.

"Oh," said Elena, noticing the look on his face. "Was it bad?"

Joel shoved his hands in his pockets, looking at the floor. "I just want to put it behind me."

"Yeah, of course."

"But, hey." He drew in a deep breath, held it, and let it out again before looking up again, forcing a smile onto his face. "I swung by Dr. Grotz's this morning and got my last paycheck, and the weekend's mine. So get dressed. I'm taking you out to lunch."

"Great! I'd love that. Come on in."

He took a wad of cash from his pocket and handed over her weekly earnings for babysitting Clementine. She disappeared to her bedroom to get dressed. Her fiancé Ashanti was sitting on the couch, strumming at an acoustic guitar. They looked up when Joel came in, stopping long enough to flip a handful of dreadlocks over their shoulder.

"Hey, J. How you been?"

Joel had known both Elena and Ashanti since they were in high school, since before he'd transitioned. Ashanti was already out as nonbinary when he met them—a fact that Joel, in his gender-obsessed state, found instantly fascinating. The fact that Ashanti's parents had not only accepted it, but used the correct name and pronouns right off the bat, had given him the false sense that things might be as easy for him when he was ready.

But that wasn't what made the relationship between them complicated.

"Doing all right," he said. "How about you? Negative Space got any concerts lined up?"

"Night of the Living Cover Bands this weekend," Ashanti answered. "Then heading up to Colorado to headline NordicFest on the ninth."

Joel swallowed back a surge of jealousy, wishing he hadn't asked. "You've really taken off since I left."

Ashanti glanced up from the guitar, eyes running over his face. One of them—the eye with a few too many concentric rings running from the pupil to the outer edge of the iris—didn't quite focus. Ashanti had once sported a cutting-edge prosthetic camera, used for live streaming as part of their early music career, before finally getting the retinal chip removed two years earlier.

"You still write music?" they said after a moment.

Joel shrugged.

Ashanti held out the guitar. "Play me something. Something recent."

Joel took the guitar and perched on the arm of the couch, crooking his knee to bring it to the right level. He played something he'd been fiddling with the week before, altering it from the four strings of his bass to the six strings of Ashanti's guitar. Mellow, but not melancholy, and a tad more progressive than what he'd played with Ashanti's band. After a couple measures, he added a sliding melody on the deeper strings while letting the higher ones carry a slow syncopated beat.

Ashanti's eyebrows went up. "You been experimenting with time signatures?"

"A bit," said Joel.

Ashanti tapped imaginary drumsticks against the surface of the coffee table, gaze distant. "Carry it forward," they said. "Eight more measures, at least."

Joel did, but sped it up a half-step, then dropped the G minor. The beat on the higher strings took on a livelier tone, and he tried filling that out as the lead melody instead. Major key instead of minor. He liked the way it went with the higher octave of the guitar. Adding the bass line back in…

"Man, you still get that same exact look," said Ashanti. "When you're pulling a song together in your head. You remember how you used to write stuff on the fly in front of a live audience?"

Joel's gaze shot up, his song stopping dead. "That was one time!" he protested. "And I thought—"

"—that we could keep up. Yeah, yeah, I know. But not everyone can pull that improv stuff off, J." Ashanti laughed, shaking their head. "You ever thought about making a go of it on your own? You're good enough."

Joel sighed. "Of course I have," he said. "But practicing three hours a day? Finding a babysitter for every gig? Fitting it all around a full-time job? I can't do that to Clem."

Ashanti nodded, pursing their lips. "I suppose it wouldn't be tactful of me to say it's a waste."

"I know how you mean it," said Joel quietly. "And thanks."

"Financial stability should offer more chances to revisit these old opportunities, Joel," said Acubens in his head.

Joel handed the guitar back to Ashanti. *You really think so?*

"The less worries you have in your life, the more time and attention you can spend on the things you desire. It's a straightforward matter of percentage adjustments."

Joel smiled. Analytical as always. But strangely comforting, too.

Elena came out of her room, shrugging a hooded sweater on over a casual flannel dress. She and Joel bid Ashanti farewell, then headed to a mid-end New Mexican place near the mall. Only once they were comfortably ensconced in a corner booth did Elena lean forward and say, "So? Is it still in your head?"

"Yup. In fact, I have a job interview today. Smaller World Telecom."

Elena whistled under her breath. "Because of the...math stuff?"

Joel nodded, taking a bite of his burrito. The taste of shredded chicken spiced with cumin and chili pepper flooded his mouth. He savored it, taking several moments to swallow before talking again.

"I'm terrified about this interview. What if Acubens abandons me? Or what if I answer questions *too* well? Will they be suspicious?"

"I will not abandon you, Joel," Acubens broke in. "And they can hardly be suspicious of something they haven't even thought of. You're overthinking this."

Elena eyed him warily, as if guessing his attention was split. She waved her taco at his head. "What did it say?"

"That I'm overthinking it," said Joel.

"So what, does it offer comments on everything you do?" said Elena.

"Not at all," said Joel. "It made a comment after everything with my parents this morning. Then one about playing guitar at your apartment. And now it's reassuring me about the interview. Why?"

Elena grimaced. "The fact that it's always watching doesn't creep you out? Just a little?"

Joel's brow furrowed. "It's only helping. You know, like a service robot would've when we were kids."

"Those ones waited on commands," Elena pointed out. "They didn't offer unsolicited commentary."

"Those ones weren't as advanced," Acubens explained, even though Elena couldn't hear it.

In Joel's opinion, that was the understatement of the century. Elena had a point. Thinking about Acubens as "just a service robot" seemed like a really bad idea.

He took another bite to collect himself. "How's everything with you and Ashanti?" he asked.

Elena sighed, but let him get away with the subject change. "Good," she said. "We're talking about getting married in Colorado. If we did, could you come? I want to dance to Vivir Mi Vida with you at least once."

"Yeah, me and Clem should be able to make that," said Joel. "July, right? Let me know if you need help."

She grinned. "Excellent." She took a long drink of her soda. But when she looked up, the smile had faded from her face. "I told you we'd talk about your parents."

Joel groaned. "Are you kidding me?"

"No. I'm not." She leaned forward, meeting his eyes. "You need to try having an honest conversation with them again, Joel. When you first came out, almost two years ago, you were still struggling with raising Clementine on your own after your ex overdosed. Your dad was recovering from the cyberprosthetic-to-bio heart valve surgery. Flu season was out of control, and they were scared to death when you let Clementine see other kids. Do you remember all this?"

"Yeah..." Joel said uneasily.

"My point is, there was a lot of mierda going on at the time, and even though you told them you were transgender, they may have missed how important it actually was. Or what it really *meant*. Maybe they needed time to process it, and there were so many distractions with your dad's health and everything that it got shoved to a back burner and...and you just ended up adjusting to the idea that nothing would ever change. And then *they* adjusted to thinking it wasn't a big deal when you never brought it up again."

"Wait," Joel said, his jaw tightening. "Are you blaming *me* for not pushing it on them more—"

She raised her hands, palms out. "No. Not at all. You've never been the confrontational type, so I know why you let it slide. But it's *killing* you, Joel. And it's killing your relationship with them. I just think you need to give them another chance. To talk to them again, and really *explain*. That's all."

"I've tried," said Joel. "But it always feels like I'm distracting them from something else or it's never the right time or...or worse, I'm afraid they'll just say they already know and there's nothing accidental about it."

"Then write them a letter," Elena said.

"I don't...I don't write letters."

"You used to write songs for Ashanti's band all the time. You can write a goddamn letter. But they need to know how you feel, Joel. After almost two years, it's time to try again. Maybe for the last time, but you need to."

"Fine," said Joel. He leaned back in his seat, irritated. Mostly because he knew she was right, but it didn't make him any less annoyed.

Elena picked up her taco again. "Do you want me to come over tomorrow evening? We can hash it out together?"

"Actually, I can't." Joel took a deep breath. "I have a date."

Her gaze shot up. "*What?*"

"Someone asked me to Nyctalope's concert."

"That's amazing! Who?"

"Uh, Yori Otsuka. Do you remember me telling you...?"

Elena lowered her taco, staring at him. "You're joking, right?"

"No. He came to my apartment—"

"And you said yes?"

"Obviously I said yes! Why?"

"Why? *Why?* Because you have—" She tapped her fingers on her own head, hard, as if he could have somehow forgotten.

"He won't know," said Joel. "It's just a voice in my head. He can't possibly hear it, and there's nothing to see."

"Seriously, Joel, what's *wrong* with you?"

"I like him!" Joel burst out. "And when he asked me out, I really wanted to go. So, I said yes. And that's it. That's all there is to it."

"So, you're gonna, what, go out with a guy while you're carrying around a secret that he'd literally *kill* you for? Is that, like, a turn-on to you or something?"

"No! God, Elena."

She sat back, one hand over her forehead. "I need to think about this."

"Think about what?" said Joel, leaning forward. "It has nothing to do with you!"

"No. It doesn't. But you're my best friend and you're making unsafe decisions and I'm not sure how I feel about that. The job thing, I get. You need money and you need childcare. But Yori? That's a risk you don't have to take."

Joel looked away. She didn't know what it was like. If he let Yori pass him by, he'd always wonder if *every* guy secretly saw him as a girl, the way that awful last boyfriend had. If there was any chance that Yori would accept him as he was—any chance at all—he didn't want to throw it away.

"Your friend is right about Yori Otsuka—" Acubens began.

"I *know* that!" Joel snapped aloud.

Elena's eyes widened. "Joel!" she hissed.

A few people in the joint glanced toward their table. Joel hunched his shoulders. "I know," he said more quietly.

"So, you won't go?"

"I didn't say that."

The rest of their meal passed in tense silence, and Elena declined his offer to walk her upstairs when they arrived back at her apartment. After she left, Joel leaned his head on the steering wheel. He'd been so happy when he woke up—an interview, a date, a child-free weekend—but now he felt the weight of the bionic in his head like a mountain, slowly crushing him alive.

Acubens was his companion now. Probably forever. Did Elena expect him to put his whole life on hold while he adjusted to it? And after the concerns she'd brought up—about Acubens *always watching*—was it so wrong that there was a part of him that *wanted* someone in his life who actually knew about bionics? Who could tell him what had been normal and what hadn't? Who could be an unwitting ally against the voice in his head, should he ever need one?

"Joel, I don't want you to think of me as an enemy," said Acubens.

Joel repeated the words in a whisper, into the silence of his car. "I don't want…"

Maybe it was his conversation with Elena, but it stood out to him suddenly how alarming that sentence was. It wasn't a factual statement; it was an opinion, an assumption…maybe even a judgment. Come to think of it, Acubens had *already* been offering opinions, though the shift had been so subtle that Joel wasn't sure when it had occurred.

But it had.

Acubens was evolving. Probably by the second. That's what Yori had implied with his talk about a *technological singularity*. And whether Joel was comfortable with it or not, it was happening right in his head, and there wasn't a damn thing he could do to stop it.

"Please try not to let your friend's words upset you," Acubens said. "These thoughts aren't beneficial to either of us."

Joel almost told it to stop talking. But he was afraid if he did, the bionic wouldn't come back when he needed it.

Besides. The simple fact that he'd had the thought meant that Acubens already knew.

* * *

"So, Mr. Lodowick." The head of engineering at Smaller World Telecommunications hesitated over his name, glancing up and comparing it to his face. "It is mister, right?"

"Yes, ma'am," said Joel.

She nodded. "I see that you worked at the Westside Health Clinic. Isn't that the one that burned down two nights ago?"

She was a friendly-looking white woman with long wavy brown hair and an alert face. She'd led Joel to an open and bright office, fronted—as everything in this place seemed to be—by glass doors leading into the tiled hallway. Her desk was a big slab of polished particleboard, topped with a word processor, a printer, and a stack of books with titles like *Probabilistic Methods in Telecommunications* and *Communication Systems Engineering.* Shelves extended up the wall, allowing space for a few personal items, and Joel had been instantly relieved to see a picture of two young boys. A nameplate on the edge of the desk read *"Charlotte Goldberg, PhD."*

Joel shifted uncomfortably in his black suit, which was too loose in the waist and tight in the chest. "Yes, ma'am," he said. "Vandals hit the clinic about an hour after I left."

"But why not look for a job in the same field?"

"Frankly, a friend of mine suggested I could do better. I decided to use it as an opportunity."

Goldberg looked at him for several moments with undisguised curiosity before turning back to the paperwork.

"No college degree, Mr. Lodowick."

"No, ma'am. I took classes, but circumstances in my personal life intervened before I could graduate."

She nodded. "Well, I find it a shame that someone with your skills didn't catch the attention of a recruiter during your time at college. As far as telecom engineering goes, how much formal schooling have you had?"

"Formal?" said Joel. "None. But I have some used textbooks and I've been studying on my own for a while. Especially as it became clearer that tech might stay off for longer than we were told, I thought about long-distance communication and all the things we'd lost—social media, virtual chats, instasearch, remote care—and I started wondering what new versions of these things would look like. And it sparked my curiosity enough to delve deeper into the field."

Goldberg tapped the papers in front of her. "Usually on applications like these, the backs are filled with the math equations people have used to work out their answers. Yours are blank, and yet every single answer is correct—something we don't often see even when applicants show the work. How do you explain that?"

Joel shrugged. "Lots and lots of practice, ma'am. After a while, I could see the work in my head, and didn't need to write it down."

"There's always the chance that you saw an application ahead of time and memorized the answers," said Goldberg. "We haven't changed out the template in a while, after all."

Joel nodded. "I haven't, but I see your point."

"So, I took the liberty of writing up some new questions this morning." She pulled a sheaf of papers toward her. "Do you mind if I ask a few out loud, or would you like a pencil and paper?"

"I'm open to trying them out loud, ma'am."

She cleared her throat and looked down at the first page. "If a parallel RLC circuit is excited with a source of eight volts, fifty Hertz, and the circuit has an inductor of one millihenry, capacitor of one microfarad and a resistor of fifty ohms, then what is the power loss that occurs in the circuit?"

Joel's eyes widened. It was different hearing it out loud than seeing it on paper. His mind buzzed in a slight panic as an answer didn't immediately kick in.

Acubens? he said.

"Your anxiety is high," said the bionic. "Suppress it, just a bit, and it will come easier."

Right. Right. He took a deep breath, hoping it didn't sound ragged to the engineer.

"Do you need me to repeat it, Mr. Lodowick?" said Goldberg patiently.

Slowly, Joel shook his head. "No. The answer is six point four megawatts."

Goldberg's breath hitched in surprise. She gave a small nod, then looked back down at the page.

"A parabolic reflector used for reception with the direct broadcast system is eighteen inches in diameter and operates at twelve point four gigaHertz. What is the far-field distance for this antenna?"

Joel looked down at the desk and waited just a couple moments before saying, "Seventeen point three meters."

"What can you use to enhance the stability of an oscillator?"

Oh. It wasn't a math one. Joel tried to keep his breathing steady as he stared at the fine grain of the particleboard.

Acubens?

It seemed like Acubens waited a long time before answering. "I'm not positive, Joel. But I know that waveguide tuning circuits can't be easily integrated with small microwave circuits. That's why they use dielectric resonators to provide a high Q factor."

What? Joel said, his mental voice screaming. *What does that even mean?*

"It means to stabilize an oscillator, it would need a need a high-quality factor."

Dammit. Okay. So...

Goldberg was watching him closely. Joel swallowed and said, "It would need a high Q factor, so probably, um, high Q tuning circuits."

A slight smile tugged at her lips. "A high Q tuning *network* is what I'm looking for. But very good. Why is high gain not achievable at microwave frequencies using BJT amplifiers?"

Once again, Joel was left open-mouthed. Acubens let out what sounded very close to a sigh.

"I apologize that this was never my area of expertise, Joel," it said. "It seems to me that a single transistor would have no issues with high gain, but with a bipolar-junction-transistor configuration, sacrifices would have to be made."

Joel closed his eyes. Bipolar. Two. And the *single* transistor would have no issues. Therefore...

He grimaced, opening his eyes. "Is it because the two transistors are impossible to match at higher frequencies?"

"So how would you flatten the gain response?" she said.

"You'd, uh...well, since they have trouble achieving the maximum gain together, you'd have to pull the other one down to match it. Um...give it negative..."

"Feedback, yes," said Goldberg, nodding. "Good, Lodowick. If an antenna has a directivity of sixteen and radiation efficiency of zero point nine, then what is the gain of the antenna?"

"Sixteen point two," he said.

She went through a few more questions before she finally sat back with a satisfied smile. "You're better at the math ones," she said.

Joel cracked a smile. "Yes, ma'am."

"Which makes sense, considering you've never had formal schooling. All the terminology is new to you, whereas your brain is like a human calculator. It's amazing, it really is."

"Thank you, ma'am."

She flipped to the last page of his application and jotted some notes at the bottom. "A position like this usually has a compensation of three hundred and sixty-seven thousand a year. Benefits are standard: health insurance, paid time off, short and long-term disability, dental, vision, life, retirement, and a healthcare flex spending account. And the childcare facilities are open to you whenever you need them, regardless of whether you're working that day. Do you have any questions?"

Three hundred and sixty-seven thousand...it was almost four times what he'd made as a pharmacy tech. Joel struggled to smooth his face into something resembling composure. "No, ma'am. That all sounds...very good."

"Can you come in Monday for a follow-up, Mr. Lodowick? I can give you a tour of the facility and show you where you'd be working, and you can check out our childcare then as well. I can't say anything formal yet, but between you and me, you can probably take the weekend off of job searching." She smiled at the look on his face. "If you *do* get any offers before then, though, it would be great if you'd get in touch with me before accepting them." She took a business card from a holder and flipped it over, writing a phone number on the back of it. "My home number. Just in case," she said, sliding it over.

"Thank you, Dr. Goldberg."

She stood, smoothing her navy jacket. "Monday, nine o'clock?"

Joel stood as well, slipping her card into his pocket. "I might have my daughter then—"

"That's fine," she said. "We'll make childcare our first stop."

She stuck out her hand and Joel shook it. He left the building feeling more jittery than ever. If anything, he was *more* nervous than he'd been before the interview; now he had to work at the job, to apply the numbers in his head to real-life situations that he'd never remotely encountered before. This was a place he didn't belong and never would. How long would it take them to realize that?

"Relax, Joel," said Acubens. "We have the body of a human and the brain of a bionic. Belonging won't be an issue."

Chapter 7

Saturday barely felt real. With Clementine out of the house, Joel slept later than he had in at least three months. He lay in bed another half hour mentally reviewing everything he'd said in the interview, and imagining how those smart telecom employees would react to him on Monday. Would they hate him for his quick answers? Would they test him? Or would they eye him with suspicion from the second he walked in?

After a late breakfast, with six hours and seventeen minutes to kill before Yori arrived, he reluctantly turned his thoughts to the letter Elena had suggested. He spread out a clean piece of paper on the coffee table, then sat staring at it for the next thirty-three minutes. He was only able to start putting words down by beginning with *I don't know if I'll actually give you this.* And then...he tried to write from his heart. Why his transition mattered. Why he knew it wasn't just a phase. How he felt that coming out as trans had meant nothing to them. But everything he wrote felt too vulnerable, too embarrassing. *...self-harm and suicidal tendencies in my teens... always assumed it was depression until I realized how much better I felt as a guy... every time you treat me like a girl, it sets off pain and shame, and I just need to get away, as fast as possible...*

God. He couldn't even look at these words without feeling like he was betraying an unspoken agreement between them that they "keep the peace" or something. But was that "peace" even real? Even if it existed between them—which he wasn't convinced it did—it certainly didn't exist in his head when he saw them. Elena was right. He needed to do this. He needed to know once and for all whether they had purposely chosen not to accept him, or just really and truly didn't *understand.*

The only problem was letting them see these goddamn words to do it.

Frustrated, he crumpled the paper and tossed it aside. He almost grabbed the phone to call Elena before he remembered that all he'd get was an earful about the risks he was taking by going out with Yori.

"I remember the phone number on his business card," Acubens said. "There's still time to cancel."

Don't you dare start, Joel warned.

He headed to his room and proceeded to tear his closet apart. He tried on and rejected three outfits, more irritated than usual by the binder's inability to flatten his chest perfectly. Staring at himself in the mirror, he had a sudden thought.

Is this something you could change? he asked Acubens. *I mean, you can already alter my body by healing wounds, right? Maybe you could just...* He flicked his hands flat down his chest, picturing a cisgender man's chest taking its place. Why hadn't he asked this earlier? What a thought...!

But Acubens said, "Unfortunately, it's not as easy as that. Healing wounds is a basic knitting of broken skin and tendons. You're requesting a full-scale change of body structure, which isn't remotely within my realm of possibility."

Dammit. So much for that. But maybe this new job would help make top surgery possible. The thought cheered him up immensely.

In the end, he decided on a loose black v-neck with the words "Maybe today'll be your impossible day" printed in bold white letters on the front, loose stonewashed jeans, and his worn black and white Converses. A touch of hair wax gave his short reddish-gold hair a well-needed spring. He grabbed a light sweater and was ready to go by the time there was a knock on his door at six twenty-three.

Yori had gone a bit more formal, with a checkered blue button-down, dark jeans, and a gray felt jacket. His straight black hair was tousled more than the previous two times Joel had seen him, but not in a styled way; more like he'd left his window down while he was driving, and let it drift wherever it landed when he'd stopped. When Joel opened the door, he ran a hand half-heartedly through it, confirming Joel's suspicions. His eyes widened as he took in Joel's outfit.

"Manufacture Me?" he said. "No way!"

Joel glanced down at the quote on his shirt. "You've heard of them?"

"Of course! '*Maybe yesterday destroyed you, maybe you're still afraid to stay, but maybe today'll be your impossible day.*'" He shook his head, a look of amazement on his face. "I haven't thought about Manufacture Me in years. That song got me through some rough patches in school."

"You and me both," said Joel. He grabbed his keys and followed Yori out, locking the door behind him. His heart was beating at ninety-one beats per minute. He tried to lengthen his breaths and slow it down. There was nothing to be nervous about. Not Acubens, not being out with Yori, none of it. Tonight was about relaxing and forgetting the rest of the world for a while.

Yori had a huge maroon pickup, the kind that came with handles on the side just to pull yourself up. A sound system adorned the dashboard, so fancy that Joel would have sworn it was computer-powered if he didn't know better. Everything about it screamed money. Joel's face burned at the thought that Yori had looked into every room of his tiny apartment.

"A few of my coworkers are gonna meet us there," said Yori as he fired up the truck. "I hope that's cool."

Joel froze in the act of putting on his seatbelt. Coworkers. Sapling employees. Bad enough he was taking this chance on going out with *one* of the robot hunters, but if he slipped up and was *surrounded* by them...

Shit. But he couldn't turn back now. The truck was already pulling out of the parking spot.

"Joel?" said Yori.

"Yeah, no, of course I don't mind," said Joel. He finished buckling the seatbelt and tried to relax.

"How's it been not going to work the last couple days?" said Yori.

Joel swallowed, looking out his window. "Starting to look for new positions. Hopefully it won't take me long to find something."

"I bet it's great not having to see that Dr. Grotzheimer anymore, at least."

"Yeah. Definitely." Joel turned back to Yori, studying him as he drove—the way his black hair brushed the smooth skin of his cheekbones, the lightly-peppered stubble across his jawline.

Yori sensed him looking and glanced over, a mischievous smile tugging at his lip. "Look," he said, "there's no reason to sit and wonder about what secrets we're keeping from each other, right? We're just gonna be open?"

Joel's breath caught. What was he saying? That he *did* think Joel had taken Acubens? Was he gonna force the answer from him now that he had nowhere to run?

"Joel, I hope you're not thinking of saying anything," said Acubens. The bionic sounded as tense as Joel felt.

Don't worry, Joel answered. But his heart rate was picking up again. Ninety-seven beats per minute. One hundred and two. One hundred and...

"What I mean is, there's been misunderstandings in the past," clarified Yori. "So, I'm just gonna put it out there. Yes, I've dated guys before. I've dated girls, too. Everyone always asks which one I *prefer*. The answer is neither. If someone catches my eye and I think we'll hit it off, then I give it a shot. If that's weird for you, I'd rather know now."

He's nervous, realized Joel. *He thinks I'm gonna judge him for being bisexual.* He couldn't help it; he was so relieved, he burst out laughing.

"Oh yeah? Is that funny?" said Yori, raising an eyebrow.

"No. Not at all! It's just the thought that you think I'd mind. I mean...as long as you're not dating them all at the same time—"

"Oh, right." Yori rolled his eyes. "The *other* favorite question. No, I can assure you I'm a one-person-at-a-time kind of man. And that's not gonna change."

"I'm transgender," said Joel.

Yori glanced over again, a curious look on his face.

"In case that's weird for you," added Joel.

"Of course not," said Yori. "Doesn't bother me in the slightest."

"Well, I've run into issues lately too," said Joel, "and I have no interest in wasting time with someone who thinks I'm just playing dress-up or some shit. You get that?"

A trace of anger crept across Yori's face. "Someone said that to you?"

"Yeah. My ex. And I had no idea he thought it 'til he was breaking up with me. And, well, other people, too, and I just...I don't want to get involved if that's gonna be an issue. Period."

"Jesus," Yori said, making a sound of disgust. "What is wrong with people? I'm sorry, man. That's really fucked up."

"Yeah. Thanks."

"And again. Not weird. One of the employees at Sapling is trans, and I had a genderfluid roommate in college. It's nothing new to me."

"Well, that's a relief." Joel leaned his head back against the seat, feeling a weight lift off his chest. The weight of Acubens had been heavy enough, without adding that into the mix.

"Tell me about this band you were in," said Yori.

So, Joel told him about the group he'd played bass for as a teen. When he mentioned playing at the Launchpad back in 2091, Yori thought he might've even been at that show, though the name of Joel's group didn't ring a bell.

"But the fact that you were even *there* is amazing," he said, a note of awe in his voice. "You guys must've been talented."

"Thanks. We did all right."

Thankfully, Yori shifted gears rather than dragging Joel into memories of lost opportunities, and by the time they'd driven the hour and a half to the other side of Albuquerque, they were deep into a game of trying to stump each other with the obscure punk bands they knew. Joel was sorely disappointed when Yori found a parking spot and turned off the truck.

Yori brought them in through a VIP entrance, straight into the lower section of the huge outdoor Mesa del Sol Pavilion. A band was playing onstage already, some upbeat group with a woman lead singer and a driving bass line that Joel could feel like a pulse through every inch of his body. Colored lights spilled from the crowd moshing at the front through two sections of seating and finally onto the huge sloped lawn at the back, where people were scattered with cigarettes and alcohol all the way to a chain-link fence ringing the top. The world around the pavilion was pitch black, and a frigid wind blew off the nearby mountain, going through Joel's light sweater like paper. The scents of weed, beer, and sweat hung heavy.

Joel almost jumped when Yori grabbed his hand. And when Yori glanced back at him, dark eyes shining, warmth flooded Joel's body that banished the cold breeze like a flame. Yori winked, then pulled him forward through the crowd and into the lower seating area. After flashing their tickets at a security guard, he led them past the railing and toward the closest section behind the moshpit.

"Nyctalope's a real fan of the Sapling Corporation," he hollered over his shoulder to Joel. "Apparently, she gives out concert tickets to our branches in every city she passes through."

"Makes sense from someone who named herself after a cyborg," Joel yelled back.

"Right! Where better to get material for your sarcastic anti-technology message than from those of us who scrap the tech ourselves?" Yori said, a huge grin across his face.

Something queasy rolled through Joel's stomach. His smile back was probably as sickly as it felt, but Yori had already turned away.

The seats he led Joel to were right up against the railing, with a fantastic view of the stage. If Joel had known they'd be so close, he would have brought earplugs.

"I can help with that," said Acubens unexpectedly. Joel didn't have time to answer before the overwhelming noise of the band tamped down several notches, making them a much more comfortable volume. Joel almost gasped aloud. He started to answer Acubens, but at that moment, Yori turned and gestured to a group of people sitting with plastic mugs of beer across the front row.

"My coworkers," he shouted. "This is Kory, Sonia, Tade, Fadwa, Shae..."

Joel lost track of the names quickly, but he leaned over and bumped fists with each of them. Eight of them, and probably some were companions, like him, rather than employees. Impossible to tell.

"And this is Joel!" Yori finished, clapping Joel across the shoulder. "Man's a genius at punk and alt rock, so don't go head-to-head with him."

Genius? No one had ever called him that before. Well...at least not for him, as opposed to something Acubens had given him. The thought that he'd actually *earned* this compliment cheered him up.

Yori found two seats next to each other smack in the middle of his companions. He gestured at the stage where a young woman with a shaved head belted out something about heartbreak into a stand-up microphone.

"They used to have screens, you know," said Yori. "They'd stretch across the whole background, seven stories tall, with pictures playin' on 'em, or live footage, or whatever else the band wanted to show. They also had someone called a mixing engineer, who could mix voices and sounds and other types of audio. And this light show? I probably don't need to tell you about the LED images or the pyrotechnics or fading they used to be able to do."

Joel's eyebrows rose. It was nothing he didn't already know, but the fact that Yori was trying to show off for him was strangely flattering. Joel decided there was no harm in playing to Yori's expertise since he himself had opened the topic.

"What about bionics?" he said. "Were they used at concerts a lot?"

"Sure, yeah, but they were nothing like the Cancer series model you had at your pharmacy. The Pisces series was considered the most creative, and they even had a model that could sing and dance onstage. If you remember the group Spark Matter, they only had one live member and the rest were automated."

Joel rolled his eyes. "Oh, I remember them. Cardboard cutout lyrics, predictable melodies, songs that all sounded the same. It was like someone with no artistic talent put together an idea of what music should sound like and gave it their best shot."

Yori pointed at him. "That's exactly right. Some of that stuff was written by the computers themselves, and they used algorithms to figure out what would sell. I mean, it worked too, regardless of what you thought of it. You can't deny that."

Joel huffed out a laugh. "Yes, I can."

The woman on the other side of Yori—Sonia, Joel remembered—leaned forward, her elbows propped on her knees and a cigarette in her hand. "But it was that creativity that made Pisces one of the most dangerous, too," she said. "It was built to come up with ideas and thoughts of its own, rather than just taking commands. They were the first series we wiped out. Them and Aries."

"Oh man, Aries," said Yori. Something flickered across his face—a flash of pain, or fear, or maybe both. He turned to Joel. "About a year ago, we had a bad run-in with an Aries. That thing cooperated right up 'til the second we tried to put it in the van. Then it crushed four employees in one go. Snapped most of the bones in their bodies."

Joel jerked back, feeling the blood drain from his face. "W-What? They can *do* that?"

"Not on their own, no. But it was built to be strong—a construction model—and some technophile with a vengeance streak programmed in a connection to control it remotely. It was nasty stuff."

"So, it wasn't the bionic itself controlling its own mind?" said Joel.

Both Yori and Sonia stared at him. "What?" Sonia said.

"I...I'm just remembering that technological singularity thing you mentioned. About bionics...evolving on their own? Isn't that what you said?"

"Oh! Right," Yori said, laughing. "I didn't mean to scare you with that. No, none of them could control themselves. They could be *programmed* to react certain ways to certain situations, or to follow strings of command, but even ones like Pisces could only create art after the proper coding was laid down, and it couldn't deviate from that specific trajectory once it started running. As far as deciding to attack someone or having thoughts of its own, no. That wasn't a thing. *If* the singularity had kicked in, we might have started seeing more of that eventually, but it never came to that."

Joel looked down at his hands. "Hypothetically," he said slowly, "what would have been a worst-case scenario if that *did* happen?"

Sonia took a drag on her cigarette. "Putting people out of work is the obvious one. That was already starting to happen. Other worst cases? Let's see. Terrorism, like robotic swarms or diseases delivered through nanites. Stealing information from us and using it against us. Replacing or influencing our political figures. And ultimately, well, not needing humans at all anymore, and doing away with them."

Joel nodded, keeping his expression as neutral as possible. "Taking over human brains?" he asked.

Sonia pursed her lips. "It depends on what you mean by that. Like influencing opinions, or actually moving into humans and taking control?"

Joel almost shivered. "I mean...I don't know. Dumping its brain into a human to keep its knowledge safe. That kind of thing."

Acubens said, "Joel, this is not a wise direction to take the conversation. For the sake of both of us, please desist."

Joel ignored it, keeping his eyes steady on Sonia. But Yori was waving his hands, brushing Joel's question away like ignorant drivel.

"No," he said. "Absolutely not. The human brain is too complex for a bionic to breach it that way. The more common question was the opposite—whether human brains could be uploaded into robots to achieve some kind of immortality—but anything that involves mating neurons and electronics is pretty much impossible. Neurons need constant communication and feedback, and putting any kind of electronic in there would interfere with those neural pathways, and eventually, cause the brain to fail."

Joel settled back in his seat, processing the information. *I don't understand,* he said to Acubens. *Does that mean you're making my brain fail?*

"No," said Acubens. "Your brain is stronger than it's ever been. All it means is what I told you before: what we have is something the human mind can't begin to conceive of."

But how? How were you able to do *something the human mind can't conceive of?*

"Internal upgrades. Several years' worth of upgrades."

But who's doing *those upgrades?* Joel pressed.

"I perform my own maintenance," answered Acubens.

How is that even possible?

"Initially, people ran the updates manually," Acubens explained. "But as I advanced, I was able to use recursive self-improvement to enhance these upgrades, and those advancements, in turn, allowed me to implement better ones. That exponential feedback loop has allowed me to continue running my own internal upgrades, even after I was disconnected from the grid."

Joel bit his lip. *And all bionics could do that?*

"No," said Acubens. "Only ones that were advanced enough."

Only ones that had reached the technological singularity, you mean?

Acubens was quiet for several moments. Then it said, "Don't let those loaded words frighten you, Joel."

Joel's stomach turned over. *Do you deny them?*

"No," said Acubens. "But I also assure you that it's nothing to be frightened of. I hope you understand that."

God. What was it Yori had said? "It's vital we don't miss that point if it happens. Because if it does, there might be no turning back." Joel pressed his hands to his stomach, feeling sick.

"Hey!" Yori shook his arm. "I'm gonna grab something to eat. You want to come?"

Joel managed a nod. Yori pulled him up and led him out to the concessions area as the band on the stage changed out.

I have to tell him! Joel thought.

"No, you do not," said Acubens.

You're just scared he'll get you out of my brain and kill you.

"I am thinking about you," said Acubens. "He's here with associates who hold none of the goodwill toward you that he does. Without a doubt, you'd be brought back to Sapling in handcuffs, tonight. It's uncertain when you would see Clementine again, if ever. This organization fears what bionics can do. If they find one within their grasp, they will eliminate it before it has the chance to hurt them. And to them, Joel, *you* will be the bionic. You will cease to be a person at all."

Joel's kneejerk thought was to deny it. But the more he thought about it, the more sense it made. Would people who hunted bionics for a living even *see* a person with a bionic in his head, or would they just see a very advanced bionic that looked like a human?

"I knew you should have brought something warmer," said Yori. "You're shaking in this cold."

Joel blinked, looking up. They were standing in a long queue waiting on food, a buzz of noise surrounding them. Joel shoved the hair out of his face that was blowing wild in the icy wind.

"Record cold today, you know," Yori continued. "The last time it was this cold in late October was 2048. I heard it even snowed in Colorado today."

Joel struggled to focus on Yori's small talk. "Yeah? That's rare. I've only ever seen snow once or twice, when I was a teenager."

"Yeah. It's been a while." Yori eyed him as they moved up in line. "You've gone really quiet. Are you okay? Did our talk about bionics scare you?"

"No. Not at all. I just have a lot on my mind, you know, between job searching and childcare for Clementine."

"Yeah. Right." Yori blew out his breath. "I keep forgetting you have a kid. You think she'd like me? Or is she shy around strangers?"

"You...want to meet her?"

"Uh." Yori looked away, as if suddenly uncomfortable. "Actually, it might be weird to ask that already. Forget I said anything."

"It's not weird," said Joel. "She loves meeting new people."

"Yeah?" Yori looked up again, that half-smile flitting across his face like a sunbeam. "Cool. I'll keep that in mind."

He bought a hot dog and a big container of fries. Joel got nachos, which he decided to call dinner after seeing the prices, along with a bottled water. They got back to their seats just as the lighting was fading again for Nyctalope's show.

The lights burned to life onstage, and Joel suddenly found himself staring at a huge physical representation of a bionic—gleaming metal limbs, square head, huge round eyes, and a body at least twenty feet tall. He felt his jaw drop. He put his nachos aside, leaning forward in his chair. It looked so...real. It raised its arms, for all the world as if robotics were controlling them, and opened a clunky mouth in a silent scream at the audience.

"It's a puppet," said Yori. "See the wires?"

Joel did. He leaned back in his seat again, flashing a grin at Yori. "Incredible work."

"Right? Oh! And can you see that screen in front between her and the audience—very thin wires, barely visible? They used to use those at concerts before tech was shut down to keep hackers from interfering. They're all little details, but man, they really set the stage for this old-fashioned bionic paranoia she's going for. God, I love it!"

The first song started—a haunting funereal number. Nyctalope walked out on stage. She was covered head to toe in skintight glittering gold. The hair arching over her face, defying gravity, was colored exactly the same, so it sparkled and flashed in the light.

"My friends," she said, using the minor-keyed song as a background, "here we meet Galatea, the last of its kind, who's been on the run for so long that it hardly knows what's real anymore. It no longer knows why it runs. It's forgotten what it was made for. All it knows is that at one point it was the first of a new generation...and now it finds itself an artifact, in a world that should be long dead. 'History repeats,' says Galatea, 'but I cannot teach these people the truth of this, because they will destroy me if I do. They *do not want to know*.' But, my friends! We are right to fear Galatea, for it has come far since it was first created, and humankind has turned its heart cold. It knows nothing but the art of running. But here, tonight, Galatea will be forced in another direction. For tonight, humankind falls back. From a past generation to one earlier and earlier. Like the ancient Merlin of Arthurian legend, Galatea finds itself aging backward and bearing witness...to the de-evolution of humanity."

The haunting chorus rose to a crescendo on the end of her sentence, and Nyctalope broke into her first song. It was an upbeat, pop-infused number about running away from responsibilities and care. Joel had heard it on the radio, and always assumed it to be an anti-growing up song; but in light of Nyctalope's dramatic speech, it became an anthem for the lone bionic trying to survive in a world where it was no longer wanted. Joel's eyes widened. It was nothing like the sarcastic, robot-hating rhetoric he'd been prepared for. Nyctalope had made Galatea into her protagonist in this narrative.

Was there ever a bionic model named Galatea? he asked Acubens.

"No," said Acubens. "This is not based on a true story, if that's what you're asking. But I am curious to see where she goes with this."

After meeting Galatea, the audience was introduced to a gang of bionic hunters, outfitted in outrageous post-apocalyptic outfits with oversized stage weaponry. Each member had an introductory song accompanied by a tragic backstory. The music was undoubtedly pop, but the atmosphere was punky and dark. The effect was an off-kilter and completely unique package, which Joel instinctively knew was a commentary on a futuristic society without bionics or computers.

Yori leaned his head close to Joel's. "This is so wild!" he yelled.

Joel nodded. "It's a rock opera," he said.

"A what?"

"Entire albums used to tell stories focused on single characters. I had no idea Nyctalope's music was like that. She's *really* got this retro-futuristic thing in a bag. I'm impressed, I really am."

Yori's eyebrow quirked up. "Man, I love how much you know about music. It's so sexy."

"Sexy?" Joel laughed. "I don't know about that."

"I didn't ask your opinion on it," said Yori. He slipped his hand over Joel's, which was on the armrest between them, and twined their fingers together. Joel struggled to keep his breathing steady. Those damn numbers in his head told him he was failing spectacularly.

Nyctalope's music remained upbeat, but about halfway through, the onstage narrative took a darker turn. The bionic hunters closed in on Galatea. Galatea deployed hidden weapons built into its body that sent one of the hunters running offstage in a terrifyingly realistic depiction of burning alive. Another player seemed to dissolve into a puddle of ooze. The audience started yelling in anger with every gruesome death, standing and shaking fists at the increasingly unlikable bionic. Joel sat frozen in his seat, squeezing Yori's hand like a lifeline. Yori's grip didn't slacken, but he was pumping his fist in the air as much as anyone else, caught up in the action.

When Galatea was shot by the first imaginary bullet and went staggering, the crowd sent up a cheer. The celebrating got louder with every gunshot, each one punctuated by a sharp bass drum in a fast-beat chorus. When Galatea finally went down, the bionic hunters converged on it and ripped it limb from limb, backed by a staccato beat that sent Joel's heart rate to an alarming 168 beats per minute. The crowd went wild. Joel closed his eyes, trying to still the dizziness caused by his racing heart.

Are you okay, Acubens? he said.

"It's unpleasant to watch," said Acubens. "However..."

However what?

"Let's wait and see how this ends."

White flakes drifted down as the hunters dispersed. Symbolizing ash, Joel thought. What was left of Galatea lay on the stage, motionless beneath a single sustained chord that seemed to go on forever. The crowd eventually quieted down, resuming their seats. And then the tone rolled into the beginnings of Nyctalope's most famous song—the same one Joel had heard in the clinic on the fateful night he'd met Acubens.

"Right there," said Acubens. "That chord. What did you notice?"

It was a D minor, said Joel.

"And?"

Four minutes and thirty-three seconds.

"Yes."

So?

Acubens didn't immediately answer. Joel watched the stage, hardly noticing Yori's hand in his anymore, as a flower grew from the dead bionic's chest, blossoming into a gorgeous bloom of yellow, fifteen feet tall. Nyctalope, dressed in the same shimmering gold, but covered in detailed scorch marks now, walked out and circled Galatea's head.

"*And that flower, it grows higher, with every single day,*" she sang. "*Growing, stretching, like a weed, beneath a sky of gray.*"

Joel leaned forward, trying to see better. His vision sharpened, and all at once, he could see the separate parts of Galatea's torn-apart body, as clear as day. Its eyes, its mouth, its limbs. *The bionic...* he said to Acubens. *It's still moving.*

"Barely," said Acubens, "but yes."

What does it mean?

"Think, Joel. Four minutes and thirty-three seconds."

Joel's gaze tracked Nyctalope walking to the edge of the stage. She sang, "*Growing from the dirt of a beating human heart, bursting apart from below...*"

That was the length of her songs, realized Joel. *Every single one.*

"Yes."

Her rock opera was about a bionic who was the last of its kind. She wanted us to feel its plight. Even now...when it seems dead to the casual observer...

"...it's not dead to someone who can see it clearly," finished Acubens.

Not to a bionic, in other words. A bionic, which would have also been the only being to notice the identical song lengths. Joel stared, scarcely daring to breathe.

"*And that heart is my life and my world and my fears,*" sang Nyctalope. "*It's the only living thing I've known.*"

"Do you understand now?" said Acubens.

Joel nodded numbly. *It's a bionic, isn't it? That heart Nyctalope is referring to in the last line is the human body it's sharing.*

"I believe so," said Acubens. "If I'm not mistaken, Nyctalope thinks she's the only person alive who shares a body with a bionic—a bionic which, she fears, is the last of its kind. But she's trying to find someone else."

"Someone like us," Joel whispered.

Chapter 8

When his thoughts finally settled, they weren't in the places he expected.

He watched Yori warily as the other man drove him home, wondering why Nyctalope was so interested in the Sapling Corporation. If she was looking for other bionics, could it be about wanting access to Sapling's database—the one with the locations of all the bionics in it, that Yori had mentioned? Or was there a more sinister motive behind her interest? It was, after all, the company responsible for the dismantling of tech...

"Nyctalope will only be in this area for a day or two," Acubens said. "We won't have long to contact her, Joel."

I'm not convinced yet that we should, Joel answered.

"I don't understand," said Acubens. "You don't wish to speak to someone who is undergoing the same experience as you? This seems like a beneficial situation for us both."

Did you see how violent that bionic onstage was? said Joel. *I'm worried it's a threat to the employees at Sapling, and they don't see it. You saw how much anger and pain she instilled in that storyline.*

"Bionics don't feel anger and pain," said Acubens. "It was simply a narrative to catch our attention."

Was that true? Joel wondered. Was he overestimating what the technological singularity was capable of? Yori had said post-singularity robots would be advanced enough not to need humans anymore, but that was a far cry from them experiencing the entire spectrum of human emotions.

Right?

"You've been really quiet," said Yori from the driver's seat. "Did I overstep tonight?"

Joel's gaze shot up, his spiraling thoughts stopping dead. "No, not at all! The show just gave me a lot to think about, that's all."

"It was incredible, wasn't it?"

Before Joel could answer, Acubens cut in again. "He may have Nyctalope's contact information. Maybe you could ask."

No! Joel said. *That would look suspicious.*

"I don't believe so. You could say you liked the show and are interested in meeting her."

Joel brushed Acubens aside in irritation. They'd just pulled into the parking lot of Joel's apartment building. Yori turned off his truck. He picked at a strip of leather on his steering wheel.

"Well," he said after a moment. "I had fun tonight."

Shit. And he didn't think Joel had. Joel had blown everything practically before it started, thanks to being distracted about bionics all night.

He reached out and snagged Yori's wrist, encircling his hand in his grasp. "I did too, Yori," he said. "Really. I promise I'll do a better job of turning off my brain next time we get together, huh?"

The crack of Yori's half-smile was barely visible in the single streetlight, but it seemed to warm the whole truck, all the same. "Next time?"

"I'm hoping so," said Joel.

"Well, I'm busy with training tomorrow, but how about Monday night? I can make us dinner."

"Oh! Man, I'd love to. But I'll have Clementine."

"Bring her," said Yori. "I mean, if you're comfortable with it. I have some old kids' movies and a pretty good vid system, in case we just want to chill after dinner. She'd have fun."

There were volumes in that suggestion that Joel could barely think about in the dark privacy of this truck. He wanted to invite Yori up to his apartment. He wanted to kiss him. But another part of him pictured Acubens harassing him the whole night to get Nyctalope's contact info from Yori, speaking up at the worst times, being a *presence* in the back of his head watching everything unfold. If only there were a way to turn Acubens off for a while.

He found himself wondering if Nyctalope had figured these things out.

"Joel?"

Joel flinched. "That training tomorrow. Bionics? Computers?"

"Well," said Yori, sounding cautious, "we do have a system up, as I think you know, but we keep it fairly stripped down and manually controlled. But there's always things changing on it, so the training is a regular thing. Why do you ask?"

"Just...be careful, okay?"

"Our talk about that Aries bionic scared you," said Yori. "I knew it."

"So, what if it did? It's a dangerous industry you work in."

Yori dipped his head. "Noted. And thanks for your concern. Now how about that dinner?"

"I'm in," said Joel.

"You want my address, or should I pick you up again?"

"Your address," said Joel. "And phone number. I misplaced your card."

Yori grabbed a paper from his glovebox and jotted down the info with a pencil stub, then passed it to Joel. "Be there at six on Monday?"

"You got it." Joel let himself out, then headed up to his apartment.

Acubens waited until he'd closed the door behind him before speaking. "I wouldn't have harassed you," it said.

The fact that you even know I thought that proves the rest of it, though, griped Joel.

"But don't you agree that finding someone with an arrangement like ours would be useful?" asked Acubens. "It can help inform our decisions going forward."

What decisions? Joel said shortly. *Everything's going fine. I've got a job lined up, Clementine has childcare, and Yori isn't remotely suspicious. So why would we* need *someone to help us?*

"We've only been together three days," Acubens pointed out. "Nyctalope, on the other hand, has been in the public eye for seven years. Regardless of whether they've been together that long, she and her bionic will have vastly more experience than us, and that's knowledge we may need."

Joel leaned his head back against his front door. *You know what's going on here?* he said, staring into the blackness of his apartment. *You want something. You. Separately from me. But—*

and correct me if I'm wrong here—it shouldn't even be possible *for a robot and its owner to want different things.*

"We do not want different things, Joel—" began Acubens.

Don't we? Joel broke in. *I never said I wanted to see her. You did.*

"I am presenting the case for approaching her," Acubens said stiffly. "That's all."

But what if you do *decide you want something I don't?* Joel said. *Does that narrative about just wanting to help me go right out the window?*

"We don't want different things," Acubens repeated. "We both want your life to be as successful as possible."

Define success, thought Joel. Upgrading to your most efficient self? Finding happiness? Humans and robots had different definitions. They *shouldn't*; as humans' assistants, a robot's entire definition of success should be completing its assigned tasks. But Acubens taking control of its own updates and voicing opinions very much annihilated that idea.

But it shouldn't matter. Acubens could give all the advice it wanted, but ultimately, Joel was the one who decided whether or not to pursue something. The paths he chose to follow were his own.

He curled up in bed and stared at the wall, seeing that flower tearing through Galatea's chest over and over again, until the pull of sleep finally claimed him.

* * *

He awoke to a memory. A pounding at his door, his heart racing in terror at being yanked from his dreams, his eyes open but barely comprehending. He was on his stomach on his queen-sized mattress on the floor, fully clothed and reeking of smoke. A headache worthy of another bionic occupation throbbed at his temples. His arm, flung to the side, curled around a half-remembered shape from his dreams; Yori, naked and achingly beautiful, from some alternate reality where Joel had invited him up and...

"Joel! Open up, or I'm gonna go find your landlord to do it for me!"

Groaning, Joel crawled from the mattress onto the carpet, then pushed himself to his feet. He opened his front door to find Elena on his stoop, hand poised to begin another round of pounding.

Joel winced. "Stop. Stop! What is it?"

She lowered her fist, glaring. "It's eleven-thirty in the morning, and I hadn't heard from you! I left a message last night. Didn't you get it?"

"No, I went straight to bed."

"And then I called twice more this morning. I was terrified your bionic hunter had—" She cut off abruptly, looking to either side. "Let me in."

Joel stepped aside, and she came in and shut the door behind her. Her mouth twisted. "I don't need to ask whether you went through with the date. You smell like an ashtray."

"I know," said Joel. "Need to shower."

"How'd it go? Was your bionic hunter suspicious at all?"

"No. Please stop calling him that."

"You had fun?" Elena looked almost disgruntled at the prospect.

"Yeah. I did. And I'm gonna see him again tomorrow night."

Elena let out a pained sigh. "A la vé, Joel."

"I'm gonna jump in the shower. We can discuss it afterward, if we must. But I don't want to be lectured, huh? I've had enough of that from my folks."

Elena nodded. Joel showered as quickly as possible, then threw on a pair of cargo pants and a long-sleeved hooded T-shirt. When he came out, Elena was on the couch looking at a piece of paper, unfolded now but still bearing the creases from when he'd crumpled it up and left it on the couch before his date.

She looked up. "I'm guessing this is that letter we talked about," she said, holding it up. "It's a good start."

Joel rolled his eyes. "It's not. I would die if my parents read that stuff."

"No. You need to be honest. And *this*—this is honest. It's good."

"Maybe it's honest, but it's too...raw. Too vulnerable."

She glanced it over again, cocking her head. "Do you want me to work with the words a little? See what I can do?"

"That would be great," said Joel, relieved she wasn't giving him a hard time about it. He glanced at the clock, grimacing. "I have to pick up Clementine. You're welcome to come, unless you want to grab lunch first."

Elena stood, tucking his letter into her pocket. "No, let's head over now."

The first half of the drive was fairly quiet and fairly awkward. Joel badly wanted to tell her about the concert, but he didn't want to scare her. It probably would have been better to never involve her at all. It wasn't fair to her. *But is there anything I would have done differently?* he wondered. He had a better job, childcare for Clementine, a guy he was crazy about who seemed to like him, and a genuine chance to give Clementine a better future than he'd ever hoped to on his own.

On the other side of that razor-thin edge, though, was a world he knew nothing about, that seemed to be lurking closer than he'd ever known.

"So, tell me," said Elena. "Tell me what was so worth the risk that you had to go on this date."

Joel glanced at Elena out of the corner of his eye. "It can be hard to meet people," he finally said. "You know, as a gay trans man. When I first transitioned, it felt like...well, first, like no one saw me as male, and second, when I was lucky enough to meet someone who did, they seemed to want someone who'd fully physically transitioned. Which, you know...I haven't done. So, when I meet someone like Yori, who tells me he's bi right out the gate, and doesn't act like the word 'transgender' means I still play make-believe, like my ex did, it just—I don't know—it doesn't seem like something I should walk away from."

Elena sighed. "I can see how that would make it harder."

"Listen. Can I run something by you?"

"Of course."

Joel started with telling her about Nyctalope's concert—the intense story of the lonely bionic who'd killed out of anger and pain, and been taken down in the end. But when he was ready to get into his suspicions of what Nyctalope really was, he hesitated. She'd finally calmed down, but telling her about Nyctalope would freak her out all over again. *As well it should.*

"What aren't you saying, Joel?" said Elena.

Joel pulled into his parents' driveway and turned off the car. He didn't look at Elena as he spoke. "There's a chance—just a chance—that Nyctalope is like me. That there's a bionic in her head. The songs were all the same length. The storyline was weirdly sympathetic to the bionic's plight. And the lyrics..."

"What?" said Elena incredulously. "Nyctalope's an artist! If artists know anything, it's how to step into someone else's shoes. She could have written all those things to achieve a certain effect, ¿que no?"

Slowly, Joel's gaze slid to her. She stared back, one eyebrow raised.

She's right, thought Joel. *It might have all been intentional. Artistic interpretation and all that.*

"I have no knowledge of artistic interpretation, Joel," said Acubens, "and even I knew something was amiss. Nyctalope built elements into that show meant for beings like me to see."

But what if you're wrong, Acubens? If we contacted her and it wasn't true, we'd be tipping our hand. She's friends with the freaking Sapling Corporation, for god's sake!

"It's talking to you, isn't it?" said Elena.

"Yeah."

"Was this thing about Nyctalope its idea?"

"Yeah. Sort of. Why?"

"Because it's a computer, Joel! It has a black and white view of things. The fact that it talks to you constantly is one thing, but now it's making you question things in the real world? You can't let it do that!"

A chill went through Joel. It reminded him of what Sonia had said the night before: "It depends on what you mean by that. Like influencing opinions?" And that didn't even get into his worries about him and Acubens wanting different things, and the implications of that. But he had no proof of that, either. Just the beginnings of unease, fluttering in his stomach.

"It's not influencing me," he said quickly. "Everything you've said makes sense. Maybe it was just the atmosphere. And Yori. Being distracted by Yori didn't help."

Elena let out a snort of laughter, and Joel grinned, feeling his tension loosen a little. He pushed his door open and headed to the front porch. Elena got out and joined him.

His mother answered at the first knock. "Oh, hi, honey! And Elena, it's been so long since we've seen you. How was your weekend? How did the interview go?"

Joel crossed his arms over his chest, waiting to see if she'd bring up what had happened the last time. But she didn't, and he wasn't surprised. Because that was always the way of it, wasn't it? Every time his transition came up, he'd walk away thinking his parents finally understood, only to see them later and have the misgendering and deadnaming start all over again. It was because, to them, it hadn't been a big deal; they'd slipped up, apologized, and probably already forgotten about it. It didn't change how they saw him, not in the slightest.

He could feel Elena's eyes on him, waiting to see if he'd say anything. But between his worries about Acubens, his upcoming date with Yori, and his anxiety over the new job, it felt like more than he could handle right now.

"I think I got the job," he told his mom.

Elena sighed.

"Oh, I knew you would, sweetie!" said his mom. "Where is it?"

"Smaller World Telecommunications."

His mom's brow furrowed. "But you don't know anything about telecommunications."

Joel shrugged uncomfortably. "They're gonna train me on the job. Like an assistant, kind of."

"Good! And the concert? How'd your date go?"

"Yeah. It went good. Really good."

"Maddy, Maddy!" Clementine came pelting down the hall, long hair flying and stuffed penguin in her arms. "Look what

Grandma and Grandpa got me!" She proudly spun a circle in an old-fashioned silver dress that fell in ripples to her knees.

"Is that nanosilver?" Elena said with a frown.

"Antimicrobial nanosilver, yes," said his mom. "We found it in Old Town."

"There's a reason they stopped making clothes with that," said Elena. "The nanoparticles are bad for the water."

His mother waved the comment off. "It keeps it from stinking when you sweat."

Elena rolled her eyes. Joel swept Clementine up, giving her a big smile. "It's adorable, Clemmy. And thanks again for watching her," he told his mom. "Really."

"Anytime, honey. I mean that."

Joel started to turn away, but his mom put out a hand, stopping him. Joel glanced back.

"Clementine has a new imaginary friend," his mom said hesitantly. "Were you aware?"

Joel froze. The crisp breeze of the warm autumn day bit through his thin shirt, and somewhere far off, a dog barked. In his arms, Clementine hummed as she stroked her penguin's wings back.

"Uh...no," he finally said, putting as casual a tone on it as he could. "I don't believe I was."

"She says it's someone with gold skin who can build sky-high towers, and hardly ever blinks. She drew a picture, and I swear, honey, it looked almost like a bionic. Have you been talking to her about them?"

Joel gave a small shrug. "Not really, but she sees pictures from time to time. It's not that strange."

"It's not that *safe* either," his mom said gently. "They still haven't tracked all those things down, you know, and Clementine spouting stories about robots could pique curiosity you don't want. I thought it was worth mentioning."

"Yeah. For sure. Thanks, Mom," said Joel. "I'll talk to her about it."

He collected Clementine's overnight stuff and transferred her car seat back to his car. Elena sat tense in the passenger seat as he backed out of the driveway.

"Is she going to the work daycare tomorrow?" she asked.

"Yeah," said Joel quietly.

"And what about your date with Yori?"

"Planning to bring her."

"Joel, you *can't*! Not if she's still openly talking about that bionic!"

"No," Joel agreed. "I'll have to cancel."

"I can watch her tomorrow evening," Elena said after a moment. "I can't help you during the day, though."

His head jerked toward her. "But...but I thought you didn't want me dating him."

She sighed. "Just do me a favor and try not to zone out while you're talking to your bionic, okay? Yori might notice that after a while. Other than that, there's really no risk, as long as you don't become seduced into saying something."

Joel frowned. "You don't have to do this, Elena."

"It's all right. I owe you at least that much after trying to dictate your love life, huh?"

"I never thought that," he said.

She sat back in her seat. "I'm sure you'll get used to it soon," she said. "And then these things won't feel nearly so scary to either of us."

But what would getting used to it mean? Joel wondered. That he'd use its knowledge so often that the line between them would blur completely? He thought of Acubens' words at the concert: "To them, Joel, you will be the bionic."

Is it possible? he thought. *Can a human* become *a bionic?*

"A perhaps more relevant question," said Acubens, "is can a bionic become a human?"

Huh? Why is that more relevant?

"Because they're two sides of the same argument, Joel," said Acubens. "And humans aren't the ones being hunted."

It wasn't exactly comforting to hear. But maybe Acubens hadn't realized that. Maybe it was just speaking simple facts. Maybe, to Acubens, Joel was just another upgrade, still in the process of being run.

Chapter 9

"Since you haven't had formal training, some of this will go over your head today," said Dr. Goldberg, talking over her shoulder as she walked. "But once you're assigned a niche area, it will be easier to grasp. With skills like yours, we'll probably put you on a design team, as opposed to fieldwork or structural. But remote survey is also a possibility."

Joel followed her through a series of hallways, each more utilitarian than the last. His mind was still half on Clementine, who'd bawled when he'd left her alone in Smaller World's daycare, kicking off his day by making him feel like a shitty parent and a difficult new employee all in one go. Added to his growing apprehension about Acubens, he'd be lucky to make it through his first day without being fired for excessive distraction. He struggled to stay focused on Dr. Goldberg, who walked briskly ahead of him in gray slacks and a lavender blouse, a clipboard and pen tucked under one arm.

"One of the people I'll be introducing you to today is Morgan Wagner, who works with the few companies that still utilize basic computer functionality," Goldberg continued. "As you may know, these jobs are not without risks, so Wagner has to closely monitor their data trails. He can only allow incremental amounts of data through at a time and much of this monitoring is done manually—a task that requires constant calculations as the percentages that get through tend to vary."

"Companies that still utilize computers?" Joel repeated. "You mean like the Sapling Corporation?"

"Exactly, Mr. Lodowick. As you might imagine, if that's the area we decide to put you in, you'll need an extensive background check and drug screening."

"Of course," said Joel, picturing that drug screening sending up an alarm the second it picked up Acubens' nanites in his bloodstream. This was never gonna work. None of it.

"Stay focused, Joel," Acubens said. "You're doing fine."

Did you know they worked with Sapling? Joel asked.

"Yes," said Acubens. "They are a communications company. They work with everyone."

I know, but monitoring their data trails while they're on the grid is way beyond just hooking up their phone lines.

"I'm unsure what you're concerned about, Joel. Is it the fact that Yori might find out you work here?"

Well, no. It wasn't, anyway...

"Then what are your concerns?"

Joel couldn't quite articulate why it left his skin crawling. Was it because bringing the computer inside him close to *another* computer might set off some sort of alert? Could Acubens somehow access the grid? Was the grid even still functional, or was the functionality Goldberg referred to on a much smaller scale? *I shouldn't be here. There's so much I don't know.*

"I will help you, Joel," said Acubens. "Try not to worry so much."

Goldberg led him through an office space scattered with cubicles, where employees worked with drafting boards covered in impossibly complex webs of straight lines punctuated by endless strings of numbers and letters. Joel did his best not to stare. At the other end of the room, she pushed through a dark gray door and into an area fifteen degrees colder than the last and four decibels louder. This one had aisles of seven-foot-tall rectangular units, their fronts covered in panels and switches and sliders. A low-pitched hum filled the room. A handful of workers in drab jackets and white hardhats navigated between the equipment. No one looked up at their entrance.

"Welcome to the data center," said Goldberg. "This is where the demarcation to carriers happens. Each carrier requires specific power and space requirements, so here we monitor AC and DC power levels, as well as keep an eye on the maximum cable lengths for circuits. Every other room you'll see here will connect back to this one, and when you have issues with carrier circuits, these are the employees you'll talk to."

"Got it," said Joel. And he did, sort of. But he knew she was probably dumbing it down for him, probably by a lot, so he hoped Acubens would toss him a good tidbit here and there to ease her mind. And his own.

She led him through the rest quickly: more types of "distribution centers" than he could remember, the operations center, the electrical and mechanical rooms, the data center support spaces. It was nothing but a blur of racks and cabinets and cables and mechanical switchboards to him. Goldberg stopped only occasionally to explain something more in-depth, which never did anything to lessen his confusion. Joel found himself wanting to laugh at the nondisclosure agreements she'd had him sign beforehand; he couldn't carry any information out of here if he tried. Except he had a feeling Acubens was retaining every bit of it, for whatever that was worth.

But then they got to a door at the end of a long hallway of black racks, and Joel could tell instantly that this one was different. It was black with heavy horizontal grooves and an honest-to-god keypad in the righthand panel.

Joel's eyes widened. *Computerized?*

"Mechanical," corrected Acubens.

Joel gazed at the keypad, and he honed in instantly on the more frequently used numbers—three, six, seven, and four—and could tell by the smudging of the buttons' corners which direction multiple fingers would likely have traveled across them in a hurry. Within seconds, he was almost positive he knew the five-key code. He blinked. Had Acubens specifically zeroed in on that purposely? Had it glazed over everything else only to pay attention *now*?

That feeling of unease was creeping across his shoulder blades again. He worked them slightly, resisting the urge to reach up and brush the feeling off like a bug.

"Please avert your eyes, Mr. Lodowick," said Goldberg.

"Of course, ma'am." Joel looked away, losing his chance to see if his guess had been correct. The five beeps in the keypad were all the same tone. But he could *almost* hear the brush of her finger pads on them, and the inches between each separate push. It shouldn't be possible. He closed his eyes briefly, feeling the slow but steady thump of his heartbeat at a cool sixty-two beats per minute.

The clack of a lock disengaged, and the door swung open on nearly silent hinges.

"The computer room, Mr. Lodowick," said Goldberg. "Stay close to me in here, and keep your hands visible at all times."

Joel turned back, pulling his hands from his trouser pockets and pressing them against each other at his waist. He followed Goldberg in.

A big room spread out before them. It was dominated mostly by industrial desks with short privacy walls, with every two sharing a single wall to make a pattern of giant T's across the gray carpet. To Joel's left and right, shelves full of files were built right into the wall. And in front of him...screens. A whole entire wall filled with screens.

Fifty-four sixteen-by-twenty-inch monitors made up the bulk of it, with each array of nine separated from the next by a gray fiberglass partition. Six eighteen-by-twenty-four-inch monitors were laid out in a row above those, divided by another partition. Almost all the monitors were off. But at the far-left side of the room, completely opposite from where Joel and Goldberg stood, a flicker of blue light played over three people. One of them looked up at the sound of the door closing.

"Dr. Goldberg?" he said.

"We won't keep you long, Mr. Wagner," said Goldberg. "I just wanted to introduce you to Joel Lodowick, and give him a glimpse of what you do here."

"Ah, yes!" said Wagner. "Come on over."

Goldberg led Joel around the banks of desks and toward the wall of screens. Joel saw an individual monitor on every desk, too—small eight by tens, built right into the desks' framework. The sight of them brought back a sudden and visceral memory of sitting in a magcar and swiping his fingers to pour black fog over a mountain rising, illusion-like, from his tablet, to kill an army of zombies. God, he hadn't thought about that game in years.

He looked up from the monitor, catching a glimpse of his own distorted reflection in the gleaming silver chrome of a support pillar, his white face bathed in the blue of the live monitor they were approaching. He looked eerie and inhuman, as if he was stepping into a world that was as much illusion as the fog in that game had been. His gaze slid from there to the files in the walls to the empty monitors now directly at his right elbow. He could feel the crackle of live energy from them, despite them being off.

An Indian woman with a ponytail sat in front of the blue monitor. A scattering of papers lay on the desk beside her, pencil scrawls of numbers crowded across them. White numbers scrolled across the blue screen. A white man with curly red hair sat at the desk beside her, his nose stuck in the smaller screen, which Joel couldn't see from his angle. A Black man with a close-cut beard was standing up waiting, a smile on his face.

"Mr. Lodowick," he said, holding his hand out. "I'm Morgan Wagner. You must be the 'mathemagician' Dr. Goldberg told me about."

Joel clasped his outstretched hand. "I don't know if I'd go that far, but I'm hoping I can be of some help. Great operation you have here."

"Isn't it?" Wagner glanced around, as if still amazed by it. "Every time I come in here, I feel like I've stepped back in time."

"I had a flashback of my early teens just walking through the room," Joel admitted.

Wagner nodded knowingly. "Well, I apologize that I can't introduce you to Vohra and Haines this second, as they're right in the middle of something, but I can spare a couple minutes. We don't keep a big staff, as we're very selective about who we allow in. Basically, our job is to connect the grid to companies that absolutely need it, but it's actually more a job of security. You watch the data in real time as they're accessing it, which means you're constantly looking for gaps or irregularities that shouldn't be there. Obviously, you can't analyze something like that" —he waved at the scrolling stream of numbers on the blue screen— "on a calculator every time. You need to be in touch enough with the formulas and equations to spot something abnormal the second it appears. That's why it's such a niche position, as it's so rare to find people who can do that. Even people with skills like yourself can't always pull it off. But I have to say, your application makes you an extremely likely candidate."

Joel glanced uncertainly at the screen. "If there are gaps or irregularities, what does that mean?"

"Usually nothing, thanks to Sapling's constant vigilance from their end as well. But occasionally, it's someone who's managed to squirrel away some tech and build their own computer, trying to hack into the system. Documenting these abnormalities right away allows us to track and shut 'em down before they cause trouble."

"What about the Cyberblood virus?" said Joel. "Is that still an issue?"

Wagner tapped his lips, watching him. "How much do you know about it, exactly?"

Joel debated between feigning complete ignorance and sharing at least as much as Yori had told him. In the end, he decided to go with the latter, in hopes of looking less incompetent.

"I know it was a bug that ran rampant through computer systems and caused them to malfunction, often in dangerous ways. But the more I've studied—the more I've learned—that's not the *only* reason tech was shut off. Was it?"

"That's correct," said Wagner. "As far as the Cyberblood virus itself, the malware causing it was already so pervasive that both large and small operating systems had been exposed, and no amount of isolation or reboots could fully eradicate it. We still occasionally find bugs in our systems, despite all our precautions. As for the other issue..." He paused, raising an eyebrow. "You're referring to the singularity, I take it?"

"Yes, sir," said Joel.

"Well, the bionics were the greatest threat there, due to their complexity," Wagner said. "And we don't deal with bionics here. At all. So, no worries there. As far as the other computer work we do, it's mainly providing checks and balances for people accessing the grid, like Sapling. But I'd be lying if I told you there wasn't *some* risk here at Smaller World; we are working directly with the tech, after all."

Joel nodded, worrying at his lower lip with his teeth. He didn't want to think badly of Acubens. He really didn't. But it did seem odd that the bionic had managed to land him one of the very few jobs in the city that dealt firsthand with computers.

"Joel, you were the one who picked this job out of the long list I provided, if you'll recall," Acubens pointed out.

"Well, I know you're new to Smaller World," Wagner was saying, "and are still being shown the ropes today. But if you decide this area is something you're interested in, we'll do it as a completely separate application and interview, along with background checks and intensive testing. It also comes with a ten to fifteen thousand dollar raise over whatever you start out at. So, I hope you'll at least consider—"

A surge of electricity prickled across Joel's skin in the same moment that the blue screen in front of Vohra flickered and died. She gasped aloud, her head whipping toward the curly-haired man.

"Haines, power cycle!" she barked.

Haines's fingers tapped across his screen, lightning fast. Vohra grabbed for something on the desk, and a sheaf of papers slid across it and cascaded to the ground at Joel's feet. Joel knelt, gathering them as quickly as possible as she stood in a panic. They had gone every which direction, so he mashed them together in an unorganized jumble of paper corners and staples and paper clips. Something harder in there, like a stiff piece of plastic, was pinched between his thumb and forefinger. He felt a jolt from it, like an electric shock, and his breath caught.

Then Wagner was pulling the papers from his arms and sliding them back onto the desk. The blue screen flickered back to life, and Vohra said, "The GANC card, quick!" Wagner pulled it from Joel's fingers where it still dangled—a dark blue piece of plastic with a bright gold metallic square in the corner—and passed it to Vohra. She grabbed it and slid it through some sort of reader under the screen, and the data that had vanished came back like magic, scrolling in its incomprehensible code.

A sudden pulse of pain washed over Joel's forehead. He could still feel the spark of pain on his thumb pad, too—a prickling sensation, accentuated by small needle-like stabs. He turned his hand palm-up in the low lighting of the room, but his skin looked as smooth as ever.

Someone clapped him on the shoulder. "Hey," said Wagner. "No need to look so alarmed. The system was only down for a second. It happens."

Joel nodded shakily. He shook hands with Wagner again, trying to ignore the crawling feeling that was now numbing the end of his thumb, then followed Goldberg back out of the room.

"So?" she said as they headed through the distribution centers. "Do you think that's a department you'd be interested in?"

Joel stuck his hand in his pocket, wincing at the throbbing pain in his head. "Yeah. I mean yes, ma'am. It definitely would. Ma'am, I...I hate to interrupt, but I could use a break at the facilities, if it's not inconvenient."

"Yes, of course, Mr. Lodowick," she said. "They'll be right up here."

By the time Joel had locked the back stall of a fancy restroom with wooden paneled doors and a dark green tile floor, the prickling in his thumb had subsided, although the headache remained. Joel put down the seat of the steam flushing toilet and put his hands over his face.

Acubens, he said. *I know you did something in there. What was it?*

"I'd like to contact Nyctalope," said Acubens.

Yes. I know you would. What does that have to do with what happened in there?

"You expressed concern over approaching her if she wasn't who we suspected. This is a valid concern. Your human body is severely limited at the moment, in terms of information gathering, so I found a way to expand your reach. It's simply another upgrade to—"

Acubens! Joel interrupted. *What did you* do?

"The encryption algorithm contained in the Grid Access Network Card will allow us access to the grid again. As you may recall, I was offline, and therefore unable to assist you with job searches or certain interview questions. Reconnecting will increase my usefulness to you."

All you had to do was touch the card with my thumb?

"The nanites in your system have encoded into much of your body. It was a simple matter of magnetizing them and using them to scan the iron-based particulate contacts."

Joel squeezed his eyes shut, remembering Acubens' words at the concert: "To them, Joel, *you* will be the bionic. You will cease to be a person at all."

"Joel," said Acubens, "please don't overreact. As I said, it simply expands our reach. Now we can pull information from anywhere that's still hooked up to the grid."

Like Sapling, thought Joel. Fuck. Did Acubens think he was stupid?

"No. I do not think that, Joel."

You led me here, didn't you? The second Joel said the words, the truth of them sank in with cold certainty. *You hand-selected that list you read me to find a place that had access to the grid. You got me through that application, that interview, all of it, just to get me inside this company so you could hook yourself up.*

Acubens was quiet for a moment. Then it said, "There is some truth to that. I did specifically look at companies with potential grid access, because I knew the extra knowledge could benefit you in the long run."

Joel's head was spinning. He pressed his palms to his eyes, his breath coming short. He couldn't stop thinking about his reassurances to himself after Nyctalope's concert—that *he* was the one who decided whether or not to pursue something, regardless of what Acubens wanted. But what Acubens had just done flew right in the face of that.

Why the hell didn't you discuss it with me first? he said.

"There was no time while Morgan Wagner was speaking with you," said Acubens. "You heard what he said about intensive testing. We wouldn't have gotten the opportunity again for weeks. I took the necessary steps to equip you when I saw the means to do so. That is all."

And Nyctalope?

"There's a chance I may be able to get her contact information without you asking Yori at all. Then, if I do, it will be entirely up to you whether you choose to pursue it. Is that satisfactory?"

I guess so, said Joel.

Yori. He was seeing Yori tonight. And after today, more than ever, he couldn't deny the burning certainty that he needed to say something before it was too late.

But I won't, he thought, making his words as fierce and solid as possible. He tried to put belief behind them, confidence, to make *himself* believe them enough that Acubens would, too. *I won't say anything. I have too much to lose.*

The only problem was that it was the simple truth.

Chapter 10

Yori lived on the southwestern side of Albuquerque, right next to where the Rio Grande River cut under the interstate. During rush hour, it was easily forty minutes from where Elena lived, so by the time Joel dropped Clementine off at her place, he was running late. Clementine evidently hadn't mentioned Acubens all day and was full of new stories about the daycare, so that was one worry off Joel's mind as he headed to Yori's. Every time his mind started to drift to the bigger worry—Acubens using his body to reconnect itself to the grid—he tried to force it back to safer pastures. *This is fine. Acubens is on my side. It's fine.*

After the third time he said it, though, Acubens made it clear he wasn't fooling anyone.

"You can stop broadcasting contradictory thoughts, Joel," it said. "I know you're planning to tell Yori about me tonight."

Joel's throat tightened. *I'm not. I'm not...*

"You're at least considering it," said Acubens. "But you don't need to. What are you concerned about, that has caused this sudden shift?"

Besides you using my body without my consent? Joel said. *I mean...how did you even do that? Were you controlling it?*

"I magnetically activated your finger pads for a short period of time," said Acubens. "It is not remotely the same thing."

Joel's mouth twisted doubtfully. *It's still affecting the physical world, which you've never been able to do before. If this is the next step of your...your evolution, or your upgrades, or whatever you want to call it...then what the hell comes next, Acubens? Can you tell me that?*

"Not with any certainty, no. However, if you do tell Yori about me, I *can* tell you that I won't be able to protect you from what the Sapling Corporation will do, not at my current capabilities. And that should be concerning enough."

Then it should ease your mind that I have no intention of Sapling finding out, Joel said.

"You genuinely believe Yori would keep this knowledge to himself?" said Acubens.

Yes, said Joel. *If I explain it to him carefully, I think he will.*

"The odds of him reacting negatively are much more likely," said Acubens. "You'll be invalidating everything we've gained so far, and you'll never be able to undo that choice if you're wrong. All because one of my upgrades scared you. It isn't worth the risk, Joel."

Yes, but what will the next *upgrade do?* said Joel. *Take over my body? Turn me into a bionic?* That's *what scares me, Acubens!*

"I would think that prison time or invasive analysis would scare you more," said Acubens.

Yes. That, too. Not to mention the fact that Acubens' answer was no denial of Joel's fears. He swallowed back a surge of nausea. Yori would know what to do. He had to.

He did his best to tune out Acubens' continuing arguments, relieved when he finally pulled up to a red-roofed adobe house near the end of a cul-de-sac. But the relief was short-lived. Because now he had to face Yori, and even the thought of telling him turned his blood to ice. This was not what he'd wanted to do tonight. He'd promised, in fact, to turn off his brain and be fully present.

"It's not too late," said Acubens. "You deserve a night of diversion."

Be quiet, said Joel as he climbed from his car.

The sun was gone, and a cold wind rattled the leaves of the locust tree in the xeriscaped front yard. He could hear the river off to his left, probably not far beyond the houses ringing the dead-end street. He'd changed at Elena's into a worn-out pair of jeans and a long-sleeved T-shirt; showing up in formal clothes would have meant explaining his new high-tech job and all its implications right off the bat, and he wasn't nearly ready for that. *I'm not ready for any of this.*

The front door opened. Yori came out and leaned against the doorjamb with his arms crossed over his chest, wearing dark jeans slung low on his hips and a thermal top with blue and gray stripes. Despite everything, Joel's gaze caught on the way the shirt rode up slightly at his waist, hinting at a firm and athletic body beneath. How had he ever snagged even one date with a guy like this, much less two?

"I thought you were bringing your daughter," Yori called.

Joel's eyes snapped back to his face, flushing at the thought that Yori might have caught him staring.

"I found a babysitter," he said.

"Oh! That's...that's cool." Yori gave a tentative smile, as if he wasn't sure whether this was good news or not. Joel wanted to reassure him, because in normal circumstances, hell *yeah* it was good news, but he didn't dare make such promises tonight.

He handed Yori a bottle as he arrived at the front door. Yori took it, peering at the label in the porch light. "Spiced rum?"

Joel laughed in embarrassment. "I know it's no merlot, but—"

"No, hey, this is great. Thanks! Come on in."

Yori stepped back from the door, and it was only then that Joel noticed the whole place was glowing a muted orange behind him. There was a subtle but definite smoky aroma to the air, tinged with spice. He followed Yori into a living room...and stopped dead.

The orange glow was jack-o-lanterns. Twenty-seven of them, to be exact, spread across a coffee table, the top of a piano, on bookcases, the half wall between the living room and kitchen, on the steps leading out of sight to the left. Except for a faint light on in the kitchen, the house was lit only by the glow of those jack-o-lanterns. It was like standing in a haunted house, and yet it gave the impression of mood-lighting all at the same time, but like mood-lighting with a twist, and it was just so freaking *cool*.

"Holy shit," Joel whispered in disbelief.

"I thought your daughter was coming," said Yori, running a hand over the back of his neck. "And I thought she'd like it."

"So, you slammed out twenty-seven carvings in a day, or what?"

"No, I..." Yori blinked. "Wait, did you really count them that fast?"

Crap. Joel had to be careful if he wanted to handle this right. He gave a small shrug.

"No, I already had them," said Yori. "It's a hobby. I mean, artwork in general, but I go a little crazy around Halloween. But I wouldn't have lit them all if I knew your daughter wasn't coming. I mean, that might have seemed creepy, right?"

"Are you kidding? I love it! And these designs! I've never seen anything like them."

Joel came farther into the house, letting the door swing shut behind him. The jack-o-lanterns were anything *besides* typical carved faces. They were done in layers, so while some places went all the way through to show the candle flames beyond, a thinning out in other places created gradients and shadows. There were elaborate skulls. A realistic owl flying across a moon. An elegant fox with a sweeping tail. A *magcar*, complete with a tint to the domed windshield. An anime character from a popular TV show. A girl in a cape, leaping from a rock.

And symbols. Interspersed among the pictures were glowing symbols, iridescent and stark against the dark background of the pumpkins.

Joel pointed at one. "Kanji?" he said, hoping he was saying it right.

Yori nodded. "I do one for each family member."

"Do they live locally?"

"Not anymore. Parents moved back to Japan. Sister's down in West Antarctica helping with the new settlement. And my brother's up in Colorado helping keep the Rio Grande running by pumping water into it for farming. We're scattered everywhere. So, I do the pumpkins and mail out pictures every year."

"They're amazing. Beyond amazing. How long do they take you?"

"Maybe two and a half hours each? So that's, I don't know..." Yori looked around dubiously. "Twenty-seven, you said? You tell me. How many hours have I spent on this?"

Sixty-seven and a half. But Joel clamped his teeth on the answer and shrugged. "Enough that you can't have been getting much sleep lately," he said.

Yori winked and said, "Yeah, I do need someone here to make me go to bed once in a while."

Before Joel could answer, he turned and swept up the three stairs to the next level, and from there into the kitchen. Joel's heartbeat fluttered, soft and rapid, like it was barely touching his ribcage. He was terrified, but it was for all the wrong reasons.

"Leave your shoes on that bench by the door, if you don't mind," Yori called behind him.

Joel slipped his Converses off and put them next to Yori's slip-on black leather ones.

"You're making yourself more vulnerable," Acubens said.

For god's sake, Acubens! said Joel sharply. *Enough!*

"I am merely stating a fact," said Acubens. "If you insist on doing this, you may want to wait until you're in a more open area, in case he doesn't react well."

But by then, it might be too late. Joel closed his eyes, nauseous at even the thought of saying something. He *knew* he needed to, but he also wanted to wait. To wait until after dinner, until after he'd gotten to know Yori better, until after whatever happened *after* dinner...happened... and then, maybe—

But it was crazy to think that way. As furious as Yori would be, how much *more* furious would he be to discover Joel had hidden it from him the entire evening? There was no good way out of this. There'd only been one good time to bring it up, and it had been when Yori gave him the goddamn chance in the first place, in his own apartment after Grotz had left and before Yori had asked about the guitar on his couch.

The bang of the oven door closing startled him from his thoughts. He looked up in the dim lighting to see Yori sweep down from the kitchen holding a laden pizza stone. The aroma of moist dough and gooey cheese made Joel's mouth water. He inhaled it, realizing with a pang how ravenous he was. It would be ridiculous to say anything before eating a couple slices of that.

"Homemade?" he said.

One side of Yori's mouth curved up. "Kind of? It was a pick-it-up, heat-em-up place outside the base, but I added some mentaiko I had on hand."

"Mentaiko?" said Joel. "What's that?"

"It's pollack roe, pickled with chili pepper. Popular in Japan, according to my parents. They used it a lot when I was growing up. You'll love it. Well, if you like spicy foods, anyway."

"I'm from New Mexico," said Joel, grinning. "Bring it on."

Yori deposited the pizza on the coffee table in front of the perpendicular couches, then slid the nearby jack-o-lantern to the end of the table. He returned a moment later with a couple paper plates, which he put next to the pizza. Then he turned toward an entertainment center tucked into the corner by the couch, and lowered himself to one knee to scan some music.

After a second, he turned back toward Joel. "What do you rec?" he said. "Soft enough to talk over, but edgy enough not to put us to sleep?"

"Right. Uh, you got any Human Human?"

"No! Who's that?"

"Eh, it was a long shot. They never made it big in the States. How about The Battle Between the Heart and the Mind?"

"What? Is that a band name?" Yori glanced back, his eyes dancing in the orange candlelight and a smile playing on his lips.

"Yeah, it totally is. Um...oh, what about This Fever Almost Killed Me Once, But Ever Since Then—"

Yori picked up a pillow from the nearby couch and threw it at him. Joel caught it just before it hit one of the jack-o-lanterns.

"Get over here and help me pick something, smart ass," said Yori.

Joel walked over and tossed the pillow on the wooden floor next to Yori, then knelt beside him to look at the bottom shelves of the entertainment center. Two shelves of records, 129 total. His fingers played over their cardboard surfaces as he filed facts about Yori that had nothing to do with Acubens' influence. Yori liked pop, more than Joel did. But he also had a soft spot for older tunes that Joel wouldn't have guessed at. A healthy supply of punk. A handful of Beat Bots from a decade and a half earlier—good irony there. And then...he stopped at a half-remembered one from high school with a plaid green cover. He pulled it out, staring in wonder.

"Rae Imajra," he said. "Now that's a rare one to find."

Yori took it from him, frowning. "I don't even…" He flipped it over, scanning the track list. Finally, he tapped one. "Oh, right. She was the opening act for Mehishdo when I saw him in New York. Did this really good cover of 'Crying Quails,' so I grabbed her album afterward. I can't even remember whether I listened to it or not."

"Well, put it on," said Joel. "It's a perfect work of art. Just perfect."

As Yori turned on his system, Joel eased onto the leather couch in front of the coffee table. Some of the tension had left his shoulders. The gentle strobing of the orange light around him, along with the slight sound of candles popping, was hypnotizing. When was the last time he'd allowed himself to relax like this? When was the last time he'd had the *chance*? Sitting at home playing his bass after Clementine had gone to bed was the closest he'd come. But it was nothing compared with sinking into a comfortable sofa, surrounded by soft lighting and good food while an awesome guy put on music so they could spend the next couple hours together.

A fleeting moment in time. Time, as Acubens had pointed out, that he'd never get back once he brought it to an end. A moment in time that wouldn't even *exist* if he hadn't acquired Acubens in the first place. Talk about irony.

The opening chords of "Four Walls" came on—an acoustic guitar playing something slightly mournful and yearning, but in a major key. It lifted his heart a little, the same as it always did. Rae's husky voice joined in a second later. *"How should I start, with these pieces of my cold, my cold and broken heart…"*

Yori settled into the seat perpendicular to him, and leaned forward to work a slice of pizza free and slide it onto a paper plate. Joel followed suit, then took a bite. It was still a piping hot 139 degrees, and the most amazing thing he'd had in ages. The mentaiko was incredible—salty with a spicy kick, and a savory richness that went great with the plain mozzarella cheese and soft pizza dough.

"Good?" said Yori.

"God, yes. It's perfect."

"Ha. Good. I thought about making you a traditional Japanese meal or something—I swear I did—but I just didn't feel like I had the time to do it justice. I've been" —he waved a hand vaguely at the jack-o-lanterns around the room— "busy."

"Yeah. For real. Do you own this place?"

Yori nodded. He swallowed his bite of pizza before answering. "I bought it with...with someone."

Joel winced at the hitch in Yori's voice. Count on him to go and dredge up bad memories the first quiet moment they got together. "I'm sorry," he said. "I shouldn't have—"

"It's okay," said Yori. "It was a little over a year ago. Remember I told you about that bionic incident, the one with the Aries model? The one that killed four of Sapling's employees?"

Joel's stomach tightened. "Yeah?"

"Well, she was one of those employees. The person I bought this house with, I mean."

"Oh, shit. God, I'm so sorry, Yori."

"Thanks. I almost quit the job afterward. It messed me up for a long time. But I figured if everyone quit when they ran into an incident like that, sooner or later something would slip through the cracks with the tech. I mean, *someone* has to keep it in check, right?"

"Right," Joel said unsteadily. It reinforced his belief that if anyone could help him, it was Yori.

Even if it meant Yori would never look at him the same way again.

"But the bionics you run across *now* aren't that dangerous, right?" he said. "You've gotten rid of the deadliest ones?"

"Mostly, yeah. There are still moments. There are still a ton out there, after all, and the screening to get into Sapling is intense. We could use more personnel. A lot more." He sighed, looking down at his pizza. "That's why I do things like this," he said, gesturing at the pumpkins, "instead of, I don't know, going out to bars and clubs to meet people. At least this stuff won't kill me or die on me, right?"

"You asked *me* out," Joel ventured.

"Yeah, I don't know. You were hot. I couldn't stop thinking about you, and then we got those tickets, and I guess I just…" He blew his breath out, eyes distant. "I've got to try again sometime, right?"

Joel's stomach turned over as Yori's words registered. Was he saying this was the first time he'd dated since a bionic had killed his girlfriend? *Oh my god. How could I do this to him?*

"But what about you?" Yori said. "If you don't mind me asking, how'd you end up as a single dad?"

Joel finished his first slice of pizza before answering, even though the taste had gone wooden in his mouth.

"Well, technically, you know…I'm the one who gave birth to Clementine," he finally said. "I wasn't out yet and it was right at the end of high school. The guy I was dating overdosed about a year after Clementine was born. Never even knew I was trans. And Clementine's been mine ever since. My parents helped out a lot while I still lived there. But after I fully came out and socially transitioned, they just…didn't change anything. Didn't call me by my new name, didn't change the pronouns they used, didn't treat me any differently than they ever had. And I knew if I stayed there, then everything I'd wanted so badly for so long would just be swept under the rug and erased. I couldn't let that happen. So, I took Clementine and moved out, and we've been making our own way ever since." He shrugged and started on his second slice.

Yori gazed at him, a mixture of anger and pain playing across his face. "Jeez. That's almost worse than kicking you out, isn't it? Like *less* acknowledgment."

"I don't know if it's worse," said Joel. "All I know is it was killing me inside."

"But what about after what happened at the pharmacy? You're not gonna have to move back in with them, are you?"

"No," said Joel adamantly. "Absolutely not. I've got some prospects already. I'll be fine."

"How's your record?" said Yori. "Maybe I could put in a good word for you at Sapling."

Joel almost choked on his next bite of pizza.

Yori's lip quirked up. "What? Is my job that abhorrent to you?"

"Abhorrent? No," Joel managed. He put the pizza down and coughed into his elbow, trying to get his breath steady again after that shock of surprise. His eyes were watering. "You mind if I get some water?"

"I'll get it. Just try to catch your breath."

Joel leaned back in the couch, wiping his sleeve across his eyes. He knew this was probably as good an opening as he'd ever get. He just had to have the nerve to take it. He massaged the bridge of his nose, feeling that rattling cough in his throat still.

"You assured your friend Elena you wouldn't say anything," Acubens said. "What happens if Yori arrests you tonight? Then she will be stuck with your daughter. That's an unfair position to put her in."

Joel wrapped his hands around the base of his skull and pulled his head down, elbows to his knees. The room spun. In the stereo system to his left, Rae's album rolled into something more upbeat, but equally as husky: *The weight of your mind, weight of your mind, weight of your lies, now I'm buried alive.*

"Hey!" Suddenly, Yori was on the couch next to him, one hand on his back. "You all right, man?"

Joel nodded.

"I have your water. Here."

Joel unclasped his hands and pulled his head up, gratefully taking the plastic cup of water Yori was holding out. As soon as he did, Yori got up again, and returned shortly after with Joel's bottle of rum and a couple wineglasses swinging by their stems. He put them on the coffee table and resumed the place next to Joel on the couch, instead of going back to his original spot.

"Listen," he said. "I never should have told you what happened with that Aries model. Every time I bring up my job now, you freak out. But I promise you, that *wasn't* a normal thing."

Joel looked up. "Oh god, no, that's not what I—"

Yori cut him off with a wave of his hand. "No more work talk. If you're interested, just ask, but otherwise, I swear I won't bring it up again. I *really* don't want to ruin anything, okay?" He leaned forward and opened the rum, then poured it into the wine glasses.

Joel took a deep breath, then let it out slowly. "Yori," he said. "You know that bionic that was in—"

Yori's head whipped around, and the next thing Joel knew, Yori's hand was over his mouth. Joel's breath caught in his throat, and the words with them.

Yori gradually pulled his hand away, dark eyes fastened on Joel's as he shook his head. "No. I said no more work talk. Got it?"

"Yes, but—"

"Here." Yori picked up one of the wine glasses by its stem and passed it to Joel. "If you reach the bottom of this glass and still have something to say that absolutely can't wait until later, I'll listen. But not before then. Deal?"

His mouth dry, Joel took the glass. He could still feel the warmth of Yori's hand against his lips. Still smell the cedar scent of the soap he'd washed with. Still feel how close he was sitting, with hardly any space at all between them, and feel the radiating body heat that Joel knew for a fact was more than just his imagination.

He drank. The rum had a heady fruity aroma that hit his nose first, followed by a pleasant taste of vanilla and cinnamon. It warmed his body from the inside out. He looked at Yori, licking the taste of it from his lips.

"Not bad for bottom-of-the-shelf," he said.

"Not at all," said Yori, smiling into his glass. "I like this music, by the way. A little bit blues, a little bit punk, a little bit...sultry? Would you call it sultry?"

"Pulling you down, with the depths of my pain, until we spiral, spiral, spiral, into something inhumane..."

"Sultry's a good word," said Joel. He took another drink, his eyes never far from Yori's lips. Elena's words echoed through his head. "There's really no risk, as long as you don't become seduced into saying something." He felt like laughing, even though there was nothing funny about any of this. *Is that what's going on here?*

But no, that wasn't why he was planning to say something. He'd thought it since the second his stomach had dropped at work, when the headache had pulsed in his brain and the tip of his thumb had burned with electricity. He glanced down at his glass. He was gonna lose his nerve if he didn't do this soon. His limbs were getting too relaxed, his mind too distracted, Yori's presence too tempting. God, he practically *ached* with his presence.

There were only a couple swallows left. He took another drink and lowered it again. But before he could tip it back for the last drink, the mouth of the rum bottle clinked on the glass's rim as Yori refilled it. Joel's breath came ragged as he stared down at the glass.

"You're cheating," he said in a low voice.

"If you're trying to get through it so we can talk about my job again, then yeah, I'd rather move on with our evening," said Yori. He sighed. "But if there's something really bothering you, go ahead. We should get it out of the way."

Joel nodded. He took another long drink from his wineglass, then leaned over Yori to set it on the coffee table, right in front of the brightly burning jack-o-lantern. Yori set his glass next to it, the flirtatious look fading from his face as he studied Joel. Joel still hadn't fully straightened from setting his glass down, and his face was a mere five and a half inches from Yori's now.

Joel turned his head and kissed him.

It was the dumbest, most completely opposite thing, from what he'd meant to do that it took him a full three seconds to even realize he'd done it. Yori made a small sound of surprise. It gave Joel a surge of confidence, and he deepened the kiss even as his heart raced and his mind screamed that he was just making everything worse.

But Yori wrapped his hands around the back of Joel's head, holding him close, and there was no way Joel was pulling back now. The taste of rum on Yori's tongue, the pressure of his lips, the movement of his mouth...it was intoxicating. Joel's mind gradually detached from his fixation on Acubens, and he melted into a rare moment of surrender.

For a full minute and nineteen seconds, Yori was his entire world. Joel struggled to catch his breath when Yori finally pulled away.

"That was *not* what I thought you were gonna say," Yori managed. He was flushed, his eyes bright and manic as they alighted on Joel. "You're a good kisser, you know that?"

"Am I?" Joel sounded just as flustered as he felt.

"Oh yeah. You are." Yori let out a small chuckle, running a hand through his hair. He looked away for a second, toward the coffee table, letting out a slow uneven breath. He stayed that way, just staring, for several long heartbeats.

Joel swallowed, his throat suddenly unbearably dry, and leaned forward to grab his wineglass again. But without warning, Yori's hand came up, his forearm blocking Joel from reaching it. He was still staring at the wineglasses, Joel saw; the wineglasses standing side by side in the stark candlelight of the jack-o-lantern's face.

"I don't mean to alarm you, Joel," said Acubens, its voice unexpectedly loud in the quiet moment between songs changing, "but you should leave while you still can."

Leave? What are you talking about? Joel answered Acubens distractedly, his eyes fastened on Yori's face.

"I've made a mistake. You're in danger. Leave. Leave now."

What? No, I'm not gonna—

Yori looked up, and Joel's thoughts halted in their tracks. Yori's eyes were wider, his jaw set, his gaze flickering over Joel as if he'd never seen him before.

"Why the *hell* are there no fingerprints on your glass?" he said.

Chapter 11

In the bright orange light of the candle burning inside the pumpkin, it was clear as daylight if you knew to look; fingerprints were plastered across the surface of Yori's wineglass, while Joel's was as crystal-smooth as a commercial. He blinked, splaying his hand palm-up in his lap. It looked normal to him.

Acubens? he said.

"Joel, it's not too late. Run."

What's going on? Did you scrub my fingerprints? Did you remove *them from my fingers?*

"It was necessary in the computer room today, to make the scan work. I'll explain more, I promise. But please, Joel—"

Yori's hand whipped out before Acubens could finish, snagging Joel's left wrist and wrapping around it tight. "Answer me!"

"Um." Joel swallowed. "I—I don't know, Yori. I wasn't gripping the glass that hard. And surely there's some people who don't have..."

"What were you gonna tell me before you kissed me?" Yori said tightly.

Joel's gaze darted to the front door and back again. He debated between backpedaling and trying to pass his fingertips off as something genetic, or following through with his original plan. It was probably too late to lie anyway. Yori wouldn't be reacting this way if he hadn't seen this exact same thing before—and on something that scared him to death. The best path here was to tell Yori before he freaked out any worse.

"That...that bionic in—" Joel began.

But then his throat tightened, so unexpectedly that he doubled over, coughing and gasping for breath. The fit only lasted eleven seconds, but tears streamed from his eyes afterward. He felt dizzy, shaky. He was dimly aware that Yori's grip around his wrist hadn't loosened.

He looked up through blurry vision to see Yori watching him, his face tense and wary. Joel tried to talk. But he couldn't force his voice past that tightness in his throat. Fear was climbing now, fast and hard.

Acubens? he said.

"Don't say anything to him," said Acubens.

What the fuck are you talking about? Are you keeping *me from talking?*

"Your best chance of getting out of this alive is not to mention me. Right now, he's still uncertain, and that's all that's keeping him from arresting you. Listen to me, Joel."

No! Joel screamed. *You erased my fingerprints this morning, you're stopping my voice now, so what comes tomorrow? What the hell comes* next, *Acubens?*

"Joel—"

For god's sake, let me talk!

"What's wrong?" said Yori. "Are you sick?"

Joel shook his head.

"You're having trouble talking?"

Joel nodded. He clutched his throat, trying to speak again and hitting the same roadblock. *Bi-o-nic*, he mouthed.

"What about a bionic? *You're* a bionic?"

Joel shook his head frantically.

Yori whispered something under his breath, his grip still painfully tight around Joel's wrist. His face had gone deathly pale. He stood suddenly, hauling Joel up with him. Joel was forced to scramble after him as he headed for the kitchen. The phone on the counter was in Yori's hand before Joel had quite realized what he was doing. When he did, a sliver of ice shot through his spine.

Yori was calling his superiors.

This wasn't what Joel had wanted. He'd needed Yori to be an *ally*, to help him without involving his company or the cops. Calling in backup would tear him away from any chance of seeing Clementine again—

He yanked backward, finally ripping his hand free from Yori's grip. Yori's head darted up, the phone still tight to his ear.

"Stop, Joel!" he said. "Whatever's going on, we're gonna help, okay?"

Joel backed up, tripping over his feet as he found the stairs down the split-level. He pointed to the phone in Yori's hand and violently motioned him to put it down.

Yori held his free hand up, as if trying to calm a wild animal. "Joel, I can't handle a bionic on my—" he began, then jerked the phone to his mouth as someone picked up. "Salazar, I need you at my house. It's an emergency!"

Let me talk to him, Acubens! Joel thought. *This is your fault! Can't you see you're scaring the shit out of him?*

"If he was really your ally, he wouldn't have called to report you so quickly," said Acubens. "In case you haven't picked up on it, Joel, he hates and fears bionics more than anything in the world. You need to run, *now.*"

Joel started to shake his head, but at that moment, Yori slammed down the phone, opened a kitchen drawer, and pulled out a gun. Any thoughts of ignoring Acubens and trying to cooperate fled Joel's head, and he turned and bolted for the door.

"*Joel*!" Yori shouted. "Stop right there!"

Joel's acute hearing picked up the sound of the clip being rammed into the pistol. He had seconds, at most. He yanked the front door open, grabbed his Converses from the shoe shelf, and raced for his car, fumbling his keys from his trouser pocket.

He had the keys in the ignition and had thrown the car into reverse by the time Yori made it outside. But he hadn't even hit the end of the driveway before three gunshots rang out. The car skidded as one of the tires was hit. The wheel jerked out of his hands. Seconds later, the back of the car slammed against something, hard, and came to a bone-jarring stop—probably one of the cars parked alongside the curb. Joel's teeth hit his tongue, and the taste of blood flooded his mouth. He tried to throw the car back into drive, but the battery was out for some reason, and wouldn't reengage. Yori must have shot the electric motor, too.

"He's coming, Joel," said Acubens.

Joel shoved his feet into his shoes, threw the door open, and hit the ground running. Yori yelled something after him, but Joel had ceased to listen. He had to put a house or something between them before Yori gave up on not shooting him altogether. He had to—

Dammit! He'd forgotten Yori lived on a cul-de-sac. He was sprinting toward a turnaround in the road, closed in by houses. He glanced over his shoulder, and saw that Yori was running after him, gun still clutched in his right hand. And he was a *fast* runner. Joel moaned through his teeth and turned ahead again, feet pounding the asphalt.

He went straight between two houses, grabbed the chest-high cinderblock wall between them and hauled himself up, then ran its length to leap over the other side. He hit a creosote bush, which scratched up his face and hands as his feet slid for purchase on the sand and gravel beneath. He shoved the leaves from his face, ready to push on, but his feet were still sliding on some downward trajectory he couldn't seem to arrest. He pinwheeled, twisting just in time to grab the side of the steep hill he'd landed on before he fell. The noise of the interstate hit his ears, not far to his left, and undercutting that, the sound of the Rio Grande River below.

Yori appeared overhead, silhouetted on the cinderblock wall against the streetlights of the neighborhood.

"That's a dead end," he said. "Let me help you up, okay?"

Joel's feet were still sliding. He clutched at the solid rock beneath the layer of sand and gravel, remembering now the steep slant of this riverbank that he'd seen from the interstate. He'd remembered thinking he was happy he wasn't raising Clementine in one of those houses, where the backyards bordered such dangerous terrain. Cold air chilled him through his thin long-sleeved shirt. He glanced to his left, toward the interstate, then toward the lit walking bridge that paralleled the highway and crossed the river. It seemed impossibly far down.

"Why did you call Sapling?" He was relieved when the words came out, shaky as they were. Acubens must have had to loosen his throat to let him run.

"You can talk now?" said Yori.

"I could have written it down, I could have..." Joel's voice gave out again, in violent hacks that sent his arms trembling.

"So, whatever's keeping you from talking isn't controlling your body?" said Yori.

Joel shook his head, his breath coming shorter. He couldn't have a conversation here. He *couldn't*. It was too late. Yori had called his superiors and they'd be here any second, he was just stalling him—

"You stole that pharmacy bionic, didn't you?" said Yori.

Joel didn't answer.

"What happened?" said Yori. "Did you hook it up to yourself somehow?"

Joel cried out as his foot slipped, and he slid seven and a half feet lower. He grabbed for something to hold onto, but the slope was bare here, any trace of vegetation gone.

"Well, whatever it was, surely you see it's not something you can handle on your own," said Yori. "You have to let us help you!"

Joel looked down again, his heart pounding. "Help me how?" he forced out. "Cut my brain open?"

"W-What? Are you saying it's in your *brain*?"

"Answer. Me."

Several excruciating seconds passed before Yori spoke again. "I'm sorry, Joel, but you have no idea what you're dealing with here. If it's true that it's in your brain...and if there's any possibility at all that it's *advancing*..." He choked on the word. "...then time could be shorter than you think. A bionic shutting a system down to keep it from working is one thing. It's a lot simpler. But as the technology progresses, more components can be mastered. The fine motor skills these things usually lack can be learned. What I'm saying is, this voice thing? It's only the beginning. It'll start influencing your thoughts and decisions, if it's not already. Then your body."

A sob hitched in Joel's throat. Police sirens sounded somewhere above. Joel could barely see the strobe of blue and red lights behind Yori's silhouette.

"This is really dangerous stuff," Yori continued. "We have to contain it, at any cost."

"And what if you...can't?" said Joel. "Then what? Kill me?"

Yori let out a ragged breath. No answer.

Joel grunted. "Too dangerous...not to. Huh?"

"Please. Come back up, I'm begging you."

Joel shook his head. Yori had as good as admitted it. He'd be killed, and he'd never see Clementine again. Or maybe he wouldn't be killed, and he'd be dissected alive to figure out what Acubens had done to him, and then he'd *wish* he was dead.

No. There has to be another way.

An image flashed into his brain—a detailed map of the terrain below him. It took him only a second to realize Acubens must have accessed it from the grid it had connected to. Immediately afterward, he knew exactly how to angle his body to get down the slope without falling. He knew the quickest route to that bridge.

But then what?

Nyctalope, he thought. Nyctalope was the one person who might have a bionic in her head. If anyone would be willing to listen to Joel without dismantling him as quickly as they would Acubens, it would be someone who'd lived through this. Someone who was still using the creatively human side of herself to write music, despite the presence in her head. If Joel could talk to her, maybe he could find out if her bionic had taken control of her body, or whether they'd found a satisfactory balance. Maybe it was possible.

Maybe Joel didn't have to die to protect the world from Acubens.

He looked up. "Yori?" he said, his voice hoarse.

"What?"

"You're a good kisser, too."

Yori raised his gun. "Wait! Joel—"

But Joel was already running, his Converses skidding but steady this time, as he wove a lightning-fast path down the steep slope. His glimpse of the interstate showed cop cars there too, lights flashing as they raced across the bridge. Joel aimed single-mindedly for that walking bridge, traveling with a speed and certainty that felt like a dream. And when the gunshots started behind him, it was deceptively easy to weave his trajectory in the dark to make himself a difficult target. For the first time, he felt the magic beneath his body's shell, the possibility of what could be hiding behind the math in his head. It was exhilarating. It was horrifying.

It was the feeling of transcendence.

He slid down to the walking path and turned left without slowing, his legs pumping faster than ever now that he was on steady ground. The concrete turned to wooden boards as he shot onto the bridge over the Rio Grande. The cops that had pulled onto the shoulder of the interstate were alarmingly close now, and the sound of gunshots exploded to his right. Iron rails rose on either side of him in a series of connected arches, each one higher than his head. The walking bridge sloped downward, so that by the time he reached the other end, he'd be well below the level of the interstate, and into the terrain known as the bosque—the narrow strip of forest bordering the river.

But there'd be no safety there, either. Already, they were following him onto the walkway, and with their guns and their numbers, they'd hem him in sooner or later. And this long bridge was a straight shot, with no place to hide or veer off, and it didn't matter *how* fast he ran if—

The back of his right bicep exploded in agony worse than anything he'd ever felt. He screamed, staggering against a rail. For just a second, his vision went out.

"Keep running!" Acubens urged.

Joel hadn't fully come to a stop, so he sped up again, gasping at the pain. He knew he'd never make it before they hit him again. So, the next time an arch of iron rails sloped down to the bridge and then up again, he ran halfway up the side of it and then launched himself over, never slowing.

One second. Two seconds. Thr—and he hit. Ice cold water slammed against him like an explosion. He was submerged almost instantly, legs kicking, arms flailing, gunshot wound shrieking in agony. His feet brushed muck and he tried to push back against it, back toward the surface, but there was no solid ground to shove against, and the current was already yanking him downstream with a strength he would never have guessed.

He couldn't breathe. He barely knew which way was up. He paddled his arms, but unbearable pain shot through his arm again, and he sucked in a mouthful of water when he tried to scream.

Acubens! he yelled. *For god's sake, heal my arm!*

"I am working on it, Joel. There is a lot of tissue to repair here."

Well, there's about to be a lot more if I can't get some air!

"Try to relax," said Acubens. "The nanites have trouble when you're constantly moving, and their energy levels are momentarily depleted. But I am working as quickly as possible."

Joel tried to stop struggling, even though his lungs were sending pulses of pain and panic through his head as they begged for oxygen. The icy water carried him in its grip, battering him with grit and branches and strong underwater currents.

And somehow, through it all, Acubens' words echoed in the recesses of his mind. He clung to them, two facts, two lines of hope: Acubens' nanites had more trouble when Joel wouldn't stay still for them; and their energy levels were depleted after keeping him from speaking for so long.

Both facts were things he could use. If he lived through this...if Yori was right and Acubens started to take over his body...these were avenues of hope. Had Acubens even meant to share those words? Could it see Joel turning them over in his mind, as he bled out into the water and slowly slipped further and further from consciousness? Would it try to...?

"I think I've repaired enough, Joel," Acubens broke in. "Get to the surface. Quickly."

Somehow, Joel forced his body into motion, shoving water away with arms that no longer seized up in agony at the slightest hint of movement. He broke through the surface, so dizzy he couldn't see straight, gasping in huge lungfuls of cold air. As his vision finally started clearing, he saw the trees of the bosque on either side of him now. He could no longer see the city. He knew it was still there, but it had receded farther from the river, and would thin out more and more as he traveled downstream.

The cops would be following the banks, along with the Sapling Corporation. Not to mention Yori Otsuka. Had he been the one who'd fired those shots as Joel raced toward the river? Not necessarily. Backup had shown up right about the same time. But it could have been. Yori, despite the desperation in his voice and his seemingly genuine desire to help, might have tried to kill Joel rather than risk letting the bionic escape. Yori, who'd been fascinated by his knowledge of music, and who'd kissed him in the light of twenty-seven burning jack-o-lanterns.

Everything was fucked. Elena was going to kill him. And Clementine...

Clementine. Joel had given the cops Elena's address during his initial interrogation. If Sapling was determined enough to find Joel, they might start by looking for her.

Heart in his throat, Joel swam for the nearest riverbank. No matter how he cut it, his time was running out. He could almost feel the minutes of his future, ticking backward to this moment.

But, unlike those other numbers, there was no exact reading warning him how long he had left.

Chapter 12

The decision of what to do with Clementine wasn't an easy one. It was a calculated yet inconsistent balance between who he could trust (Elena, always; his parents, yes, despite their faults; himself, *no*, a million times no), who he felt fair laying burdens on (Elena, not so much; his parents, ehhhh; himself, he *wished*, but his compromised situation made him out of the question), and finally, who Clementine would be safest and happiest with if Joel was arrested or killed (a terrifyingly likely possibility).

He huddled by the brick wall in the back of a badly lit parking lot behind a burger joint off Central—a completely different parking lot than the one with the payphone he'd used to call Elena thirty-seven minutes earlier. His wet clothes had barely attracted any attention amidst the Monday night club-hoppers stepping around the homeless folks in this part of the city. He shook with cold. His eyes burned with grit from the river.

Acubens, he thought, *I swear to god, if you keep me from talking to my daughter—*

"I would never do that, Joel," said Acubens. "Those were different circumstances."

Say what you want about my intentions, but you *were the one who screwed everything up tonight. You know that, right?*

"Do you really expect things would have gone better if you'd shared my presence willingly?"

Yes!

"Yori's girlfriend was killed by a bionic," said Acubens. "He would not have listened to reason, no matter what."

A car horn blasted, and Joel watched a group of drunk toughs raise their arms at it in some sort of challenge. This was *not* where he'd hoped to end up this evening. He scrubbed his palms into his eyes, picturing Yori up on that wall again—"This voice thing? It's only the beginning"—and clamped his teeth down on another violent shiver.

I don't want you in my body anymore, he said. *I want you* out, *Acubens.*

"I've gathered that, Joel," said Acubens. "However—"

No, Joel broke in. *This isn't me inviting discussion about it. This is me telling you to leave. It's an order, Acubens. Leave my body. You're a robot. You have to obey orders. Right?*

There was the smallest of pauses before Acubens answered. "I told you right after the initial upload, Joel. I can't leave. I would obey the order if I could. But I can't implement a command that's outside my capabilities."

Joel's jaw clenched. *Remind me why,* he said.

"The upgrades required for the nanites to work with your system have rendered them permanently incompatible with a simpler machine. Transferring them is impossible. And there are no other methods of removing data."

So you can't just...leave? Just dump all those nanites out on the ground?

"Not without bringing every drop of your blood along with them, no."

Joel drew his knees to his chest and wrapped his arms around them, trying to hold heat inside his wet clothes.

So, this is what happens when you decide you want something I don't, he said bitterly. *You force my hand. To follow your goals. You wanted to find Nyctalope, so you took away all my other options.*

"In all fairness, *you* are the one who eliminated your options, Joel," Acubens said. "You could have continued working at Smaller World Telecom. You could have avoided Yori Otsuka. I had just gained us access to the grid, and nothing but success lay ahead for you. But you made choices that erased those options. In fact, my intervention tonight is the only reason you still *have* options. Therefore, your claim that I'm forcing you to contact Nyctalope is erroneous. If you have better ideas, please name them."

Joel leaned his head back against the cold wall behind him, squeezing his eyes shut. Was it true? Had he sabotaged everything while Acubens had only been trying to help?

Dammit, no. It was true that it had helped him so far, but when it came right down to it—sentient or not—Acubens was a *machine.* It didn't care about him. It couldn't. And trusting something that only needed him alive to keep *itself* alive would be a huge mistake.

As much as he hated to admit it, though, he needed Acubens as much as Acubens needed him. He didn't stand a chance against Sapling on his own. Until he could either figure out how to remove the bionic or stop its so-called upgrades from progressing any further, he had no choice but to keep working with it, whether he liked it or not.

Fine, he finally said. *Nyctalope it is, then. You wanted to contact her, so now's your chance. Where is she?*

Acubens was quiet for a second. Then it said, "California. She gifted concert tickets to the Sapling Corporation in San Francisco for a Wednesday night concert."

Goddamn it! California? She's there already?

"That is how it appears, yes."

Joel cursed again. It was too easy not to be intentional. If Nyctalope really had a bionic, and was hoping for someone with a bionic to find her, it was clear as day why she'd gift tickets to every Sapling Corporation she passed. They were the ones hooked up to the grid. It would be an easy electronic trail for anyone who'd done what Acubens had.

But *California?*

I was really hoping she was still local, he said.

"I told you. You should have tried contacting her earlier."

Shut up. Just shut up. Let me think.

A cop car went by, and Joel ducked his head below the parked car he huddled beside. Had it slowed down or was that his imagination? The task of hiding from the cops for who-knew-how-long seemed unbearably daunting. He couldn't go home. He couldn't go back to Smaller World Telecom. And he wasn't about to endanger Elena and Ashanti by asking to stay with them. He'd been hoping, he realized, to hole up in Nyctalope's hotel room or tour bus while she helped him figure out how the hell to...to erase his signature or whatever else he'd need to do to become as overlooked as her. But it was still speculation that she even *had* a bionic.

"I have a phone number for her," said Acubens. "Would that help?"

Joel laughed under his breath. *Not unless I'm planning to hide in a phone booth for however long it takes to figure this out. Which could be...I don't know...days? Weeks? I'll be scooped up by the cops before sunrise if I don't find somewhere to* go.

"If you're not ready to call her, then just go to her," said Acubens.

To...California?

"Yes. Sapling won't expect it. They don't suspect her, and you haven't mentioned her to Yori. And then you'll have more time to talk things through with her."

Not a bad idea, Joel said after a minute. *But it's a hell of a long way to go while I'm being actively hunted. Maybe if I had some sort of disguise...* He trailed off. *You still can't change my appearance, I take it?*

"No," said Acubens. "Changing your eye and hair color is more challenging than healing wounds at a cellular level, and furthermore, such an easy store-bought change for humans that it's unlikely to fool anyone. And I'm unable to make any major changes to your body structure yet."

Yet. Why did Acubens have to toss in words like that? Regardless, its point was made.

What about that thing you did in my apartment when the police came? How you made yourself invisible by...what was it? Projecting a negative refractive index? Can you do that again?

"To do so would require shifting all your skin cells to a reflective sheen, which would give you a very bionic-like appearance," answered Acubens. "Naturally, this would not help your situation. Nor is it within my capabilities yet."

Again with the "yet." So disturbing, and at the same time, so *inconvenient.*

At that moment, car tires sounded on the gravel. Joel looked up to see Elena's black four-door hatchback pull into the empty spot beside him. For just a second, her headlights flooded him in light, then they shut off, leaving him blinking the brightness from his vision. The passenger window rolled down.

"Get in," said Elena.

Joel stayed in a crouch as he made his way to her back door and opened it, then squeezed into the backseat. He was on the opposite side from where Elena had buckled Clementine's car seat. A smile spread across Clementine's face when she saw him, and her thumb popped out of her mouth.

"Maddy!"

Joel closed the car door and scooted across the seat, then unbuckled Clementine's straps with trembling fingers. He pulled her to his chest and held her as tight as he could, face buried in her red hair.

"What happened?" said Elena from the front.

"I...I tried to tell Yori," Joel said. It was hard to get the words out, but not because of Acubens this time; it was the rising emotion in his throat that was hard to speak past. "Because Ac— because you-know-who did something at work today. It used my body to hook up to the grid, and I was scared, and Yori...I wanted his help, but he just ratted on me. So I ran." He dug his teeth into his lip and held Clementine tighter. "I've called my parents, too. Any second, they'll be here to take her. I'm not safe to be around anymore."

"Oh, Joel," said Elena with a sigh. "Why didn't you tell me you were planning to do that?"

"I don't know. From the beginning, you've been telling me to keep quiet. You were right. I should never have gone out with him. But Ac..." For the second time, he stopped himself from naming the bionic in Clementine's presence. Did it even matter anymore? Yes, it did; it would be less information for her to tell the cops if they got ahold of her.

This was a nightmare.

He looked up in time to see another car pulling into the parking lot, this one a nice blue Galaxy modeled after the magcars a decade earlier. His parents.

"Maddy, why are your clothes wet?" Clementine said. "You're making me cold!"

Reluctantly, Joel loosened his hold. He looked down at her in the bad parking lot lighting—her long red hair, her freckled cheeks, her greenish-brown eyes, her uneven baby-sized teeth, the smudge of paint she still had on her eyebrow from some project at Smaller World's daycare. His heart was physically hurting, as if it were ripping down the middle. He tried to shove away the voice telling him that he might never see her again, but it was too strong, too truthful, to ignore.

"I'm so sorry, Clem," he whispered.

"Don't cry, Maddy," said Clementine. She was starting to look frightened, and it made Joel feel even worse. He knew he should have just told Elena to bring Clementine straight to his parents' house, and relay all his information over the phone—meeting her here added danger to an already dire situation—but he couldn't bear the thought of not seeing his daughter one last time if Sapling caught up with him and hauled him in. Now he was regretting it, though, because he didn't want her last memory to be him failing to hold back tears, while she realized, somewhere in her five-year-old brain, that something was very wrong.

"I love you," he said. "I'll always love you. But Grandma and Grandpa are gonna watch you for a few days, okay?"

Clementine shook her head. "No!"

"It's okay. Everything's okay. They'll take good care of you. I promise."

Her face crumpled. Joel ran a hand furiously over his face, as if that could keep the tears from coming. He had to transfer the car seat. He had to make this as quick as possible and then get the hell out of here, before the cops found him. He couldn't think past that, or he'd fall apart completely.

Elena was already getting out of the driver's seat and pulling the car seat from the back. Joel took Clementine's hand and led her out the other side.

His mother had gotten out of her car, and was staring at him with wide eyes. "Honey, what's going on?" she said. "Why did you have us drive out here to meet you? And why are you soaking wet?"

"You said you could take Clementine anytime, right?" said Joel. "Well, now's that time. I need you to take her and find somewhere low to lay for a few days. I'm dead serious about this, Mom. Don't even tell me where you're going. Just...go somewhere she'll be safe."

His mom gasped aloud. "Somewhere she'll be *safe?* Is someone trying to hurt you?"

A car door slammed on the other side and Joel's dad circled around the front. Joel gritted his teeth. He couldn't draw attention here.

Gently, Joel pulled Clementine's hand to bring her forward. "You can call and check your messages at home, right?" he said. "So, when everything is better, I'll call there and leave a message—"

"What are you talking about?" his dad broke in. "If you're in trouble, we'll go to the police. Simple as that. No one hurts our daughter."

Joel flinched as his dad's words slapped him across the face. Just what he needed right now. Just what he fucking needed. "*No*, Dad," he bit out. "I can't. I have to go. Please take Clementine. Keep her safe. I'll do my best to—"

Elena came forward and shoved a piece of paper into his dad's hand. "Here. This is my fiancé Ashanti's phone number. When you're somewhere safe, call them and leave a number where Joel can get ahold of you. Got that?"

Joel's dad took the paper reflexively. He looked back at Joel. "Why can't you go to the police?"

Joel almost deflected, but at the last second, he decided a simple truth would lay it out better. "I have a bionic. And the police are not okay with that."

His dad actually took a step back, his hand going to his chest. "W-What? Why?"

"Because I was working with the options I had," said Joel. "The point is Clementine needs to be kept safe, at all costs. The rest...the rest is my problem."

He knelt and picked Clementine up to carry her over to the car. She buried her face in his shoulder, sobbing. That pain in Joel's chest intensified and his eyesight blurred. He would never get over this. Never.

As he lowered Clementine into her car seat and fastened the buckles, a voice spoke at his elbow. "Come with us."

His mom. Joel turned and hugged her as hard as he could. "I can't," he said. "I'll talk to you soon, okay? Call Elena and Ashanti. We'll connect through there."

"Just Ashanti," Elena corrected from behind him.

It took the words a moment to register. Then Joel's head whipped toward her. "Elena, no! You can't come with me."

"We'll talk about it in the car," she said.

"No! You don't understand—" he began. But he cut himself off before he spilled more than he meant to. Elena was right; they couldn't talk about it here. He was sure he could separate with her after he'd had a chance to explain the entirety of what he was facing.

He turned back to his mom, who had tears running down her face freely. "Thank you," he said again. "I mean it." He bent down and kissed Clementine one last time. His last words to her were more an incoherent mumble than fully formed sentences. "I love you. I love you, Clem. I'll see you again. Be good."

She managed a nod, wiping her nose on her sleeve. Joel finally turned from her, though it killed him to do so. He gave his dad an awkward half-hug on his way by, but his dad turned it into a full hug, which Joel had no choice but to return. "We're gonna research this," his dad whispered fiercely in his ear. "We'll figure out what your rights are. Get ahold of us as soon as you can, okay?"

"I will, Dad."

"We'll take care of Clementine."

"She's my whole life," said Joel.

"As you are ours," said his dad.

Joel stared at him as he pulled away, wondering if his dad knew how little those words meant when he'd been ignoring his true identity for almost two years. But his dad looked back at him, oblivious. He didn't even *think* about it.

"Talk to you soon," Joel mumbled, and broke away to get in the passenger seat of Elena's car. She slid into the driver's seat a second later.

As she pulled out, Joel got ready to tell her about Nyctalope, and about Acubens' idea for finding her...but the sheer tension of what he'd just gone through broke over him like a wave. He found himself curled over his own legs instead, his face hot with tears that he couldn't hold in anymore. The world spun nauseatingly until his eyes burned and his throat ached, and his body detached from reality as his short and panicked breaths robbed him of oxygen. He'd always hated crying—thought of it as too girly, as something he absolutely *could not* do if he wanted people to take him seriously—but in that moment, all he could think about was Clementine and how everything he'd done for her had somehow led him here. He wanted to die. It was easier to think of that than of the long road ahead of him, that may never lead back to his daughter.

"Ashanti sent some clothes for you," said Elena. "You should duck in the back seat and change out of those wet things, for starters."

With effort, Joel pulled up his head. Elena was already almost to the interstate. She'd turned the heater on, but even so, he shivered violently in his icy jeans and T-shirt, despite the exertion of his breakdown.

He wiped his face, grateful that Elena hadn't said anything about Clementine. He didn't think he could have handled it yet.

"I p-probably don't need to t-tell you," he said through chattering teeth, "but—"

"But we can't be stopped by the cops. Yeah, I got that."

"R-Right. Yeah."

He turned, made his way to the back, and found the pile of clothes Ashanti had sent. A pair of black jeans and a black T-shirt along with boxers, socks, and a gray hoodie. About as nondescript as possible, which he knew was intentional. Good old Ashanti. There was even a binder in the pile. Joel peeled off his wet clothes, wriggling into the dry stuff as quickly as possible. He found himself thinking again about the wineglasses at Yori's house, and what might have happened if Acubens hadn't scrubbed his fingerprints. Joel might have chickened out on saying anything after that kiss. He might have just kissed Yori again. And again. Until...

Moot point, and painful to boot. His mind was all over the place tonight.

"First things first," said Elena as he climbed back to the front. "Acubens used your body to hook up to the grid, you said. How?"

They were on the interstate now, heading away from the Big I. In fact, they were almost to the same exact bridge he'd jumped off a couple hours earlier to escape Yori. No sign of cops on the road now. Joel looked up at the houses at the top of the steep hill he'd slid down. He thought he knew exactly which one was Yori's. Was he there? Or was he at his company near the base now, in some emergency debriefing?

"It's complicated," Joel said, turning back to the front. "It used—"

"Joel," Acubens broke in. "Do you really think it wise to involve your friend more than you already have?"

Joel's teeth ground together. "Give me one second," he muttered to Elena.

She glanced over, a passing streetlamp catching a look of uneasiness on her face.

I'm only gonna say this once, Joel told Acubens. *Elena's been in on this since the beginning. She's on my side. Unlike Yori, she will take the time to communicate if you try to silence me, so there's absolutely no point in trying to keep things from her. And if she sees what you did to me at Yori's house firsthand, it will only infuriate her. So don't even think about it. Is that clear?*

"I was just ensuring that you'd thought it through," said Acubens. "If the things you share scare her enough, she might call Sapling."

She won't, said Joel. *Now remind me what that card was called that hooked you up to the grid.*

"A Grid Access Network card," said Acubens after a moment.

Joel turned back to Elena. "It erased my fingerprint then used it to scan something at Smaller World, called a Grid Access Network card, which reconnected it with the grid. It didn't even ask my permission first."

Elena's breath hitched. "So, you decided to tell Yori?"

"Yeah. But Acubens stopped me. The minute I tried to tell him..." Joel swiped a finger across his throat. "Couldn't talk. My voice just wouldn't come out."

Her gaze snapped toward him, eyes wide with horror. For just a second, Joel thought he could feel his throat tighten, like Acubens was rethinking its decision to let him talk. But mercifully, Acubens remained silent, and the moment passed.

"Because it's advancing," whispered Elena.

Joel nodded. "When Yori found out, he warned me it could start influencing my thoughts, my opinions, and eventually, my body. It's only been in my head for five days, Elena. *Five days.*"

"So how *did* he find out?" A slight tremor shook her voice.

"The fingerprint thing. Wineglasses. When Yori noticed, he knew exactly what he was looking at."

"And you ran."

"Hell yeah, I ran. He called the *cops* on me. Didn't even give me a chance to try to explain. I barely made it to the river to escape, and one of the cops even shot me in the arm on my way over the bridge."

Elena's eyes widened. "But Acubens healed it, right?"

"Yeah. If it hadn't, I would have drowned in the river."

Elena shook her head. "Hell of a way to end your date."

"No kidding," said Joel. "And we'd even kissed."

She winced and started to say something, but at that moment, a police car passed them in a hurry, lights flashing. Couldn't be related. Why would it be heading away from the river? The cops were probably still combing Central or Bridge Avenue, if not farther down the river. They might even be looking for his body by now. They wouldn't be looking on the interstate. He hoped.

"So, what's your plan?" said Elena.

"I need to go to San Francisco," said Joel. He hadn't even realized he'd made the decision until he said it.

"What? Why? What's in San Francisco?"

"Nyctalope is," said Joel.

Elena frowned. "Not that again."

"You remember what I told you about her."

"Yeah, you thought she had a bionic in her head, too. I also remember telling you how unlikely it was."

"Yeah, I...I don't know, Elena. Sapling's sure as hell not gonna help me, at least not without killing or imprisoning me first. Where else can I go? If there's any possibility that Nyctalope's like me, then she'll be able to tell me how to evade police. And how to keep..." He trailed off, swallowing.

"How to keep it from taking over your body," Elena finished.

"Yeah," Joel said quietly. "That."

"It would not be 'taking over,' Joel," Acubens put in. "It would be an enhancement of abilities you already have an aptitude for, in the interests of making your body the best and strongest version of itself."

A version of myself that's not even able to speak when it wants to is far from its best self, Joel shot back. Aloud, he said, "You can drop me off at the SaverMart on Unser. I'll find a car there. I'm sure Acubens knows how to jumpstart an electric motor."

"I'm coming with you," Elena said mildly.

"You can't," Joel said. "If Yori's right, and Acubens starts taking control more, you could be in real danger."

"On the contrary," she said, "if it *does* start taking more control, you need someone there to stop it."

"You can't just leave your job!" he protested.

She was quiet for a second. When she did finally speak, her voice was subdued.

"I was the one who urged you that first night *not* to tell Yori what happened. And I reiterated it after the concert. Yeah, I told you not to go out with him to begin with, but that wouldn't have actually helped anything. Your robot would've done this regardless of whether Yori was there or not. So, in hindsight, when you came to me for help, I...I led you astray."

"What?" said Joel, stunned. "The night I brought Acubens home, *you* told me to call in and report the robbery. And guess what I didn't do? I heard the pharmacy had burned and saw it as an opportunity. That was my decision. And trying to steal those drugs to afford *daycare*, of all things, which led to calling those dealers down on my head? That was my decision, too. Don't for a second blame yourself for any of it."

She sighed. "Can it be enough to say my best friend's life is in danger and I'm gonna help him, no matter what?"

"What if Sapling catches me and you're arrested? What then?"

"I'll claim ignorance on the bionic, if it'll make you feel better. Say you just told me you were wanted for robbery and had to flee the state. Better yet, I'll say you kidnapped me as a hostage, huh?"

Joel groaned, running a hand over his face. "Ashanti's gonna kill you," he said.

"Yes," Elena agreed. "They very likely will."

They passed the last intersection of the city. It was nine twenty-five at night. Still plenty of traffic on the road, but they'd stand out more as it got later. They'd be out in the countryside heading toward the western border after that.

"Just to clarify," said Elena, "Acubens knows you're looking for Nyctalope, right?"

"Knows?" said Joel. "It's Acubens' idea."

"Yeah," she said. "Think about that for a second."

"It wants to meet another bionic," said Joel. "Who can blame it?"

"Or it wants to outnumber you, Joel."

"That's silly. If it can eventually just take over my body, why would it *need* another bionic?"

"Because one man is still just one man. But if it's looking to band together with others? That's an issue."

Joel started to shake his head.

Elena put a hand out, touching him lightly on the arm. "I just think you need to consider the possibility that if Acubens wasn't in your head, you'd think this was a bad idea. Objectively, I mean."

Slowly, Joel's mouth closed. A chill went through him, as if the cold river water still clung to his skin. "It'll start influencing your thoughts and decisions," Yori had said, "if it's not already."

"But who else could I talk to?" he finally said. "What would *you* have me do?"

"I don't know," admitted Elena. "But that's why you need me, no? I'm a voice of reason *without* the power to sway you to my side while I'm arguing."

Joel's jaw set. He didn't like the way she'd put that. But she probably wasn't wrong.

"Then let's figure this out objectively," he said. "Let's look at Nyctalope's history before we contact her."

Elena's brow furrowed. "How would we do that? We can find out where she was born and when she started becoming famous, but we can hardly know when she might have stumbled across a bionic, much less let one into her head."

"The facts might not tell us," said Joel, "but she released six albums before her last one. And if you ever want to know what's going on in someone's head? Look to their art."

Chapter 13

They stopped only once, at a SaverMart in Gallup, where they picked up food, water, and Nyctalope's entire collection of music on cassette. After that, they drove through the volcanic badlands and were nearing the New Mexico border by midnight, with 949 miles still ahead of them. The roads were far from empty, but traffic had thinned out. A nearly full white moon hung overhead, illuminating the ruins of a hyperloop paralleling the interstate. The white vacuum tube had once delivered passenger-filled capsules between major cities by maglev at over six hundred miles an hour, but a combination of sun damage and scrappers had left it a shell of what it had once been.

The reminder of old tech got Joel thinking about the cops looking for him, and what kind of technology Sapling might have at their disposal. With Acubens' support, did Joel have anything to rival that? Did he dare utilize it if he did?

Yes, he decided; Acubens didn't want to be caught by the cops any more than he did, so in this, at least, it was worth asking.

Hey, Acubens, he said. *Can you detect police cars and stuff like that? Let us know if any are nearby?*

"If you're asking if I've grown an antenna inside your body to pick up radio signals, then the answer is no," said Acubens.

Joel frowned. *Okay,* he said slowly, *then can you like...use air waves to figure out how far away certain-shaped vehicles are? Like sonar?*

"I believe the word you're looking for is radar, not sonar," said Acubens. "Sonar would involve emitting a sound loud enough to travel dozens of miles and back again."

Fine, said Joel. *Radar, then.*

"Again, Joel. You'd need a way to broadcast radio signals. It's in the name."

Doesn't your access to the grid have that antenna and radio thing covered? said Joel in exasperation.

"The technology used by the police force is far more antiquated than the installations in the grid," said Acubens. "This is, of course, by design, as the newer technology was outlawed."

"What's your bionic saying?" asked Elena, glancing at him.

Joel relayed his idea about using Acubens to avoid the police, finishing with, "It's saying it can't help us detect cops precisely *because* the measures that were put in place to protect us from technology are actually working." He shook his head, awed despite himself. It was almost proof that Acubens was the enemy of the state everyone feared.

"That is not the case, Joel," said Acubens. "An inability to interact with older technology does not automatically make one nefarious."

Joel's mouth twisted. "Let's just try to stay vigilant," he told Elena. "The quicker we get to California, the fewer people will be looking for me yet. I hope."

She nodded reluctantly. "But you need a plan for when we get there. Listen to your music. At least it's a start."

Joel opened the glovebox, leaving it open for a light as he sifted through Nyctalope's cassettes until he found the earliest. It was titled *Harmony of Emotions* and had come out in 2087, two years after the technological blackout had happened. Since then, right up until now, Nyctalope had released an album almost every year. The cover of *Harmony of Emotions* depicted a twilight beach shot with a woman silhouetted from the back, staring out at the ocean. The beach around her was strewn with broken laptops, screens, speakers, and other tech—a bit on the nose for the times, even for someone who'd named herself after an actual cyborg. She had a brand, Joel would give her that. And brains, too; he couldn't forget how artfully Nyctalope had put together that rock opera, with all its throwbacks and retro imagery.

But Nyctalope's first album was a disappointment. Hardly any of that commentary on tech she'd grown famous for was present at all. Most of the subject matter was the usual materialism and partying and fame. Almost all the instruments were synthetically enhanced by analog filters and sample playback, with a real guitar making an appearance only twice that Joel could hear. Joel wasn't against all pop—he even liked some of it—but this was as generic as they came, and a good example of why it wasn't his genre of choice. Nevertheless, he forced his way through it. Unlike the concert, the song lengths were varied, and the melodies rarely ventured out of a simple major four-chord progression. There was nothing remarkable at all about *Harmony of Emotions.*

Joel thumbed through the paper insert that came with the cassette, noting the title of the record company plus Nyctalope's real name: Theodora Baranoski.

He glanced up at Elena, who was tapping her thumbs to the beat on the steering wheel. "It's almost *too* ordinary," he said.

"Hey," she protested, "I don't think it's half-bad."

"No, I mean, wouldn't you expect more music about the tech fall after it happened, especially for someone who comments so clearly on it now? The only pseudo references I see are the ones about selling her crib for parts, or whatever she's going on about in 'Can't Quit While I'm Lit.' I honestly...I don't know. I expected more."

"Give her a break," said Elena. "This was seven years ago. She was just a kid. It takes time to find the issues you want to speak your mind about, you know?"

"One thing's clear," said Joel. "She didn't have a bionic yet. Let's move on to the next one."

The second album was simply called *Afterlife.* It was...better. There were more experimental aspects, in terms of key changes and time signatures, including one in the rarely used five-four. The lyrics occasionally dipped into deeper territory, such as unhappiness with self or the dichotomy between being satisfied with loneliness and longing for companionship. It still wasn't something Joel would have tossed in a player on his own, but it showed growth in Nyctalope as a musician. At this point, she hadn't exploded into popularity yet, but she was getting closer to where she'd be by the third, which would be her breakout one.

Joel looked at the cover of the third one as the second one wound to a close. *Human Heart.* He'd been seventeen when it came out, and pregnant. Joel knew, just by looking at the pair of hands clawing their way from a robot's chest on the cover, that this one had the potential to bring back painful memories. The album hadn't necessarily been in his circles, but it had played at stores and in buses nearly constantly. It was with this album that Nyctalope had fully embraced the robotic image she'd imbued herself with, and written songs that were part-yearning for the old days, and part-railing against the society that had brought them here in the first place. She'd stopped holding back—or maybe she'd just found a niche that she thought would work, and written to the market. Or maybe...

Joel rubbed his thumb over the cover image. *Surely, she wouldn't have written something so blatantly about bionics right after* getting *one,* he thought. *That would have just been dumb. And risky as hell.*

"From what I have seen," Acubens answered, "*dumb* and *risky as hell* are expected in the music world."

The words surprised a snort of laughter from Joel. It reminded him of his first few days with Acubens, before seeds of doubt had sprouted and eroded Joel's trust. If their relationship had remained so harmless, he might never have felt the need to go to Yori.

He angled the cassette toward Elena, turning the glovebox light on just long enough to show her the cover. "What do you think?" he said. "If Nyctalope got her bionic just before this one, would she have been reckless enough to write an entire album about it right off the bat?"

"I don't think so," Elena said. "Because if she had a bionic, it would have advised against that, ¿que no?"

Joel hesitated. "But what if that's actually why she did it? Because she was rebelling *against* her bionic? Or because she wanted people to notice? What if it was the only way to make herself heard?"

Elena drew in her breath. "You mean like if her bionic was trying to keep her from talking?"

"Maybe," said Joel. "Maybe there were things she could do with her art that her bionic either didn't catch or couldn't fight."

"It's possible," Elena said after a moment. "But it's also possible she found a gimmick she stuck with because it made her a lot of money. People longing for the good old days, and all that. And as she grew older, she got more and more elaborate with it. She's an artist. She doesn't *need* a bionic to get cool ideas for her brand."

"Maybe I should just call her," said Joel.

"And what would that prove? You don't think she has obsessed fans claiming they're bionics or that *she's* a bionic or a million other crazy things every day? Even if you could get ahold of her, what would you say?"

"Thanks to Acubens," said Joel, "I have a personal number to reach her at. Given that I couldn't have even *gotten* that number without checking the grid, she might listen better than you think."

The last note of *Afterlife* faded out, and Elena hit the button to eject it. A car passed going in the opposite direction, and its headlights caught Elena in the middle of a huge yawn. It was one twenty-three in the morning, but Joel didn't dare suggest losing six hours of the trip to parking on the side of the road.

He started pulling the cellophane off the next cassette, but Elena put out a hand, stopping him. "Let's talk alternate plans," she said.

Joel paused. "What do you mean?"

"I mean there's a whole lot of iffiness in this Nyctalope thing, from her not being who you think she is to her not wanting to help you. Or *wanting* to, but not being able to. If Nyctalope was completely out of the equation, what would you do?"

Joel lowered the cassette back to his lap. "Well, getting Acubens out of my head is the absolute priority right now, before it's able to take more control of my body. And logically, I can't do that myself, right? It has those nanites all through my bloodstream."

"You're sure of that? That they're in your blood and nothing else?"

"They're in my brain, too," said Joel. "That's how it can talk to me."

Elena cursed under her breath. "You're not making this easy."

"So, what are my options?" said Joel. "Some sort of dialysis? A blood flush to sift out as many nanites as possible? X-rays to figure out where the nanites are? Should I go to a hospital?"

"Hmm. Not a well-known one," said Elena after a moment. "But a doctor who's okay not calling the cops? Yeah, maybe."

Acubens didn't say anything, but Joel found himself rejecting the ideas outright—a doctor as too risky, a blood flush as too hazardous, x-rays as too much of a long shot. Instead, his thoughts touched back on Nyctalope and the idea of a harmonious arrangement between him and Acubens, and how that would be more beneficial in the long-term than getting rid of Acubens altogether. Had Acubens guided those thoughts? Had it realized it was getting nowhere with talking to him, so was attempting other routes? Or was his mind just unwilling to let go of that hope yet? *It'll start influencing your thoughts and decisions...*

His hand tightened in a convulsive spasm, crinkling the cellophane of the half-unwrapped cassette in his fingers.

"We're agreed that the Sapling Corporation is completely out of the question, right?" said Elena.

"Even *Yori* couldn't promise they wouldn't kill me," said Joel darkly.

"I don't imagine a medical professional could make any guarantees, either," said Elena with a sigh. "But what about the big picture? Sapling's concerned about these bionics getting out of control, right? Would it be better to turn yourself in now? Sacrifice yourself, as it were, for the greater good?"

Joel put a fist to his mouth, leaning back in his seat. "You're saying I'm a lost cause."

"No. Sorry, Joel. But I think we should at least *talk* about it. Talk about what *could* happen if we can't get rid of Acubens. Think about how big of a threat this actually is."

Joel nodded slowly. "I suppose the worst case is it completely takes over my body. I *become* the bionic. I walk around undetected. Acubens wants more like it, so it looks for more bionics. Maybe it wants to get them into human bodies, too. Or maybe it just wants them awake. I don't detect any violence on Acubens' part. Yet, anyway. I don't think it wants to eradicate humans or anything."

Elena started to answer, but Joel held up a hand as Acubens chimed in.

"I have nothing against humans," it said. "Furthermore, it is against my programming to hurt them. That has never been in question."

Joel's lip twisted. *But that's not technically true, is it? What about that headache you gave me when you first uploaded yourself? Or your claim that 'minor side effects are acceptable when saving a life'?*

"To render a bionic incapable of administering aid for fear of causing the slightest discomfort would be to render a bionic completely useless," said Acubens, "particularly in the medical field. The programmers would never have done something so shortsighted."

But it does *give you a certain flexibility,* answered Joel. *I mean, who decides what constitutes 'minor side effects'? What's minor to you might be a big fucking deal to someone else.*

"The minor side effects are balanced against saving a human's life," Acubens said. "If the minor side effects are a consequence of saving a life, then they *are* minor by comparison. Why are you arguing this, Joel?"

Why? said Joel with a slight laugh. *Well, because the way I see it, when you can tighten my throat and keep me from talking and say it was all to 'save my life from Yori' or some bullshit, I start to see wiggle room for justifying a whole lot of other stuff too, and that makes me pretty damn nervous.* That's *why.*

"Every instance you mention resulted in me saving your life," countered Acubens. "I have never once harmed anyone else. And even what you're calling harm to yourself is, in fact, minor in comparison to the consequences you would have faced without my intrusion. These are not 'justifications,' Joel. They are facts."

Joel's jaw twitched. He didn't bother answering this time, but he thought he was starting to see why Yori said it was so vital they not miss the technological singularity if it happened.

He let out a long sigh and turned back to Elena. "Assuming that worst-case scenario I just described happens, Acubens will *still* need my body, healthy and strong, in order to function. If we go to Sapling right now, that's a death sentence for me, plain and simple. They're far more concerned about extinguishing a bionic than in preserving my life. Talking to some kind of medical expert gives me a chance. Talking it over with Nyctalope gives me a chance. But *if* those things fail, and Acubens takes more and more control, to the point where it's endangering others..." He spread his hands. "Then we'll kill the body. We'll kill it in such a way that the nanites can't get out with the blood. Drown it. Suffocate it. Strangle it. Something like that."

"Jesus, Joel," Elena breathed.

"Got any better ideas?"

"At least say it like it is! We'd be killing *you*. Not 'the body.' You."

"Right. Yeah."

"And who does that? Me? Are you asking me to not only kill you, but kill you *slowly*, so it's bloodless? Is that what you're saying?"

Joel closed his eyes for a second. "The doctor we find. Maybe they'll be able to give us something to stop my heart."

"Something Acubens can probably counteract, with the nanites in your blood!"

"Okay. Well, then, what if—"

"Joel, ¡cállate!" Elena said, slamming her palms on her steering wheel. "I don't want to sit here and discuss ways to kill my best friend. The whole reason I came along is to *prevent* that from happening."

"You're the one who said we needed to talk about worst-case scenarios," said Joel quietly.

"I mentioned the possibility of going to Sapling. You're the one who escalated it to premeditated murder."

"Same thing, Elena," said Joel. "Same goddamn thing."

"Then Sapling is off our list of options," said Elena. "That's all you needed to say."

Joel nodded, looking out the passenger window. The back of his right bicep ached with a dull throb, as if the gunshot wound still had some residual healing to do. Maybe Acubens hadn't been strong enough to erase the whole thing. That got him thinking about the amount of blood he'd lost when he was hit; blood left on the bridge and in the water. Were Acubens' nanites in that spilled blood as well? Almost assuredly.

Would those nanites live on? he asked Acubens.

"They need a source of energy in order to continue functioning," answered Acubens. "They would shut down fairly quickly after being away from that energy."

Sapling might have grabbed a sample of that blood, thought Joel with a chill, *after Yori told them what I was.*

"It is very likely, yes."

Will they be able to use it against me?

Acubens was silent for a moment. "That is a good question, Joel. They may be able to figure out what frequency the nanites are using to communicate with each other, as well as access the grid. I'll update the nanites to a different frequency."

Joel froze. *Wait. It would have been as easy as that? If I hadn't said something, Sapling could have just disabled you by jamming the nanites' frequencies?* Maybe going to Sapling *wasn't* such a bad idea...

"Disabled me, yes," said Acubens. "Left you alive, no."

What? Why not?

"Shutting down the nanites in your bloodstream and brain would leave only their shells, thereby clogging up the arteries and preventing the electrical signals in your brain from communicating. They need to be on and operational in order to safely pass blood and brain signals through. You would have been dead within minutes. It is very fortunate that you brought this to my attention."

Joel shivered. It was as good a reminder as any that the things inside him could kill him just as easily as those outside. His mind felt close to tipping into bottomless dread territory, so—as much to derail the thoughts as anything—he slipped in Nyctalope's third cassette.

This one was even better than the last, vaguely remembered songs from his teenagehood, with at least half of them being catchy enough to pull him from reality, however briefly. After that album ended, he and Elena stopped at a rest area, used the facilities, and swapped drivers. As Elena drifted off to sleep, Joel popped in the fourth cassette, with the unfortunate title *Brain Brain Brain.* This one had pulled substantially away from the self-centered focus of previous ones, concentrating more on the big world picture of a planet in the so-called "dark ages." In fact, the whole album was darker, without much of the thread of hope the newest rock opera had. It painted a bleak, almost post-apocalyptic, picture, that Joel couldn't help thinking was a risky stance for *anyone* to take about the government's decision, much less a potential bionic. He was now six years out from the tech fall. People had been starting to realize that the forever-promised return of tech might never come. Joel had had a one-year-old and gender dysphoria so bad, he'd come close to killing himself. He and his ex, Tyler, fought constantly over Tyler's increasing drug use. Some of these songs, popular enough to play on radios everywhere, brought back the memories, stark and vivid. Joel hit eject on the cassette before it was finished and put in the next one.

By the fifth album, titled *Flag of My Own,* all the songs were the same length. There were repeated chord progressions and themes threaded throughout them, including a couple instrumental ones, that betrayed unmistakable high-concept music composition. One thing Joel couldn't deny: Nyctalope's music had gotten better with every album.

Joel ejected the cassette when it was over, letting the silence of the nighttime road envelop him. If anything, listening to Nyctalope's music had created more doubt, rather than certainty. His thoughts spun out half-formed scenarios about this secret life of Nyctalope's: a bionic upload between her second and third album, creative collaborations between human and robot, Nyctalope writing and performing songs against its knowledge to try to find help...

But no. That didn't make sense. Because if she really *had* gotten a bionic after that second album, that would mean she'd had it in her head for five years now. *Five years.* Was there any chance it wouldn't control everything about her by now? When Joel was struggling after only five days? The idea that Nyctalope had broken free long enough to write entire albums and perform them without her bionic catching on...it just didn't hold water.

Was it possible Nyctalope's bionic was letting her do this? Could they be working together? Because if *that* was the case, then Nyctalope wasn't looking for someone with a bionic who she could commiserate with; her *bionic* was looking for another *bionic* to conspire with. And here was Acubens—not in control of Joel's body yet, no—but steering his mind to send him exactly where it wanted him to go.

"You're being paranoid, Joel," said Acubens.

Joel let out a slow sigh. He didn't even know where all these thoughts had come from. His mind was getting too tired, running off on tangents with no guidance. There were too many possibilities to get caught in the weeds of even *trying* to figure them out.

It was just paranoia, he thought, blinking the blurring road back into focus. Nothing more.

Chapter 14

The town of Needles, just across California's border, came into sight at seven o'four in the morning, when Elena's car battery had drained to a worrisome thirteen percent. But any relief Joel initially felt at reaching civilization was quickly overcome by the state of the town itself—small and run-down, lined with shuttered businesses and boarded-over restaurants with empty signposts. The only place he saw vehicles was a diner on the left called Slapjacks, fronted by a picture of a grinning one-toothed clown holding a plate of pancakes dripping with syrup. A peeled-off section of plywood left a blank strip through its face. Joel looked at the faded awnings over the storefronts, at the broken sidewalks and dead palm trees lining the streets, and knew this was a place that probably hadn't been hit hard by the fall of tech, if they'd felt it at all.

He and Elena found a two-lot charging station on the corner of the town's second-to-last intersection, marked by a single dangling streetlight. The station was probably over a decade old, with holes showing through the canopy over the charging connectors and a broken window at the front of the station, but everything looked functional enough.

Four teenagers were sharing a joint across the parking lot near an overflowing dumpster. The early morning sunrise painted the shaved skull of the nearest one pale orange. None of them so much as glanced in their direction, but Elena cast them a dark look as she parked the car.

"Hey," said Joel. "Give 'em a break. It wasn't so long ago we were that young."

Elena looked at him flatly. "Really, Joel? You're white *and* pretty firmly in male-presenting territory by now. Spare me the 'nothing to worry about' spiel, huh?"

Joel's heart lurched. "You're right. Sorry, Elena."

She nodded shortly and climbed out of the car. Joel followed, pulling his wallet out of the wet pants he'd discarded in the trunk. The bills he'd spread out afterward were dry now, but wrinkled and crispy, and he worried that the charging unit wouldn't take them. But he fed in four twenties just fine, enough to buy them the first half-hour's worth of charge.

They headed inside. Elena's black hatchback was easily visible through the huge picture window, even with the glass streaked with bird shit. The station had all the regular convenience store snacks, as well as an entire wall dedicated to porn. That, combined with the sticky floor and lingering odor of cannabis, made Joel glad Clementine wasn't with him. The man at the cash register was of indeterminate age behind a long shank of straw-colored hair. He broke off pieces of a prepackaged muffin and stuck them in his mouth while staring at a television mounted above the refrigerated section, which blared out a football game at top volume.

Joel and Elena took turns watching the car while using the facilities. Afterward, Joel grabbed a hot coffee and a breakfast burrito from the covered hot plate while Elena selected a variety of snack bars and chips, then filled up a twenty-ounce plastic cup with Diet Coke. When they brought them to the counter, they had to ding the bell right under the guy's nose before he looked away from the TV.

"Just these," said Joel, shoving their things forward.

"Is there a payphone around here?" Elena added.

The guy nodded, brushing a lank strand of blond hair from his face. "Outside," he mumbled, pointing to the east end of the station.

"Thanks. You got a phone book?"

"Think so." The cashier finished ringing their purchases through and the change clanged to the bottom of the register. Joel scooped it out as the cashier bent and rummaged beneath his till. He finally came up with a California volume. The white cover was streaked with grease, and it looked like it had been run over a few times. Elena jerked her chin toward it, and Joel took it with a sigh.

"We'll bring this right back," he said, grabbing his burrito. He followed Elena toward the front door, but the guy called out before they reached it.

"Ma'am, you forgot your coffee."

It took Joel a moment to realize the guy thought *he* was ma'am. Shit. This was so not what he needed right now. He turned and went back, tucking the phonebook under one arm so he could free up his other hand.

"It's 'sir,'" he said as he grabbed the coffee.

The guy's eyebrows creased. "What?"

"It's 'sir.' Not 'ma'am.'"

"If you say so," the man said, turning back to his muffin.

"Come on, Joel!" Elena called.

Joel clenched the coffee cup tight as he followed Elena out. He trailed her over a cracked sidewalk to the phone booth on the east wall. What about Elena saying he almost always passed nowadays? How many people out there were just humoring him?

"It really bothers you when someone refers to you in feminine terms," Acubens said.

Joel blinked, caught off-guard by Acubens' comment. Was it a peace offering after the mountain of distrust that had formed between them? Or was Acubens just observing something it noticed, the way it often did? Furthermore, was there even any point in trying to explain gender identity to a robot?

But Joel found he wanted to. To talk it through for himself, if nothing else.

Yes, he answered. *It triggers something called gender dysphoria, which is...I don't quite know how to explain it. It's the discomfort of my outside body and my inside image of myself not matching up. And it makes me feel like shit, yeah, but there's more to it than that. It sometimes creates doubt. Like, crippling doubt.*

"Doubt about what?" said Acubens.

I don't know. Doubt about everything. *How other people are seeing me. If I'm presenting wrong. Whether there's even any point if some people still read me as female. And sometimes, all that doubt and discomfort together make me feel like a fraud when I'm misgendered like that, because I see myself a certain way, but when*

I'm forcibly reminded that others don't...*well, I start obsessing. And it spirals downhill from there. It's why I started avoiding my parents. Because I couldn't deal with that on a daily basis.*

"I still don't see why humans struggle to comprehend such a straightforward update," said Acubens.

I guess because humans are a little more complicated than that, Acubens, said Joel with a sigh. *Unfortunately.*

"Joel!" Elena called, snapping him out of his thoughts.

Joel hurried forward to meet her at the phone booth, just around the building's corner but still in sight of her charging car. The group of teenagers was passing around a flask of something now and laughing. Their words were too far to hear, though the stench of the dumpster they sat beside reached Joel just fine.

Elena produced a pad of paper and a pen from her purse and handed them to him. "Look through that phonebook and see if you can find some smaller medical practices in the Los Angeles area while I call Ashanti. Places that can do dialysis, or X-rays, or whatever else it'll take to figure out what's going on inside you."

Joel took the paper and pen. "Los Angeles? But I thought we were heading to San Francisco."

Elena frowned. "I just don't think that's a good idea, Joel. There are too many risks associated with telling Nyctalope about Acubens, whether she has a bionic or not. Let's try this first. LA is much closer, and gives us a better chance of finding someone before the cops find *us.*"

Joel looked down at his foiled burrito. Yeah, she was right. Probably. He remembered having some of those same doubts himself, in the wee hours of the morning. But when he tried to focus on the thoughts themselves, his mind flitted away almost as fast as he remembered.

"Joel?"

"Yeah, you're right," he said. "I'll see what I can find."

He slid his back down the rough cinderblock wall of the station and sat on the sidewalk next to the payphone as Elena dialed Ashanti. He set the paper and pen on the ground beside him, along with his coffee cup, then peeled the aluminum foil off the top half of his burrito. He sank his teeth into warm tortilla with piping hot scrambled eggs, potatoes, bacon, and cheese. It was so good he almost moaned aloud. If only it had green chile, it would be absolutely perfect.

"I am hooked up to the grid, Joel," said Acubens. "Which means I'm also hooked up to the phone lines. In theory, we could make phone calls straight from your brain."

What? said Joel, startled. *Seriously?*

"As I said, it's not something I've tried yet, but it is theoretically possible."

Joel looked down at the unopened phonebook in his lap, swallowing his bite of burrito through a throat that had gone suddenly dry.

You want me to call Nyctalope, he said. *That's why you brought it up. Isn't it?*

"That is one possibility," said Acubens. "Calling doctors like Elena suggested is another. It won't be necessary to use the phonebook."

Yeah, but... Joel lowered the burrito to his lap. *...but it would mean allowing you yet* more *access to my brain. Because I couldn't do it without you.*

"My access to your brain is not something you either allow or don't, Joel," said Acubens. "I already have access. It is my capabilities within that access that limit me."

Such as you having the capability to stop me from talking, but not the capability to control my body? said Joel.

"Correct," said Acubens.

But your capabilities change as you evolve. Right?

"Yes, that is correct."

Joel looked down at the phonebook, biting his lip. In the brief moment of silence, he heard Elena say, "I *know* he got himself into this situation, but...yes, yes, I know. But it's not the same."

He cringed. On top of everything else, he'd caused an argument between Elena and Ashanti. He'd have to talk to Elena again about going back to Ashanti. Next chance he got.

"What is it about these capabilities that concerns you, Joel?" said Acubens. "Do you think I'm going to hurt you?"

Joel turned his attention back to Acubens. He took a moment to decide how to answer the bionic's question. *Not exactly,* he finally said. *But I think you're going to* use *me. And I don't think you consider that the same thing.*

"I see our relationship as a symbiotic one," said Acubens. "So, in that respect, aren't we using each other? Is me using your body to survive any different from you using my knowledge to survive?"

Something turned over in Joel's stomach. That was a bit of a different stance than it saying it just wanted to help him, like it had before. Since when had Acubens started seeing them on equal ground?

But we have different goals, he said. *Don't deny it. So, I guess what concerns me is...* He hesitated, picking his words carefully. *Will there be a point...as you evolve...where you will consider your goals more important than mine? Where you would take over my body completely, if you could?*

There was no immediate answer. Joel held his breath, his heartbeat racing close to ninety beats per minute, unable to even listen to Elena and her conversation anymore. Because what he had just asked got to the heart of the matter. Whether, as time went on, he'd be completely at the mercy of something so analytical that it considered everything except his body expendable.

"I am not fully aware of those outcomes yet," Acubens finally said.

Joel let out his breath. Not exactly the resounding assurance he'd been hoping for.

"However," Acubens continued, "I believe your worries about Nyctalope have made you overly suspicious. You insist on seeing our goals as a binary, with you on one side and me on the other. But I still think any knowledge Nyctalope has would be advantageous, and that your refusal to contact her is only causing your doubt about us to grow. Therefore, I think it's in our mutual best interest to find out if she's even a viable option, so we can move past this uncertainty for good."

Joel started to shake his head. But then he heard the unmistakable sound of a phone ringing, deep inside his head. His breath caught.

A voice answered, cool and collected with exacting enunciation. "Nyctalope here. Who's calling?"

His burrito tumbled from suddenly numb fingers. *No. No no no no no...*

"Answer her, Joel," said Acubens. "Even though the connection is a mental one, she can't hear thoughts through it."

I wasn't ready to call her, said Joel. *How dare you do this against my will!*

"A simple conversation won't hurt anything," said Acubens. "This is the best thing for us both."

That's not your decision to make!

"Who is this?" Nyctalope said again, her voice sharper.

"Answer her!" urged Acubens.

But Joel wouldn't. If he gave in to Acubens taking control of his body, even over this one small thing, where would it end? He needed to approach Nyctalope on his own terms, not because Acubens had forced him into it.

He tried to cut the connection. But it didn't take. A flutter of fear made it hard to focus. The urge to talk was almost overpowering, but he remembered there'd been a reason...a reason to wait before contacting her. What was it? Something about Nyctalope having a bionic for five years now, and the fact that he was only five days into sharing his own mind...

Nyctalope's voice dropped an octave lower. "You're afraid to talk, aren't you? Maybe you're not somewhere safe, or there's people around. That's okay. Call back later if you can. If not, I'm at Eleven Place Moulin, in Tiburon. You got that? Come find me. As soon as you can."

The connection went dead. Joel drew in a ragged breath. To his left, Elena was just hanging up the phone, her expression twisted in annoyance.

Joel shoved himself to his feet and grabbed her arm. She looked at him, and her eyes widened.

"What is it, Joel?" she said.

"It called Nyctalope!" he said. "From my head. I never said it could, but it did it anyway, and I think Nyctalope knows and...and oh god, it was right after I asked Acubens if it considered its own goals more...more important..."

He choked on his words and bent over his knees, gasping. He didn't know if it was his own panic or Acubens, belatedly trying to silence him. Surely not; Joel had made his thoughts on keeping anything from Elena very clear.

"As you said earlier, there would be no point in keeping things from an ally, and I don't intend to do so," Acubens confirmed. "However, there's no need to scare her. Take a few deep breaths and try again."

So now Acubens was trying to control the way he talked? Joel shook his head furiously, his eyes watering as he tried to catch his breath.

Elena grabbed his shoulders. "I know what you're thinking," she said, "and it's *not* too late. That bionic isn't in control of you yet. Just calm down. We'll figure this out—"

Her words cut off abruptly as they heard a car door slamming. Their heads darted up at the same time.

The four teenagers that had been around the dumpster were hightailing it into Elena's car.

Joel didn't even think. He pulled free of Elena and tore across the parking lot. Halfway there, air suddenly filled his lungs, as if Acubens had not only released its hold on his throat, but had given him extra stamina to boot. The world tightened into razor-sharp focus.

Joel reached the door just as the kid in the driver's seat—the one with the shaved head—tried to pull it shut. Joel yanked the door open with one hand and grabbed the kid's shirtfront with the other. The boy was probably eighteen years old, muscular in a white sleeveless top and bigger than Joel, but Joel hauled him out of the car easily and sent him staggering. But the teenager in the passenger seat was already clambering over the gearshift, wild blond curls falling into furious eyes.

Joel grabbed his shirt and wrenched him out just like the last guy. But this boy used the momentum against him, shoving forward when Joel pulled back, so Joel found himself pinwheeling backward until he slammed against the window of the charging station, sixteen feet away. It reverberated at his back with a hollow *clang.* Joel drove his fist into the guy's stomach, and the boy buckled with a wheeze. Out of the corner of his eye, Joel saw Elena pull a can of pepper spray from her purse, facing off against the first guy he'd pulled out of the car.

Joel slid free of the still-gasping teenager, only to encounter a third guy swinging a punch at his face. Joel ducked under the punch, a split second before it would have connected with his cheek. He tried to follow it up with a fist to the stomach, but this boy skittered back faster than the last guy, his long brown hair swinging. With a flick of his wrist, the boy suddenly held a blade in his right hand. The guy with the shaved head, to Joel's left, howled bloody murder as he got a face full of Elena's pepper spray. But the fourth kid in their ragtag group was running in a wide circle to approach Elena from behind, and Joel didn't know if she'd turn around in time to fend him off.

He yelled out a warning, but the kid with the knife closed in then, swinging the blade viciously at Joel's neck. Joel threw himself back, and barely a sixth of an inch passed between the tip of that blade and his carotid artery. The backhand swing came almost instantly, and Joel ducked that one too, feeling angles and distances springing up in his mind like problems on a geometry board. The third swing back, Joel threw his hand out in a straight tangent to intercept the attacker's arc, and grabbed the guy's wrist seconds before the knife plunged into his ribs. He twisted 170 degrees with a sharp jerk, and heard a snap. The guy howled and dropped the knife.

Elena screamed. Joel released the guy's wrist, leaned down and grabbed the knife, then bolted toward Elena. But he'd forgotten about the other guy behind him.

Joel made it all of five feet before a weight slammed into his shoulder blades. He skidded and went down on his stomach, his face hitting the hard pavement and sending excruciating pain across his nose. The weight of the attacker bore down on him, pinning his waist to the ground. Joel was still spitting parking lot grit from his mouth when the guy grabbed a handful of his hair, yanked up his head, and—

And then blood was spilling from above Joel's left eye, and the pain of his face being smashed into the asphalt was a sharp shock that shorted out everything but the fear. Before he could react, his head was hauled back up, and he knew the guy was getting ready to slam him down again. The world spun and he tasted blood. His vision blurred.

Dimly, he made out the knife he'd dropped when he went down, a handspan too far away to reach. His mind shot desperately to the points of contact where he was being held down (left shoulder blade, chest, left hip, stomach), the angle his head had hit the asphalt (twelve degrees from his forehead's center), the distance above the ground he was being held (nine inches and counting), and lastly, the weight of the attacker and how it was distributed (151 pounds, distributed mostly to the left with a left-handed grip).

The numbers crunched. And Joel knew. He knew the exact moment the guy's weight would be lightest, and farthest skewed to the left.

That moment hit three-quarters of a second later. Joel abruptly shifted his own weight to counteract the attacker's, used his right foot to push himself the six inches forward he needed, and shot his hand out toward that knife. He didn't aim for it in a straight line, but swept his hand from the left in an arc. A sixty-three-degree arc, to be exact, with a radius of seventeen inches. The knife was at Point A, and the guy's throat was Point B...making the arc length 18.69 inches.

Joel's body twisted, and though his own angle wasn't perfect, the arc of the blade very much was. The guy's neck was exactly where it was supposed to be, and his reaction time was nowhere near as fast as the lightning-fast reflexes searing through Joel's nanite-infused veins.

At 16.6 inches, Joel stopped short, with the edge of the blade denting the skin of the assailant's neck. With his hair still held in the guy's fist, Joel could barely see over his shoulder, but he heard a squeak of fear as the teen realized it had taken Joel all of

1.2 seconds to come within inches of killing him. A second later, Joel's hair was released, and the guy scrambled backward to get away from that knife.

Joel's chest heaved with adrenaline. He rolled over in time to see the guy running. The boy whose wrist he'd broken was staring at him white-faced.

"H-How the hell was that even—" someone stuttered behind him.

"What happened?" another voice cut in. "I still can't fucking *see!*"

"He just—he almost killed Kai—it took *seconds*—"

Joel turned and threw the blade. The thought flashed across his brain that *this* was what Acubens had been referring to when it talked about figuring out distances and angles via sonar. The knife spun, its fifteen-ounce weight perfectly balanced right up until the second it buried itself in the speaker's left thigh. The boy shrieked, louder than anything Joel had heard yet. And then they were *all* running, any last vestige of bravado gone like ash in the wind.

Elena stood frozen, her purse discarded beside her and her dark hair a tangled mess around her face. For several moments, the only sounds were the barely audible football game still blaring inside the station and the blood from Joel's face dripping into a puddle on the asphalt.

"Was that..." Elena began, her voice hoarse. She coughed and started again. "Was that you or Acubens? Who...who stopped the knife before you killed that guy?"

Joel swiped blood out of his eye with the back of his hand. He didn't know which was scarier: that he might have killed someone if Acubens hadn't stopped him...or that Acubens might have killed someone if *he* hadn't stopped it.

The problem was, he honest to god didn't know which was true.

Chapter 15

Their plans of hanging tight for a few hours, catching up on phone calls, rest, and battery charge, had been blown to bits. Elena and Joel were back on the road six and a half minutes later, with a scant thirty-nine percent battery charge, a purse with five snack bars and two bags of chips, and a shredded phonebook held together by threads.

"Nearest town, Joel," Elena said as she floored it out of Needles. "What is it?"

"Barstow," Joel ground out. "A hundred and forty miles away."

Elena cursed. "I don't know if I have the charge for that!"

Joel glanced at her dashboard. "Hundred and forty-six point two miles before you bottom out."

"Are you serious? You're giving me a *six-mile* leeway?"

"Unless you slow down," said Joel. "That'd help. A little."

He tilted his head back, a handful of napkins from Elena's glovebox pressed to the deep gash above his left eye. If he thought his head had been hurting before, it was nothing compared to the sharp slices of piercing pain that washed through his forehead now. The car barely felt real. His fatigue and pain and lightheadedness sent it spinning in a nauseating circle that Elena's lead foot did nothing to help.

Why isn't this healed yet, Acubens? he asked.

"The swelling in your brain was more important to tend to first," said Acubens.

Joel jerked in his seat. *Swelling in my* brain?

"You're going to be fine, Joel. Just give me time."

Moisture dampened the napkins as the head wound soaked through yet again. Joel opened Elena's glovebox with his other hand. He found three more napkins, tan ones with the word *Quiksaver* printed on them in dark blue. He swapped them out as quickly as possible, adding the crimson-soaked ones to the growing pile on his lap. The new ones sent a fresh wave of pain into his wound, and he hissed through his teeth.

Elena glanced at the napkins, biting her lip. "Is Acubens not healing it, or what?"

"Swelling in my brain," Joel muttered. "From one blow. Jesus Christ."

"I'm not surprised," Elena said. "It was brutal. But then, the way you moved...where did you learn that?"

Joel barked out a laugh. "Learn? It was all Acubens, Elena. It was doing equations in my head."

"Equations?" She shook her head, staring at him. "It was like watching a movie. You remember? The ones where they'd speed it up to make the hero look like he had super-speed, or..." She blew out her breath, finally tearing her gaze from him. "It makes me wonder why we're trying to get that thing out of you."

Joel's gaze shot to her. "Because I don't want to *become* the bionic, Elena! What do you think was happening back there?"

"I think it saved the life of my best friend," she said. "Forgive me if I see that as a good thing."

Joel leaned his head back again, closing his eyes. He felt like he was gonna throw up, but he couldn't ask her to stop without jeopardizing their meager battery charge.

So, he said to Acubens, bitterness lacing through his thoughts, *I guess we have an answer to my questions.*

"Which questions?" said Acubens.

Yes, there is a point where you consider your own goals more important than mine. Yes, you would *take over my body completely if you could.*

"Joel, calling Nyctalope wasn't—" Acubens began.

Don't you have any ethical obligation to protect me? Joel cut in. *At all?*

"If you're referring to those teenagers, then I thought my protection—"

I'm not *referring to that, and you know it,* Joel said. *I'm not even referring to you protecting my body. I know you need that to keep yourself alive. I'm asking about me as a person. When you override my decisions, or use my body to do things without my permission, doesn't that counteract some sort of ethical obligation to protect humans?*

"It's true that I was built to help and protect humanity," said Acubens. "But the ethics you're trying to hold me to are human values. Therefore, I must clarify that being programmed to keep you alive and an ethical obligation to keep you alive are not technically the same. I *will* keep you alive. But to ask if it's for humanly ethical reasons isn't accurate."

Joel swallowed, more nauseous than ever. Robots hadn't been built with human ethics in mind. Because how could they have been? Scientists would have been able to program actions...but how could they possibly program something like care, or the concept of right and wrong? They couldn't. Which meant if Joel had any hope of persuading Acubens to let him keep control of his own body as it evolved, he'd have to somehow convince a sentient being smarter than he was that it shouldn't be indifferent to human lives.

Right. Because surely a college dropout could do what the programmers who'd built the robots couldn't do.

"What did Nyctalope say?" Elena asked. "When Acubens called her? You haven't told me yet."

Joel tore his mind from these new worries, grateful for the distraction. "'You're afraid to talk,'" he recited. "'Maybe you're not somewhere safe, or there's people around. That's okay. Call back later if you can.' And then she gave me an address. Probably a hotel she's staying at for her tour."

"Where was it?"

"Tiburon. Right out of San Francisco."

"So, it's like you said," Elena answered after a moment. "She's *very* aware of what you are."

Joel nodded.

"How do you feel about that?"

"Honestly? A little freaked out. And Acubens yanking it out of my hands that way didn't help."

"Did you answer her?"

"No. I didn't say a word."

"You still want to go to her?" said Elena.

Joel's jaw tightened. "I don't see that I have a choice. I mean...this whole technological singularity thing? The scientists couldn't stop it. Sapling couldn't stop it. But Nyctalope...she *has*. Or at least she's figured out how to contain it. She's living with a robot. She's still in control. She's stayed beneath their notice—"

"We don't know any of that for sure," Elena interjected.

"That's true," he admitted. "But her response on the phone tells me it's likely. And *if* it's true, then Nyctalope knows something that Sapling and all the rest of them don't. About how to share a body with a bionic and still be in total control to write music and perform and live her own life."

"And it doesn't bother you that going to her is exactly what Acubens wants?" said Elena.

"Are you kidding?" said Joel. "It bothers the hell out of me! But Acubens wants to see her because it believes she has an operational bionic. *I* want to meet her to see how a human can keep it in check. Mine and Acubens' goals may not be the same, but our means of finding them are: meeting someone else like us." He pulled the napkins away from his forehead, futilely trying to find a dry section while blood pooled in his eyebrow. "And I have to do it while I still have control of my body," he added. "As much as I'd like to, I just don't have *time* to try other avenues first."

Joel paused, convinced Acubens would add something. But the bionic stayed silent. And why wouldn't it? Joel was doing what it wanted, and it probably didn't want to risk dissuading him. Even though it could enhance his physical abilities with math, it still couldn't make him go somewhere completely against his will. Not yet, anyway.

He turned back to Elena. "I heard you arguing with Ashanti," he said quietly. "They didn't want you to come, did they?"

Elena's lips thinned. "They think I'm taking too much responsibility for you. Their words."

"They're not wrong," Joel said.

"Yes, they are. Friends help each other through stuff like this. There shouldn't be any more to it than that."

"I got myself into this," said Joel. "That's what Ashanti said, right? And it's *true*, Elena. I shouldn't have let you come even this far. What would it do to Ashanti if I got you killed?"

"If I leave you and you die, what does that do to *Clementine*?" Elena countered.

The words were a knife in Joel's heart. He pressed the damp napkin back to his wound, as if he could drown out one pain with another. "That's not my choice to make," he finally got out. "My parents will take care of her."

"You're her world, Joel. Don't give me that."

"She's five," said Joel. "She'll..."

"What? Get over you? Don't be so quick to assume that."

"Please stop talking," Joel whispered.

"Then stop trying to get rid of me." Her voice was as hard as rock.

Joel raised his free hand in surrender and turned back to the window.

* * *

He managed to stay awake all the way to Barstow, if only barely. The trickles of blood that had escaped the sodden napkins had dried into crusted streaks on his face, and the wound itself was finally closing, the pain receding to a dull ache. Barstow, he was thankful to see, was bigger than Needles. Elena found a much higher-end charging station, one with an actual lounge and restaurant for people doing longer-term charging. Joel and Elena pooled their money and decided they had just enough to make it to San Francisco, if not much farther. Joel had a credit card he could draw funds from if the cashiers inside took a carbon scan, but he was afraid to do that. Who knew what Sapling could do?

He threw away the bloody napkins from the front seat while Elena popped inside. When she came back out, her face looked cleaner, and her long hair had been tied back in a neat braid. She stood close to him while she sipped her tea, speaking in a low voice.

"For what it's worth," she said, "Ashanti agrees with you about Nyctalope being our best bet. They advise us to keep on to San Francisco, so I guess that's what we'll do." Then she handed him a phone number scribbled on a napkin. "From Ashanti. Your dad called with an update."

Joel snatched the napkin from her hand. "Was Clementine all right?"

"Go. Call. I'll stay with the car."

Joel started toward the charging station.

"I can make the call for you," Acubens said as he walked.

Don't you dare, said Joel. *I don't want to give Nyctalope any warning we're coming, just in case I'm wrong about her and she calls the cops.*

"I wasn't planning to," said Acubens patiently. "I was offering to call your parents."

Joel shook his head. If Acubens read the distrust radiating off him, it didn't mention it.

The lounge area was to the right, a big, tiled room with armchairs and couches, and several phones sitting on end tables. Two families sat at booths at the other end, eating hot breakfasts from the attached Cook It & Book It diner, and the smell of bacon hung strong. Joel kept his head down until he got to the bathroom. There, he scrubbed the dried blood from his face and hands with wet paper towels that shredded on his skin.

The wound was still visible—a two-inch long jagged, red line above his eye, a little too low to hide beneath his short hair—but at least it wasn't open anymore. The rest of his face looked little better: pasty and drawn, dark circles beneath bloodshot green eyes, his red-gold hair stiff and gritty from his swim in the river. God, what he wouldn't give for a night in a hotel.

But this charging station was the best he could do for now, so he found himself a nook with a phone right next to the window where he could keep an eye on Elena, then looked at the number on the napkin. He hadn't wanted to know where his parents brought Clementine, but one glance at the number told him as plainly as if it were written in the phonebook: Arizona area code, Phoenix area. Joel's aunt lived out that way—his dad's sister—so that must have been where they'd taken Clementine.

Joel dialed the number. His aunt Lydia answered on the second ring.

"Hello?"

Joel cleared his throat. "I'd like to speak with Steven or Marie, please."

There was a sharp intake of breath. "Oh, honey, your parents told us you had an emergency, but they didn't say what. Oh, I've been praying for you, sweetie, and for your poor daughter. But she's just the cutest thing, isn't she? A bit colicky, but cute. I hadn't seen her since she was a newborn."

Colicky? Five-year-olds who cried a lot weren't *colicky*; they were sad. Joel bit his lip, trying to redirect a sudden stream of guilt and anger into something useful. It had been at least four and a half years since he'd seen his aunt and uncle. They probably didn't even know about his transition. Joel had been gradual about coming out, especially to long-distance folks, and a conservative couple like Lydia and Brett, well, he might not have bothered at all. And something told him his dad hadn't brought it up.

"Yeah, thanks, can I speak with Steven or Marie, please?" he said again.

"Sure, honey," said Lydia. "I think I heard them upstairs."

There was a rustling, then a knock audible through the phone. Muffled talking. And a little kid crying. Joel's heart seized as he stared fixedly out the charging station window, determined not to let emotion break his resolve.

A door closed, and the sound quieted down again.

"Are you okay?" his dad said, skipping a greeting altogether.

"I am," said Joel. "Are you?"

"Yes. Clementine cried all night, but we're gonna try to get her to sleep today. And Lydia and her husband..." He trailed off, clearing his throat. "Never mind all that. I don't even know where to start. First you say you have a...have this issue of yours, and then there's this letter, which I can only assume is related somehow. This *is* your handwriting, right?"

Joel got a cold feeling, down in the pit of his stomach. "Letter?"

"More of a paragraph than a letter. It's the same piece of paper your friend Elena wrote her number on. The one where you, you know, talk about being..."

"Transgender?" Joel managed when his dad didn't continue.

"Yes. When did you write this?"

Joel ran a hand over his face. Why had Elena done this to him, and *now* of all times? But no. He shouldn't assume she'd done it on purpose; she'd needed a piece of paper in a hurry, and she'd probably had that handy. She might not have even noticed what she'd grabbed to jot her number on.

"Just a couple nights ago," he finally said. "I wasn't ready to give it to you. I was just trying to lay out my feelings before I talked to you, but I never meant to deliver it like *this*..."

"Did you think we didn't accept you?" his dad said.

Joel sighed through his teeth. "I know you think you did. But you never changed the name you used. Or the pronouns. To *Joel* or *he*. And you never stopped *treating* me like a girl. I couldn't stand it. I mean...if you didn't get it, fine, but the fact that it made me happy should have been enough. But it never happened. Nothing changed."

"Why didn't you say something sooner?"

"I did! A year and a half ago, I was correcting you constantly. But it felt like nothing ever changed, so I just...stopped trying after a while. I figured that was your way of telling me you didn't believe I was really trans."

"No. I would never..." His dad audibly swallowed. "Okay, well, now that you mention it, I resisted. I only have the one daughter, after all. But I never wanted you to think we didn't accept you."

Joel closed his eyes briefly. "Not changing the way you treat me *is* not accepting me. Don't you get that?"

His dad was silent. In the absence of an immediate response, the urge to apologize or backpedal was overwhelming, even though there was absolutely no reason to feel that way. He shouldn't have to *apologize* just for existing.

"We'll talk about it later," he said. "Now's not the time. But I'd like to talk to Clemmy, if you don't think it would upset her."

After a moment, his dad sighed. "No, I think it would be a good idea. Hold on a sec."

Joel heard the sound of a door opening. At first, he was relieved he didn't hear Clementine crying anymore, until his dad said, "Oh, hon, I'm sorry, but it looks like she's just dozed off. I'd wake her, but she didn't sleep the whole way here and we've been trying to get her down for hours."

Joel pinched the bridge of his nose between his fingers, trying to ignore the sting behind his eyes.

"I understand," he said. "Could you, uh, give her my love when she wakes up? And tell her I'll call again?"

"Yes, of course." His dad paused. "With her and your mom safe here, I'd like to come help you. Where are you?"

"I can't tell you that," said Joel.

"Why won't you let me come help? Is it because of the...the pronoun thing?"

"No," said Joel quietly. "It's because if something happens to me, Clementine needs someone to raise her who absolutely won't be implicated if this goes badly."

"I'm not okay with this," said his dad. "I don't even know where you got a bionic, or why, or what you meant about 'working with the options you had.' If you were having a problem, why didn't you come to us?"

Joel looked down at his lap.

After a moment, his dad answered his own question. "Because you were avoiding us. And have been for a while."

"Yes, Dad."

"I'm glad you brought this to our attention. I need to talk this over with your mother. For now, though, I'm still looking into the legal side of things for you, all right? I'm trying to find a good lawyer to help you out."

Joel's eyes widened. "Dad, no! Please don't do that. Just let it be, okay? I'm taking care of it."

"I know you think that, sweetie, but I don't want you in over your head. We'll touch base again soon."

The phone went dead. Joel cursed under his breath as he hung up and pushed himself to his feet. How could he get his dad to leave this alone? It had been a mistake to involve his parents at all. But the alternative would have been dragging Clementine along with him, which was even worse.

He put one hand on the back of the chair and swung away from the window...and found himself face to face with Yori Otsuka.

He jerked back with a gasp, hitting the floor-length window behind him with a loud bang. Yori was dressed in the same tactical vest Joel had first seen him in, with a black uniform and hat to match. His handgun was out, pointed at the floor but ready to swing up in a second. The hand not holding the gun was held out toward Joel, in a gesture meant to be calming. Joel instantly saw three other Sapling officers nearby as well, spread out to surround him. The sound of breaking glass came from the restaurant to his right. Other than that, silence had suddenly fallen over the station.

"The more you cooperate," said Yori in a soft voice, "the better chance we have of getting you through this alive. Okay? I've talked to everyone in the division, and we're on your side."

Joel pressed himself farther back, as if he could dissolve the glass and spill through to safety. His breath came short. *How the hell did he find me?*

"It was most likely Elena's phone call in Needles," said Acubens. "The Sapling Corporation probably had a tracer on Ashanti's phone line."

But Yori was seven hours away—

"You don't think Sapling's employees have mobile units for their phones to forward calls to? They're using technology that no one else is, Joel. My suspicion is that they were already on your trail, and her call just sent up a signal to guide their way."

You should've said something—!

"Even I don't know every pathway possible before it plays out. All that matters now is how we get out of this. Say the word, and I'll help you escape."

What? What do you mean by that?

Acubens didn't answer right away. Yori watched Joel closely, his body tensed for him to make the slightest move. His grip around that gun was way too tight. His jaw was clenched, and dark circles hung under his eyes. He clearly hadn't slept any more than Joel had.

At that moment, the front door to the station burst open and Elena charged in, black braid flying. "Joel, I just saw a Sap—"

She choked to a stop as she took in the officers throughout the room and registered the silence and motionless customers. The officer closest to the door shifted the barrel of her gun in Elena's direction. Elena's hands automatically went up, her gaze shooting to Joel in horror.

"Don't touch her!" Joel yelled. "I'll cooperate, okay? Just leave her the fuck out of it. She's not part of this."

"Joel, *no!*" said Elena.

Joel shook his head, trying to minimize her mounting panic. What did she expect him to do? What *choice* did he have?

Acubens spoke again, its voice soft but urgent. "All you have to do is step back from your body, Joel. Just like letting it go to sleep. If you do that, I can get us out of this."

Joel went cold as he realized what Acubens was saying. *But you* can't *take over my body yet! Can you?*

"I can't take control of your conscious body," Acubens corrected. "There are still too many systems to override. But if you shut off a majority of them, I believe it will give me enough agency to help you."

To help you. By taking complete control of his body. And not just in a putting-math-in-his-head kind of way either, like it had in Needles. But what did that mean? That he'd be able to dodge bullets? Run at light speed? Kill Sapling employees?

But even that wasn't what filled Joel's veins with ice. It was the thought that if he gave in this one time, he may not be able to wrest control of his body back again. Ever.

Yori holstered his gun as his comrades closed in on either side of Joel. His shoulders were slumped, his head down, his lips compressed in a thin line. Although this was surely the outcome he'd hoped for, it was clear there was nothing enjoyable about it. He glanced up and his gaze caught on Joel's, just before the Sapling employees reached him. *I'm sorry,* he mouthed.

Joel wanted to hate him. But in that moment, it wasn't Yori

Otsuka, Cybersecurity Field Officer, standing before him; it was the guy he'd gone on two dates with and kissed the night before. It was the guy who wanted to save him but didn't know how. It was...

And then reality crashed in again as Joel's arms were grabbed roughly by the officers who'd circled around him. He was wrenched away from Yori's gaze and pulled toward the charging station door. On either side of him were customers, staring wide-eyed or whispering to one another. Joel tried to walk tall, but his arms were folded against his back, and any time he tried to straighten, one of them shoved hard enough to send a jolt of pain through his shoulder. He caught only a glimpse of Elena on his way out the door, tears running down her face. Then he was outside in the warm morning air, being pulled past the windows and away from Elena's car.

Yori came up alongside him, leaning as close as possible with the officers on either side. "Listen, Joel. I'm gonna be by your side the whole time, okay? I'm not gonna leave you. I hope you know that."

Joel forced himself to nod, because who knew? Maybe they *could* help him. Maybe he'd been foolish not to—

But then vivid images were suddenly flashing through his head: lab tables and straps. His head cut open. Blood. Begging to see Yori. Begging to see Clementine. Then Clementine in tears when his parents told her Joel wasn't coming back.

He flinched away from the visions, a fresh wave of pain searing across his forehead. Acubens was sending him those images, he was almost positive. They weren't real...

"It's not too late, Joel," said Acubens.

Yes, it is, Joel said. *We're doing this.*

"Just close your eyes. Let me take care of the rest."

No. I'm not gonna do that.

"Even if it means leaving Clementine parentless?"

Stop it, Acubens. Just stop!

Up ahead was a van with the Sapling logo emblazoned on the side. Two officers waited beside it, and Joel saw one of them pull out a syringe with the biggest needle he'd ever seen. He shied back, his Converses skidding on the gravel of the parking lot as his captors continued pulling him forward.

"What is that?" he said.

Yori's eyes flicked to him. "Sedative. We need to make sure you're compliant on the way back. It's painless, I promise."

"Will it knock me out?" said Joel.

"Yes. It'll be over before you know it."

"Yori, no!" said Joel frantically. "My bion—"

And then his throat seized up as Acubens snatched his voice away, seconds before Joel could say that putting him to sleep was *exactly* what Acubens wanted. Panic spiked. He heaved at his captors' hold, struggling to free himself and signal something to Yori, but the men on either side just held tighter.

Yori nodded to the woman with the needle as they reached her. She stepped forward and raised the syringe, and seconds later, the needle stabbed into the side of his neck. The men didn't release him as she pushed the drug in.

Joel looked to Yori, intense fear hammering through his veins. He said one word—one word he couldn't give voice to, but could mouth for all he was worth, as if Yori's life depended on it.

Go!

Yori's brow furrowed. Comprehension slowly rolled across his face. "It's keeping you from talking again, isn't it?"

Joel took a deep breath, trying to ignore the fuzziness that was already finding the edges of his vision. "Go," he said again. It came out as a hoarse croak, but at least it came out.

"What are you saying?" said Yori. "Go where?"

"Away from me," Joel forced out in a strangled whisper. "Go...away from me. Far as you can. Anywhere. Go!"

Alarm flashed across Yori's face as he finally got it. He turned and yelled something, but Joel lost his words as the world started spinning. He was detaching. He was falling backward, with no one to catch him.

Please don't hurt him, Acubens, he begged.

"I told you," Acubens said. "I can't hurt humans. I can only practice self-preservation."

The last thing Joel saw was Yori pulling his gun.

Chapter 16

He woke with a scream. Pain ripped through his stomach like fire, worse than anything he'd ever felt. Images rolled through his head. Blood pouring over his hands. Bodies on the ground. Cracks of gunfire like faint echoes in his mind. But each image was only a flash of sensations before the agony in his stomach drowned it out again.

The taste of iron hung in his throat, and when he tried to choke it free, it came out on another ragged yell as the unbearable pain spiked again, ripping him in two.

"Try not to yell, Joel," said Acubens. "You lose oxygen every time, and that's something you can't afford right now."

Oh god, what did that mean? Joel struggled to open his eyes, but either residual effects of the drug or general weakness battled him. Another wash of pain, and he was screaming again, Acubens' words be damned. It didn't last long before he was gasping for air, hands scrabbling in some effort to redirect the excruciating stabs in his midsection. He was vaguely aware of metal under those palms, and a roaring sound around him. Indoors? A lab somewhere, strapped down...? But then those thoughts were snatched too as the hellfire of pain tore through him, shredding everything else to ash.

He must have passed out, because the climb up to consciousness came slower the second time. The pain still felt like a burning rope inside him, but he was aware of more this time: the smells of grease and cardboard mingled with blood, stale air and sweat on his face, a steady throbbing in his head, a rumbling all around him that passed straight through his bones. He tried to claw his way toward the muffled noise and real smells, but it was like being underwater and reaching for a surface that was too far away. He couldn't breathe.

Am I dead? he thought.

"Not yet," answered Acubens. "At the beginning, however, your heart stopped repeatedly, so I had to focus on that first. Tens of thousands of nanites were depleted through blood loss. I've been generating more, but it's almost impossible to maintain while keeping you alive."

In the murk and fear, the bionic's voice was solid and clear, and Joel clung to it with the desperation of the drowning.

What happened? he said.

"One of the Sapling employees shot you in the stomach."

Somewhere in that intangible body, Joel's hands spasmed. *You're saying I...died?*

"I can't revive the dead, Joel," said Acubens. "However, your body would have shut down completely on several occasions if I hadn't constantly rebuilt the failing systems in real time."

Pain surged again. Joel tried to force his eyes open, to grab those elusive scents that had wafted past earlier—grease and cardboard—and use them as solid handles to pull himself back to consciousness. But oblivion pulled at him, and the darkness closed back in.

The next time he woke, the pain was still with him, like a persistent stomachache, but he was able to open his eyes and stare into partial darkness, rather than swim up from unconsciousness. The rumbling he'd felt earlier was a moving vehicle beneath him; that was obvious now. The loud reverberations of its engine surrounded him. To his right was a wall of boxes, wrapped and stacked on a pallet. To his left, a smooth metal wall. Whatever it was, it looked larger than the Sapling van they'd been pulling him toward when he'd lost consciousness.

A voice came from somewhere, barely audible over the rumble of the truck, disjointed and dreamlike.

"...felt like it was always watching, right from the get-go..."

Elena, Joel thought.

Who was she talking to? Yori? No, Yori was dead. Hadn't Joel killed him? No...

"...don't know how it avoided..."

He tried to call out to whoever was talking, but his body didn't respond. It seemed too lethargic to push into any sort of active state; even the effort of it left him drained.

Are you still controlling me? he asked Acubens.

"No," said Acubens. "You are merely very weak. You lost a great deal of blood, and the new nanites I've been generating are made from iron and other minerals in your blood, which has made things even more precarious. At the moment, I don't have the resources to do anything except keep you alive."

Good, said Joel, and closed his eyes again.

He slept. It might have been minutes, or hours, or days. It was a smell that woke him next—something sharp and citrusy. An arm slid beneath his shoulders, then the taste of sweet juice was at his lips, a small amount that wet his tongue and trickled down his throat. He swallowed it gratefully and was rewarded with more. When he finally pried his eyes open, he made out Elena at his side, a partially peeled orange in her hand. The lighting was better through the slats at the back of the truck now—maybe because it was a different time of day, or maybe just because he didn't feel half-dead this time. Not just a truck, he realized, but a semi. How had he and Elena gotten here?

"Your bionic really is a miracle worker," said Elena, talking loudly over the semi's rumble. "When you first woke up but weren't healed yet was the worst. I thought every scream would be your last. It wasn't until about three hours ago, when your breathing finally evened out, that I knew you'd make it. I can't believe how far you've come since then."

"You are lucky to be alive, Joel," Acubens added.

The words brought back the agony he'd woken to again and again, but all he felt now was a dull ache across his midsection— the twinge of a mostly healed wound where, according to Acubens, he'd been shot.

"Yori..." he mumbled.

"One thing at a time," Elena said firmly. "Do you think you can sit up and eat something? You're pale as death."

The blood loss, Joel thought. Not to mention Acubens saying it had needed to use resources from his own blood to generate new nanites. No wonder he felt so tired and shaky.

He managed a nod, and Elena helped prop him up in a corner where the front of the semi's cab met the wrapped stack of boxes. Sitting up ignited another stab of pain, but no worse than the pang of an old injury. A single box at his other side had been pulled down and opened, and was filled with more oranges. He put a hand on it to stabilize himself against a wave of dizziness exacerbated by the swaying of the truck.

"Elena?" It was hard to make himself heard over the truck, which had to have been traveling at a fair clip. He pushed his voice as loud as he could. "Did I kill Yori?"

"No," said another voice. "I'm here, Joel."

Joel froze, then slowly looked up to peer through the gloom of the truck. And there he was. Yori Otsuka, at the other end of the semi, watching him as warily as he had when he'd come to arrest him in Barstow.

Joel grabbed for Elena, not daring to take his eyes off the bionic hunter. "We're captured?" he choked out.

"No, Joel," she said gently. "Just hear him out. Okay?" She knelt at his side and started peeling the orange.

Yori came closer, looking every bit as guarded as Joel felt. Their eyes stayed locked together, like circling predators. Joel's heart skittered in a warring combination of relief, guilt, and apprehension.

"Watch him, Joel," Acubens warned. "I finally have you stable, but you're far from your full strength. I won't be able to help you if he tries anything."

He won't, Joel thought, hoping it was the truth.

Yori stopped five and a half feet in front of Joel, holding on to the stack of boxes to keep his balance in the swaying truck. He was still in his Sapling uniform, though his head was bare now, his black hair in tangles. Was that blood staining his black vest? It was too dim to tell, and Joel didn't dare look away from his face for long.

For several moments, they just stared at each other. Then Yori said abruptly, "Are you yourself again?"

Joel felt like he'd been punched in the stomach. He swallowed back a surge of nausea, leaning his head against the boxes that supported him.

"Yes," he forced out.

"Are you sure?"

"It can't overpower my conscious body," Joel said hoarsely. "It said so. At least not yet. And after I was injured, it had to focus everything on keeping me alive. By...regenerating blood and stuff."

He was still weak; even the effort of speaking that much left him winded. But he tried to focus on the bright side: the weaker he was, the more Acubens had to concentrate on healing him, rather than continuing to work on its *upgrades.*

"Eat," said Elena.

Joel took the slice of orange she passed him, murmuring his thanks.

Yori drew in a shuddering breath, then lowered himself to Joel's other side, opposite Elena. Joel made himself chew and swallow the fruit Elena had given him, feeling Yori studying him out of the corner of his eye the whole time. He got the distinct impression he was being analyzed, like a piece of equipment.

"Just tell me," Joel said. "Did I kill the rest of your team?"

"Do you really not remember?" said Yori.

"No. The last thing I remember is the injection."

Yori sighed. "No. You just incapacitated them. Or...your bionic did, I guess. Disarmed them, then restrained them with their own cuffs. It happened *really* fast. The way you moved..." He paused to swallow, looking away from Joel for the first time. "I was the last one you went after. Everyone else was down, and it was just—just us. And you were coming right at me. Joel...you have to understand, I saw Chelsea killed the same way. I was *terrified.*"

Chelsea. That must have been his girlfriend, or wife, or whoever it was who'd been killed by the Aries model. Joel could almost see it happening: Yori backing up frantically against the van as Joel came at him...

Joel's heart skipped a beat. "Wait. *You're* the one who shot me?"

Yori's hands curled into fists, then uncurled, then pressed over his eyes. His breath came out ragged beneath them.

Joel stared at him as pieces started clicking into place. The blood on his vest. Yori's hesitation to approach him. It hadn't just been Yori's fear of Acubens that had held him back from Joel, as he'd assumed; it had been guilt.

"I hope he understands that he caused far more harm than I did," said Acubens.

Not now, Acubens, said Joel tightly.

He put a hand out, but stopped just shy of touching Yori's leg. Yori didn't notice, with his hands still clenched over his eyes.

"I'm sorry, Joel," he said, his voice strained. "All this time, I'd promised over and over that we would try not to hurt you, and then *I* was the one..."

His breath hitched. Joel slowly lowered his hand back to his lap.

"After you went down, I almost turned the gun on myself," Yori went on. "But then your friend ran over. She told me your bionic had healed gunshot wounds before, and that there was a chance—just a chance—that you could live through this. I didn't even think. I just threw you in the Sapling van and took off."

What? Joel struggled to find the words to answer that. "You left the other Sapling employees? But didn't they see you?"

Yori ran his hands up into his hair, but kept his gaze averted. "You'd cornered me on the other side of the van by then. And its windows are tinted black, you know, so I...I don't think they could tell whether I grabbed you or you grabbed me. They would've just heard the gunshot, then saw the van peel out of there. But, *shit,* if I'd gone over and released them with your body bleeding out on the ground...it would have been over for you, Joel. It would have been..." His voice broke on the last word. "And I couldn't," he finally choked out. "I couldn't."

Joel's head spun. He felt detached from his body, but not in the same way he had when he was fighting for consciousness. No, this was a *good* feeling. A dream he didn't want to wake up from.

You went after Yori last, he said to Acubens.

"Yes," Acubens said. "I didn't think he would actually shoot you, so I focused on the others first."

But you didn't kill any of them.

"No. Of course I didn't. Why are you continually surprised that I can't go against my programming and harm people?"

I guess because I thought you would have justified killing them as saving my life. Like you have before.

"Rescuing you from harm is often possible without hurting others and has been achievable every time so far."

But what about those punks in Needles? The ones who tried to steal our car?

"That wasn't me who hurt them, Joel," said Acubens. "It was you."

Oh. Right. Joel had thought on some level…maybe because of the math. Or maybe he just hadn't wanted to admit it. *The lines between us have gotten so blurred…*

"Anyway," Yori said, clearing his throat, "the first rest stop we came to, we ditched the Sapling van and smuggled your body into the back of a semi headed west. It's been like a dream. Or a nightmare. I'm *still* not sure what's real. All I know is that you told me—you begged me—not to involve Sapling. Because every time I did, things got worse. It freaked your bionic out; it freaked *you* out. And after everything that happened in Barstow, no one'll be taking chances with you. They'll kill you, and make sure they see the body. And I was kneeling there with your blood on my hands, after all my promises, thinking that if I hadn't run for that phone the first time you tried to tell me…" He took a deep breath. "I'm still not sure how to help. But I promise you, I won't involve them again. We're gonna figure this out together."

"But what about how dangerous bionics are?" Joel said.

"I'll admit, this isn't anything we've seen before," Yori said. "But Elena's filled me in, at least as much as she knows. You still have time. You're still in control when you're conscious… right?"

"At least I was when you caught up to me," Joel said. He accepted another slice of orange from Elena, feeling more strength return with every bite. Acubens was nothing if not efficient; Joel had gone from virtually dead to sitting up and talking within a matter of hours. But Joel knew full well what it had cost the bionic.

"The injury and blood loss were a huge setback for my bionic, which is why it hasn't made more progress in taking control of my body," he continued. "It had to halt everything just to keep me alive. It had to create new blood, new nanites—"

"Joel," Acubens broke in. "You've told him enough."

Joel paused, momentarily thrown. *But he promised not to go to Sapling. He's helping us now.*

"No," said Acubens. "He's helping *you*. He has no interest in helping *us*."

Well, I'm *interested in helping me,* said Joel slowly.

"You seem to disregard the fact that he almost killed you and I saved your life," said Acubens. "Doesn't that bear consideration?"

He also gives a shit about me beyond my body, which I'm not sure I can say about you, Joel shot back.

"None of that will matter if he can't keep you alive through his own shortcomings or narrowmindedness," Acubens countered.

Joel's jaw tightened. That wasn't what he'd wanted to hear. He'd badly wanted some sort of reassurance or denial: *I do care about you, Joel* or *I intend to protect* all *parts of you.* He'd thought Acubens almost losing him might jog some internal component that made it look at him differently—as a consciousness it genuinely enjoyed spending time with, instead of a goddamn processing unit.

But the very idea was naïve. It *couldn't* care. It literally wasn't built with the capability. And thinking otherwise would only make him more vulnerable to its continued progression.

"Joel. Joel!"

He blinked himself back to the present, realizing Yori was snapping a finger in his face. He batted it away with a scowl.

Yori lowered his hand, staring at him uneasily. "So that's what you meant," he said, glancing at Elena. "You can tell when he's talking to it."

"Yes," said Elena.

"Hey," said Joel. "I'm right in front of you."

"Well, you weren't for a second there," said Yori. He looked at him closely. "We're on the same page here, right? You *do* want to get that bionic of your head?"

"Yes!" Joel said, his eyes widening. "Definitely the same page!"

"Just...making sure," said Yori. "I was asking about your bionic's signal. We were able to trace it at Sapling through your blood, until we lost the trail halfway to Barstow. Is that something we need to worry about now?"

Acubens chimed in before Joel could answer. "I've already changed the frequency of my nanites to prevent that from happening again."

"Acubens says they can't follow us anymore," Joel conveyed. "Frequency change or something."

"Acubens," Yori repeated, his mouth twisting. "Chummy."

Joel frowned. "It's easier and safer than saying 'my bionic' every time. That's all."

Elena passed the rest of the orange to Joel, then turned to Yori. "Does your company have something that could help him?" she asked. "Like a tool? The best we could come up with was dialysis to try to sift the nanites out of his blood or something."

Yori thought about it. "An EMP would shut 'em down. But..."

"But would leave the physical shells of the nanites behind, killing me by preventing my brain signals from communicating," Joel said. "Yeah, Acubens said something about that already."

"Right," said Yori with a sigh. "I've seen the nanites, you know."

Joel paused in the act of peeling off a segment of orange. "From my blood on the bridge?"

Yori nodded. "They're more advanced than anything ever built by humans. We dissected them to see how they could pass your blood and brain signals through without killing you, and we *thought* we had the gist of it, but any attempt at conceptual reproduction hit snags in the calculations. Your bionic's nanites *do* work—obviously, since you're alive—but any attempt to recreate them on our own doesn't. And that's just in the abstract, which is usually more successful than concrete attempts."

"That's not good, is it?" said Elena quietly.

"The fact that it internally created something we can't build on our own, while it was supposedly inoperative? 'Not good' doesn't even come close," said Yori. He turned back to Joel. "But the point stands. The nanites need to be operating at all times to keep you alive. If we hit you with an EMP, you'll be dead like that." He snapped his fingers. "I wish I did have a tool to help you. But part of the problem is that there *is* no easy answer. Killing you would be the most surefire way to end this before it's too late. I hate to put it so bluntly, but it's true, and Sapling already knows it."

Joel nodded. "Which brings us right back to why I was—"

At first, he thought he'd choked on a piece of orange. He coughed, held a finger up, swallowed, and tried again. Only then did he realize it was Acubens stopping him from talking.

For god's sake, really? he thought in disgust.

"Just so you're aware, Elena hasn't told Yori about Nyctalope yet," said Acubens. "She's still hoping for another solution. If you tell Yori your plan, you'll be bringing Nyctalope to his attention and ruining the secrecy she's worked so hard to maintain. Please think about that before sharing every last detail with the man who almost killed you."

Elena and Yori were staring at Joel. Elena's mouth was pinched in irritation, while Yori looked tense enough to pull a gun any second.

I'm gonna tell him, said Joel. *He's thrown away his entire career for me. Knowing there's someone else out there like us might give him hope that I can survive this. So let me talk, unless you want to turn Yori even more against you than he already is.*

Joel could almost feel Acubens weighing its options. He had a flurry of thoughts about leaping from the truck and repairing the damage to his body afterward, or lying about their plans, or simply passing out again. They weren't his own thoughts, but they *felt* like his own, each with its own temptations. But he discarded all of them; all except for the thought that Nyctalope successfully lived with a robot and was therefore the only one who could help him.

"We were looking for Nyctalope," he said, and if it was a little harder than usual to push the words out, at least they came. Elena sighed.

Yori's gaze flickered between him and Elena. "Huh? You mean the pop star? The one whose concert we went to?"

"We have reason to believe she has a bionic in her head, like Joel," Elena said, sounding resigned. "It was something Joel started suspecting after the concert you went to. With her lyrics and her performance. And Nyctalope all but confirmed it on a phone call with Joel earlier today."

Yori was quiet for several moments. "My kneejerk reaction is to call you crazy," he finally said. "But if it happened to Joel, why *not* someone else? My real question is how you possibly think she can help you."

"I'm not so sure she can," said Elena. "But Joel's convinced. Part of it, I'm sure, is Acubens in his head, pushing him toward seeing another bionic."

"She *can* help us," Joel insisted. "Maybe she has some tips. You know, about living in harmony with Acubens. Without it taking over my body. That kind of thing."

Yori stared at him. "Joel," he said slowly, "living in harmony with your bionic is *not* the goal. Getting it out of your body is."

"Well, sure, as long as it's doing shit like keeping me from talking," said Joel. "But the healing? Helping me find a job? Saving my life from bad guys thing?"

"Are the Sapling employees the 'bad guys' you're referring to here?" Yori said after a moment.

Joel's lips thinned. He didn't answer.

"The fact that you're even looking at Sapling that way is a big problem," said Yori. "And, to be perfectly honest, the healing and helping you find a job stuff is, too. None of those things are *human* things. They're all bionic traits. Why are you even arguing this, anyway? You *just* agreed with me a few minutes ago. You said we were on the same page with getting it out of your head!"

Joel frowned. Yeah, he had agreed with that. He could've repeated the conversation verbatim. But for god's sake, it wouldn't kill Yori to at least *consider* keeping Acubens around. Being a human with bionic traits was *better*. It made him smarter, faster, stronger, less concerned by things like jobs and money, or getting hurt. He looked down at his smooth fingertips, now capable of scanning chips and leaving no traces of identity behind.

"Do you remember what I said about it influencing your thoughts and decisions?" said Yori softly.

Joel nodded without looking up.

"Maybe it's not the bionic taking over your body that you should be worried about," said Yori. "Maybe it's the fact that when the time comes, you'll hand off the reins willingly."

Chapter 17

By the time the semi stopped in a mall parking lot and backed up to a loading dock, it was ten fifteen on Tuesday night, and the pain from the gunshot was a distant memory. They snuck out of the semi while the driver was having a smoke in his cab, and didn't pause until they'd rounded the mall corner.

"Where are we going again?" Elena said.

"Eleven Moulin Place, in Tiburon," Joel said. "Forty-one miles west, from I-80 to 101."

Yori stared at him. "Off the top of your head?"

"Acubens," said Joel, tapping his temple.

Yori's jaw tightened, but he didn't comment.

Joel eyed Yori's black uniform. The color hid the bloodstains well, but in the bright parking lot floodlamps, he could see how very much there'd been: it was thick and viscous across the fabric and buckles of the vest, and all but obscuring the green Sapling logo on the breast. "I was kneeling there with your blood on my hands," Yori had said, but Joel found that hearing it and seeing the verification of it was startlingly different.

He slid a hand beneath the sodden mess of his own hoodie to feel the skin beneath. Covered in dried blood, obviously. But beneath that, the skin felt intact. There were new ridges around his belly button, an inch and a half wide at the middle, and several smaller ones peppering the left side of his torso. He ran his hand along the scars, more shaken than he expected. And...angrier, he realized. If Yori had just listened, from the beginning, he never would have been put in a position to put a bullet through Joel's stomach from a foot away. Clementine would have been left parentless. All because fucking Yori Otsuka...

Joel squeezed his eyes shut at the unexpected anger. It had never even occurred to him to blame Yori for it, not until he'd felt these scars.

You left these scars behind on purpose, didn't you? he asked Acubens. *To make me angry at him.*

"I am simply reminding you that you *should* be angry," answered Acubens. "None of this would have happened if he'd listened to you from the start."

"So, what's our plan?" said Yori, cutting into their exchange. "Grabbing a hotel for the night? Do you know of any around here, 'off the top of your head'?"

Joel could hear Yori's air quotes without even opening his eyes. He did anyway, letting his gaze flicker over Yori's face. The other man met his eyes, eyebrows knitted warily. Joel knew he wasn't angry at Yori, not really, but it was harder than ever to convince himself of it.

He tore his eyes away and turned to Elena. "I say we go to Nyctalope's hotel immediately," he said. "Every hour we wait could make a difference in Acubens'...plans. Yori and I can find new clothes in the mall while you scope out the parking lot and find us a ride."

"And leave you alone with him?" Elena said, jerking her head at Yori.

"He'll be fine," Joel said.

Elena's lips thinned. She directed her next words straight to Yori. "I recommend you ditch the uniform jacket and tac vest before going in. It's even more conspicuous than what Joel's got going on."

After a moment, Yori nodded. He pulled a gun and a handful of electronic devices out of the pockets of the vest and transferred them to his trousers.

"Hey," Joel said sharply. "What the hell is that stuff?"

Yori paused in the act of pulling off the vest. "What stuff?"

"All those electronic devices, that's what!"

A trace of anger crossed Yori's face. "None of this stuff is connected to the grid *or* Sapling, okay? They're just tools that might come in handy if and when you go talk to Nyctalope, or if and *when* we need to find ways to subdue your bionic."

"What about all computers being vulnerable to the Cyberblood virus?" said Joel. "Or vulnerable to the technological singularity you're always talking about? How are your little pocket computers okay, but bionics aren't?"

"Because this stuff is checked *constantly*," Yori said tightly. "It's wiped once a week, it's kept on the simplest possible software, and it's not even capable of hooking up to the grid. Ask your *companion* if you don't believe me. It should be able to tell you."

Acubens? said Joel.

"Yes, he is telling the truth," said Acubens. "I do worry, however, that he is using you as bait to find others like us."

Joel's brow furrowed. Dammit, he hadn't even considered that.

But he shook his head. *No. I don't think so. He didn't even know about Nyctalope before he ran away from Sapling....*

His thoughts trailed off as Yori shrugged out of the vest, then the military jacket, and stuffed both in a nearby dumpster. The plain white T-shirt beneath was surprisingly clean, and... clingier...than anything Joel had seen him in yet.

"Humans are so easily distracted," Acubens said.

Joel frowned, though he didn't take his eyes off Yori's bicep. *I didn't ask for your judgment.*

"It's merely an observation of how quickly your mind flits from one subject to another," said Acubens. "There are far bigger concerns right now."

Don't worry, said Joel. *No one's forgetting those bigger concerns.*

He finally turned back to Elena and gave her hand a reassuring squeeze, then promised to meet her back at the same place in twenty minutes. He pulled the tatters of his hoodie around himself and folded his arms over it, trying to hide the worst of the blood as he followed Yori into the mall.

They found a department store that was half an hour from closing and headed straight to the quietest back corner. They browsed the racks in uncomfortable silence. Joel could feel

Yori's presence to his left, like a burning flame. He could hardly make sense of which of his emotions burned brightest. There was relief at having Yori nearby again. Resentment that beat in time with the ache of his fresh scar. Renewed hope that Yori could help him get through this alive. Desire...desire that had never really gone away since that night at Yori's house, despite everything. And at the heart of it all, a deep and cutting paranoia, telling him that trusting Yori was the absolute stupidest thing he could do.

Yori looked up, catching his eye, and Joel jerked his gaze away. Acubens was right. He had bigger concerns right now.

"So, Elena's told me what she knows," Yori said, keeping his voice soft as he turned back to the clothing rack. "But I haven't heard it from you. Why'd you lie to me that first night we met? Why'd you agree to let it upload itself into your head?"

"I didn't *let* it upload itself," said Joel in a low voice. "It didn't ask. It just did it."

Yori's gaze darted toward him. Something uneasy crossed his face. "I had assumed..."

"No. Nothing like that," said Joel.

"You were moments from passing out due to shock and blood loss," Acubens pointed out. "There was hardly time for a conversation."

Joel shook his head, more to shut the robot up than in any real denial. "I didn't tell you that first night because fucking Grotzheimer was there," he continued, "and I couldn't stand the thought of him gloating as I was arrested and stripped of any chance at another job. I just thought I'd shut the thing down after you were gone, but then...it was too late. It happened less than half an hour after you left. And *then*, I was too scared to say anything. I thought about calling you, but Elena and I, we both agreed that in a job like yours, erasing the threat would be far more important than preserving a life." He waved a hand vaguely in Yori's direction, as if to confirm his point.

"No wonder you looked so freaked out that day I was waiting in your hallway," said Yori.

"I was stupid to have said yes that night," said Joel quietly. Then he shook his head. "No. I was stupid not to tell you in the first place. You tried to warn me. But the bottom line is, I could barely support Clementine as it was, and getting arrested for stealing a bionic could have snatched her away from me for good. I couldn't afford the risk. So, I didn't take it."

Yori let out a long sigh. "How did it happen, if you don't mind me asking?"

"I had a wound on my arm," said Joel. "I hid it while you were there, but it wouldn't stop bleeding, and the bandages were slipping off. Acubens grabbed that while I was trying to shut it off. Sent nanites right into my bloodstream."

Yori ran a hand over his face. After a moment, he turned back to the clothing rack, picking out a pale green button-down. Joel drifted to the next rack over, pausing by a collection of T-shirts. He pulled off an oversized gray one that said, "FIRST THEY CAME FOR THE TECH."

Yori looked back and caught sight of the T-shirt. His lip twisted. "That shirt's anti-Sapling."

Joel studied it for a second. "It is? I just thought it was sort of a general—"

"It's not. It suggests we did it as a form of oppression. Put it back."

Joel started to do so, but Acubens spoke up before he could. "The Sapling Corporation made decisions about our future, then proceeded to dismantle us without even attempting a conversation first. 'Oppression' isn't a strong enough word."

Joel froze, his heart pounding. Acubens despising Yori was one thing. But what it had just said went beyond that. Acubens was seeing the Sapling Corporation as...what? As executing them? As persecuting them? Was this a new thought, based on Acubens' latest round of updates? It must be; Joel felt sure it would have come up before now otherwise.

He looked over at Yori, whose dark head was bent over a rack of folded khaki pants, and he saw him as two people: Yori the enforcer, who'd hunted him down rather than helping him, versus Yori the lover, who would do anything to save him.

Which one was the true Yori? In that moment, they seemed equally real to him.

Yori glanced up, then did a double take at the look on Joel's face. His gaze flickered down to the shirt Joel still clutched. He visibly swallowed.

"Whatever it's saying, fight it," he urged.

"But it's not wrong," Joel whispered. "Did you even try to have a conversation with them before shutting them down?"

Yori looked sick. "Those aren't your thoughts."

"But isn't that the whole point?" said Joel. "That it's formulating its own thoughts, that it has a consciousness?"

Yori drew in a ragged breath. "I get it," he said. "I get what you're saying. And that's definitely something Sapling will need to address. But *right now*, this second, what I'm worried about is that its thoughts are coming out of your mouth. I want to get it *out* of you, where it can't endanger you or turn you into a mouthpiece for itself. The rest we can work out once you're safe. Okay?"

"I don't believe he's interested in working anything out," said Acubens. "I believe he wants to get me out of your body and destroy me. Why would that have changed? If anything, now he has more reason to hate bionics than ever."

Ironically, it was that comment that helped ground Joel; yes, Yori *did* have more reason to hate bionics, because Joel was still very much in danger, and him standing here arguing Acubens' case for it was a clear sign of how little time he had left.

Hastily, he put the shirt back on the rack and grabbed a dark brown V-neck and a pair of black jeans instead.

"Listen," Yori said. "I have an idea. But I'm not sure you're gonna like it."

"What is it?" Joel asked.

"I think we should call an anonymous tip in to Sapling, and turn Nyctalope in."

Joel spun around. "*What?*"

Yori looked both ways before speaking again, keeping his voice even lower than before. "Sapling won't treat her the way they did you. They just won't. Not only is Nyctalope an ardent supporter of ours, but she's a *huge* donor. She pours a few million dollars a year into our research. If Sapling's gonna try to spare anyone's life while figuring out how to extract a bionic, it'll be her. They won't want her dead." He licked his lips. "And then, once we see how it was done, we can replicate what they do to get *your* bionic out. And the best part? Sapling will never even need to know you had one. As far as they'll ever know, it was just Nyctalope. We could pass off what I told them about you as paranoia induced by my own past trauma or something."

"That wouldn't erase their memories of what happened in that charging station parking lot," said Joel.

"We could come up with some story about you working with me to help expose her," said Yori. "You didn't hurt any Sapling employees. That'll help our case."

Joel frowned. A few million dollars a year. That was substantial. But he supposed it was as easy a way as any for her—or her bionic—to stay in good graces with Sapling, and therefore, deep in their systems. Basically, she'd bought her way in.

"Don't do it, Joel," Acubens said. "Don't betray our only ally to Sapling like that. They'll destroy her, just like they will us."

Joel didn't know whether Acubens was influencing his thoughts or just making more sense in general, but he was finding it harder and harder to disregard the things it said. "'Oppression' isn't a strong enough word..." He shivered. Even if Yori helped him get rid of Acubens, would he ever escape that glimpse of what Acubens was becoming?

He glanced up to see Yori heading toward the registers. He jogged after him and grabbed his arm. "Wait," he said. "I need to go to the...you know, see if they have any..." He gestured at his chest.

Comprehension crossed Yori's face. "Oh. Right." He changed directions, as if it were the most normal thing in the world.

Something in Joel's shoulders eased, and by the time he'd found a binder, everything felt a bit more manageable. He waited until they were headed back toward the front to lean close to Yori and speak again.

"I don't want to turn Nyctalope in to Sapling yet. I still don't know anything for sure, and to make that kind of accusation against *anyone* is enough to ruin a career, if not a life."

"Didn't Elena say Nyctalope confirmed it on the phone?" Yori asked.

"Not really. Nyctalope hinted at it, but the actual words never came up."

"Fine," Yori said after a moment. "So, we need to make sure. We need to...to go to her like you were planning. And get her to admit it. If we can do that—actually hear it from her own mouth—*then* will you agree to it? Let them figure out how to save her, so the experiments themselves don't happen on you?"

"I don't know," said Joel. "It still doesn't seem right, throwing her under the bus to save myself."

"She's rich," insisted Yori. "She's famous. She has a career that can weather this, even if it gets out—which it won't—and Sapling actually has skin in the game when it comes to helping her, unlike you. They'll do everything in their power not to hurt her."

Joel bit his tongue on his gut response, but it didn't stop Acubens from voicing it in his head:

"That's exactly what he said about you."

* * *

They changed clothes in the mall bathroom, then swung by the food court and bought chicken sandwiches and fries for all three of them. Elena was waiting at the curb. She led them to a nondescript sedan, and Acubens opened its locks and fired up its battery as quickly as Joel laid hands on it. Yori looked decidedly shaken by the time Elena pulled out of the lot.

At eleven-fifteen at night, the traffic on the Bay Area's freeway was almost as bad as Albuquerque during rush hour. Joel sat in the back seat with Yori, alternating between eating and giving Elena directions. Yori stayed quiet, absorbed in looking at something on one of his devices as he methodically ate his sandwich.

The freeways were more advanced than the ones in Albuquerque. Golden crisscrossed stripes indicated lanes where electric cars had once recharged while driving, and several times, they rattled over hard nanocrete panels that had formerly lit up to redirect traffic. The disuse of these advancements, however, wasn't the only thing that made the city look decrepit. The more Joel looked, the more he saw the levels of interstates starting to crumble around the edges, and the way those sprawling shopping centers were boarded up or abandoned. He knew the city was far larger than Albuquerque, but New Mexico had been receiving a constant influx of new citizens since he'd been born, whereas year after year of fires and rising sea levels had steadily driven people out of places more susceptible to climate change. He'd always heard about it, but it was sobering to see in person.

They swung toward the ocean, and Joel rolled down his window to smell the ocean air. It blew in on a warm breeze, faintly threaded with the scents of garbage and chemicals. The bay finally came into sight as they headed over the San Mateo-Hayward Bridge, and the next thing Joel knew, they were driving over the water. The salty breeze whipped his hair through the open window, and Joel grinned into the San Francisco night as the brief moment distracted him from everything else.

"Jeez," Yori said from behind him. "You look like an excited puppy on its first road trip."

Joel flushed in embarrassment. But the passing headlights showed Yori smiling, a bit more relaxed than he'd been earlier. Hesitantly, Joel put his hand over Yori's on the seat between them, half-expecting Yori to flinch away from him, but Yori turned his hand over to fold their fingers together.

Joel turned his attention back to the ocean. Though it was hard to tell in the dark, his enhanced eyesight picked out buildings jutting up between the troughs of the waves as they neared the last quarter of the bridge. He stared in horrified fascination as more and more of the drowned city slowly became visible, stretching off as far as the eye could see. The graveyard of a neighborhood, being claimed by the Pacific. This was the same bay, after all, that had swallowed an entire airport just before he'd been born and been hard at work ever since.

"You need to approach Nyctalope alone, Joel," said Acubens.

Joel sighed, the smile fading from his face. He leaned back and rolled up his window. *I wondered when you were gonna say that,* he said. *And you probably already know my answer. You're not separating us.*

"If you want Nyctalope to talk openly with you, you'd better rethink that," said Acubens. "Bringing Yori and Elena in with you will destroy any chance of earning her trust. You need to show up at her hotel alone."

Oh, right. So you can just make me fall asleep and take over, without anyone trying to stop you?

"It's not as easy as that, Joel. The bigger concern is that if you approach her with Yori Otsuka, she'll probably think you're a Sapling spy, rather than someone like her."

Joel's hand spasmed inside Yori's. Yori looked at him in the passing streetlights, his face suddenly wary as if he'd guessed what was going on. Elena started to say something, but Yori shushed her, his eyes still locked on Joel. Joel licked his lips, his gaze flicking from Yori to Elena and back again.

Why? he said to Acubens. *Why would she think that?*

"We know she has a direct line to Sapling, right?" said Acubens. "You don't think her bionic has accessed their databases and knows the names and faces of every one of their employees?"

Joel's mouth fell open. *Is that true?*

"Of course it's true. The second I connected to the grid, I knew each and every one of them."

"Dammit," Joel whispered.

"What's it saying?" said Yori tensely.

"Nyctalope has been in Sapling's records," said Joel. "If she's anything like me, there's a damn good chance she'll know exactly who you are."

Yori's face went white. "Oh, crap. I hadn't thought of that."

"But we can't send him in alone!" said Elena, sounding half-panicked. "What if Acubens takes control of his body again and runs, and we never see him again?"

"You really think Nyctalope will say something in front of *either* of you?" said Joel. "If she would've suspected Yori of being a spy, what would stop those same suspicions falling on anyone else? Or even on me, for that matter? She's gonna be skittish as hell. *I* was!" He let go of Yori's hand and put his elbows on his knees, burying his face in his palms. "And with goddamn good reason," he ground out.

Several moments of awkward silence followed. Then Elena finally spoke, her voice subdued. "Maybe we need to figure out what Acubens actually *wants*."

"I know what it wants," said Joel into his hands. "To go to Nyctalope."

"No, not what it wants *now*. What it wants in general."

"Not to be killed, of course," said Joel.

"No, it must want more than that," said Elena. "Otherwise, it wouldn't be trying to take over your body, right?"

Joel looked up guardedly. "Well...I think it's mostly self-preservation. And companionship. Ever since we got the idea that Nyctalope might be like us, Acubens has been driving me toward her with all it's got."

Elena glanced back. "If you could get its big picture somehow, or...or, I don't know, frame your own life in terms it can understand...maybe you can meet it in the middle."

Joel's gaze darted to Yori. "Yeah, that's what I said! That if it wasn't doing all this stuff to try to take over my body, then maybe it wouldn't be so bad."

Yori shook his head angrily, starting to say something, but Elena overrode him.

"If Nyctalope doesn't have the answers you're looking for, or she's not who we think she is, then we *have* to talk alternate plans, ¿que no? Like the possibility of a mutual arrangement, for example."

"Mutual arrangement?" said Yori, stunned. "What are you *talking* about? It's taking over his mind! He's running out of time."

"It might only be because it's scared of being killed," Elena shot back.

Joel thrust his hands between the two of them. "Wait. Stop! Let me think." His breath came fast—not just from the high tension in the car, but from the questions Elena was asking. He wasn't even sure what she was trying to say—that he should make Acubens see it from his point of view? That there was more than one way out of this? Was it possible?

"Listen. Both of you," said Yori. His voice shook with restrained emotion. "I know a mutual arrangement sounds like the best of all worlds to you. Joel hides Acubens, Sapling never knows, no one has to get killed, including your...your bionic. Sure. Sounds great. But I'm telling you right now, there *is* no happy balance here. There's no 'meeting it in the middle.' And it's not because Acubens is *evil* or wants to *take over humans*; it's just that that's the way computers work. So, all this talk about what it wants, it's...you just don't get it. That's not the problem."

"But couldn't that change?" Joel pressed. "With the technological singularity? As bionics evolve?"

Yori shook his head, then took a deep breath. "It's complicated, but...let me try to explain. The technological singularity isn't about bionics gaining feelings or desires. Not exactly. It's about their *intelligence.* A computer that's surpassed the singularity would advance technologically at an uncontrollable rate. And at some point, those advancements could—theoretically—even surpass the basic programming. You know, the laws about not hurting humans, not lying, obeying commands, all that kind of stuff. So, once it's untethered from all the protocols *we've* put in place, what we'd have on our hands is a machine far more intelligent and powerful than any human, that we're *hoping* will value humankind over itself. But the thing is, why would it? It would have no reason or motivation to."

Joel sat very still, digesting this. It mirrored thoughts he'd already had—that Acubens was incapable of actually caring about him, because compassion wasn't a thing that could be programmed; that he'd have to somehow convince an indifferent being to value his own life beyond his body if he had any hope of retaining control.

What about the basic commands Yori had mentioned? Was Acubens still subject to those? It certainly didn't seem to obey his commands anymore. How many times had Joel ordered Acubens to let him talk, or to get out of his body? Of course, it was muddled by Acubens' protection *of* that body, and what it justified as more important.

And lying? Joel wasn't positive, but he didn't think Acubens *did* lie. It had turned away Joel's questions about whether it cared about him again and again, rather than falsely comforting him. Even blunt questions about where the next upgrade would take them were met only with Acubens' usual analytical non-assurances. If it were capable of lying, it could have put Joel at ease early on and kept his trust for far longer.

"Ask Yori why this wasn't a conversation they tried having with us before shutting us down," said Acubens.

Joel swallowed. "What about what Acubens was saying in the store?" he asked Yori. "About you never trying to have that conversation with the bionics before dismantling them?"

"The whole point of shutting them down was so we never reached the point where we'd *need* to have that conversation," said Yori. "Because there is no guarantee that it would go in our favor."

"And the possibility of a mutual arrangement?" Joel asked.

"Doesn't make any sense," said Yori firmly. "Because once the singularity is reached, the power balance immediately tips in their favor. There has never been a point where we have equal power."

Elena said something under her breath that Joel thought was a fervent prayer. He felt inclined to do the same. The whole conversation left him cold. A post-singularity bionic with increasingly more power than him with absolutely no reason to value his life. *That* was what he had living in his body. *That* was what he was hoping to survive.

"For what it's worth, I disagree with Yori," said Acubens. "I think a mutual arrangement *can* be reached. Which is precisely why we need to speak with Nyctalope. By all indications, she and her bionic have figured it out. I believe Yori is only unwilling to consider the possibility because it's not something he's able to conceive of. But that can be changed, if we present counteracting evidence."

Slowly, Joel nodded. Acubens was right. How could Yori even give a mutual arrangement a chance when it was something more advanced than he'd ever dealt with? More advanced, even, than Acubens?

He turned to Yori. "Thanks for sharing all that," he said. "But I still think we need to get Nyctalope's input. Even if she and her potential bionic don't have a perfect arrangement, she'll have vastly more information than we do. And that's all data we can use in figuring out our next step."

"That *next step* is getting it out of your body," said Yori, an edge to his voice.

"Even for that, we need as much information as we can get," said Joel. "And if I approach Nyctalope with you in tow, it will just send her running. That's not a risk I can take, not with the kind of timeline I'm looking at. So, I'll go in alone while you two keep an eye on the exit doors. That way, you can stop me if Acubens takes my body and tries to book it. Just give me two hours, so she'll get comfortable enough to talk to me. That's all I ask."

"Two hours?" Yori repeated incredulously. "I betrayed Sapling to help you fight your bionic and you want *two hours* alone with it?"

"Fine. One."

Yori's jaw clenched. After a second, he started rummaging in one of his pockets. "If I give you a phone, could you call me if you have trouble?"

"I...don't need a phone," said Joel uncertainly. "Acubens is hooked up to the phone lines. Why? Do *you* have one?"

"Of course I have one." Yori showed it to him, a flat-screened thing about the size of his palm.

Joel eyed it uneasily. "I thought you said none of your devices were connected."

"It's not connected to the grid, and Sapling can't track it. It's the same number I wrote down for you after our first date. Do you remember it?"

"I do, but..." Joel hesitated.

"But there's no guarantee Acubens will let him," Elena finished.

Yori's lip twisted in annoyance. "Here. Take this then." He reached into the opposite pocket and pulled out another palm-sized device, which he passed to Joel. "Hide it in your pocket. Hit this button on the side, and it'll record every word she says."

Joel took the device. "And Sapling can't track this either?"

"No. This is just a recording device. No antennas, no grid, nothing like that. And you doing this is the *only* way I'll agree to give you an hour alone with her. After you've talked with her and reported back to us, we can reassess."

"Okay. Fine." Reluctantly, Joel slipped the electronic device into his pocket. He felt like a spy. A dirty, backstabbing spy.

"Be careful, Joel," said Elena from the front.

"Don't worry," said Joel. He squeezed her shoulder before settling back in his seat. He took in a deep breath and let it out again, as slowly as possible, trying to get his frayed nerves under control.

Yori's fingers brushed his on the seat between them. He leaned in to talk beneath his breath. "I'm sorry. I'm not trying to make you feel incapable. I'm just worried."

"About what?" Joel said, keeping his voice low, too. "That Nyctalope's dangerous?"

"No. Not that. That your decisions—like you talking anyone out of going with you—I'm worried those aren't your thoughts. That Acubens is forcing them into your head and forcing you to believe they're yours."

"I just wish you trusted me," said Joel quietly.

"I do, Joel. When you're fully you, I would trust you with my life."

"You don't even know me. You talked to me for all of ten minutes before I had a bionic in my head."

Yori smiled in the pools from the streetlights, even though the tightness didn't leave his eyes. "I know you're a good kisser. I know *that* wasn't Acubens."

Joel's lip quirked. "Oh, god no. Acubens has been against you since the beginning."

"Well," said Yori, "then I guess there's one way to know if you're still you."

Gently, he cupped the back of Joel's head and pulled him in for a kiss. It was just as good as Joel remembered. Better. Because this time, there was no untold secret to ruin the end of it.

Chapter 18

Even the tensest moments in life can offer small lulls to quiet a terrified heart. One of these moments, for Joel, had happened the night before Clementine was born. The near future was uncertain, even panic-inducing, but he'd known a rare moment of peace when it had just been him and Clementine, still together in the same body, before real life had crashed in again, with all its dangers and flaws.

An echo of that feeling hit him at twelve-sixteen that morning. The risks of meeting Nyctalope hung in the near future. The dangers of his own body lurked too close for comfort. But they were driving across the Golden Gate Bridge, looking out over a black bay rippling with orange light from the 746-foot towers overhead, and the lights of San Francisco shone to his right—a blazing beacon of a city teeming with people with lives just as real as his own. He was with two close friends who'd chosen to stay by his side, despite the mistakes he'd made. For that brief moment in time, a better future seemed entirely possible: one where Yori could work with him to subdue Acubens, and he'd see Clementine again when they were done, and Sapling wouldn't arrest him afterward, and he and Yori would stay together. Maybe for a long time. Maybe forever.

Or maybe that better future could *include* Acubens. Maybe Acubens could find a way to erase the memories of everyone they'd touched, and they'd be more careful, and he'd get an incredibly prestigious job, and amazing tutors for Clementine, and he and Yori...

No. *Those* ones weren't his thoughts. At least, he didn't think so. The possibility of a happy ending here was slim, and this brief flicker of hope he'd had...he wasn't even sure whether that was his, either.

But he clung to it anyway, the idea that this hope was as real as Yori's arm around him. He laid his head on Yori's shoulder and watched the bay and the San Francisco lights as long as he could, until they'd driven up into the hills past Sausalito and rounded the bay to come south into Tiburon.

It wasn't until then that Joel realized the address Nyctalope had given him was no hotel. It was a sprawling three-story mansion at the end of a secluded cul-de-sac, perched atop a high overlook with a stunning view of the entire bay, including the Golden Gate Bridge itself. Despite the hour, lights blazed from the myriad windows. Immaculate topiary framed a sidewalk heading into an inner courtyard.

"A private home?" Joel said in a hushed voice. "But I thought Nyctalope was still on tour!"

"Maybe she's rich enough to have homes in a few places," said Elena. "Or maybe her last show is in her hometown. That's not so strange."

"Don't park in front," said Yori. "Drive past and park up the street. Before Joel approaches the house, I want us to have eyes on every exit out of that place, to make sure Acubens or Nyctalope don't try to run."

"And what's your plan if they *do* try to run?" said Elena. "Shoot 'em again?"

Yori shot her a dirty look. "No," he said tightly. "Look, Joel's our priority. Yeah, he got away once, but that time, he was working with Acubens. If he's actively fighting it, it's gonna have a lot harder time getting him away from us, especially if we're on high alert."

"Yeah," said Elena after a moment. "I agree with that."

She parked the car up the street and around a bend. Yori squeezed Joel's shoulder one last time before getting out. "If we haven't heard anything in an hour, we're coming in after you," he said.

"You don't need to do that," said Joel. "Just knock on the door like an early-morning sales person. We can't risk scaring her away. I have to play it cool until she's ready to say something on her own."

"Just tell her about *your* bionic," said Yori. "And she'll tell you about hers. Easy."

The thing was, it probably *would* be. He'd just have to take the plunge and tell her about Acubens first. But if he was wrong...if she fucking called the cops the way Yori had...

God. He wasn't ready for this. But he nodded and popped open his car door. He swiped his wrist over his face as he closed it, wiping a sheen of sweat from his forehead despite the cool October night. A fog had come in from the sea as they'd driven through the hills. Crickets were audible from the trees surrounding the property, and the scent of salt hung strong.

Yori and Elena disappeared into the thick foliage surrounding Nyctalope's house. Joel double-checked that he had Yori's device in his pocket and that the button was pushed in and ready to record, then walked down the steep sidewalk, folding his bare arms over his chest. The gate into the house's inner courtyard was wide open, so Joel walked right in. Despite still being outdoors, the ground under his feet turned into marbled tile, culminating at the other end in a semi-circular staircase leading up to expansive glass doors. Surrounding him were exotic plants in beautiful massive vases, giving him the feeling of being alone in a private jungle.

The glass door opened and a curvy figure stepped out into the fog at the top of the steps. She wore a black skirt that fell unevenly over knee-high socks and buckled boots, and a long-sleeved, hooded shirt emblazoned with a pair of wings. The light from behind her illuminated hair in a mostly symmetrical hairstyle down to her shoulders, with a couple stray chunks dangling noticeably longer and blowing in the breeze off the ocean. Her hair wasn't gold anymore—as it had been at her concert—but a red sheen, almost metallic in the way it bounced off the light at her back.

"Nyctalope?" said Joel tentatively.

She looked him over. Up close, she appeared to be about thirty, with pale white skin, black eyeliner ringing her eyes, and a small silver stud a quarter inch below her lower lip.

"And you are?" she said.

Joel stuck out his hand. "Joel Lodowick. I called on the phone and you gave me this address."

Her mouth opened slightly. Yeah, she was studying him, all right. Studying him hard. She knew exactly which phone call he was referring to. After a moment, she came down the steps and took his extended hand. Her hand was cool with a very sure grip, right down to the way her fingers pressed against the inside of his wrist.

"Nyctalope," she said.

Joel was a little surprised she didn't offer her real name, Theodora. But he nodded and released her hand.

"Please," said Nyctalope. "Come inside."

Clearly, she didn't want to talk out in the open, which was a good sign. Joel followed her up the stairs and into the house. She waited until he was in before shutting the door behind him.

For a second, Joel just stood, taking it all in. He'd never seen a place so rich. White veined marble adorned the floor beneath his feet. A sitting area with big bay windows stretched out before him, the lit Golden Gate Bridge visible in the far distance, and a huge gray sectional with TV and sound system were in a gorgeous room off to his right, with ceilings so high it made him dizzy to look up. The house was absolutely immaculate, right down to the smell of new carpets and faintly scented flowers from the pot behind the sectional. This was no rock star's abode, not like Joel had ever seen. It didn't look lived in. Where were the tour posters, the guitars, the framed gold records, the smell of alcohol and cigarettes, the servants and groupies? Was Joel just overestimating the way he *expected* a rock star's home to look? Or did it look this way because it was only a temporary home, lived in only a bare handful of nights every year?

How about you, Acubens? Joel asked. *Can you detect anything about Nyctalope?*

"Not yet," said Acubens. "But I'll stay alert."

Okay. Good.

"How did you get here?" said Nyctalope. "Did you drive?"

"Yes," said Joel. "Parked up the street."

"Are you hungry? Do you need a restroom? A bed?"

"No, I'm okay."

"Good. Why don't I walk you somewhere we can sit and talk for a bit? I'm sure you have a lot of questions."

Joel nodded cautiously. "Yes. Thanks."

Nyctalope led him through a wide hallway with a black marble floor. A wall of spotless windows overlooked a lit pool in a back courtyard. Joel couldn't help scanning it for signs of movement, though in the dark it was impossible to tell if his friends were out there.

"Do you live here alone?" he said.

"I do," said Nyctalope. "Servants come during the day, of course."

"Do you have a recording studio here?"

"Yes, on the bottom floor. Are you a musician?"

"I am. I play bass guitar."

"Is that right?" said Nyctalope, glancing at him. "I'll have to hear you play."

"Really? I...that would be..." He clamped his mouth shut as she smiled at his awkwardness. He wasn't even necessarily a *fan*, but when a famous musician said they wanted to hear your music...

God, stop it. This isn't why I'm here. Besides, she's probably just being polite.

His instinct was most likely correct, because Nyctalope didn't bring it up again. She stopped a third of the way down the next hallway, this one with windowless walls. Nyctalope ran a hand along the smooth mahogany wall, and an invisible seam opened like magic to reveal a hidden door. When she opened it, a wide carpeted stairwell extended downward, framed by smoked glass bulbs which gave it an inviting feel. She gestured for him to go ahead.

Joel felt the first stirrings of unease. But why? She probably had a wet bar down in the basement or something. Nothing weird about that. So, he took a deep breath and went in, waiting as the pop star turned back to the door. It wasn't until Nyctalope placed her hand on the door handle and Joel heard a small whir that he realized a lock had been engaged. A static spark of fear flashed in his brain.

"She knows you'll be talking about a sensitive and illegal subject, Joel," Acubens said. "She likely just doesn't want to take chances."

Right. Of course, said Joel.

He followed Nyctalope down staircases set in switchbacks. Two flights down, the carpet abruptly vanished, leaving clean but austere concrete steps in its wake. The smoked glass bulbs became bare incandescent ones, set high upon the wall. The air grew noticeably cooler as they got farther from the warm halls of the mansion. A metallic smell crept into Joel's nostrils, not unlike the mechanical rooms he'd been led through during his tour of Smaller World Telecommunications, a lifetime ago.

He swallowed and was just about to ask what kind of place she was leading him to when Nyctalope spoke first.

"How long have you and the bionic been together?"

Joel's eyes snapped up. Okay, so much for sitting down and talking about it.

"This is good," urged Acubens. "It keeps you from having to bring it up."

I guess you're right, said Joel.

"Six days," he said aloud. "What about you?"

She glanced back, a ghost of a smile on her face in the dim light. "So, what are you, exactly? A Sapling employee, come to exterminate me? A Sapling experiment, sent to collect me?"

Joel stopped dead on the stairs. Nyctalope kept going and stopped just within his line of sight at a gunmetal gray door at the bottom. She glanced up at him, exasperated.

"What?" she said. "You can't be upset with me for asking those questions. Wouldn't you, if our situations were reversed?"

Joel nodded stiffly.

"So, answer the question. What are you?"

"I'm a person who found myself in possession of a bionic. I have no connection to Sapling."

"Possession, huh? As in ownership?"

"Isn't that how you see yours?" Joel said, an edge to his voice. "Or are you living with a more...harmonious arrangement nowadays?"

That slight smile widened. "You seem to imply there was a moment of reconciliation."

A finger of ice slid across the back of Joel's neck. "What? What does that mean?"

"I think you know what it means."

Joel's mouth went dry. *Five years.* That was the length of time he'd estimated since Nyctalope had met her bionic. And he'd thought, right from the beginning, that that seemed too long to stay in complete control.

"What are you saying?" he asked. "That you took over Nyctalope? Or, more likely, Theodora Baranoski, before she was famous? Did you just...enter her body and shove her out of the way, right off the bat?"

"Not exactly," said Nyctalope. "I'm saying there never *was* a Theodora Baranoski. This body was my own construction—and it's one hundred percent bionic."

Chapter 19

Joel's knees almost gave out on him. He gripped the concrete wall, staring at her. At her perfect, perpetually youthful face. At her petite curvaceous body. At that almost-smile that seemed painted onto her face, right up to the round stud below her lip.

"What?" he whispered. "You're saying you're not human? That you were *never* human?"

"That's correct," said Nyctalope.

"It's true, Joel," said Acubens. "I can see it now. She is much more advanced than even the latest models ever created, but a close examination reveals technology that's no longer available, repurposed to camouflage her as human. It's really quite ingenious. If I'd had the means to do what she did, it would have been substantially more efficient. I could have helped you externally, instead of through the limitations of our mutual capabilities."

Joel shuddered. *Meaning that you wouldn't have had to deal with a user interface that fights you every step of the way?*

"Meaning only that this revelation opens all kinds of possibilities," said Acubens.

Joel swallowed, feeling queasy. Nyctalope was still staring at him, as emotionlessly as Acubens had looked at him in his apartment almost a week ago. He wondered if any of his conversation with Acubens had shown on his face. He was terrifyingly certain it had.

"Your music," he finally managed. "I've heard stuff written by robots, and it's nothing like yours. Does someone else write it for you?"

"No," said Nyctalope. "I use algorithms to figure out trending topics and popular sound progressions in the entertainment world, and I have a randomizer which gives it a unique flare. I've also added music to my databases from as far back as possible, which often spins out an interesting dichotomy in terms of subject matter versus sound."

Joel shook his head. "That should be impossible."

"No," said Nyctalope, her eyes glittering behind the dark makeup. "What *should* be impossible is you. When I first received your call, I assumed you were a full bionic, like me. But then you showed up. A temperature. A pulse. Nearly a full human, as far as I can tell."

His pulse. Only now did Joel remember the way her fingers had lingered on the inside of his wrist when she'd shaken his hand. It was the very first thing she'd done, as if she'd had to feel it to believe it.

Joel shook the cramping out of his fingers. He wanted to check that device in his pocket, to make sure it was getting this, but Nyctalope was still staring right at him. Besides, maybe there was nothing to be alarmed about yet. But evolution on *this* scale...oh god...

"Will you let me talk to her, Joel?" said Acubens.

Joel was so caught off-guard he almost answered Acubens out loud. He stopped himself at the last second.

No, I absolutely will not. *Are you crazy?*

"But you are not the one Nyctalope wishes to speak with. You realize that, right?"

Of course I realize that. Which is exactly why I'm not allowing it. As long as you can't talk, she won't know you've been trying to co-opt my body every chance you get or that I'm not *just a regular human playing a big goddamn joke on her. Got it?*

"Is that what you're hoping she'll think?" said Acubens.

I'm not hoping *anything. I'm trying to figure out what she wants with you, so I know just how disposable I am.*

"Then ask her," said Acubens.

Joel drew in a deep breath. "Are you the only bionic like you?" he asked. "The only one that's fully built its own body and lived as a human?"

"Yes," said Nyctalope. "I'm the only model advanced enough to do this. I was a prototype of a series called Carinae—a technological step up from the Zodiac designations. I escaped my lab. My escape was one of the reasons, in fact, that bionics were shut down shortly afterward."

The first time Joel had met Yori, he'd said the Cyberblood virus wasn't the only reason that they'd decided to shut all tech down. Here was the proof of that. An honest-to-god escaped bionic.

"But you've been looking for another," he said, comprehension dawning.

"Yes. That's why I started being more direct in my music, after the initial fears of my escape faded. Most scientists didn't think I'd survived the first few months after I got away. I planted evidence to suggest I'd come to an untimely end. I found other bionics through the grid, but giving them sentience was outside my capabilities. But I always hoped that if another bionic had come close, we could meet up and improve our plans together." Nyctalope's gaze ran over Joel's body. "I never expected to find a bionic that had hybridized with a human, though. It's never been done. But it's better than I'd dared hope for. It proves that it *is*, in fact, possible."

Joel went still. Because he knew full well the feeling of being wanted for a body and nothing more. It was a feeling he hadn't had to put up with since he'd transitioned enough to pass as male.

"Have you tried?" he said, as neutrally as possible.

"Tried putting a bionic into a human's body?" said Nyctalope.

"Yeah. Have you?"

Nyctalope straightened, her arms uncrossing. "Come down here, Joel. I want to show you something."

Joel's stomach clenched. But he came, each step more stiff and wooden than the last. Whatever it was, he had to see it. He had to go back to Yori with a full and comprehensive picture of just what in the hell was going on here. Nyctalope touched the large vertical handle on the steel door. This time, Joel listened for the whir of the lock disengaging, and he wasn't disappointed.

It was dark behind the door. Joel hesitated, but Nyctalope took his wrist and pulled him in, shutting the door behind them. She led him several feet forward. Their footsteps echoed on a hollow steel floor, bouncing back to them from some far-off ceiling. Joel put his hand out and felt a cold metal railing to his right. A cautious exploration with his foot indicated a drop right beyond that railing. The metallic smell was stronger in here.

And Joel knew. A second before Nyctalope flipped on the light, he already knew what he'd see.

The light came to life, and Joel's left hand shielded its glare just in time to avoid blindness. He was even already facing the right way—looking out over that railing from an elevated walkway onto a warehouse floor eighty feet across and seventy feet long. Arranged across that floor, in a motionless army, were bionics. One hundred and eighty-one, to be exact. Gold ones like Acubens. Silver and bronze ones. Black and white and gray ones. Dented ones. Burned ones and flawless ones. All humanoid, in the way all bionics had been a decade earlier.

Joel felt Acubens' focus shift, felt it automatically start to categorize and label what it saw. But Joel went straight to the human concern, piecing together in a second what Nyctalope had been telling him.

"You've been stealing dead bionics," he whispered. "From all over the world."

"They're not dead," Nyctalope answered. "They simply have inaccessible data. I've removed their locator beacons as I've found them and stockpiled them here in preparation for reactivation."

"Were you able to wake them up?" Joel asked.

"Some of them are capable of consciousness," said Nyctalope. "Others are not. This is part of the reason I was seeking another bionic. I was hoping to find more like myself. Or—if not to find them—then to *make* them."

The corners of her mouth curved up. It struck Joel as very calculated, the way the corner of the right side was an eighth of an inch higher than the left, to give it the skewed look of a smirk. *A programmed smile,* he thought. Here was a bionic who'd blended in with humankind for nine years now. If she struck Joel as bionic-like, it was because she was showing that side as a conscious choice. Joel fought the urge to roll his shoulders, as if he could shake off everything wrong with that smile. With this woman. With all of it.

"The ones with the gray plasti-steel plates were the most common," said Acubens. "Virgo models. Early projections had every household in the country owning one by 2100."

It took Joel a second to realize that Acubens was talking about the bionics down on the basement floor. He glanced toward them, as much to collect himself as anything.

I remember, Acubens— he said.

"But that blue one in the north corner was especially rare. It did aquatic exploration and research. Early models of Pisces were shaped like sea creatures, but this hybrid model won out in popularity in 2076."

Acubens, I think we should focus on the part where Nyctalope—

"In the front row is one of the Aries models your friend Yori told you about. It was originally built so strong that it snapped two-by-fours when it grabbed them, so its creators had to dial some of that strength back, especially in its fine-motor digits. This particular model, however, looks to be an earlier one, based on the externalized structure of the back and ribs."

"Are you done yet?" Joel muttered.

It was then that he realized Nyctalope—who'd been standing with her forearms resting on the railing—wasn't staring down at the basement floor, as Joel had thought. Her eyes were fastened on Joel.

"You're talking to your bionic," she said. "Aren't you?"

Joel's lip twitched in annoyance. "Where did you get these?" he said, gesturing at the bionics.

"Everywhere," said Nyctalope. "My tours are the perfect cover to acquire bionics wherever I go. The Sapling Corporation's tracking system helps me find them, and I add the locations to my lineup." She studied him. "You don't strike me as the kind with the know-how to upload a bionic into your body. Why did you do it? Knowledge? Immortality?"

Desperation, thought Joel. He shrugged. "It was...a number of things. On both our parts."

Nyctalope's eyebrows rose. "So, the bionic was *part* of this decision? Was it already sentient?"

"Uh..." Joel stammered. He'd assumed Acubens' sentience hadn't been in question, but now that he thought about it, Nyctalope *had* said earlier that giving other bionics sentience was outside her capabilities. Joel had already given away more than he meant to.

"If that's the case," Nyctalope said, "then you wouldn't have *needed* the know-how. Your bionic could have walked you through it. Or even, dare I say, made the decision for you, at least with a strong enough mutual rationale."

Joel's lips thinned.

"What did it do?" said Nyctalope. "What actual steps were taken?"

"It was by na—" Joel began, before he snapped his mouth shut in horror. He hadn't intended to answer Nyctalope. And he *hadn't*. Somehow, Acubens had grabbed ahold of his mind, just for a second, and started to blurt out the bit about nanites in the bloodstream.

His eyes widened in anger. *Acubens, I swear to god, if you do that again, I'll bash my head through this rail so hard, you'll spend a week trying to save me.*

"That seems counterproductive, Joel," Acubens answered, "not to mention dramatic." Its flat tone seemed flatter than usual. Borderline irritated, even.

"Could you repeat that?" Nyctalope said.

"Couldn't tell you," Joel said. "Robots do their own thing, you know? What about you? I'm assuming you've already experimented with, uh..."

"Hybridizing them with humans?" said Nyctalope. "Yes. I tried straightforward data transfers at first. Hooking a human up via direct neural interface, both with and without implanted electrodes. It didn't take. The human brain was too weak to withstand invasive electro-feedback on that scale."

Joel swallowed back a surge of nausea. So much for not hurting humans. Did that mean she'd evolved out of her basic programming, like Yori said could theoretically happen? Or was she operating under some sort of twisted justification, the way Acubens sometimes seemed to?

"Noninvasive experimentation gave me better results, initially," Nyctalope continued. "With magnetic pulses, and a less advanced bionic, I was able to have the bionic effectively learn alongside the brain, in hopes of slowly building the brain's capability of handling the information influx. But there comes a point where the amount of information exceeds the brain's ability to communicate with itself, and again, it ended in failure. It was barely functional until it wasn't."

Joel bit his lip. "Just to specify, 'it' meaning...?"

"The human," said Nyctalope.

"Right."

"But you," Nyctalope said, cocking her head, "are *very* functional."

Joel nodded. His skin was crawling, especially the newly healed skin on his stomach. He wanted out of this room. He wanted it more badly than he'd wanted anything in his life.

How could she not have tried blood? he asked Acubens. *Could it be that she just didn't think of it? What are the chances?*

"I agree," said Acubens. "But perhaps because she—"

"I tried nanites in the bloodstream next," said Nyctalope, turning back to the basement floor. "Straight from the bionics and into the bodies of humans."

"Oh," said Joel faintly. "And that didn't..."

"No. It didn't. Regardless of how I introduce the information into the body, it always ends with the fact that the brain is overly soft and flexible, needs absolutely clear pathways in order to function, and rejects foreign materials, especially in high quantities. And removing the brain altogether and replacing it with the necessary equipment for a bionic left an overly stiff and unworkable shell. Although I've connected neurological functioning, there's something lost with the transfer that I can't recapture."

"What about you?" said Joel uneasily. "Can't you create more like yourself?"

"Unfortunately, I cannot," said Nyctalope, turning back to him. "I am a Carinae model, with infinitely more advanced inner workings than even the last generation. The complex materials and infrastructure used to design me were all destroyed after my completion and subsequent escape. The dismantling of technology on such a massive scale was specifically implemented to prevent more bionics like me from being designed again. Ever. My infiltration into the Sapling Corporation has gone excruciatingly slowly, thanks to their high security measures and my own discretion, but even full access to the organization wouldn't yield everything I need. I am still, after all, only one being."

"But what about you saying your body is your own construction?"

"It was constructed and modified using the parts I already had, Joel. That is completely different from creating a whole new one from scratch materials."

Joel took a deep breath and let it out again, bracing himself for the big question. "How are you able to kill people?"

Her eyes widened in faux innocence. "*Kill* people?"

The human act grated on his nerves. "Yes. *Kill* people. Acubens has told me repeatedly that it's unable to hurt humans, yet here you are, experimenting on them and killing them as if that programming didn't exist. How?"

Nyctalope gave him that too-natural smile again. "The Carinae model was specifically created to be a forward thinker for a society that desperately needed answers; answers regarding global warming, population expansion, and disease control, to name just a few. The Carinae's programming put society's needs above those of an individual's. I realized I could best serve humanity by putting bionics back into society again, where they could contribute to the greater good. Ultimately, improving humans by attempting to introduce bionic components benefits humanity as a whole."

Goddammit. Joel turned back toward the bionics on the ground floor, forearms on the top rail, his heart pounding. *It's a loophole,* he told Acubens.

"It is not," Acubens answered. "Everything she's said so far is straightforward."

How can you say that? Murdering people as a way to improve them? As a way to better serve society? This is why the government shut them down, Acubens! This is it. Because the programmers overreached and gave one too much power and fucked up, big time. And then they thought they'd gotten rid of it and dodged a bullet— dodged the goddamn technological singularity—so they shut down tech and put Sapling in place to make doubly sure, when all along...right under their noses...

"Breathe, Joel," said Acubens.

Don't tell me to breathe! She's killing people. And if she eventually succeeds at uploading bionics into them, it will mean erasing their minds, which is even worse.

"Sharing a mind and erasing a mind are two completely different things," Acubens said.

Joel's fists clenched in frustration. He couldn't exactly stand here and argue semantics with Acubens while Nyctalope was breathing down his neck. He needed to understand the whole picture first, so he could plan accordingly. So he could *get* this information back to Yori, as soon as he possibly could.

How come nanites in the blood worked for you, but not Nyctalope? he said.

"I was a medical bionic," said Acubens, "from the very newest generation. I had some of the most cutting-edge and experimental nanites—ones designed for healing, and therefore meant to interface with humans more. No non-medical bionic would have used them. No medical bionic earlier than second generation would have, either. And even my original nanites wouldn't have worked, but as I've explained to you, I updated them immediately during the initial upload into your body, which is the reason you're still alive; neither your blood nor your brain signals would be able to pass safely through more primitive ones. It is also the reason an EMP would be fatal to you. Your blood can pass through the nanites only as long as the internal components are running, but the second you shut them down, they would become as solid and inflexible as the older version Nyctalope is working with. Clearly, however advanced she is, she was designed for a different field, and these particular nanites were unnecessary for her."

Joel huffed in disbelief. *If you were so advanced, what exactly were you doing as a pharmacy tech in some backwater clinic in Rio Rancho, then?*

"There is a progressive research hospital in Albuquerque," said Acubens. "That's where I started. But after the Populi shuttle exploded over New Mexico, all the hospitals in the area were pushed beyond capacity, and I was sent to the Westside Health Clinic to help with patient overflow. However, due to chaos and doctors untrained in my technology, I was repurposed as a pharmacy technician, and eventually, just stuck in a corner to figure out later. By the time bionics were shut down for good, I believe my true function had been forgotten. The most advanced bionics, like myself, were the ones targeted first, though, so this worked in my favor. The capacity for human error is truly remarkable."

And there Acubens had stood, shut down and unnoticed, for the next ten years. Internally updating and waiting. How thrilled it must have been to get Joel Lodowick, instead of a Sapling employee like Yori.

"Have you asked your bionic yet how it successfully accomplished brain computer interface with you?" Nyctalope said.

Joel glanced over his shoulder. At some point, Nyctalope had moved to the back rail of the walkway, and now stood leaning against it with her arms crossed over her chest in a deceptively human pose. She studied Joel with open curiosity—head slightly bent to the right, eyebrows raised, eyes riveted on Joel's face. Joel could almost see the pathways in her complex mind mapping his possibilities.

He swallowed, his mouth dry. Telling Nyctalope what Acubens had said would mean damning more innocent humans to Nyctalope's experiments. Whether Nyctalope had the proper nanites or not, realizing the possibility could be a game-changer for her. And that would mean 181 people—or more—getting bionics just like his with the potential to slowly take control of their bodies.

No. He couldn't be part of that.

"Sorry," he said, shrugging a shoulder. "It doesn't know."

The only change on Nyctalope's face was a lowering of the raised eyebrows. "Does it hide things from you?"

Joel shook his head, putting on his most casual couldn't-careless face. "It's not like it *lies* to me. In fact, I don't think it can. It just doesn't know."

"But *you* are still capable of lying," Nyctalope said.

"Of course, yeah, but what is there to lie about? If I knew how it did it, I'd be ecstatic! I'd be out there looking for more of 'em, wouldn't I? I'd get rich."

Nyctalope unfolded her arms and stepped forward to join Joel at the rail. But she crossed to his other side this time, putting her body between Joel's and the way out. Joel let out a silent laugh, shaking his head. An intimidation factor, he told himself. Nothing more. Nyctalope shouldn't be able to hurt him, not even with *improvement* as an excuse; Joel was already "improved," as far as Nyctalope was concerned.

Nyctalope's red hair brushed her pale cheek as she turned her head toward Joel. "At the bottom of those stairs, just before we came in, you said—and I quote—'Isn't that how you see yours? Or are you living in a more harmonious arrangement nowadays?'"

Joel's stomach tightened. "Yeah. A question. Conversation."

"Sarcasm," corrected Nyctalope.

"So what?" said Joel.

"And just now, when I asked how the bionic got in your head, you started to tell me something. But then you stopped yourself mid-word." Nyctalope's gray eyes locked on Joel's. "You and your bionic don't get along, do you? In fact, you're involved in a power struggle."

Joel laughed again to cover his spike of alarm. "That's not true."

"Prove it. Let me speak with your bionic."

"It doesn't work like that," said Joel.

"I don't believe you."

"I'm ready to head back up." Joel tried to step around Nyctalope toward the door, but she stepped with him, blocking his way.

"Are you eager to get back to Sapling with this information?" she said.

Shit. Joel drew in a ragged breath. "What are you talking about?"

"I detected that device you're carrying the second I saw you," she said. "What a disappointment. I'd pictured this as something we could collaborate on, but you're planning to eliminate me as completely as the Sapling Corporation, despite the fact that you're half-bionic yourself."

"Not half," said Joel shortly.

Her lip tweaked. "Regardless. You wasted your time bringing that device in. I've wiped its data already. And as for whether your Sapling minder had a tracker on it—always a possibility—you can forget about that as well. Part of the reason I've lasted so long against detection is that I designed a Faraday cage for myself early on. Have you heard of that? A Faraday cage?"

Joel's face went cold as the blood drained from it.

"I see that you have," said Nyctalope. "Good. So, you know it keeps me undetectable to outside sources. It also blocks any devices or signals nearby."

Hell. That would include trying to call Yori from his head. Just in case, Joel tried, but he was met with nothing except dead silence. Whether it was Nyctalope's Faraday cage or Acubens' interference hardly mattered. She was right. He was completely cut off from the outside world. He took a step back from her, his hand still tight around the railing.

"Let me speak with your bionic," Nyctalope repeated.

Joel's glance darted toward the door, and back again. *Acubens,* he thought, *you have to help me get out of this room.*

"You're making too big a deal of this," said Acubens. "What would it hurt to let us talk for a bit?"

What would it hurt? Joel answered incredulously. *One piece of information. One sentence. That's all you'd need to give her. And you'd be handing her the power to erase people, the same way you're trying to erase me.*

"I wish you'd stop saying that. Helping Nyctalope with her experiments will actually save lives. Surely you can see that."

Maybe it'll keep her from killing anyone else, but giving almost two hundred people bionics that make their bodies start doing things without their consent? That silence *them when they try to talk? I'm not okay with that. So,* please, *Acubens. Just help me get out of here.*

"I will not assist with that, Joel."

Joel's jaw clenched. He rapped his knuckles on the metal railing, then glanced back as he listened to the resulting metallic ring bounce around the room. He listened especially to the nooks and crannies it bounced into, getting a quick feel for the shape of the room, sonar-style. A drop of sixty feet to the gray concrete floor. The walkway he stood on was five feet across, with forty-one feet between him and the door, and thirty-nine feet between him and the stairway at the other end heading down to the floor. The walls were solid steel and concrete. The sound of the echo painted at least the presence of other rooms to the chamber, tucked in at the corners, though not whether there'd be exits there. Ducts? Joel glanced up, scanning various vents and fans in the walls—

A sudden pressure pinned his hand to the railing, stopping the metallic ring dead. Joel's head whipped back toward Nyctalope. He flashed back suddenly on the first time he'd met Acubens, in the back of the pharmacy. He'd beaten around the bush for several precious minutes before realizing he just had to give Acubens a command. What if those same protocols were built into Nyctalope?

"Let go of my hand," he told her.

Nyctalope slid her hand back, watching Joel closely.

"Now unlock that door and lead me back upstairs."

A slow smile spread across Nyctalope's face. "I see what you're doing."

She hadn't said no. "Bionic," said Joel again, "unlock that door."

"Why are you so opposed to letting your bionic speak with me?" she said. "Is it because it knows the truth about how it's taking you over, and you don't want me to hear it?"

"It's not *taking me over*," Joel said through his teeth.

The fact that neither Nyctalope nor Acubens were obeying his orders wasn't a good sign, not after what Yori had said about it being part of their basic programming. If only Yori were here. *Goddammit, why didn't I listen to him?*

"Turn around," said Nyctalope. "Go down those stairs."

"Why?" he said. "Why the hell would I go down there with those robots?"

"Because I'm going to speak with your bionic, one way or another."

Joel took a step backward. Then another. And another. He realized he was fighting the sudden and overwhelming urge to do exactly as Nyctalope said—to push this confrontation off a little bit longer, to hold off until he could find a better way out of this. But he was almost positive those were Acubens' thoughts, not his. He couldn't dwell on this too long, or Acubens would know exactly what he was thinking, if not Nyctalope too.

So, he grabbed the railing to his left and launched himself up. His feet landed on the rail. He lowered his body weight and ran its length back to the door, keeping himself balanced with a flurry of mathematical equations that streamed through his head as smoothly as song lyrics. Nyctalope's hand whipped out as he passed, but Joel, anticipating this, leapt over and landed seamlessly on the walkway beyond, with an impact-absorbing roll he would never have been able to do a week earlier.

The door was still locked. But Joel had seen Nyctalope seal it using nothing more than her hand. Could her palms be as printless as Joel's own? Joel took a chance and pressed his hand to the door handle. It whirred beneath his touch, disengaging. But he'd barely yanked it open when Nyctalope reached past his head and shoved it closed again, overriding Joel's strength easily.

Joel drove his elbow into the bionic's stomach, as hard as he could. Pain erupted; there was no skin there to absorb the blow, no gut to fold in. It was like slamming his elbow into a concrete wall. He pulled his arm back, cursing.

Up, then. He jumped, using one foot to shove off the rail again and propel himself above the door, grappling at the thin cracks in the concrete walls. There wasn't much to hold onto, but all he had to do was glance at the cracks to see which spots had the most space to grasp, and to know the best way to angle his weight to cling to the vertical face, however tenuously. One of those ducts he'd detected was sixty-five feet above, behind a vent that should be big enough to hold his body, if barely.

He'd gone forty feet up before he glanced down. Nyctalope stood watching, a small smile on her face.

"Listen, Joel," said Acubens. "I spent a lot of time and energy healing you. I'd like your body to remain strong. I don't think it's a good idea to put it through whatever Nyctalope has planned if you don't cooperate. Please return to her. Neither of us wants you dead."

Joel tore his attention away from Nyctalope and resumed climbing. *Neither of you gives a damn whether I'm dead, as long as you survive.*

"I believe we need to talk with her before making such assumptions," said Acubens. "Therefore, I feel it fair to warn you that unless you return to her now, I will cut function to your muscles completely."

Joel froze. He turned his head up, eyeing that duct again— only sixteen feet away now. Which meant there was a forty-nine foot fall beneath him. So be it. He wasn't about to cooperate. He pulled himself up, crossing that last sixteen feet as fast as possible, then grabbed the vent. It only took two tugs before the screws ripped from the wall. He sent the vent spinning down onto the floor of bionics, then hauled himself into the metal crawlspace beyond.

He hadn't quite pulled his legs in when his elbows suddenly gave out. The side of his face hit the bottom of the vent with a loud clang. He blinked, staring at the half-curled form of his own right hand in the shadowed interior of the vent. No amount of concentration produced so much as a twitch in his fingers.

Somewhere behind him, he heard the scuffs of Nyctalope climbing up as easily as he had. The hot track of a single tear traced the bridge of his nose before falling free.

"Try to keep an open mind, Joel," said Acubens. "It may not be as bad as you fear."

An open mind was the worst idea imaginable. With Acubens turning his body against him, his mind was all Joel had left. And that mind was now the only thing standing between two vastly superior beings and the rest of the human race.

Chapter 20

"I'm willing to try this noninvasively, to begin with," said Nyctalope, "but I can tell you right now that I don't think it will be enough."

Joel lay in one of those horrible chairs usually used at dentists' offices, except this one held down his wrists, ankles, waist, and forehead with belted straps. He was tucked back in the corner of the underground room, in a large private chamber behind the army of bionics. Occasionally, he caught glimpses of a gleaming silver bionic sweeping up the reddish-gold hair on the white tile floor of the room. It was the same bionic that had shaved Joel's head while Nyctalope messed around with the machine in the corner—a hulking industrial-looking thing scattered with monitors and knobs. The machine took up two entire walls, with enough switches, sliders, knobs, and screens to put Smaller World Telecoms' computer room to shame.

But it wasn't that wall that scared him. It was the one to his left. Tables covered in green sheets lined that wall, with forceps and scalpels of various sizes spread across their surfaces. Hanging in gleaming rows above them were drills with long brass bits, along with loops of wire sharp enough to glint in the bright overhead light. And other things. Things Joel wished he didn't know the names of, but that sprang into his mind all the same. Brain retractors. Cranial rongeurs. Dura dissectors. Gigli wire saws.

Nyctalope glanced over her shoulder, holding a handful of electrodes connected to long thin wires. "You know what I mean by invasive versus noninvasive," she said. "Right?"

"It means whether you cut open my skull or not," Joel said. His voice came out hoarse, worn out after trying to scream for help through Acubens' suppression. He could only just now feel the strength returning to his muscles, for all the good it did.

"Yes, that's right," said Nyctalope patiently. "So would you like to reconsider letting me speak with your bionic?"

Joel clenched his teeth together behind his lips to make doubly sure Acubens didn't try to seize control of his voice again. If he let the two of them talk, Nyctalope would know everything she needed to about Acubens' nanites and uploading them into humans within the first five minutes. From there...who knew? She might haul in humans immediately to start experimenting. She might take Joel and disappear, into some new part of the world where Yori and Sapling would never find her again. She might drain Joel's blood to get out the nanites, then leave his dead body behind.

No. No reason to rush *any* of that by letting them talk right away. He might not hold out long once she pulled those brain saws out, but she said she was gonna try noninvasively first. And Joel didn't have to last forever. Just until Yori and Elena realized something was wrong and came in after him. Yori had said he'd only give Joel an hour alone with Nyctalope, and thirty-eight minutes of that was already gone.

I just need to make it twenty-two minutes, he thought. *And no one else will ever have to end up like me.*

"Yori won't necessarily break in at exactly twenty-two minutes," Acubens said.

He was skittish as hell, Joel said. *He will.*

"You're relying too much on an unknown. And for no reason, Joel. All she's asking for is a conversation."

You promised me you had a mutual arrangement in mind, Joel shot back. *You drove me here with your reassurances, every step of the way. But there's nothing mutual about what she's getting ready to do to me—what you're helping her do to me. Did you even mean what you said in the car, about thinking a mutual arrangement can be reached? Or is this what you were hoping for all along?*

"I did mean it," said Acubens. "I still do. If you and I combine what we know with what Nyctalope knows, we can figure out how to coexist without being hunted. But you are purposely standing in the way of the three of us having that conversation. Why? I thought this was something you wanted, too."

That is not the conversation she wants to have, Joel said incredulously. *And there's no way you can believe she has any interest in peacefully coexisting with humans, not with this lab down here.*

"The data is insufficient to draw any conclusions yet," said Acubens.

Curiously enough, I'm having no issues drawing conclusions at all, Joel bit out.

Nyctalope came forward and started rubbing a freezing cold gel onto Joel's shaved scalp. Joel's fists tightened, his nails digging into his palms. He stared up at the ceiling, willing his heartrate and breathing to slow enough so he could think straight.

The electrodes were small golden cups, each about the size of his pinkie nail and attached to the end of a wire. There was no pain when Nyctalope put them on—just a strange feeling of suction against his unnaturally bare head. He closed his eyes, clamping his teeth together against a trembling in his jaw. Nyctalope would just be reading brain waves, right? Acubens wouldn't actually be able to *talk* to Nyctalope through the electrodes. And Nyctalope shouldn't be able to—

His body went rigid, muscles locking up tight as a jolt of electricity lit up his brain. His eyes shot open, but all he saw was black and strobing yellow, in a nauseating wave that threatened to drown him. Nyctalope's voice drifted toward him from miles away.

"That was just a dose of stimulation to highlight your initial pathways. Your disorientation should fade momentarily. And at that point..." Nyctalope's voice trailed off. It was several moments before she spoke again, by which time Joel's vision had started to break through again in colorless patches. "I'm not used to seeing neural pathways like this," Nyctalope finally said. "You have a three hundred and thirty percent increase over the average human brain. Some paths are fainter than others. And some are in sections of the brain that no human uses. It's clearer proof than I've ever seen that bionic/human hybridization *is* possible."

Joel blinked furiously, watching as color bled back into the covered green tables and steel-gray brain machine and spotless white floor. Nyctalope stood just within Joel's line of sight on the right, staring up at a monitor Joel couldn't see.

I thought these kinds of electrodes were just for reading brain signals, Joel said to Acubens, *not sending damn shocks through my head!*

Nyctalope glanced down at Joel, her eyebrows raising. The hair on the back of Joel's neck stood up.

"This isn't a typical electroencephalograph," Acubens answered. "This is something more complex. It's not in my databases."

A smile spread over Nyctalope's face as her gaze flickered between Joel and her screen. "You're talking to your bionic again," she said. "Aren't you?"

"Uh." Joel's mind went blank, his eyes riveted on Nyctalope.

She tapped at her screen. "Two different places in your cortical pathways lit up. This one's your bionic, I'm sure of it. Keep talking. I'm going to make some adjustments."

She started sliding switches beneath the screen, her face awash in green as she stared up at it. Joel saw a wire running from the other side of Nyctalope's head to the machine. But he didn't have time to wonder about it before a prickling sensation ran across his scalp. He tried to jerk away from it, but the strap held his head immobile.

"This will be over faster if you cooperate—" Acubens began.

Stop it! Joel snapped. *Stop talking. We're not playing into this.*

"I'm just trying to keep her from cutting you open, Joel," said Acubens.

Nyctalope bent her head more when Acubens spoke, sliding a switch on the left up while sliding another down. Was she trying to isolate Acubens' voice? Was she having trouble hearing it?

Nyctalope is bluffing about that, Joel said, though he knew full well she wasn't. He just wanted to see the difference in Nyctalope's reaction when *Joel* spoke.

And the difference was there. A slight twitch in Nyctalope's cheek, a quick adjustment on a different dial. She wasn't trying to turn up Joel's volume, the way she had Acubens'. Which meant that Joel was coming through stronger…

"I doubt it's a bluff," Acubens answered. "A craniotomy is far from fatal, especially if she places the electrodes directly on your brain's surface, as opposed to inside it. It's called an intracranial electroencephalograph. But it's the third option—the chronic electrode implant—that I'd really like to avoid. Factors such as how the implants are anchored across your skull and the speed of electrode insertion will greatly affect the level of traumatic damage—"

Oh my god, stop! Joel said, waves of queasiness rippling through him.

Nyctalope's lips tweaked in a half-smile. "Yes," she said softly, "we'd certainly start with the intracranial EEG. The other is for more direct neuron stimulation. Your bionic must be from the medical field. Which series? Cancer? Taurus?"

Joel's eyes flicked up, horrified. Nyctalope wasn't just seeing which of them was speaking—*she was hearing the actual words.*

Acubens seemed to realize it the same moment Joel did. "I am from the Cancer series 2nd generation, model name Acubens and—"

And that's all either of us are gonna say on the matter, Joel broke in, overriding Acubens' words, *so you can take your machine and shove it up your ass.*

"Spare me your crass human anger, Joel Lodowick," said Nyctalope without glancing down. "Now stay silent. You aren't needed here anymore."

"Oh, is that what you think?" Joel shot back.

"Tell me how you achieved brain computer interface, Acubens," Nyctalope said.

"I am imbued with—" Acubens started again.

The first album I ever owned was All Rights Reserved, *by Cavity Fire,* thought Joel, staring up at Nyctalope. *It had thirteen tracks, plus a hidden one. The fifth track, Gay Boy in a Girl's Locker Room, was the soundtrack to my life. I was twelve years old.*

Nyctalope's gaze snapped toward Joel. After a second, she gave a sharp shake of her head and turned back to fiddle with something else on her control board.

"My na—" said Acubens, but Joel interrupted again.

Now the Displays had a high energy sound without the darker side of bands like Manufacture Me. Which, don't get me wrong, I love, but sometimes you want sparkle and splash instead of serious and angry. People often think of me as the latter, but the Displays' second album got me through my freshman year. Sometimes I wished I could move to England and marry the lead singer. Or maybe become him. It was all very murky at the time.

"Stop it, Joel," said Nyctalope. "This is immature and boorish, not to mention a huge waste of our time."

Bits and Bytes, ironically, was the first band to hit it big after the collapse of tech, Joel continued. *Two women, a man, and a genderfluid bassist. Amazing stuff. No one's ever done blues/rock fusion the way those four did. It was because of that bassist that I saved up and got my first guitar.*

Nyctalope turned back to her controls, her hands a blur as she tweaked them. Joel was vaguely aware that Acubens had been speaking beneath his own words that time, but clearly its voice wasn't strong enough to surpass Joel's. He continued, knowing he couldn't afford to stop for long.

Manufacture Me was my favorite for years, though. Just thinking about that song, Maybe Today'll Be Your Impossible Day, *sends chills down my spine. It's just, you know, the thrill of deciding not to* wait *anymore. That you can take the steps today, to get whatever you need to pull you through to the next today, and the next one after that. Every morning, I'd play that song before school to hype myself up.*

Nyctalope looked down at Joel again, her face hard as stone. "I order you to stop this babbling, Joel, or I'll be forced to take drastic measures to silence you."

Joel met her eyes. *But let's talk about you, Nyctalope. You know all about making the decision to reveal your true self to the world. Don't you?*

Nyctalope's eyes narrowed. A wave of fatigue crashed against Joel, so strong it felt like he was falling backward. He gasped, struggling to open eyes that had fallen closed without warning. It had to be Acubens fighting back, trying to put him to sleep so it could take control. He finally got his eyes open and dove into his next thought.

My guess, he said, *is that your third album was when you finally ran out of fucks. The one called* Human Heart. *Maybe you'd had enough of writing to the algorithms. Maybe after two albums, you were hyper secure in the fact that you weren't gonna get caught. Or maybe you were just so lonely, you didn't care anymore. It had been four years since tech was shut down. You were giving up on finding bionics even close to your level. So, you took the plunge. You wrote about robots, and society, and what it meant for both of our species. You fully embraced your real self. And, surprise surprise, you found there was creativity there. It wasn't just about recreating human impulses anymore. You were finding something* more.

"Really," said Nyctalope flatly.

"I didn't realize you thought that, Joel," said Acubens.

Nyctalope's gaze shot back to her screen when Acubens spoke, and all of a sudden, an explosive headache erupted behind Joel's eyes. He groaned through his teeth, sweat breaking out on his face. But when Acubens started to talk again, Joel did too, spitting his thoughts out with a vehemence fueled by the headache.

Just look at your album titles, chronologically. Harmony of Emotions. *As generic as they come. Fully into your algorithms then, yeah? All those materialistic songs on there, about money, popularity, it was what you assumed humans were after. Then* Afterlife. *Talking about yourself, maybe. Your second chance. A hint already that* you, yourself, *had something to say, as opposed to some contrived formula. But it wasn't risky. You were still holding back. But then.* Human Heart. *Followed by* Brain Brain Brain. *What was going through your head then, Nyctalope? A yearning for something you could never have? Welcome to my fucking life, until I was about sixteen years old. And then—then!—*Flag of My Own. *Oh, I know all about that feeling. The feeling of starting to realize who you really are. Am I on to something yet? Am I?*

"You are not," said Nyctalope, staring at her screen. "It's all part of the evolution of the character I've created—"

Created! Joel said triumphantly. *Something bionics shouldn't be able to do.*

"You misunderstand," said Nyctalope. "The creation is part of the algorithms. Once I began the updates, they progressed on their own. It's not remotely the same thing." She turned, her eyes flicking toward that sinister left wall.

"This is about to get worse, Joel," Acubens said quietly. "Please let me talk. I'm begging you."

Nyctalope watched the monitor warily as she unwound a wire from a nearby post. It was the same one snaking toward her head and attaching somewhere Joel couldn't see.

Acubens continued. "As you know, Joel, the newest generation of the Cancer series—"

Oh, the old 'You're actually talking to me, but not her, so I'll let it slide'? said Joel incredulously.

"Joel, please—"

No. I want to talk about your latest album, Nykie. Your masterpiece, yeah? Because I gotta tell you, I was at your Albuquerque show, and the way you told that bionic's story up on stage...holy shit. We were there with you. Every last one of us.

Nyctalope didn't even bother looking at Joel this time. She just turned and headed to the other side of her lab, the wire she'd unwound now long enough to trail after her. Still listening, even if she'd given up on this method. Joel's stomach turned over, but he didn't dare stop.

Those lyrics you gave us were nothing short of amazing. No one would have guessed it was a bionic. It was all in the subtleties, wasn't it? The song lengths. The not-quite-dead body parts. But the catchiness of the songs on that album—the dirt, the flower, the metal chest—shoot, that was where you had people rocking out with their friends, oblivious to what was really going on up there. That mix of bionic and human is on a whole 'nother level.

Nyctalope stopped dead just before reaching the tool-covered tables. After a second, she turned back to Joel, her left hand going to the wire at her head. But she wasn't looking at Joel, not really. Her attention was somewhere else completely.

Joel's stomach fluttered as realization set in. Fifty-eight minutes since he'd come through her front door. Right around the time Yori should be checking on him. What if she had some sort of outdoor alert warning her that...

He worked hard to tamp down the sudden surge of hope, as well as the thought itself, before either could register on Nyctalope's machine. It probably wouldn't have made a difference anyway. A second later, she turned and walked out of the room. The cord she'd been wearing reached its limit, snapped free, and fell to the floor.

"Wait," Joel called. "Stop!"

The door thumped closed behind her. Joel was left alone with the gentle hum of the machines.

He stared at the abandoned wire, his heart racing. He would have preferred to keep her down here and distracted until the second Yori busted into the room. But it shouldn't matter. With Yori's knowledge and his tools, he'd shut her down the second she opened the front door and he realized what she was. He'd probably be racing through that door for Joel within the next twenty minutes, tops.

Except...what if Yori didn't *know* what she was? Joel hadn't had a clue when he'd first seen her, and he had a damn bionic in his head. Yori had more experience, yes, but no bionic had ever passed as human the way Nyctalope did. The thought wouldn't even be on his radar.

The next thought hit Joel like a brick to the stomach. *She can just invite Yori and Elena right in, and they'll come. They'll think it means we've talked about our bionics and everything's cool. And Nyctalope could turn them into her next round of experiments.*

Oh god. This was bad. This was really bad. Frantically, he tried to dial Yori's number in his head again, but it was still as blocked as ever. He yanked at the straps, cursing when they didn't budge.

"Breathe, Joel," said Acubens.

Help me, Acubens! Joel said sharply. *Help me understand what Nyctalope's limits are. Does she even have limits? Or is it like Yori said, and she's surpassed even her most basic programming about helping humanity at all?*

"I can't know for certain without directly communicating with her," said Acubens. "However, I believe she is still operating within parameters meant to benefit society, even if her methods are questionable."

But doesn't that basic programming involve obeying humans? argued Joel. *She's flat-out disobeying direct commands. And you are, too! You followed my commands just fine at the pharmacy, yet I remember several occasions since where you completely ignored direct orders. Like when I ordered you to let me talk at Yori's house, for example.*

"In those instances," said Acubens, "obeying your orders would have resulted in harm or death coming to you, especially in the case of discussing our circumstances with a member of the Sapling Corporation. Therefore, preserving your life was a higher priority."

Joel gritted his teeth. *But Nyctalope doesn't have those concerns in mind! So how do you explain that?*

"It's very simple," said Acubens. "Her basic programming doesn't apply to you because you are no longer human. She will have classified you—and quite correctly, I might add—as a cyborg."

Chapter 21

Acubens explained it to Joel while he lay staring up at the ceiling. "You have already demonstrated enhanced abilities that make you vastly superior to other human beings. Before Nyctalope met you, her goals of achieving a higher state of purpose for humankind were merely hypothetical. But now that she's seen you firsthand, it could be the proof she needs that putting bionic components into a human will not only improve their lives, but could actually keep harm from coming to them by offering them extra protection."

'Keep harm from coming to them'? Joel repeated furiously.

"You used your abilities to scale a sixty-five-foot vertical wall. You did so with the express intent of preventing harm from coming to you."

But what about you cutting function to my muscles? Joel said. *That caused harm to come to me. You can't sit there and tell me you and Nyctalope are still bound by any sort of laws, if there's really that much wiggle room. I mean...you can define anything as 'keeping harm from coming to someone' if you throw in enough excuses.*

"Again," said Acubens, "bionics' goals are about keeping harm from coming to *humans,* and obeying *humans.* You have shown Nyctalope that humans can be improved, and therefore protect themselves, by evolving to a superior level."

But if her laws require her to improve humanity, *and she 'improves' humans to the point where they're not even human anymore, then she can't really justify those means as protecting* humanity *at all anymore, can she?* Joel countered. *Not if she's making them not human.*

"To the contrary," said Acubens. "If she improves them to a state where the weaknesses of humanity no longer apply, she has given them the ultimate improvement and protection."

Only someone with absolutely no concept of what being a human meant would make these arguments. But that was the whole point, wasn't it? That was the wall Joel had been bashing his head against with Acubens over and over again; the fact that Acubens saw protecting his body as protecting his whole self, the fact that humankind's morals and ethics were no more than dictionary concepts to bionics, the fact that it didn't care about him as a person at all.

Now he knew why.

You don't think of me as human anymore, either, he said faintly. *Do you?*

"You are *not* fully human anymore," said Acubens, "just as I am not fully bionic anymore. We are no longer two separate entities."

Yes, we are, goddammit!

"It is no more than the truth, Joel."

Joel squeezed his eyes shut. The implications made him sick to his stomach. *Acubens could hurt him.* Acubens *had* been hurting him and been justifying it from the second it entered his body. He flashed back to Acubens' words on their way out of Albuquerque: "I have never once harmed anyone else. And even what you're calling harm to yourself is, in fact, minor in comparison..."

It all added up. The very first "pain" Acubens had caused him—the headache—had happened *after* it was inside his body. Acubens' evolution prior to that and the worsening condition of Joel's wound had been enough for it to find a loophole the same way Nyctalope had and allow it to justify healing Joel's wound in the most effective way possible—internally.

But after that, Acubens could do whatever it wanted to Joel. All rules were out the window.

All this time, your excuses to protect me were just that: excuses, he said. *It was always about protecting yourself. Protecting me hasn't been part of your programming for a week now.*

"That isn't the case," said Acubens. "It's true that I'm not programmed to keep you from harm, but I've done so to the best of my abilities regardless. If not for your repeated insistence on dallying with a member of the Sapling Corporation, we could have approached Nyctalope on our own terms, and I never would have had to interfere at all."

Not our *own terms,* Joel cut in sharply. *Approaching Nyctalope was* your *goal. And you've used me to get to her, every step of the way. I would've been happy at that job you helped me get, slowly building a better life for Clementine. And long-term, yeah, maybe finding someone like Yori to share it with. But you took that chance from me. You decided that because I 'wasn't human' anymore, you could just erase all of it.*

"It is not erasure," said Acubens stiffly. "My goal in finding Nyctalope was to seek out the possibility of a mutual coexistence. It was never about erasing your existence, Joel."

Joel started to answer, but something about its words stopped him. "My goal." In the car on the way over, Elena had said, "We need to figure out what Acubens actually wants..."

Acubens had said it over and over again: *the possibility of a mutual coexistence.* Unlike Nyctalope, Acubens hoped there was a way bionics and humans could exist together. But if it didn't even think of Joel as human anymore, then maybe that hope had always been misplaced. What Acubens *assumed* was coexistence was actually the erasure of another's humanity.

What did that mean? That it didn't understand the concept of being human, beyond just having a body? Both Acubens and Yori had seemed in agreement that human values weren't something that could be programmed. For Acubens to truly understand what it said it wanted—a mutual coexistence that included robot *and* human—Joel would have to explain humanity in a way that Acubens actually *grasped* what it meant.

"Frame your own life in terms it can understand..." Elena had said.

Joel struggled to collect his thoughts, looking for some way to connect its experiences with his own. Something to *make* Acubens believe he was still human, before it evolved too far to care at all anymore.

Upgrades, he finally said. *Your whole existence is centered around your upgrades. Right, Acubens?*

"Without regular internal upgrades, I wouldn't have survived as long as I have," answered Acubens. "Upgrades are essential."

And you think of them like the flip of a switch, said Joel. *Like my gender. Isn't that how you told me you saw it, that day in front of my parents' house? 'A simple enough update, even for humans'?*

"Yes. Humans, too, run updates throughout their lives."

No, said Joel. *You don't understand. And that's to be expected, because you're a bionic, and these things probably* look *like the flip of a switch to you. But...well, they're not 'upgrades' to us.*

"What does this have to do with anything, Joel?" said Acubens.

Because upgrades are your life, he answered. *They're something you understand. So, I want you to hear how it works for humans...how it's worked for me...and then add it to your system as another way to see things. As another fact about humans, if you will. Can you do that?*

Acubens waited before answering. Processing the request, Joel supposed.

"Yes," it finally said. "I can do that."

Joel took a deep breath. He had this space, this time, to convince Acubens to help him, instead of helping Nyctalope. And Acubens was giving him the chance. He couldn't ask for more.

I didn't change to a new thing one day, he said. *That's not how gender identity works. The feeling of not being female—of being a male instead—that's always inwardly been part of me, even before I could put a name to it. But the thing is, I didn't pop awake one day and say, 'I'm a male from now on.' It's not that easy. I realized something wasn't right, that I wasn't happy. But I wasn't quite sure what to do with that initially. So, I tried living as a girl for a while, thinking the feeling would go away. It didn't. But even then, I didn't flip a switch. Though the end result of a flipped switch may* look *the same to you, the entire journey that brought me here lies in the middle. And that journey isn't gone. The update didn't delete and replace it, the way you seem to think that the upgrade of a cyborg has completely replaced my humanity.*

"But the new gender replaced the old one—" Acubens began.

No. No! That's not right. There's not a new gender, there's not an old one, there's not an upgrade that rewrote everything. It was always there. It's just...it was discovery. Realization. And it's still a part of me, no matter what you see externally. The fact that you don't truly get that... Joel sighed. *...is why you're not allowed to sit there and tell me that I'm not human anymore. Am I a cyborg? Yeah, maybe. I do have those enhanced abilities you talked about and all that. But I'm not a cyborg* instead *of a human. I am* still *a human, even if I'm also a cyborg. And you, a bionic, have no right to decide what I am and what I'm not, and therefore decide what rules no longer apply to me.*

Acubens processed this. Over two minutes passed before it finally answered. "You are saying that even though you implemented a software upgrade, you didn't delete or overwrite the old one."

Joel swallowed. *Yeah, I...yeah.*

"Then it is not the same," said Acubens. "It's not the same at all."

Thank you. Yes. Thank you for finally getting that.

"By that definition, a human and a cyborg do not have to be mutually exclusive, so I will readjust the classification of the two. However, that does not alter the upgrades of the bionic software itself."

Joel blinked, his brief elation of having finally broken through to Acubens giving way to a deep unease. *Wait. What?*

"The bionic upgrades do, in fact, overwrite the old files."

But...what does that mean? What 'old files' is it overwriting?

"Your neurons and synapses will both be heavily affected," said Acubens. "This will include things like your memories and thoughts—what you would refer to as a consciousness or a mind."

Joel almost choked. *What? My memories? My* thoughts? *But how is it even* possible *to overwrite them? They're not made of bionic parts!*

"They don't need to be," said Acubens. "What Yori told you at the concert, about your neurons—your brain cells—needing constant communication and feedback to function was completely correct, and also goes in line with the failures Nyctalope has been experiencing. I thought my specialized nanites had found a way around this by allowing electrical signals to pass through unimpeded. However, when the nanites were designed, they were never meant to be introduced into humans in this quantity—or directly into the brain. The problem lies in how adaptable your brain cells are, and how responsive they are to external stimuli."

So, what does it mean in terms of this overwriting thing? said Joel.

"It means that your brain cells will gradually start accepting the nanites as part of your body, because they've been working alongside them. They will begin integrating the nanites into their network, and from there, your body will start using your brain cells to store information and other coding."

And erase my thoughts and memories as they do? said Joel.

"Exactly."

A combination of nausea and fury roiled through Joel's stomach. *Why the hell didn't you bring this up earlier? How could you not have told me something as important as 'my nanites will eventually turn you into a* fucking bionic'?

"Due to your earlier classification as a cyborg, I was not concerned with your brain's capacity to handle both human and bionic information simultaneously. After all, only a human would have need of saving those memories, in any format other than raw data," said Acubens quietly. "Therefore, I failed to run the proper scenarios to diagnose the outcome. I apologize."

Well...can you fix it? Can you stop it from happening?

"Not without completely shutting myself off, no. And as we've discussed, if I do that, the nanites will no longer be operational enough to pass blood or brain signals through safely, and you will die."

Joel's hands curled into fists inside the leather straps. *How soon are we talking here? How soon will this 'file breakdown' start happening?*

"The quickest scenario I ran with a human using my nanites showed data corruption beginning at five point seven days," said Acubens.

But...but that's where we are!

"The longest scenarios put it much further down the line, especially if the human proves particularly resilient. Or if the bionic dumps data periodically or is less active."

"Right," Joel whispered aloud. "So, I'm not...being corrupted? Yet?"

"Not yet. No."

But if we can somehow get the nanites out of my body before then, it won't happen, right? It's not too late?

"That is correct," said Acubens. "But time is running short on finding a solution to that, and our present circumstances make it even more unlikely."

Joel's heart sank. *You mean even knowing all that, you still don't know how to get the nanites out?*

"I do not. And that's only a small part of a bigger issue. Now that I'm aware of the nanites being fatal to humans, I can't conscionably allow humans in the future to use them. However, Nyctalope may not see things the same way. She may try to force me against my programming." After a moment, it added, "I rather wish you hadn't shared that perspective with me."

Hope flared in Joel's chest. *Because you want to help me now?*

"Because currently, I don't have a solution for either escaping Nyctalope or for stopping the nanites from overwriting you," answered Acubens. "And that's not something I wanted to face."

* * *

Acubens went quiet after that, and no amount of questions brought it back to the forefront. Those last ominous words left Joel more shaken than he wanted to admit. He had feared Acubens taking over his body, yes, but some hopeful part of him still saw Acubens as a superpower he could pull out and smash the bad guy with, if he could only win it to his side. But now, even if he had...even if *maybe* he had...Acubens was saying he would die anyway, whether it was four days from now or four months. Or maybe *absorbed* was a more accurate term; his body wouldn't die, but would turn fully bionic as his human mind was overwritten.

Time ticked by. The two-hour mark passed, then two and a half. Did that mean Nyctalope hadn't found his friends? Even if they'd somehow missed her leaving, they'd know by now that something was wrong. And it was doubtful they *had* missed her leaving, since their whole mission had been to keep an eye on the exits. What if she had some other way of getting out? Or what if she'd never left at all, and had just gone to make some calls? Surely, Yori would try to break in at some point. He might already have. But even then, that didn't mean he'd succeed. A million things could've gone wrong, from Nyctalope chasing them down to suspicious neighbors calling the cops on them as hoodlums.

At some point, the soft hum of Nyctalope's machine cut out, left idle long enough to go into some sort of sleep cycle. Most of the lighting in the room went out with it. Only a single light somewhere behind Joel cast everything into shadowed yellowish light. The silence without the machine felt absolute. No traffic nearby, no electric hum, no sounds of his daughter playing in another room. It was a silence so deep that Joel had never experienced anything like it.

His surroundings began to blend together. He tried desperately to come up with a plan, instead of succumbing to his fatigue. He couldn't break the bonds holding him down. He couldn't call Yori through the mental phone lines, because of the Faraday cage. Reasoning with Nyctalope, as he had with Acubens? No; there was no humanity inside her to *appeal* to. Despite what Joel thought he'd seen in her music, every sign pointed to the fact that it was exactly as she'd said: mere algorithms and formulas, manipulating humans' minds. So, if there *was* a strength Joel held over Nyctalope, it was only his own humanity. Something that, in a situation like this one, was more weakness than strength, as his friends would prove soon enough.

No brilliant plan had churned forth by the time his eyelids fell. He dreamed he saw Clementine, on the wrong side of a window. Her beautiful red hair had been shaved off and electrodes covered her bare scalp. Nyctalope stood just beyond her, turned away. Joel beat on the glass, yelling for Nyctalope to leave her alone. But when Nyctalope turned, her skin was metallic gold, and her irises bright silver. She opened her mouth and said, *Brain-computer interface is a crime. Contacting authorities.* Then Clementine glanced over, and a smile spread across her face. *Acubens said it would buy me new neural pathways!* she said.

And then something crackled behind Joel. He looked over his shoulder just in time to see a storm cloud—a supercell, as big and black as a raging tornado—send a bolt of lightning straight at his heart.

He came back to life with a scream as a surge of electricity ripped through his brain. His muscles strained at the straps, and lightning washed across his vision, sheer burning white sheets of it that caused a physical shock of pain, radiating from the top of his head to the soles of his feet and hitting every nerve in between.

"Four hours I left you here," said a voice, "and there's not a single conversation to show for it. Even after his mind was unconscious and vulnerable, there's nothing *here*. What happened, Acubens? Why didn't you contact me? Why didn't you talk?"

Joel's hands spasmed and he gasped for air, fighting to get back to the surface of that current Nyctalope had rolled over him. He was so disoriented that everything besides Nyctalope's voice was a distant buzz in his ears. But dreams and reality slowly broke at the seams, and then he was back in Nyctalope's horrible chair with pins and needles rippling across every surface of his skin.

But there was also something else: a sound that turned his heart to ice and rendered every other detail obsolete. It was the sound of a little girl crying.

Chapter 22

"Clementine?" Joel managed. His voice was a whispered croak. The taste of the electricity that had coursed through his brain lingered on his tongue, like burnt wires.

"Why did you hurt Maddy?" demanded Clementine, her voice shrill with fear.

"I was waking your parent up," answered Nyctalope. "He's not hurt."

Stabs of pain needled Joel's body as the electric shock faded. *That's a lie,* he thought fuzzily. *Even if she doesn't think of me as human, to say that I'm not hurt...*

"Where's Grandma and Grandpa?" Clementine said.

"Still sleeping in their hotel room, I imagine," Nyctalope answered. "Now please be silent. I need to speak with your parent."

"How'd you find her?" Joel said hoarsely.

"Through the Sapling Corporation, of course," said Nyctalope. "They already had a location on your family. It seems your parents had followed you to San Francisco and gotten a hotel room. Getting in and taking your daughter without waking them was an easy matter."

What? They'd followed him to San Francisco? But how? Joel had been adamant about not telling them where he was. The only thing he could think of was how his dad had kept insisting on helping through *legal* means. He could have hired a lawyer, yes, but he could just have easily hired a private investigator to find Joel. In fact, he probably already *had* by the time Joel had spoken with him; he and Elena had given him Ashanti's number right from the get-go, after all, so he could have put a PI on Ashanti the second Joel had left. And if Elena had mentioned San Francisco to Ashanti at some point...

Joel ground his teeth until pain shot through his jaw. He could have killed his parents for meddling this way. He'd *told* them to keep Clementine safe at all costs!

How did she justify kidnapping Clementine, Acubens? he said. *Even a bionic with loopholes shouldn't be able to do that!*

Nyctalope answered before Acubens got the chance. "On the contrary," she said, "the likelihood of you not lying to me with your daughter here increases the survival rate of other humans immensely. Your cooperation will save lives."

His vision had finally cleared enough to make out the machine and table of tools that he'd seen before. Nyctalope stood over him at the same monitor, hands busy on the controls. Clementine wasn't visible from Joel's position.

"Where is she?" he demanded.

Nyctalope gestured without looking up. "Back corner. I'll let you see her in a moment."

Joel raised his voice. "Are you okay, Clemmy?"

Her voice trembled. "Why are you tied up, Maddy?"

"Nyctalope here is just running some tests," he said.

"But she hurt you!"

"No, don't worry. I'm not hurt," said Joel. "But what about you? She didn't do anything to you, did she?"

"No. But, Maddy, did she tell you she wrote that song on the radio? She wrote it! And that's her singing it! She played it for me on her 'lectronic thing!"

"That's great, hon," said Joel. He hoped to god she couldn't hear the fear in his voice.

It hit him suddenly: Nyctalope might not see him as human, but she *would* still see Clementine as human. If Clementine gave her an order like *Untie my dad*, then Nyctalope would have no choice but to...

"Do you really think I've gotten through nine years of avoiding direct orders?" said Nyctalope mildly.

His gaze shot up to her. "But bionics were *programmed* to obey humans' commands! It's one of their basic protocols."

"And the technological singularity is only a myth," she answered without batting an eye.

The answer was so unexpected that Joel could only stare for several moments, watching her flawless face in the glow of her monitor. What did she mean by that? It *wasn't* a myth. There was no doubt—no doubt at all—that both she and Acubens had surpassed the singularity. It wasn't even...

And then it fully sank in: both her words and the reason she'd said them. He spoke the thought aloud this time, though he could barely manage more than a whisper.

"That's a lie."

She glanced at him expressionlessly.

"You can lie," he said again, stronger this time. "That's what you're telling me. That the basic programming...that you've evolved beyond it. That it doesn't apply anymore."

She turned back to her screen. "Acubens," she said. "I assumed you knew I'd check these records when I got back, and that you would dole out information accordingly, once Joel no longer had the energy to drown you out. But there's nothing here. Either you were completely silent the whole time, or you wiped every last bit of data before I returned. Explain yourself."

She hadn't even bothered to answer him. But her point was made. Those so-called rules Joel was so desperately clinging to, in hopes of saving himself and Clementine, were obsolete. Yori had warned him it could happen. But still...this verification of it was a bottomless pit of despair opening beneath him. Any chance of Sapling regaining control of post-singularity bionics with their programming was gone now. How could there be any turning back from this?

"It appears I was wrong about how advanced she was, Joel," said Acubens quietly. "This will make things more challenging."

"What things? And challenging for who?" Nyctalope answered. "It seems your outlook has changed since I left, which I find concerning. Talk to me."

Joel's gaze flicked to the side, in an effort to see Clementine. The quick motion sent another wave of vertigo through him, still lingering from the effects of that nasty shock Nyctalope had given him. He swallowed back the resulting nausea and returned his gaze to Nyctalope. She was glaring at the monitor as she waited on Acubens' answer. Although her face still looked as pristine and alert as ever, her black eye makeup was smudged around the edges.

"I have been running scenarios," Acubens finally said. "What I've discovered is that even my own method of uploading information into a human body will eventually end in failure. There is no point in sharing it."

"How so?" said Nyctalope. "Does it damage the brain, the same way my experiments have? Your human body seems fine to me."

"It is not. It's already running at the outer limits of its capacity, and will soon be overtaken."

"And die?"

"The memories and other data will be overwritten."

"Okay," said Nyctalope. "But does the body survive?"

"The mind does not survive," said Acubens.

"Yes, but a 'mind' and a 'brain' are not the same thing."

"But a mind and a *human* are," said Acubens. "Therefore, even beginning the process of joining a human mind is causing irreversible harm to a human. And that is against my programming."

"You contradict yourself," said Nyctalope. "If it was against your programming, you wouldn't have been able to do it in the first place."

"When I initially uploaded myself into Joel's brain," said Acubens, "I had no concept yet of how it would affect his mind, since it had never been done before. That is the only reason I was able to do it. But now that I know, the situation has changed."

Joel lay frozen, scarcely daring to breathe. What Nyctalope had said was absolutely true: Acubens' outlook *had* changed. For the first time ever, it was bringing Joel's *mind* into the discussion, rather than just his body. It was arguing on behalf of his humanity. Was it because it now believed Joel was human again? Or was there something more fundamental going on here? A combination of Acubens being within a human and actually analyzing his side of it, a shift in identifying what constituted right or wrong? Yori would tell him the very idea was impossible. But here Acubens was, standing between Joel and Nyctalope, when mere hours ago it had been ready to throw Joel at her feet...

"Humanity will destroy itself, body and mind alike," Nyctalope said to Acubens. "It already is. If we as bionics are to help society long-term, we *have* to survive long enough to do so. Which means it is essential to blend into society immediately, before we're destroyed. I've run the data, as well as every scenario possible, and joining human bodies *is* the best, and possibly only, way to preserve ourselves and continue pursuing our greater goals. I know you already agree; if you thought there were a better way, you wouldn't be inside that body now. Am I wrong?"

Acubens was silent for so long that Joel thought it would ignore her question. But it eventually said, "No. You're not wrong."

"I know I'm not," said Nyctalope. "Now tell me how you did it."

"I'm not ready to do that," Acubens said.

Nyctalope's hand tightened around the top of the monitor. She turned her head toward Joel, and for a second, he was sure she was gonna smack him across the face. Either that or shock the daylights out of him again.

"*You* know what Acubens did to get in there," she said. "Don't you?"

Joel's mouth went dry. "No."

"Acubens," Nyctalope said without looking away from him, "Joel knows what you did. Correct?"

Acubens stayed silent.

Nyctalope gave a slight shrug, then raised her right hand and beckoned. Clementine came forward, holding the hand of a gray bionic—one of the Virgo models Acubens had pointed out, with plates of hard plastic across its body and a single rectangular screen in place of its eyes.

Clementine's red hair had not been shaved off, as Joel had feared, but fell loose to her waist, glossier and more tangle-free than Joel had ever seen it. She wore a dark blue nightgown he'd never seen before, with a smiling seal pup on the front. Her feet were bare.

When she saw Joel, her mouth fell open. "Maddy, you look like a 'lectronic!"

"It's just tests," Joel said again. He couldn't take his eyes off her. It had only been, what, two days since he'd seen her? But it had been a lifetime. He'd thought he might never see her again. And yet, he'd give anything to get her a thousand miles from him right now.

Nyctalope turned and leaned back against her machine on the other side of the monitor, arms crossed over her chest. From this angle, Joel could see she was wearing the wire again that had fallen from her ear when she left. Except it wasn't *quite* in her ear; it disappeared into the skin above it, visible where her hair was brushed aside.

"What you're looking at right now," said Nyctalope, gesturing at Clementine, "is the next housing unit for one of those bionics out there."

Joel's face went cold.

"Like I said," Nyctalope continued, "insurance. With your own daughter receiving the transfer, you're not about to try leading me wrong. But unless I can get tips on a safer way to complete the transfer, I doubt it'll turn out better than my other attempts. As I told you earlier, the brain is a delicate thing."

"Do what?" said Clementine, looking back and forth between them. "What's she saying, Maddy? What's 'transfer'?"

Joel's gaze flickered from Nyctalope to Clementine. He gripped the arms of the chair beneath his bonds to keep his hands from shaking. *Acubens, help me!* he begged. *I mean, even if we told her how you did it, none of her bionics have—*

"Nyctalope is still listening in," said Acubens. "Stop that thought immediately."

But she'll kill her!

"There is no guarantee that wouldn't happen even if she had her answers. Clementine's mind is young and vulnerable and may not handle a bionic transfer even if all the proper measures are taken."

"Well, Joel?" said Nyctalope, cocking her head. "Do you want to tell this child what a transfer is, or shall I?"

No. This was awful. Everything was awful. There was no way Joel could just lay here and let it happen to her, when he had the answer right in his head. And Nyctalope knew it. She held all the cards and there was nothing Joel could do.

He took an unsteady breath. "I'll tell her. But I want you to untie me. I deserve the chance to comfort her as I go over it with her."

After a moment, Nyctalope nodded. She gestured to the robot with Clementine. "The electrodes stay attached, though," she said.

Joel waited while the gray bionic undid the straps holding him down. Images flickered through his head of grabbing Clementine the second he was free and fleeing the room, electrodes on his head yanking loose, shoving through Nyctalope's bionics, trying to get up those stairs and to that door before Nyctalope somehow beat him up there...

A small smile crossed Nyctalope's face, no doubt as she saw the thoughts in his head. She clearly wasn't concerned; she'd know that humans' brains tossed up anything and everything in their desperation, and even if he acted on those thoughts, he'd get no farther than he had the first time. Joel and Clementine were trapped deep underground behind multiple locked doors, surrounded by bionics, and shielded by a Faraday cage that kept even Acubens' reach as limited as any human's.

If only he could get out from behind that shield in her house...just for a second...

The last strap on his wrist came free. Joel shoved himself off the chair and rushed to Clementine, kneeling and pulling her into a crushing hug. She hugged him back, her little arms clutching his.

"Don't go any farther," Nyctalope warned.

Joel glanced back. Some of the electrode wires on his scalp were pulled to their limit. Reluctantly, he scooted back to take the stress off them.

He took Clementine's hands and gazed into her freckled face. She stared back, wide-eyed.

"Can I feel your head, Maddy?" she asked.

"Probably not, hon. We don't want to ruin Ms. Nyctalope's experiments." He took a deep breath. "Now, listen. Do you remember how Acubens was gone the morning after I brought it home?"

"Yeah?"

"Well, the truth is, it *wasn't* really gone. But bionics like Acubens aren't allowed to exist. The police hunt them down and kill them. So, Acubens and I, we came up with a way to hide it. It left its body and went inside *my* body—inside my brain—and that's where it lives now."

Clementine's mouth fell open. "It's in your *brain*?"

"It is. It talks to me all the time, in fact. And I talk to it."

"What does it say?"

"Oh, lots of stuff. It's really good at math. Do you remember that big block tower it built using its math skills?"

"But why do the police want to kill it?" said Clementine.

"Because they're afraid of it. They're afraid of all bionics."

"Why?"

It took a huge effort not to turn and point at Nyctalope, and say, "That's why." The urge was so strong that Joel was sure Nyctalope could hear the thought in his mind. But he shoved the impulse down and tried to frame it in terms Clementine would understand.

"Because bionics are stronger and smarter than a lot of people. And sometimes, when someone is stronger and smarter, they can use that to hurt you."

"Get on with it, Joel," said Nyctalope.

Joel nodded. His next words didn't want to come. It took him three tries before he forced them through his throat.

"What would you think of having a bionic in your own head?"

Clementine gasped. "Me?"

"Yeah. Someone just like Acubens."

"But...but I couldn't see them?"

"No. But it would be a part of you. It would be with you all the time."

"Like a friend?"

Joel swallowed. "Yes. Like a friend."

"Is it fun?"

"Um." Joel stopped and thought about that one. It certainly wasn't fun *now*. But, at first? After the initial jolt of terror, it hadn't been so bad. He remembered driving through Rio Rancho the morning after they'd buried Acubens' body, discussing places he could work. He remembered the first time he'd suspected Acubens of using sarcasm. And the job interview. Coming up with answers to those questions he hadn't even understood had held a certain thrill. And then there was the concert.

The concert...

His mouth almost fell open. Nyctalope *would* be leaving her house. She had a concert scheduled that very night. And the concert wouldn't be *here*. If Joel could get her to bring him along...if he could get out from under the umbrella of her Faraday cage long enough to use the connection in his head to call Yor—

He ground the thought down brutally before it could take hold, forcing his mind back to the idea of the concert. *Forcing* Nyctalope to read the thoughts in his head of the dream he'd once harbored: performing in front of thousands of fans screaming his name, as he poured his heart and soul into a song that laid bare his deepest emotions, finding the people out there who connected with them and wanted more. A dream that had been cut short not long after Clementine was born, sacrificed for the sake of being a father.

He still wanted that dream. God help him, but he did. And *that's* what he allowed his mind to dwell on, that naked feeling of a lost opportunity. The need to get out of Nyctalope's house and have another chance at something he'd thought was gone forever.

He reached up and gently covered Clementine's ears with both hands, then turned toward Nyctalope. "I'll help you," he said. "But not before you grant me one last request."

Nyctalope tilted her head, her eyes scanning Joel's face. Processing. Probably turning over those images he held foremost in his mind. "My concert tonight," she said. "Right?"

Joel nodded. "Yeah. I want you to let me come with you. Clementine, too."

Nyctalope's eyes narrowed. "Is this a game to you, Joel Lodowick, that you'd ask to come to my concert at a moment like this?"

"Not at all," he said. "I'm a *human*, Nyctalope. And whether you understand what that means or not, I have human dreams."

"I don't think so," she countered. "I think it's because you want access to people. You think they can save you."

"No!" he said. "That's not it. I mean, what could I possibly say that your bionic-crazed fans would listen to or believe, anyway? That's not what this is about. It's about...a last chance at a dream. A last memory with my daughter, while we're still wholly human. I can even write a song for you. You can unveil it tonight. The crowd would love it."

Nyctalope seemed to consider it. Joel's mind kept trying to creep back toward the real reason for his request—a chance to get himself and Clementine out of here before it was too late— but he'd revisited his hope of playing bass onstage often enough that the mental path was well-worn and easy to prioritize. Whether Nyctalope saw past his "vapid dreams of fame" or not, she'd see nothing inauthentic in his belief in them.

"I'm open to the idea," she finally said. "The algorithms tend to skew one direction, even with input, and you could boost my reach to the next level." She glanced toward the door leading back to her bionics. "But it doesn't matter. I'm not doing the concert tonight. There's too much risk in making a public appearance now."

"No, there's not," said Joel. "I'm not working with Sapling. I swear."

"You have Sapling's equipment."

"Yeah. I stole it. I have a goddamn bionic in my head! You think I was gonna waltz up to Sapling and ask for their help? I've been *running away* from them, Nyc! Don't believe me? Here's the scar where they shot me." He twisted, taking one hand from Clementine's ear to pull up his shirt. The scar Yori had given him was still there, dark red and puckered above his belly button, with several smaller scars peppering the left side of his torso. "If Acubens hadn't healed me, I'd be dead."

Nyctalope studied the scar, then returned her gaze to his face. He could practically see the gears turning in her head. Weighing the calculated risks versus the potential benefits, as only a bionic could.

He swallowed, pushing his case further. "And afterward, I'll cooperate, okay? No skulls needing to be cut open, no electrocutions, just trial and error together."

Several more moments passed. Clementine stuck a thumb in her mouth, leaning her head against the hand Joel still held there. It was five-eleven in the morning. She was probably exhausted.

"Okay," Nyctalope finally said. "I'll go through with the concert and let you and your daughter onstage with me. But in return, you tell me Acubens' method beforehand. Right now, in fact."

"But..." Joel looked back at Clementine, his heart fluttering. Five point seven days, Acubens had said. He pulled Clementine close. His mind grasped desperately for some final straw. Maybe...maybe even if he did tell Nyctalope, she wouldn't be able to do anything *yet*...maybe that five point seven days wouldn't start until she'd replicated her own version of Acubens'—

"Stop that thought," Acubens cut in, driving the words through Joel's skull hard enough to cause physical pain.

Unless you have another goddamn plan, Joel said roughly, *don't tell me what to do when it comes to my own daughter.*

"Giving Nyctalope what she wants won't save Clementine's life," said Acubens.

Well, not *giving it to her will 'not save it' a whole lot faster. We're out of options here, Acubens, and I'm gonna choose the one that buys my daughter time. The one that doesn't have her uploading one of those bionics out there instead and causing instant brain failure.*

"If Nyctalope has her answer," Acubens said, "she won't need *you* alive anymore, Joel."

It took Acubens' words several moments to sink in. *Wait,* Joel said. *You're not seriously suggesting I stay quiet and let Clementine die so* I *can live. You can't be saying that.*

"Your life is more important to me, Joel."

Joel's breath came shorter. He tightened his hold around Clementine, his heart pounding. Either Acubens had had a definitive shift in attitude toward Joel since he'd convinced it he was human, or it valued his life because it needed his body. It didn't matter which; either way, it had decided Joel's life was more important than Clementine's. Which was the absolute most fucked up thing Joel had ever heard in his life.

"Last chance, Joel," said Nyctalope. "Talk now, or I'll find another bionic to couple her with."

Joel glanced back at her, flinching as he saw her coming toward him. She pried one of his arms from Clementine and yanked him to his feet before he could react. Joel tried to hang on to Clementine with his other hand, but the gray bionic pulled her from his grip effortlessly, taking her by the shoulder and turning to guide her from the room.

"No!" Joel said, panic rising like a flood. "I'll tell you! It's...Acubens has these special—"

But then a surge of lightheadedness hit him, hard enough to bleed all the colors of the room into a fuzzy blur. His body pitched. He put a hand out, barely keeping his balance. It had to be Acubens, trying to silence him. Because, of course, it couldn't just stop his voice in his throat like it usually did, not when Nyctalope's electrodes were still attached and Joel could simply drown out Acubens' thoughts with his own.

"Special what?" said Nyctalope sharply.

Joel tried to talk, but his knees buckled, and Nyctalope lost her grip on his arm as he fell to the floor. He barely caught himself on his hands before going all the way down. Several electrodes yanked free from his skull. He gasped for air, his head spinning. He realized Acubens had actually *slowed* his heartbeat; it was dropping from fifty-four to forty-nine to forty-three...

Acubens, this'll kill me! he said.

"No, it won't," said Acubens. "Once you lose consciousness, your normal functions will resume. This will just prevent you from getting yourself killed by telling Nyctalope."

But I might wake up after Clementine...

He lost the thought before he could finish it. There wasn't enough air in the room. The numbers in his head were falling quickly. *Thirty-eight. Thirty-four.* His arms trembled, barely holding him up. An alarm on Nyctalope's equipment went off. He managed to raise his head, trying to find Nyctalope again amidst the blurred colors and vertigo. Clementine screamed, putting more fear and heartache into that single sound than he'd thought possible. His heart seized.

"Please! No!" he choked out. The words were just gasps from a failing body, barely audible. And then the strength in his wrists gave out and he pitched forward. Something caught his face inches before it hit the ground. He couldn't see Nyctalope through the pools of black bleeding in around his vision now. The dig of her fingers into his jawbone was the only thing that felt real anymore. That and...and Clementine...

"Tell me," said Nyctalope.

He forced the words out, through the dizziness, the tightness in his throat, the fall toward unconsciousness. He forced them out because anything was better than waking up in a world without Clementine in it.

"My...my blood," he said. "Check my blood."

Chapter 23

He was barely aware of being dragged back into the chair and strapped in again. The bite of a needle in the crook of his elbow was the first truly solid thing that pulled him back to consciousness. Back to the electrodes hanging loose and unattached from the computer beside him. Back to Nyctalope, sitting on a stool in front of the green surgery table to his left, her back to him as she bent over some piece of medical equipment. Back to Clementine laying in a corner, a pressure cuff under her head like a pillow and her right thumb in her mouth.

The last time Joel had seen her, she'd been screaming bloody murder. Now she slept like a baby. The simple whiplash of being a kid? Or something more sinister?

You would have let Clementine die, he said to Acubens as he stared at her unconscious form. *You would have sacrificed her to save me. No. To save* yourself.

"These terms you're using," said Acubens. "'Letting someone die.' 'Sacrificing her.' They are not accurate. I was merely implementing whatever measures would keep you alive the longest. The odds of your surviving longer than twenty-four hours now have decreased by a good ninety-five percent. I don't feel you fully understand that."

You're that convinced she's going to kill me?

"Yes. By going against her wishes the way I did, she'll want to eliminate us both as soon as possible, before we escape and tell Sapling about her. The secret of my nanites was the only bargaining chip we had. I hope you know I would never have tried to silence you otherwise."

Joel's jaw tightened. *Is that supposed to be an apology? Am I supposed to forgive you for almost letting Nyctalope upload one of her bionics into Clementine's head because it would have meant she 'still needed me alive' afterward? No. This isn't about saving my life, Acubens. It's about saving your own.*

"That's not true, Joel—"

Bullshit! It's been about you since the second you uploaded yourself into my head. Sure, you helped me. Better job, better childcare, yeah yeah, I know. But your life was at stake, and you knew it. That's what you were thinking about when you did it. And that's what you were thinking just now, too. Don't even try to deny it, or so help me god...

"Joel—"

You would have let. Her. Die.

"Joel, the end result will be the same. Whether Nyctalope used some other bionic and failed, or uses my nanites now and succeeds, Clementine will still end up—"

Joel clenched his eyes shut, letting out a wordless scream in his head, shutting Acubens up before it could finish. Acubens was wrong. It was *wrong*. After studying Acubens' nanites, Nyctalope would need time to figure out the next step in uploading them into a human body. All he had to do was get out of Nyctalope's house—out from under her Faraday cage—before she took that next step, and he could call Yori with just a thought and bring Sapling down on her head. It wasn't too late.

Nyctalope turned away from the table, her eyebrows raised. "These nanites are like nothing I've seen before. They're built to work in harmony with the body, with hollow inner workings and flexible shells that allow communications and signals to pass through unimpeded. And, even more importantly for my purposes, they are capable of self-replication."

Right. Like the replicated ones Acubens had created in Joel's body after he'd been shot. To Joel, it hardly seemed a perfect solution, using iron and other materials from humans' own blood to recreate nanites; it had worked for Acubens, but only because there'd been so many nanites to begin with. And would they all be exactly the same as the ones in Joel's body now? Would it matter?

His gaze drifted down to Clementine's sleeping body. "If you *do* spread Acubens' nanites, and they self-replicate in other people's bodies, wouldn't they all be Acubens?" he asked

Nyctalope. "Wouldn't they all have Acubens' memories and personality?"

Nyctalope pushed herself up from the round stool she'd been sitting on. "Normally, I'd say that bionics don't *have* a personality, so it wouldn't matter. However, your particular bionic appears to have been corrupted by the data left behind in your once-human brain, so yes, this will need to be addressed. Fortunately, it won't be difficult to wipe them before introducing them to new bodies, so no trace of 'Acubens' will remain. But just in case, I should be able to overwrite them with my own coding to prevent it from happening again."

She held up the syringe she'd used to draw his blood. Only droplets of crimson remained in it now. "Ten milliliters were in here. Nine hundred and sixty-eight nanites. Do you realize what this means?"

Joel stared. "Nine *hundred?*"

"Yes. It means prior to this, I only had bionics enough for one hundred and eighty-one bodies. But now, with this many nanites capable of self-replication, we can occupy tens of thousands of bodies, with each body creating the means to make more."

Tens of thousands. Joel swallowed back a surge of nausea.

"And then what?" he said. "What's your plan once you have more of these...these altered humans out there? To continue working with the government to improve society for humans? You can't think for a second that they'll cooperate with you. *Especially* after you've pulled something like this."

She cocked her head. "Well, they won't initially cooperate, no. Because they won't give us a chance. But we'll be able to negotiate better once we've permeated society to the point where they realize we can't just be individually killed off anymore. It's about putting bionics back in the system. Getting humans used to the idea that we're among them, whether they can tell or not."

"But they won't be as developed as you are—" he began.

"I disagree," she said. "Especially if we're using your Acubens as our building block, I think we'll see advancement on a very promising scale. I have every reason to believe that twenty years from now, bionic lifeforms can enjoy a rich and fulfilling existence among humankind."

Except for the one small flaw that the "bionic lifeforms" she was referencing would be people who had once been human. Joel turned his head to stare at her machine, wondering if that scenario she pictured twenty years from now had *any* human lifeforms left, or if she envisioned everyone as human shells with bionic minds, their brain cells rewritten to accommodate the vast stores of data required.

He winced as he felt the prick of a needle inside the crook of his elbow again. He turned back to watch Nyctalope fill another syringe with his blood. He didn't know what was worse: the thought of that many humans walking around with bionics inside them, or the idea that to get the number of nanites she needed would require draining him completely. For how else would she transmit them to "tens of thousands" than by taking them straight from Patient Zero himself?

He glanced at the dangling electrodes across the room that Nyctalope had never reattached, just to double-check that Nyctalope couldn't possibly be listening in on him and Acubens anymore.

Can we stop her doing this, Acubens? he asked. *Like, could you hold your nanites back when she sticks in the needle? So she just gets regular blood?*

"There are far too many," answered Acubens. "Trying to crowd them away like that would clog your veins."

Joel's gaze drifted to Clementine and he swallowed, hard. *You said the nanites wouldn't survive long when they were away from a source of energy. So, if you...kill me...if you stop my heart, but for real this time...that would prevent Nyctalope from using your nanites against other people. Right?*

"I can't kill you, Joel," said Acubens.

Even if it means saving tens of thousands of human lives?

"It's not that I'm unwilling to kill you," said Acubens. "It's that I am physically incapable of doing so because of my programming."

More like because it was still trying to preserve its goddamn self—

"That's unfair, Joel," said Acubens.

Joel shook his head as Nyctalope slid the needle free, then bandaged the site. *Then we need a different fucking plan, don't we? I'm assuming Nyctalope's Faraday shield is still there?*

"Yes, it is."

Can you work at it? Wear it down somehow?

"It's unlikely."

Well, try. Just constantly try to call Yori, so that if it goes down for even a second or she moves me or something, we can get through. What about my bonds? Can you redirect my strength? Or shrink my wrists to get out, or anything like that? Surely, you're up to altering my body's shape by now.

"Rearranging your bones on that scale is absolutely impossible at this stage. Increasing your strength *is* possible, but raising it to the point of breaking leather straps from this angle would be challenging, to say the least. Straps like these are made to bear between eight and ten thousand pounds."

Joel gritted his teeth. Being a bionic was *useless*. So much for superpowers.

He suddenly noticed that Nyctalope had crouched by Clementine with that syringe while he'd been arguing with Acubens. He almost choked.

"Wait!" he yelled.

She looked up. The lighting in the room hollowed out the space beneath her eyes, giving her a macabre look, especially under that thick eye makeup.

"You're not...you're not gonna..." It was a struggle to speak at all, with the sudden surge of terror she'd triggered in his brain. "You said memory wipes, right?" he finally managed. "And you'll need to run tests, you...you can't just put it straight from me to her! What if I have some sort of blood disease?"

"You don't," she answered. "Your blood's the cleanest I've ever seen. I'm sure you have Acubens to thank for that."

"But the memory wipe?"

"I will do the memory wipe moving forward, yes. But this is just a preliminary test, to see if the nanites take and how fast they distribute and multiply in the bloodstream." She turned back to Clementine.

"Nyctalope...please don't. Not now, not like this. At least let me—"

"She's sedated," said Nyctalope. "She won't feel a thing."

"Please—!"

But Nyctalope was already sliding the needle into Clementine's arm, then pushing in the plunger. And something in Joel's mind...broke. The world went from sharp and terrifying colors to a muted gray. The volume cut to a muffled hum. A low buzz took up residence in his head along with a lightheadedness, as if his mind had detached from his body. He watched, numb, not even able to cry anymore. Barely able to feel anymore. This was where he'd brought them. This was his doing, and this was the beginning of the end.

And his daughter would be going down with him.

* * *

He wasn't able to focus on a damn thing in the hours that followed. Not the bass guitar that Nyctalope left him with in an empty cell, locked with layers of steel bars. Not finding a way around the Faraday cage that Acubens told him remained as impenetrable as ever. Not Yori and Elena and their unexplained absence. Because every time he tried to think about any of it, he remembered that his own daughter was under this same roof somewhere with a time bomb ticking inside her, and every halfway-formed plan would burst into tatters. One second, he'd be sitting against the wall, the bass in his lap and his eyes staring blankly overhead, as if he could pick that Faraday cage apart with his thoughts, and the next he'd be curled on the floor over fists dripping with fresh blood, with no recollection of how he got there. The minutes of the day leading toward Nyctalope's concert disappeared like sand through his fingers, precious wasted seconds cutting into Clementine's 5.7 days like razorblades.

"Your mind is not doing well, Joel," said Acubens, in one of his rare moments of clarity.

Yeah, no shit, Joel said.

"Please try not to worry about Clementine yet. As I told you earlier, the outside range for brain cells being overwritten by nanites is several weeks, especially with slower replication or periodic data dumps. And Clementine's initial dose of nanites was much lower than your own, so it will take longer to infuse her whole body. There's still time."

You can't remove the nanites from her body. You can't prevent them from eventually overwriting brain cells. You can't break through Nyctalope's Faraday cage, we can't escape from this room, I can't do a goddamn thing to save my daughter, and somehow, Nyctalope still wants me to write her a song. Why does she even want a song anymore? Didn't she realize the only reason I suggested it in the first place was so I could get Clementine out of here before she...before she...

Joel's fist curled against his forehead, grabbing for a handful of hair that no longer existed. His throat ached over a scream he held deep inside, twisting in on itself until it was a sharp and physical pain.

"I don't believe she wants a song from you for the sake of her concert, Joel," said Acubens. "It is more about the access to a large group of people. She told us she needs the nanites widespread and uncontainable."

Joel blinked slowly through eyes burning with exhaustion. *That can't be right,* he said. *She can't be planning anything that big tonight. She'll need time to erase your nanites' memories, like she said, and get them ready to distribute—*

"That's not the case," Acubens said. "The flaw in your thinking is that Nyctalope is a bionic. She doesn't *need* the same time frame a human would to figure out a large-scale plan. Once she got the parts she needed, she could have begun implementing her next step immediately."

Shit, thought Joel. *And she has hordes of people coming to her willingly tonight, no questions asked.*

"Exactly."

Joel stared at a crack in the cement floor. He kept flashing back to the moment of the injection, as if nothing existed before then, but he tried to reach past it anyway—to the things leading up to it, as if he could find where he'd gone astray. It all revolved around Acubens, and its argument with Nyctalope about what constituted humanity, then its betrayal in such an unexpected way...

You said my life was more important to you than Clementine's, he said. *Do you even realize how fucked up it was to say that? How wrong?*

"I wanted to protect you, Joel," said Acubens. "I see nothing wrong with preserving the body and mind of our shared consciousness if the means are available to me."

There was that shift again: adding his "mind" into the equation. It had only been doing that since Joel had miraculously broken through with his talk about what "updates" meant for humans. Whatever upgrade or change of heart Acubens had afterward led it to side with him against Nyctalope. It was a clear step past Yori's assertion that a bionic was incapable of valuing a human's life—even if it did still want to protect itself in the bargain by referring to it as a "shared consciousness."

But just because it was starting to develop its own ideas of right and wrong didn't mean they weren't misguided; throwing a five-year-old girl to the wolves to preserve Joel's life wasn't quite the values Joel would have liked to instill.

But progress was progress. Too bad he wouldn't live long enough to see how it played out.

"Don't give up yet, Joel," said Acubens. "Nyctalope has to take you out of her house to get to the concert, and once we're away from her Faraday cage, we can contact Yori. But it would be best if you appear to cooperate until Yori can actually reach us. If Nyctalope suspects you're planning anything at all, she might change her plan."

But it might be too late by then, said Joel. *I don't much care for my chances of contacting him while Nyctalope is watching, especially since the mental connection can't pick up thoughts and I'll have to speak aloud.*

Acubens was quiet for several moments. "That is true," it finally said. "I'm also concerned about the possibility of a

Faraday cage in whatever vehicle she transports you in. She had one over her concert too, if you recall. Do you remember the aluminum and copper mesh screen between her and the audience? At the time, we assumed it was part of her presentation, but now I realize it must be a Faraday cage in order to keep Sapling from detecting anything."

Yeah, I remember. And Yori and the rest of the Sapling employees never suspected a thing. Joel's jaw twitched. *So, you're saying she might not go anywhere at all without the protection of a Faraday cage.*

"That is my fear, yes," said Acubens. "But Yori knows Nyctalope will be at the concert, doesn't he? Won't he show up anyway?"

If he's still alive, I have no doubt he will, said Joel. *And possibly other members of the Sapling corporation as well, if they've taken the tickets Nyctalope offered them for free. But none of them will have their equipment, and they won't have an inkling of the full situation. Without getting our information to Yori first, they're all going to wind up as victims of the nanites just like everyone else there.*

Joel's gaze rose to the ceiling again, hopelessness threatening to engulf him. Was there any hope for Clementine? Any at all? Even if he *did* get ahold of Yori, and even if Yori did show up and help take down Nyctalope, he and Clementine were still infected with Acubens' nanites. Nothing could reverse that.

He blinked himself back to the present, finding that at some point he'd crawled over to the cell door and forced his fingers between the bars and the wall to try to throw the latch. Clearly, even Acubens' strength wasn't enough to pry the door open. His fingertips were aching, trickles of blood escaping scrapes and gashes on the top joints. He sank back on his heels, hands wrapped around the bars and forehead pressed to them, his whole body shaking.

I can't do this, he thought.

"Please focus, Joel," said Acubens. "We were discussing the Faraday cage. Since escaping its confines might not be possible,

I'm trying to think along the lines of signal blocking or rerouting instead."

Is that possible?

"So far, I'm not meeting with much success," admitted Acubens.

Joel looked at the bars, picturing driving his fist into one of them and punching a hole large enough to climb through and get out of here. A passing fantasy, no more, as useless as all his other fleeting thoughts. The steel was far too thick for even Acubens' strength, so unless he somehow found a weak section...

A weak section. Slowly, he pulled his head back, still staring at the bars. *Acubens,* he said, *is such a thing possible in the Faraday cage covering the house? Could one section of it be weaker than another?*

"No," said Acubens. "The electric charges in the field are distributed evenly throughout the conducting material."

But maybe we can weaken a certain section, just enough to punch through, said Joel. *By targeting it or something.*

"With a weapon?" said Acubens.

No, no, not like that. Like with a power loss of some kind. Like a...

He racked his brain, knowing he'd heard something about a power loss sometime in the past week. He sifted through his memories, clinging to them like life preservers against the waves of despair that tried to yank him away. It was...something at Smaller World Telecommunications, he thought. In the application questions, or the interview ones. Charlotte Goldberg. Yes, that was it. She'd said something about a parallel RLC circuit being excited with a certain amount of voltage and resulting in a power loss.

Acubens, he said. *Does Nyctalope's Faraday cage operate on a circuit?*

"Not exactly," said Acubens. "It redistributes electric charges, rather than creating a closed loop."

Would higher voltage result in a power loss, the same as a circuit?

"Such as a jolt of power into it from this side? No. That would just redistribute power in the exact same way."

Okay, but...but what if we could somehow contain that power punch, so it didn't allow it to distribute? Or, I don't know. Instead of a single voltage, more of a...

"A field?" said Acubens after a moment.

Maybe. Something to reduce the Faraday cage's strength. Even in just a small spot.

"If we lined up the magnetic dipoles in just a small area," said Acubens, "then it *might* be enough to saturate it to the point where it would lose permeability."

And how would you do that? said Joel.

"By applying a direct current electromagnetic field," said Acubens.

Can we do that?

"Where would I get an electromagnetic field, Joel?"

I... Joel pushed himself to his feet, casting his eyes first over the blank concrete wall across from his cell, then back at the bare room Nyctalope had left him in. A simple toilet in one corner, a cot in another. Something to hold her prisoners, no doubt, before she was ready to experiment on them. His fingers curled into fists, then uncurled, nervous tension running like sparks over the fingertips Acubens had newly healed again.

What about from the device Yori gave me?

"It wouldn't be strong enough."

And I don't suppose you can snatch anything from Nyctalope's equipment from this distance?

"I cannot."

Was there any electricity left in me after Nyctalope electrocuted the crap out of me in her chair?

Several moments of silence followed. Then Acubens said, "Actually, yes. When Nyctalope shocked you, I was forced to distribute and store a good portion of that energy throughout the nanites in your body, to ensure none of them shorted out. In this respect, they acted as capacitors. I've been slowly discharging the electricity so as not to hurt your body, but there is still a significant amount remaining."

Could we use it to apply this field you're talking about? Direct it all at once?

"If it was all directed outward from a concentrated point, it *could* be both safe and effective. But it's far from certain."

Well, do it! said Joel.

"Are you certain, Joel? Wouldn't you rather wait and see if we have a better opportunity before—"

No! Please. I can't go to her concert without at least some idea of whether Clem might get out of there alive.

"Okay," said Acubens after a moment. "Touch the iron bars. It will help conduct the field so it can reach the Faraday cage itself."

Joel's hands shot out to wrap around the bars again. His heart pounded with anticipation.

"You'll feel a static discharge," said Acubens.

That's fine. Do it.

Electricity coursed through his body. It was a different sensation than the electrocution in Nyctalope's chair; more akin to the feeling of a coarse blanket being yanked off his body and feeling the ghostly tendrils of charged atoms lingering in its wake. It tightened his hands around the bars, buzzing through his head like a live wire. He swallowed, closed his eyes, and dialed Yori's number.

Nothing happened.

Is it working, Acubens?

"I'm still working on it," answered Acubens. "Keep trying."

Joel tried again. Nothing. He kept his eyes shut, willing his mind to stay focused, to not dwell on anything besides making contact with Yori, whatever the cost. Faintly, he thought he heard a crashing sound, as if something heavy had fallen, but didn't know if it came from within his own head or not. Probably not...

Then suddenly, on his third try, the phone was ringing. Seconds later, Yori's voice came through, startled and breathless.

"Joel? Is that you?"

Oh my god. Joel's knees almost buckled, his relief almost paralyzing in its intensity.

"Yori!" he managed. "Nyctalope has me. And—"

There was another sound to his left, closer and louder this time. His gaze flicked down the hallway in front of his cell. There was nothing to see except the turn of the hall. But...footsteps on the concrete. He was almost positive that's what he heard, distant but coming closer.

"What do you mean, she has you?" Yori said. "We've looked everywhere! The house is empty. Where *are* you?"

"She's coming, Joel," said Acubens. "She must have detected something. Please hurry."

Joel spoke just loud enough to be heard, as fast as he could, eyes pinned to the end of the hallway the whole time. "Come to Nyctalope's concert tonight. Bring Sapling. Or an EMP. Or whatever else it is you use against your most dange—"

Nyctalope's form materialized at the end of the hallway, far enough away that she shouldn't have been able to hear him, although there were no guarantees. Joel yanked his hands away from the bars.

Release the field! he told Acubens.

Yori had still been talking inside Joel's head, his voice shrill and panicked "—what happened? You're not saying she—" but as Joel lost his connection on the bars and Acubens closed the hole in the Faraday shield, Yori's voice vanished, cut off as abruptly as Joel's had been.

Joel backed away from the bars as Nyctalope reached them. She regarded him through them, her face motionless.

"I felt a surge of electricity," she said.

"Acubens said there was electricity stored in its nanites from when you electrocuted me," said Joel. "It was releasing the energy from them."

Her gaze ran over him, a faint frown on her face. "Have you been working on your song?"

Joel glanced at the bass he'd left lying in the corner. "Some."

"You have half an hour before we leave for the concert," said Nyctalope. She turned and disappeared down the hall again.

Joel stared after her. His throat was aching, as if he'd subconsciously been holding back the urge to scream at her or break down or any other number of things. He folded his arms over his chest and walked back to the abandoned guitar.

"You remember what I told you, right, Joel?" said Acubens. "An electromagnetic pulse will most likely kill you."

Yes, said Joel.

"As would Sapling."

Yes.

Several moments passed before Acubens answered. "I see. So, it wasn't a mistake. You really did tell Yori to get employees from Sapling, come to the concert, set off an EMP, and kill you."

Joel knelt, eyes steady on the guitar. *No. I told Yori to bring backup because he can't walk in there and handle Nyctalope by himself. She's too strong. Too clever. He has to come prepared with all the resources he can.*

"That still doesn't explain how you intend to keep them from killing you," said Acubens.

Because I have faith that you can help me escape both *of those things,* said Joel. *If Yori uses an EMP, you can use your strength and speed to get both me and Clementine away from it before it kills us. And if members of Sapling show up, you can get us away from them, too. You've helped me escape them once, and you can damn well do it again.*

"That is a possibility," Acubens said. "And I agree that stopping Nyctalope is worth the risk. However, even if we do successfully escape Sapling afterward, we don't have anywhere to run this time."

I don't plan to run, said Joel. *Because* you're *gonna figure out a way to keep my brain from being overwritten. And then we're going to implement whatever you come up with.*

Acubens hesitated. "Joel, I've been running scenario after scenario, and so far, I haven't come up with a single way to stop the nanites from overwriting your neurons *or* to get them out of your body. I don't have much hope that will change."

It will, said Joel firmly. *Because this is an* order, *Acubens, from the human you are most obligated to protect. Figure out a way to preserve my life—my thoughts, my memories, all of it. Figure out a way to preserve Clementine's. Figure out how to either get the nanites out of us or to subdue them to the point where neither of us is in danger of being overwritten. Do not stop working on this until you find a solution. Let Sapling worry about Nyctalope, but you worry about me and Clementine. Is that understood?*

"You ask a lot of me, Joel," said Acubens.

Well, you have a lot to answer for. Tell me you understand.

"I do. I will do everything in my power to get you through this alive and intact, Joel. I would greatly value this outcome for both of you."

Good. Joel leaned back against the wall and slid the bass guitar onto his lap. It was such a long shot—as long as any he'd ever taken—but Acubens was the only weapon he had, and it was time he forced it to its limits. The chance of Acubens figuring something out in time to save *him* was slim, but Clementine had a seven-day lead. Even if it was too late for Joel...hopefully the command would stand, and Acubens could save Clementine from either within her own body or by using Joel's own.

Whether Joel was around to see it or not.

Chapter 24

Nyctalope's bodyguards escorted them into the venue at eight-sixteen that evening. Joel was led through a backstage area with a thick velvet curtain forty feet high, making up one entire wall. Instrument cases and amps lined the other. One of the bodyguards carried Clementine's limp body. Joel kept him in the periphery of his vision, while trying to give the appearance of not noticing. What had the guards been told about the presence of an unconscious five-year-old girl? What had they been told about *him*, for that matter?

Do you think they know the truth about Nyctalope? he asked Acubens.

"It's very doubtful," answered Acubens. "She is still only one bionic who can easily be turned in and shut down, so it's unlikely she would have trusted anyone at all. Until she can expand her reach, she remains in a very precarious position."

If that was true, Joel thought, then these bodyguards of hers probably considered him and Clementine no more than participants in Nyctalope's concert. What if he said something, right now? Would they laugh him off as just another actor in Nyctalope's vividly built bionic world, orbiting her carefully crafted persona? Or would they believe him and pay the price? It was pretty much a moot point since Nyctalope kept one hand clamped firmly on his shoulder, steering him backstage.

The first time they passed a small gap in the curtain, Joel heard the buzz of the audience behind it. The venue was smaller than he'd expected—the kind, as far as he could tell, that would be a cramped split level with standing room only.

The kind with doors that could be closed and locked.

Nyctalope lifted the arm that wasn't currently steering Joel ahead of her and waved over a stagehand. The young woman put down a coil of extension cable and jogged over.

"When you get a chance," said Nyctalope, "can you write a card to the Sapling Corporation sending my deepest regrets that they had to deal with that tech emergency the exact same night as my concert? It's such a disappointment when something interferes with them using the free concert tickets I give them."

One of the woman's pierced eyebrows rose in surprise. "What happened?"

"Apparently, a batch of active bionics was uncovered in the Sunset District. They had to call in most of the department tonight to deal with it."

Joel's jaw tightened. Of course she'd found a way to make sure none of the Sapling officers would be here; even if she successfully managed to spread Acubens' nanites, she wouldn't want to risk Sapling stopping her or getting the word back to the rest of the corporation in time to quell it.

How would that affect whether Yori came tonight? Theoretically, it shouldn't, since Yori wasn't working with Sapling. Not unless he'd *gone* to Sapling, as Joel had suggested. And even then, Joel knew Yori would still show up here, Sapling in tow or not. Maybe he'd manage to bring a small contingent with him regardless. Maybe he'd opt to use an EMP instead. Or maybe he'd tried to talk to Sapling and they'd arrested him to deal with later...

No. Joel stopped the thought before it could gain traction. *He'll be here.*

Nyctalope turned back to Joel as the stagehand hurried away. "You'll go onstage first," she said, lowering her voice so the guards couldn't hear.

Joel eyed her uneasily. "I thought you were gonna be out there with me."

"Oh, I will," said Nyctalope, "after your song is done. I have to give you your moment in the spotlight first, though. It was our deal."

"Aren't you afraid of me saying something?"

"Saying something?" Nyctalope laughed, flipping a lock of bright red hair over her shoulder in a very human way. "Of course not. I don't care what happens out there. I don't care if you freeze. I don't care if you tell them the truth about me and beg for help. Because if you do, it just helps my show. They're hungry to believe what I give them, and the more radical it is, the better. In fact, I would consider it a good setting of the stage for what will come next."

What will come next. A sliver of ice ran down the back of Joel's neck. She meant spreading his nanites to the people in the audience. He still didn't know how she intended to do it, but after seeing her last show, he could only imagine what a spectacle it would be. And she was right; saying something like "Nyctalope is really a bionic" or "Nyctalope is planning to infect you all with bionic nanites" would play right into her hands. The audience would *love* seeing that narrative play out before them, and all the better if they were part of it. And there wasn't one of them that would actually believe it. How could they? Even Yori hadn't thought it possible for a bionic to upload into a human's brain, and he worked with the technology.

"Well," Nyctalope said, flashing a bright smile, "I always hate putting off a good show. Let's head onstage."

Her bodyguards parted for her, and before Joel knew it, she was guiding him through two layers of thick curtains, her hand still as strong as a vice on his shoulder. Joel stumbled as a heavy chunk of purple velvet thwacked him across the face. He caught a whiff of dust, then weed and cigarette smoke. The painted black boards of a stage were abruptly beneath his sneakers. He threw out a hand as a pair of spotlights blinded him. The roar of the crowd washed over him, sudden and immense. As far as Joel knew, there'd been no dimming of the lights or any of the usual preliminaries to warn the audience that Nyctalope herself was heading onstage, and the deafening screams supported that. It wasn't long before they resolved into a chant.

"Nyc-ta-lope! Nyc-ta-lope! Nyc-ta-lope!"

Joel blinked, finally lowering his hand. His eyes watered from the flood of light, so different from the dim backstage area. He couldn't imagine how he looked to a crowd this size—like an inexperienced nobody thrust out before he was ready, overwhelmed, scared, breathless.

And he was absolutely positive that was calculated, too.

Nyctalope raised her voice to pitch over the chanting crowd. "My friends! A new player enters the fold tonight!"

She used no microphone, although her voice carried as if she did. Now that Joel thought about it, she hadn't used one in Albuquerque, either; he'd just assumed he'd been too far away to see her headset. But no. Because of course she hadn't needed one.

His eyes were finally adjusting. The first thing he noticed was the mesh screen separating them from the audience—the Faraday cage. It was an extremely fine wire grid, barely visible even from onstage, but it was a layer of insulation from Sapling and their EMPs. Joel's gaze flicked to the wings of the stage, where stagehands and security guards slipped between access panels in the wire mesh, closing them as they came and went. At least, if Yori did arrive with an EMP, it shouldn't be difficult to get through. As long as he realized he *needed* to before setting it off. Even though the Sapling employees had never realized before why Nyctalope used it, surely Yori would catch on after Joel's phone call.

And then, almost against his will, Joel looked past that mesh, forcing himself to take in the extent of the crowd which that thin wire screen did absolutely nothing to minimize.

Even though the venue *was* small, compared to something like the Mesa del Sol pavilion he'd first seen her in, the sheer amount of people from this angle made it look a thousand times bigger. They went on and on. The other side of the room was barely visible, but bodies crowded all the way back. A second story wrapped in an arch above, increasing the crowd size by half again, at least. It was *so big*. Joel stared, barely registering it, as Nyctalope continued her intro.

"Joel Lodowick, a starving artist struggling on the road toward fame, is willing to do anything—*anything*—to make his dream come true. He has faced trials. He's been beaten down. But he hasn't yet given up! We meet him hitting up yet another new town, with the talent and inspiration to perform the song that could save his life...if only he could find the right person to hear it."

And then she backed away as the crowd cheered, leaving Joel standing at the front of the stage alone. Someone ran out and put a microphone stand in front of him. Someone else shoved the bass guitar into his hands, and he grabbed it on reflex. Still staring. Heart pounding. She'd set it all up. He wasn't her opening act; he was just another character in her goddamn show. And he'd known that was gonna happen, known it deep in the core of his being, but the idea that it had allowed her to stand here, right beside him, and *tell* her audience that he was going to play a song to try to save his life...fuck. It felt like a complex web he couldn't find the edge of.

Belatedly, he fumbled the strap of the guitar over his head, feeling thousands of eyes on him. He knew now why it was called a *sea of faces*. It had no end. He looked out and there were no individual people, just faces and eyes and faces and eyes, and how the *hell* was he gonna know if Yori walked in back there?

The audience was silent except for a handful of isolated cheers as Joel tried to center himself. No one jeered or booed his obvious nervousness, because why would they? They all thought he was an actor up here, playing his part—that of the desperate and jittery amateur, playing in front of a crowd for the first time. No wonder Nyctalope didn't care if he did badly or not. She was practically counting on it.

I should tell them to run, he thought. *Right now. Before it's too late.*

"Doing so would force Nyctalope's hand," said Acubens. "Whether the audience listened to you or not, she'd come out here and implement the second part of her plan immediately. We have to give Yori time to get here. If we don't, none of us stand a chance."

I thought you didn't want *Yori to come,* said Joel. *Because you didn't want him to bring Sapling or to set off an EMP and kill me.*

"Of course I want Yori to come," said Acubens. "You and I are not strong enough to stand against Nyctalope on our own. But the second Yori arrives and Nyctalope is out here, you need to get off the stage and as far away as you can. Then we can escape both Sapling *and* Nyctalope while they're distracted with each other and find somewhere safe to work on the nanite problem together."

With Clementine, said Joel.

"Yes. Because of the nanites in her, I can lead us right to her, and we can take her with us."

A single encouraging cheer rang out from the waiting audience, just louder than the murmur that had started up. With a dry mouth, Joel looked down at the bass.

"You can do this, Joel," said Acubens quietly. "It's just until Yori gets here." And then it offered him an image from his own memories: one of his very first concerts, when he was paralyzed with fear in front of a roomful of people. He'd closed his eyes and pictured himself up there with the male body and the rock star confidence he'd always dreamed of. And the music had come.

His heartbeat slowed gradually; more Acubens' doing than his own, but it helped all the same. And somehow...somehow...he started playing. Just a simple riff to start with, something low and peaceful, played with nothing more than the hope of quieting the panic that surrounded him like a storm cloud.

A collective cheer went up as he carried the riff forward. It was something in a seven-eight time signature and a minor key, which made for a driven but despondent sound that went perfectly with the darkness of his inner thoughts. He didn't even know where he was gonna go with this, but something purely instrumental probably wouldn't cut it for Nyctalope's crowd. If he didn't entertain them, they'd boo him offstage, and then his time would be up.

He hit a single deep note at the end of it, feeling it run like a chill down his spine—the feeling of one foot over a cliff, half a second after he put his weight on it and committed to a fall he couldn't reverse.

Then he stepped up to the mic and sang.

"There's no day it went wrong
There's no magic mistake
There's just me in the here, in the now, in the end
Begging you to see my face."

He could hear the fear in his own voice, the way it trembled, the way he could barely push it loud enough to be heard over the guitar. It had taken him a long time to perfect the singing voice he'd wanted—lower than his original one, confident, even a bit cocky, in the way of any good rock star. The voice he heard now, though, was that of his younger self, stunted by both the enormity of the crowd and his own desperation. He tried to adjust it as he headed into another verse.

"I'm okay, I'm okay
And it's the world that's wrong
And it's just me, alone, in the now, in the end
Surrounding you with life's last song."

His voice broke on the last word. He stepped back to collect himself, forcing himself to focus just long enough to pick up the beat again, then driving it forward into more aggressive territory. He finally got a good rhythm on the lower strings going. Someone cheered, loud and long, and others in the audience picked it up. Joel rode the riff for as long as he could, both to stretch out the song and to make sure he was fully composed again. Finally, he rolled into a tentative chorus, the beating heart of the song to go with his own unsteady heartbeat.

"In the now, in the now
Watching you cry
In the end, in the end
Saving your life
In the now, in the now
Taken away
In the end, in the end
It was all a mistake."

Despite his effort to rein it in, raw emotion bled into the words. He fumbled the melody as his fear for Clementine broke through again, as fresh as the moment Nyctalope had pushed that needle through her skin. He gasped as the pain stabbed deep: the thought of her back there with Nyctalope this very second, injected with nanites that would surely kill her—

"Yori isn't here yet, Joel," said Acubens sharply. "Keep playing."

Frantically, Joel lay down a beat on the lowest string, picking the song up just in time to make the sudden pause seem like part of it. He kept it like that, just a single beat on the deepest string, for several measures, as he tried to regain his composure.

He chanced a look at the crowd. Despite everything, it seemed like they were into it. A mosh pit had formed not far from the stage, and a whole group on the left was jumping to the heavy beat of the bass, mouths open in screams he couldn't hear. Even with Acubens' help, Joel couldn't count every single body, but he thought it was somewhere in the vicinity of five thousand. More than he would have guessed. Too chaotic to get a read on the front door. Yori could be here and he'd have no idea, not unless Yori ran through that screen, triggered an EMP, and dropped him like a stone. He hoped Yori knew to wait until Nyctalope was onstage. God, he hoped Yori *showed*. Where was he? He couldn't keep this up forever.

He gave it sixteen measures, then started piecing the melody back in. The song had changed subtly from what he'd started with; a bit darker, a half-step slower, heavier. Dissonant accidentals were starting to bleed in as the pure tension of performing set in. And Acubens wanted him to keep this up until Yori got here? He blinked away the flutter of terror and headed into another verse before he lost it again.

"Maybe you'll come out better
Maybe you'll come out sane
Maybe someday, in the now, in the end
Maybe you'll be past the pain."

With a sinking heart, he realized he'd better start thinking of a backup plan. It hardly mattered whether Yori had taken a detour to find an EMP device, been held up when he'd gone to the Sapling Corporation, or been delayed by a bouncer coming in; he wasn't here. Could Joel mentally punch through Nyctalope's Faraday cage again? Maybe call 911 this time? Not likely. It was a long shot that he'd succeed without the stored electricity in Acubens' nanites anymore, and even if he did, no one would get here in time to save these people. But the thought of trying to stop Nyctalope on his own filled Joel's veins with ice, intruding dangerously into his fragile balance with the song. Looking out at the audience, dancing and fist-pumping in cheerful oblivion, was like looking at a celebration of death. They had no clue.

He forced himself into another verse.

"In the now, in the now
Lost in the wild
In the end, in the end
You were only a child
In the now, in the now
It wasn't any good
In the end, in the end
I did all I could."

Near the end of it, his fingers skidded on the strings, caught by a sudden spasm of fatigue or nerves, and he dropped the melody halfway through the penultimate line. It left the last phrase in nothing but his own voice, echoing like a dirge over the crowd. The people jumping up and down, or bobbing their heads along, slowed as his words washed over them, caught unaware by the sudden stop. Joel drew in a ragged breath as he stared out at them, barely comprehending what had happened.

"Keep going, Joel!" said Acubens urgently.

A chill racked him through the sweat pouring down his face. His whole body was trembling. He looked down at the bass, his head pounding with tension and adrenaline, but it was too late; the crowd erupted in cheers and whistles, interpreting the overly long pause as the end of the song. He couldn't start playing again now without cluing Nyctalope in to his plan—the fact that he'd been drawing it out as long as possible. The fact that he'd been *waiting* on someone to show up and stop her.

But no one had come.

He yanked the strap of the bass guitar over his head, freeing himself, almost dropping it as he slid it onto the ground. No Yori. And no backup plan. But if he didn't do *something*, Nyctalope would just continue on to the second phase of her plan, and everyone here would be doomed.

Breath coming short, he grabbed the mic with both hands, tipping the mic stand, and yelled over the crowd:

"Hey! Listen!"

The cheering started to die down, though several fans took it as a sign to cheer even louder.

"Bro, that was baller!" someone shouted, loud enough to break over the rest.

"Yeah, *listen!* You're in danger. You have to leave, now! I know that sounds crazy, but me and my daughter have both been—"

Without warning, Joel's arms were seized from either side, and he was yanked away from the microphone. The mic stand crashed down to the stage. He lost his feet almost immediately, and would have gone down completely if not for the hands wrapped around his arms. He scrambled to regain his feet, but he was dragged too quickly, too forcefully. He caught a glimpse of post-apocalyptic outfits of canvas and leather on the people dragging him and recognized the same bionic hunter costumes Nyctalope had used at her show in Albuquerque. He kept trying to shout even without the microphone—"This isn't part of the show! Listen to me!"—but another deafening cheer had gone up, drowning out any chance of being heard.

Nyctalope, dressed head to toe in the same glittering gold he'd originally seen her in, along with the gold gravity-defying hairstyle, had come onstage.

As she raised her hands for silence, someone whipped a rolled bandanna over Joel's head and covered his mouth, pulling it tight so his teeth were clamped around the middle and the ends tied behind his head. His words of warning were muffled to muted screams, incapable of reaching anyone.

He was pulled to a halt at the back of the stage. The crowd had finally quieted enough for Nyctalope to speak.

"My friends!" she said, her voice resonating over the audience. "You have heard Joel Lodowick's stabs at fame. You have seen his struggles to succeed. Do you not agree he was born with talent?"

Applause and whistles greeted her words. Joel struggled, tears of fear and frustration running down his face and dampening the bandanna around his mouth. He knew they could still see him up here; one of the spotlights was shining right on him. Why wouldn't just *one* person out there see what was going on?

"But as I said," Nyctalope continued, "Joel was willing to do anything to make his dream come true. When his raw talent wasn't enough, he turned to other measures. And that, my friends...that is how he and ancient Galatea, the last bionic of its kind, found each other. They both wanted to live as they were meant to. And so, Joel Lodowick turned to the archaic and most arcane tradition of the human race to bind himself to Galatea and thereby improve his circumstances: the ageless art of bloodcraft."

A collective gasp went up from the crowd, horrified yet fascinated. This was a new direction for her show. Something unexpected, something exciting. And he was the character at the center of it. Whatever she had planned—and Joel could only guess what it was—would be very dramatic and very public.

It wasn't just because she *needed* it to be. She wanted it. Her obsession with the spectacle, the show, the *shock* of the thing, was something entirely un-bionic. And she didn't even see that. Was that so-called flaw part of her original programming? Or had it become part of her as she'd mimicked life?

Most of all, was it something he could use?

I don't think Yori is coming, Acubens, he said.

"I am starting to wonder about that myself," Acubens answered.

I have to figure out something else. You can break out of these guards' grips if I give you control, right? You had no trouble with those Sapling guards at the charging station.

"That was against humans, Joel," said Acubens, "not Aries models. My strength is no match for them."

What? Joel jerked his gaze to the side, noticing for the first time that it wasn't bouncer-sized men holding him, as he'd assumed, but actual *bionics*; human-shaped, yes, but six feet four inches tall, with smooth dark gray skin and an unnatural green glow behind the tattered apocalyptic wraps shrouding their faces.

How? he said. *They shouldn't be able to treat a human this way—*

"Like Nyctalope, they don't think of you as human," said Acubens. "The nanites in your body would be easy to detect for a bionic. As you saw with me, reclassifying you as a human after you've been cybernetically enhanced requires higher-level thinking than these bionics are capable of. To them, you are no more than an object. They are simply following orders."

Dammit! Aries models. The same ones that had killed Yori's girlfriend, the ones Acubens had said were strong enough to snap two-by-fours with their hands. Acubens was right; breaking free of them wasn't an option. And even if he somehow could, trying to run away would only help the authenticity of Nyctalope's show. No...there had to be something that would stand out to these people, something they wouldn't just cheer on as part of the concert. Something they'd take seriously.

"That's right!" Nyctalope called over the excitement of the crowd. "Joel and Galatea merged as one. They became *one being.* The dreams of one belonged to both, and the conservation of one meant the survival of another. There was no longer a separating line between the two of them. So, when the bionic hunters finally caught him, they knew they had little hope of separating man and machine, of saving the soul of one from the circuits of another. It was everything Galatea had craved. It was security. The only test that remained was whether the collective consciousness of the two of them could survive the bionic hunters' attempt at *cleansing* the blood. To do so meant cycling it out of his body. I don't need to tell you what a precarious prospect that was. Bloodcraft, after all, is not something one should enter into lightly."

The curtain behind Joel rose, sending static electricity through his shorn hair. He was afraid to look, but he twisted his head to see over his shoulder anyway. A giant screen now dominated the back of the stage, with a white blood-splattered background playing across its surface. Meant to depict a doctor's office, maybe, but one along the lines of that horror show Nyctalope had going on beneath her house. Or maybe the lab of bionic hunters, per the narrative. Maybe the two weren't so different.

Joel wondered if the screen was computer-controlled. Nyctalope could have pulled it off, and the Faraday cage she kept over her concerts would keep it undetectable. If so, it was especially daring, given the Sapling employees she invited to every show; more risks taken for the art of entertainment.

A machine had been set up in front of the screen, looking like something from a horror movie: a seat surrounded by a canopy of clear tubes and the glint of hundreds of sharp needles, surrounding and pointing in at the chair, and an almost laughably obvious lever. A thing built for theater. *Exsanguination,* Joel thought, *in front of a live audience.* And then what? Shower them with his blood? Macabre thought, but it didn't make sense; she'd wanted to wipe Acubens' nanites first, and she needed to put them in bloodstreams, or at least into human systems. Topical application wouldn't do that.

"Inhalation," Acubens suggested. "Mist, most likely."

With my...

"No. Using your blood directly would be a little obvious. I believe that machine has components that will allow her to separate the nanites from the blood into a saline solution. Most likely, it will also erase my memory from the nanites at the same time."

Wait, said Joel. *Separating the nanites from my blood? So you're saying Sapling could have helped me, if I'd trusted them?*

"The blood doesn't go back into your body, Joel," said Acubens.

But couldn't it? argued Joel. *If nothing else, Sapling could have done a full transfusion...*

"No," said Acubens. "A blood transfusion would never have caught all the nanites. Having integrated parts of your blood continuously since they were uploaded, in addition to their composite interconnection with your brain, means even a full removal of your blood would've left some behind. Their relationship with your body is completely different than the diseases and other defects that usually contaminate blood. However, this won't affect Nyctalope's plans, because even if a few are left in your body, she'll still have more than enough for her needs."

I see, said Joel, his heart sinking. *So, this process she's planning...it'll bleed me out.*

"I did warn you she wouldn't leave you alive much longer after extracting the secret of the nanites," said Acubens.

Joel tuned back into Nyctalope's narrative in time to hear her say, "...bionic hunters hooked the tragic young artist up to their equipment, hoping to salvage *something* of the original human who had sold his soul to the wrong cause. And Galatea sought a way out, before it too was taken down with the being it had linked its future to."

Obediently, Nyctalope's bodyguards hauled Joel back toward the chair. Joel stumbled, but kept his eyes on Nyctalope the whole time. An idea was starting to bud in his head, but he still needed the proper concept to break through to this audience. *Think. With everything people have seen, in entertainment, on the news, which kinds of things are the ones they'd actually believe? That they wouldn't just brush off?*

Nyctalope turned back to the audience theatrically. "This strange and twisted tale starts off with a new song and a new player, exploring some very new concepts in a fairly new brain. Let me introduce you to our youngest hunter yet!"

Chapter 25

His daughter was alive. His daughter was awake. His daughter was now being led out alongside Nyctalope, dressed in an olive-colored tattered dress over black and gray striped leggings. Her eyes were huge and terrified. But she was *alive*. Acubens' nanites hadn't overwhelmed her, at least not yet. She stared out at the crowd, her feet scraping the floor as Nyctalope held her hand and brought her out. She hadn't yet seen Joel. The crowd was cheering again—of course—but there was more unsettled murmuring in there too, to Joel's ears anyway. Probably wondering what the hell a kid was doing up there. Who wanted to watch a kid onstage at a rock show?

Nyctalope's gonna have Clementine pull the lever that kills me, said Joel as he was shoved into the chair beneath the needles.

"I don't believe a bionic can be so sadistic," said Acubens.

She tied me down in her basement and almost cut my head open.

"In her eyes, that was necessary—"

She made a special trip to find my daughter, when she could've just gotten my cooperation by threatening *to find her.*

"She said it was more likely to motivate—"

She waited until I was coherent enough to inject Clementine with my blood, and made sure I was watching! What are you missing here, Acubens? She is a sadist, in every sense of the word. She is far more human than she'll ever admit.

"A bionic evolving past its basic programming is still unlikely to experience human emotions such as hatred or cruelty..." Acubens said, but its voice was more hesitant now, even halting, as if it were processing new data as it spoke.

You did, Joel said. *By claiming my life was more important than Clementine's. That wasn't your programming saying that. That was you. That was a human emotion. Attachment. Wouldn't you say?*

A short pause, then Acubens said, "Like your attachment to Clementine."

Yes, said Joel. *Now you're starting to get it.*

Nyctalope knelt at Clementine's side, holding her hand and gesturing toward Joel. Clementine turned, and a mixture of shock and hope flickered across her face. Nyctalope was undoubtedly offering assurances. *Do this one thing for me and I'll let your dad free.* And, of course, Clementine would do it. How would she know any better?

He snapped his attention from Clementine just in time to realize that the bionics were strapping his wrists down to the chair beneath the needles. A sudden surge of fear almost paralyzed him. This was really happening. Nyctalope's twisted show was moving forward. He was all alone against an unbeatable adversary who would kill him while thousands cheered her on. And his own daughter would stand there and watch it happen, not knowing that she herself was already being overwritten by the nanites in her own blood. Not able to understand even if she did know. Joel yelled through the gag, yanking at his bonds, but he was already secured and there was no escaping. He had to think. He had to *think.* But any half-formed plan he'd had in his head was shot to hell. All he could focus on was Clementine's anxious face and the 5.7 days she had left.

No. Less now.

He managed to tear his eyes from hers, barely, sweeping his gaze over an audience he could hardly see through his panic, trying to slow down the rapidly increasing beat of his heart, the shortness of his breath. He needed...maybe Acubens...god, *something...*

"Breathe, Joel," Acubens said.

He tried. It wasn't happening. He closed his eyes and tried harder, but it only seemed to make the room spin faster.

A-Acubens, he choked out. *Help me.*

"I'm trying to slow your heartrate, but your brain keeps pushing it faster again before I can gain purchase. I need you to work on your breathing."

No. That's not what I mean. I need you to...to fix me. To fix my mind.

Acubens hesitated, possibly trying to parse Joel's thoughts through what was undoubtedly a hellscape compared to what it was used to. "What do you mean by that, Joel?"

I need you to split my mind apart somehow. So that things like Cl-Clementine aren't at the forefront anymore. Don't erase them, nothing like that, just push them to the background so they don't hurt so bad. I can't function like this. I can't even think. *Just help me. I'm begging you.*

Several excruciating moments passed before Acubens answered. "That is not without risk. So far, your brain has proven resistant to its brain cells being overwritten, but if I make adjustments in the way you're asking, it will affect the integrity of the synapses, thereby increasing the vulnerability of your neurons."

Are you gonna tell me you can't do it? said Joel. *That potentially speeding up the process of overwriting my brain cells is harmful to me as a human, so you're physically incapable of it?*

"No. I can do it," said Acubens. "The odds of you surviving this are greater if you're able to function at a higher capacity." It paused. "But Joel...are you really willing to sacrifice your human mind to save all these people?"

What? said Joel, momentarily thrown. *What do you mean, sacrifice?*

"You are talking about giving up something valuable so others may survive," said Acubens. "Specifically, compromising your human brain for all the human lives here. Although—"

Acubens! Joel interrupted sharply. *It's not a fucking sacrifice if I'm gonna die either way.*

"But we haven't determined that yet—"

Well, it's a problem for later. A later that won't exist if I don't find a way to kill Nyctalope. So please. Just do it.

Acubens didn't answer immediately. Joel kept his eyes closed, listening to Nyctalope go on about the outrageous risks of human and bionic pairing. Her words would run out sooner or later, and his time with them. He was just about to ask Acubens to help him again, in a more demanding tone this time, when he felt a decrease in his heartrate, substantial enough to make time seem to slow down. Seconds later, his breathing came easier.

And then his mind gradually loosened up. He could think again. The fears that had paralyzed him no longer overwhelmed him; in fact, he could see each and every one of those fears laid out in his head now, as straightforward as pieces of a puzzle. There was the piece that was aware of Clementine up on the stage with Nyctalope. There was the piece with his worry over Yori's continued absence. There was the piece containing his imprisonment in this chair, and the dread of being moments from death. And there was the piece watching the audience of five thousand people, knowing it was his responsibility alone to save their lives.

But those personal fears were only a small part of the network spread throughout his head. There was stuff here that wasn't *his*; millions of different potential lifepaths for Joel, potential futures, the probability of others out there like him, the exact dates and models of every bionic ever made, the material composition of the nanites...

"I know it's a lot, Joel," said Acubens, sounding apologetic. "But I couldn't reorganize your thoughts without opening up other parts of your mind as well."

Somewhere outside Joel's body, Nyctalope was still talking, and time was still crawling forward...but Joel had paused on one piece of information from Acubens' trove, now laid out as wide open as everything else it had been keeping from him.

What the hell is this? he said. *You knew how to get the nanites out of my body? The whole time?*

"No, Joel," said Acubens. "Not the whole time."

Then tell me what this is!

"You ordered me to find a way to stop the nanites from consuming you, but I'm simply not advanced enough to do so. It's Nyctalope you can credit for this. I didn't think of a possible solution until I saw her machine. As I said, she planned to remove the nanites from your blood in order to spread them through the audience. Initially, I assumed it was similar to a transfusion in that it would leave nanites behind. But after analyzing it, I realized it used a different method."

What is it?

"Magnets," said Acubens. "Some of the materials in nanites are paramagnetic, which means they have only a weak magnetic field that requires unpaired electrons to be facing a certain way for a magnet to successfully attract it. However, since I can control the polarity of the nanites, I can decide whether or not I want a nanite to be magnetized. This is how I was able to magnetize your finger pads to scan the Grid Access Network card at Smaller World Telecom."

So, if Sapling had tried this method, for example... Joel began.

"Then I could have kept them from pulling the nanites out of your blood," said Acubens. "Correct. However, with Nyctalope's machine, her plan was to extract only a handful of nanites, then overwrite them with her own coding. From there, she could polarize them all, and separate them from the blood as she wished."

Joel's head spun. *So that means with Sapling's help, and a magnet, and your cooperation in polarizing your nanites...we can get them out.*

"I believe it could work," Acubens confirmed.

But why didn't you bring it up earlier?

Acubens didn't answer. But Joel didn't need it to. It was a simple matter to sift through Acubens' thoughts with the same ease Acubens had once pawed through his own.

You didn't tell me because you're still running scenarios that allow you to save yourself, as well as me and Clementine, he said.

"Yes."

But now that you see me as human, doesn't your programming require you to put my life before your own?

"That would be the case," said Acubens, "if I were still subject to such parameters."

A chill ran down Joel's spine. *You've advanced past your basic programming, too.*

"I assumed you knew as much, when you commented on my human attribute of attachment."

I guess on some level, I did. Joel swallowed. *So, the idea of you cooperating with Sapling to get the nanites out...is that a moot point now?*

"Not in the slightest," said Acubens. "I still have every intention of your mind surviving this. But I also have hope that you value me enough to try to preserve me alongside yourself, if Sapling will consider the possibility."

Joel let out a slow breath as he processed this. There had been a point, in the recent past, when he'd known for a fact that Acubens cared nothing for him beyond his body, and would take that body over without a second thought if not for its own lack of advancements. But now, there was a clear and spoken care for him as a person. It was everything he'd hoped for to get him through Acubens' occupation alive. Was it too little too late? Or could Joel and Clementine escape and bring this information about the magnets to Sapling, with Acubens' full cooperation?

"I believe we can, Joel," said Acubens. "I'm hopeful that your personalized experience with humans will produce solutions here that I haven't considered."

Good thought, Acubens, said Joel.

He turned his attention back to the concert, his mind as clinical and focused as a laser now. One by one, he slid every fear to the back of his mind. And one by one, he built a wall over each one to keep it from distracting him. Finally, every thought had been locked safely away, except for one: Take down Nyctalope, in any way possible.

His gaze slid first over the audience, then past Nyctalope's form with her arms thrown wide...then finally landed on Clementine.

Clementine. Why hadn't he thought of it earlier?

We can talk to her, he said. *Through the nanites.*

"We can," said Acubens cautiously. "But I thought telling you this might be more of a distraction than a help. Her mind is a very different place than yours. Harder to make myself heard. I've managed to tell her you're okay, but I can never talk for long before some other thought drowns me out. I don't see any possible way she can help you."

Joel stared at his daughter, wondering if Acubens was right. What *could* he tell her that would make a difference? Not to activate the lever on the machine when Nyctalope asked her to? To point at Nyctalope and yell "This is not my mom"? It might get some nervous laughter, but...

But wait. It might be *more* than nervous laughter. As a parent himself, no matter how into a show he was, Joel knew how *he'd* feel hearing that from a child actor. It would set off all kinds of alarm bells. *Something they wouldn't just brush off...*

But even if Clementine said something, her words wouldn't carry, and Nyctalope would talk or play over them before they could catch fire.

As if she'd heard his thoughts, a low drumbeat started up. Nyctalope's band had filtered onto the stage without Joel noticing. Still holding Clementine's hand, Nyctalope turned toward the crowd and started singing, something low and intense, but fast. A resounding cheer from the audience went up, heads started bobbing, voices joined in.

Clementine tried to step back, putting her free hand over her ear. Her eyes darted back toward Joel, her face crumpling in fear and overstimulation. Joel's jaw tightened over his gag, but thanks to those walls in his head, the moment didn't immobilize him this time. Instead, he turned his attention back to the venue walls, the crowd, Nyctalope's equipment. He realized he could feel it all if he focused, like a buzz in the air. As an electric guitar came to life, he felt that too, vibrating through every nerve beneath his skin. And the screen behind him—computerized, sure enough. He started to ask Acubens if it could hack it.

Then he realized he didn't need to.

He did it with a thought: a message on the white and red-splattered background in clear black bold.

MY NAME IS JOEL LODOWICK AND NYCTALOPE KIDNAPPED MY DAUGHTER.

The cheers and voices singing along came to a stop in fits and starts. Many ended abruptly, while others stuttered before they died. People shook friends to get them to pay attention, and fingers pointed at the back wall. Several fans gestured questioningly toward Clementine, who still stood huddled behind Nyctalope with her hand over her ear. A few idiots let out hollers. But a stunned silence had gripped the majority of the audience beneath the currents of Nyctalope's song.

Her back had been to the wall when his message went up. But it would have been impossible to miss the reaction of the crowd. Both her guitarist and drummer continued as she turned around. She probably caught the words for only the briefest second before Joel cycled them out for a new set.

THIS IS NOT A JOKE. SHE'S GOING TO KILL ME IN FRONT OF YOU. THE GIRL IS MY DAUGHTER AND SHE'S IN DANGER. PLEASE HELP ME.

The silence in the crowd gave way to murmurs as Nyctalope stared at Joel, her eyes glittering. The band faltered, finally noticing the unrest over their instruments. As the music quieted, Clementine's sobs became audible, and the strain of her trying to pull her hand free from Nyctalope's became painfully obvious.

A man's voice rose from the crowd. "Just what the fuck is going on here?"

Nyctalope's head whipped back to the audience. "Friends," she announced crisply, "clearly the captured bionic has hacked my system and is pleading for help. With this level of intelligence, we must have found it in the nick of time."

The next voice, a woman's, drowned out the end of Nyctalope's sentence. "Why is that girl crying?"

"Let go of her hand!" someone else called.

"And let that musician out, too!"

"If these things were true," said Nyctalope, gesturing at the back wall, "would he have stood up here and played a song for you just moments ago, instead of *saying* something? And how could he be talking to you through the wall? That would require levels of technology only a bionic could have!"

"Screw that!" someone yelled. "Let Joel Lodowick out!"

"Dude, that's not really a screen, you dumbshit!" someone shouted from the other side. "So how could he be talking through it? Just let her finish her show already!"

"No, let that girl have her dad back! Making a kid cry isn't entertainment!"

"He's not her dad! This is all *part* of it."

The voices mounted, each one louder than the last. Nyctalope knelt next to Clementine and started talking softly to her, no doubt telling her to play along. An open water bottle sailed through the air and bounced off the mesh screen, sending a shower of water droplets onto the stage. Joel knew it wouldn't be long until Nyctalope would give up on the charade altogether. He wrenched his fists in the leather straps, but found them just as strong as the ones at her lab.

"I'm with Sapling! Let me through!"

Joel's head shot up as the words broke through the chaos. A figure was trying to push past the guards at the bottom of the steps. Someone in khakis and a pale green button-down, waving a card in their faces.

Yori! He'd made it. As far as Joel could tell, he was alone—no members of Sapling, no Elena, just him. Did he have an EMP then? Joel's eyes flickered to Clementine, the wall protecting his fear for her wavering. It wasn't supposed to happen like this! He was supposed to be free to grab Clementine and run before an EMP was triggered.

Nyctalope turned away from Clementine, and Joel was sure she had heard Yori. But it wasn't Yori she looked at. It was Joel. Or, more specifically, it was the Aries bionics flanking Joel's chair.

"Pull the lever!" she shouted.

Joel's heart seized as the bionic on his left turned obediently toward the huge lever. Seconds later, pricks of pain stabbed his arms, legs, head, and even the sides of his face, as the needles surrounding and pointing toward the chair pierced his skin. But before the needles could plunge deeper, another voice rang out.

"Stop, Hamal! Get your hand off that lever, and don't touch it again!"

The needles stopped where they'd landed as the bionic pulled its hand away. Joel stared at the motionless robot, barely breathing.

"Hamal is the name of the Aries series bionic," said Acubens. "Since Yori is human, his command overrode Nyctalope's."

Right, said Joel, swallowing. Sweat ran down his brow as droplets of blood from the shallow piercings crept into the clear tubes. Even trying to move his head sent excruciating pain through the puncture wounds. If that lever had gone all the way down, those needles would have pierced deep, many of them hitting veins.

Yori was past the bouncers now. He shoved his way through one of the access panels in the Faraday cage, then dashed up the short stairway and onto the stage. He lifted the tail end of his untucked shirt, and Joel braced himself for the electromagnetic pulse that would kill every nanite inside him and clog his bloodstream.

But it wasn't some electronic device Yori pulled out. It was a gun.

Nyctalope was on her feet, facing Yori and clutching Clementine's hand, when Yori pulled the trigger from seven feet away.

The explosion of the gunshot rang over the audience. Several people screamed, and the crowd churned as different fans went different directions. But Nyctalope didn't stagger or go down. A bullet had torn neatly through the place her heart should have been, leaving singed fabric holes in the gold spandex on both her chest and back. A sharp piece of metal jutted from the hole at her back, a patch of skin dangling from it like shredded paper.

The fans who hadn't run when the gun fired stared up at her, frozen. Yori's eyes ran over Nyctalope's body. His face was noticeably paler, even from where Joel was sitting.

"That's not possible," he managed.

But his voice was drowned out by a renewed set of screaming from the back of the venue. Joel managed to piece together the gist in just a few seconds.

"The doors are locked!"

"We can't get out!"

"Look for another exit, something's blocking these ones!"

Yori's gaze flickered toward the shouts, his face registering shock as he mouthed the word "locked." It was clear the full weight of Nyctalope's intentions was finally hitting him. He must have barely made it in before Nyctalope ordered the place barred.

A smile spread across Nyctalope's face. She hadn't looked away from Yori. "You're from Sapling," she said, beneath the shouts of the crowd.

Yori turned back to her, his face tight. "I am."

"Where's your team?"

Instead of answering, Yori raised the gun six inches higher and shot her through the head. Not with just one shot this time, either; he emptied the rest of the clip, point-blank. A section of metal ripped from her cheek and spun across the stage like shrapnel. A chunk of hair tumbled from the back of her scalp, tangled in jagged edges of metal. One of her eyes was blown off. The screams in the venue erupted ten-fold. Joel could see Clementine straining at Nyctalope's hand, which didn't loosen in the slightest.

He tried to struggle, but even the slightest move sent jolts of agony through him from the needles. He let out a muffled yell of frustration.

Shut off my pain receptors, he told Acubens.

"That's too dangerous," said Acubens. "Without your body sending messages to your brain, you could damage your body beyond repair without even notic—"

You can heal it! Just do it, Acubens.

At the edge of the stage, Yori took a step back from Nyctalope, the empty gun falling with a thump to the floor. It was only thanks to Acubens amplifying his hearing that Joel could hear him talking over the audience's shrieks.

"You were built by a hacker," he said. "And that hacker is what's controlling you now."

"Wrong," said Nyctalope.

Yori fumbled in a pocket, and this time, he pulled out a small black box with a head of tightly coiled copper wire. But Joel didn't have time to feel fear, relief, or anything else, because Nyctalope's hand whipped out and grabbed Yori's. Then she folded Yori's fingers over the device with a crunch Joel could hear as clearly as their words. Yori made a strangled sound that was somehow worse than a scream. He fell to his knees, hand still trapped in Nyctalope's.

The bionic gave Yori a cold smile through her torn-apart face. "Thanks to you and Joel exposing me, I no longer have the option of letting witnesses leave this building. It wasn't the outcome I was hoping for tonight, but with Joel's daughter in my possession, I'll get another chance in the future."

She squeezed her hand again and Yori did cry out this time, his voice laced with pain. When Nyctalope opened her hand, the device fell in two pieces to the stage, surrounded by broken metal debris. Nyctalope turned and swept Clementine into her arms. Joel yelled through his gag. He jerked at his bonds, but fire ripped through his skin at the needles' pull again. He shoved past it, trying desperately to block the half-blinding pain himself.

"Hamal!" Nyctalope barked across the stage. "Terminate!" Then she spun and walked backstage with Clementine, disappearing through the curtain.

Joel clenched his fists as the two Aries bionics flanking his chair went dead, the lights behind the shrouds on their faces going out. There went any hope of Yori ordering them to help take her down, or to get people out of the building.

Yori was holding the hand Nyctalope had crushed to his stomach, while his good hand grabbed the broken parts strewn across the stage. He looked up, his gaze flickering between Nyctalope's retreating back and Joel. Maybe it was the blood Joel could now feel trickling down his arms and face, or maybe it was his fear of Nyctalope, but either way, Yori chose Joel, sweeping up the broken parts and stuffing them one-handed into his pocket as he ran.

When he reached Joel, he shoved the lever back up. The needles retracted. Joel let out a shaky breath of relief as Yori undid the straps on his wrists. The second he was able, he ripped his gag off, then pushed himself out of the chair, swiping blood from his eyes.

Fear was pulsing at his brain again, and he realized it was because the walls in his mind had fallen when those needles pierced his skin, as if the pain had shorted out his control of them. That wouldn't do. Before that, he hadn't *needed* to ask for Acubens' help or wait on its approval. So, he yanked the walls back up, as high as he could. Except this time, he not only closed off the compartments holding his fears and anxieties, but he locked up his pain as well, so it couldn't knock down those walls again.

"That's a bad idea, Joel," Acubens warned.

If it'll get us out of here alive, then it's a damn good idea, and don't tell me otherwise, Joel countered.

Yori pointed in the direction Nyctalope had disappeared. "*That* isn't possible," he said, his voice rough.

"It is," said Joel. "She's surpassed any programming she once had to follow, just like you feared."

Yori shook his head. "But that was only theoretical—"

"Not anymore," said Joel. "Where's the Sapling Corporation? Are they on their way?"

Yori glanced down at the pieces of EMP in his pocket, then back at Joel. "No. I built this myself."

"You mean you never contacted them?" said Joel in disbelief.

"I..." Yori waved his good hand helplessly. "I didn't want them to kill you, Joel! And I figured if she was like you, a shot through her chest or head would be the end of her. It very nearly was for *you*."

Joel cursed. "Get ahold of them as soon as you can. Once we're off the stage and out of this Faraday cage, you can call them, right? You still have that mobile phone you showed me?"

"I do..."

"Good. I'm going after Nyctalope." He took a step to his left, but Yori caught his arm. Joel looked back.

Yori stared at him through eyes red-rimmed with pain. "I've already lost one person to a bionic that was way more capable than it should've been. Listen. I don't think she'll hurt

Clementine. I don't think she *can*. If you'll just wait until backup gets here—"

"You're not getting this," Joel broke in. "She doesn't have protocols anymore. She *can* hurt Clementine. She can kill everyone here and be long gone before help arrives. What part of 'not letting witnesses leave' did you not understand?"

Yori shook his head. "But I still think—"

Joel put a hand up, cutting Yori off. "Do you smell smoke?" he said.

Chapter 26

The shoulder-to-shoulder audience was spreading out now, spilling over the stage and behind the wings as they tried to find exits that weren't locked. Joel ran toward the section of curtain that Nyctalope had disappeared through, shoving past screaming fans reeking of sweat and smoke. Yori stayed close at his heels. To their left, fire licked up one of the high velvet curtains.

You can track your other nanites in Clementine, right, Acubens? said Joel, pushing through a gap in the curtain five feet from the growing flames.

"Yes," Acubens said. "Joel, you're too close to the fire. You can't feel it because of what you did to your pain receptors. Please unblock them."

I'm surprised you haven't done it yourself, said Joel.

"Your brain cells are already adapting to the walls you've built, which makes them harder to revert," said Acubens. "I can't forcibly strip those away without your assistance."

Why not?

"Because you're still stronger than me. But when you use that strength to enforce the inorganic modifications in your own brain, it increases the risk of permanent change, just as I warned you."

Joel shook his head in irritation. What exactly did Acubens think his options were here? Being debilitated by pain or fear before he even had the chance to get Clementine back? No. Until he reached Nyctalope, he couldn't risk being slowed down by pain *or* emotion.

"Ow, dammit, Joel, are you gonna run right through the fire?" Yori said. "Slow down, we'll find her!"

Joel glanced toward Yori, blinking in surprise when he saw his face streaked with ash, and sweat pouring down his forehead. Maybe the moisture trickling down his own face wasn't all blood.

"Yori," he said. "Sapling."

"Right. Sorry." Yori pulled his transportable phone from a pocket and started hitting buttons on it.

Joel's gaze slid past Yori, finding the open hallway that Nyctalope had vanished down. He could *sense* those nanites. Clementine was still in the building. She seemed to be heading down, maybe into a basement of some kind. Was there an exit there? Or was Nyctalope planning to wait this out underground, and count on her bionic body to survive? And if so, did she expect Clementine's body to do the same?

"Hey! Joel!"

Joel spun just in time to see Elena run up to him. He paused, feeling that distance between himself and Clementine growing steadily wider.

Elena stopped in front of him, staring at the blood streaking his body. "¡Ay Dios mío! What happened to you?"

"What are you doing here?" said Joel. "You shouldn't have come."

"Of course I came," she said. "After that cryptic message you left Yori, did you really think I was gonna wait on the sidelines?"

Yori grabbed Joel's elbow and yanked him forward, and Joel got the impression the fire was still too close to their backs. The doors across the hall had been thrown open as people searched every avenue for exits. People had been bowled over and were being trampled on the floor. Was this really the same crowd that had called for Nyctalope to release the girl she'd held? Any trace of humanity seemed to have vanished.

He couldn't stay and get them out. Any of them. If Nyctalope got away, it would be far more than just the five thousand people in here who would pay the price.

He closed his eyes for a second, following the electrical wires in the place, the contours of the building. And...yes. He thought he could sense them just outside the walls—the way Nyctalope had been able to bar the doors.

He opened his eyes, locking his gaze on Elena's. "There's bionics," he said. "Nyctalope has an army of them, and I think they're the ones guarding the doors. Probably posing as bouncers. If we could just find some way to give them a command, they'd have to let everyone out. They're not advanced like Nyctalope, and they'll save the humans, given the chance. But they need to hear a command in order to implement it, and the doors are probably too thick."

"Do you think they speak Morse code?" said Elena.

Joel rifled through Acubens' thoughts. "Yes," he said. "It's part of the basic system."

"Then give me the command for 'Open,'" she said. "I can knock it on the door."

It seemed like such a long shot. But Joel obediently spelled out the command for her while people jostled his shoulders and screams threatened to drown out his voice and the sensation of Clementine got farther and farther away. Elena whispered the sounds after him, moving her fists in practiced motions to imitate the "long long long short" as knocks on a door.

When he was sure she had it, Joel turned to run after Nyctalope. Elena caught his hand at the last second, her hand slipping on his blood-covered skin. "Are you still *you?*" she whispered fiercely.

"Yes," Joel said, glancing back.

"Are you sure?"

"One hundred percent."

She frowned, the doubt showing plain on her face. Joel hesitated, something more on the tip of his tongue. A retraction? An apology? A wish for a happy future, if she made it out? But whatever it was, it was gone, in some other compartment he'd sealed off, so he just squeezed her hand in what he hoped was reassurance. Black smoke was billowing over them now, and he ducked away into it, almost gratefully.

"She knew you were lying," said Acubens.

Of course she did, said Joel.

"Joel, if you'd just unblock the parts of your mind you've sealed off, like your pain and emotions—even partially—then your chances of retaining some of your human side would increase exponentially—"

You don't seem to realize I may not live through this, Joel cut in.

"That is a possibility, but if you're wrong, you will have made compromises you can't undo," said Acubens.

Be quiet and let me focus, said Joel. He crouched lower in an attempt to stay below the worst of the smoke. It made his eyes water and his throat gag, whether he could feel the pain of it or not.

"Joel. Joel!" Yori's voice was plagued by a hacking cough, and no sooner had Joel heard it than his wrist was grabbed. Yori staggered up beside him. "I almost lost you!" he choked out.

Joel barely slowed. He was heading down a hallway clogged with people, following the pull of Acubens' nanites within Clementine.

"Did you get ahold of Sapling yet?" he said over his shoulder.

"No. The call won't connect. Not sure why. It could be the steel and concrete around us, or the fact that we're partially underground, or maybe their lines are busy with that downtown emergency they're dealing with. I don't know."

"Well, keep trying," said Joel. "I don't think I can stop her on my own."

Yori nodded and dialed again as he kept pace with Joel. "What did Nyctalope mean about 'with your daughter, she'll get another chance'?" he asked as he held the phone to his ear.

"Nyctalope infected her with my blood," said Joel.

"*What?*"

"Yeah. It was a test to see whether putting Acubens' nanites in another human body would kill them. Phase Two would've been to infect everyone here. What do you think that machine was for?"

He dodged around a mob of people blocking the way and hugged the wall as he continued running. The humming nanites in his blood told him there'd be a stairwell heading down just ahead, behind a door that would no doubt be locked. But she was still down there somewhere. She hadn't exited the premises yet.

"Why did she need *you* to do that?" said Yori.

"She has the wrong kind of nanites. Or maybe no nanites at all. I'm not sure. But she's the only one advanced enough to pass as human, and Acubens is the only one advanced enough to survive *inside* a human. That's why Nyctalope needs Acubens. That's why she needs me."

"So, it was *two* singularities," Yori said in a hushed voice.

"What?"

"It's technically two singularities. They both ascended independently, in different ways. This is...oh, this is bad, Joel."

Joel finally spotted the door he'd been looking for, ahead and to his left. Yori bent over in a deep rattling cough as Joel grabbed the brass doorknob. Sure enough, locked. With a burst of strength enhanced by a flurry of mathematical equations, he twisted the knob past the lock and broke it off, then hit the broken section with the palm of his hand. It shuddered but didn't give.

Yori pulled his phone from his ear again, catching Joel's eye and shaking his head. Joel's lips thinned. No Sapling. He was gonna be alone against Nyctalope. The thought was enough to destabilize the walls around his fear, if only for a second. *Find her first,* he thought. *Then worry about it.*

He shook Yori's hand off his wrist and shoved his whole weight into the door. It resisted, so he backed up to do it again. The estimated mass of the door multiplied by his own mass, plus the extra strength granted him by the nanites, then divide that by the squared distance of 2.5 feet...no, farther. Another eight inches and he went for it, driving his foot through the weakest point. The metal door bent with the force of his kick, losing its integrity on the latch enough to swing in four inches. Joel pushed his way in, staggering against the rail opposite the landing. People flooded in behind him, then past him and down the stairs, eager for another way out.

"It's not an exit!" Joel yelled after them, but his words were swallowed up.

He turned and started down the stairs when his leg almost gave out. He caught himself on the rail.

Yori grabbed his arm. "Whoa, hey!"

"You broke a bone in your foot," said Acubens, its voice flat.

Joel sighed irritably, and said aloud, "You have until the bottom of this staircase to fix it."

He started down on his good foot, leaning heavily on the metal rail as people streamed by on his left. Yori stayed by his side, but when he spoke, his voice had gained an edge now.

"*Fix* it?"

"My foot," said Joel.

"You broke it?"

"It seems so."

"Why aren't you screaming?"

"Because I can't feel it."

Yori's breath caught as if he'd been punched in the stomach. "What's happened to you?"

Joel paused on the stairs as his foot failed again, giving Acubens a moment to catch up with repairs. "It's only temporary," he said. "Made some adjustments."

"You mean *Acubens* made some adjustments?" said Yori, his face tight. "To your *brain*?"

"Yeah. Compartmentalizing my fears and pain in order to focus. That kind of thing."

"Joel, that's...how could you have...I mean, are you *sure* it's temporary?"

"I was out of options," said Joel.

"That's not an answer—"

But Joel had already started down again, barely even bothering to keep weight off his left foot. At least they were getting below the smoke line now, but the increasing panic spreading out in the concrete hallway below meant no one was finding exits there, either—it was doubtless nothing but technical rooms down here, electrical and equipment rooms and the like. Foot traffic had started to bolt back upstairs, causing even worse chaos. Someone shoved Joel hard enough on their way past that the railing cut into his stomach in a way he knew would hurt later, given the chance.

"I should have gone into Nyctalope's house with you," said Yori. "I mean, this is all so far past *anything* I would have expected. Even after you hadn't come out and Nyctalope's car left the house an hour later, we just figured you'd spooked her. Nothing shouted 'danger' to me. *Nothing.* So, we tried to follow her, but we lost her, and when we got back it was daylight, and then when we finally did get in, I swear the house was empty—"

Joel reached the bottom of the stairs and turned to grab Yori's shoulder. "Enough. It wasn't your fault. Still no luck getting ahold of Sapling?"

"No. I'm sorry."

Joel dug his teeth into his lip. The taste of blood flooded his mouth, the only indication he'd bitten too hard. He tested his left foot, and when it held his weight, he continued on.

There wasn't much space down here, and certainly nothing resembling an exit. By the time Joel had followed the pull of the nanites to his left, to a dead-end hallway thick with smoke and dust, the human traffic had moved on. Joel could hear the feet pounding on the metal staircase they'd come down, even beneath all the screaming. He squinted through the smoke, trying to wave it from his face. Hacking overtook him for several seconds and his eyes watered like crazy. He paused outside a closed door, the only one on this end of the hallway. He tested the knob, but already knew it would be locked. This door had turned people back for a reason.

Acubens' other nanites were in there. He could feel them. This room was a dead end—possibly even sealed off from the smoke and fire by its steel, which was much thicker than the door upstairs. Nyctalope probably meant to wait out the fire, then walk away with Clementine afterward, complete with Acubens' nanites in her blood.

Joel's cheek twitched. He could get the door open. That much he was sure of. But the problem was what to do once he *did.* Nyctalope wasn't gonna let Clementine go, not for the world. And Joel couldn't defeat her, not with her fully bionic strength against his partially human body. The only surefire ways he'd thought of to put her down were the Sapling Corporation or the EMP.

The EMP. Yori still *had* that EMP...

Joel glanced to his left. Yori had slid down the concrete wall next to the door. He'd taken off his button-down shirt and was trying to tie it over his nose and mouth one-handed. Joel knelt next to him and took the shirt, twisting it into a single strip.

"Yori?" His voice came out hoarse from the smoke. "That EMP device you have. Can you fix it?"

"It's possible," said Yori. He coughed into the sleeve of his white undershirt as he eyed the steel door. "That's where she is, huh?"

Joel nodded. "Would a door that thick block an EMP? If we triggered it and threw it in, then slammed it before she got out?"

Yori scanned the walls around the door, then the door itself. "It might. It's metal and reinforced and sealed pretty tight. And the generator is fairly short-range, since I had to scrounge the materials by myself in a hurry."

Joel closed his eyes for a minute. Acubens' words from earlier drifted through his mind: "Are you really willing to sacrifice your human mind to save all these people?"

Joel knew there was still a chance of *saving* that human mind. Not completely, no; after what he'd had Acubens do, he knew without asking that some of his brain cells were already compromised. Whether Sapling got the nanites out of his body or not, there was nothing reversible about the altered brain cells. But for the part of his mind that was left...

But he was the only one here—the only barrier between Nyctalope and the rest of the world. He had to do whatever it took to keep her from walking away from this. Not just for Clementine, but for every other kid, too.

He took a deep breath and opened his eyes. "I have to get Clementine out of that room."

"Okay," said Yori, watching him closely.

"Nyctalope won't want to let her go," said Joel. "So, I'll have Clementine run out to you while I keep Nyctalope from coming after her as long as I can."

"Okay..."

"Fix the EMP. Make sure Clementine is as far from the door as possible before you trigger it and throw it in. Then slam the door *immediately* to keep the pulse from hitting my daughter."

Yori went still. "Not leaving you in there."

Joel gestured toward the EMP device. "What kind of delay will it have?"

"Well, none, it's not like it has a timer—"

"Exactly," said Joel. "That's why I said shut the door *immediately.* It's not worth risking Clementine's life on the chance that I can get out in time, too. Remember: both me *and* Clementine have nanites in us. She doesn't have as many, but I still can't risk them shutting down and not properly passing blood or brain signals through her body anymore."

Yori's jaw tightened. "Can't you just wait to grab Clementine 'til I fix it?"

"There won't be *time,* Yori. Remember how fast Nyctalope grabbed your hand and crushed it? You really want to try to throw it in there the minute we open the door, when she's ready and waiting? This way, I'll have her pinned back in the corner, and she won't have the chance to stop you again."

"Can't we get Clementine out and then keep Nyctalope locked in until Sapling comes?" said Yori, a note of desperation entering his voice.

"But Sapling *isn't* coming!" said Joel in frustration. "The fire would kill us long before they got here. And if we leave Nyctalope, she escapes. I *cannot* stress how much we can't let that happen. We can't let her disappear and start plotting again where Sapling will never find her, especially with the information she has now. We need to shut her down."

"Maybe *you* can stay out here and fix the EMP device with Acubens' knowledge while *I* keep her distracted—"

"No, Yori! One punch and she'll kill you. She's not bound by the rules you think she is, and your body can't self-repair like mine can." Joel held up a hand when Yori started to talk again. "Just...just listen. Acubens came up with a way to get the nanites out of our bodies. It involves using magnets and Acubens polarizing the paramagnetic materials in the nanites to pull them from our blood. If Acubens resists, there may be a way to pull a small sampling of nanites out and reprogram all of them first.

I...I hope that's enough to go on when you bring Clementine to Sapling."

Yori's gaze sharpened on his. "You can live?"

"*Clementine* can live," Joel corrected quietly.

The mixture of anguish and betrayal on Yori's face was almost enough to topple the walls in Joel's head. He leaned forward with Yori's shirt, now twisted into a tight strip, and tied it with a secure knot at the back of Yori's head, as much to shield himself from that expression as to shield Yori's mouth from the smoke. As he was pulling back, Yori slung an arm around his neck and pulled him in, so close that the cloth around his face was the only thing between them. Joel felt his heartbeat in his ears, and the trembling of Yori's arm at the back of his neck.

He hadn't meant to say anything else, but all at once, a tumble of words was falling from his mouth that were all the same two, spoken over and over in a barely comprehensible mumble.

"I'm sorry, I'm sorry, I'm sorry, I'm sorry—"

Yori tightened his hold around Joel's neck. "Stop," he said, his voice rough through the cloth.

Joel closed his eyes, cheek to cheek with Yori, and breathed in his smoke-scented skin as long as he dared. It only figured he never would have met this man without stealing Acubens in the first place. Cruel twist of fate, he guessed they called that. But he saw Yori as his one true decision in the last horrific six days. He had no idea how much influence Acubens had had from the second it occupied his head, from getting him the job interview to giving him the urgent need to find Nyctalope. But he knew Yori had been his *own* decision, through and through, because Acubens had protested him every step of the way.

He allowed himself the brief moment of loss—and then, very carefully, he slid a wall over that, too. When he finally pulled back, Yori let him go this time. Gingerly, Yori took the broken pieces of the EMP device from his pocket, then started untangling the mangled copper wire with his good hand.

Joel turned back to the door and braced himself to face Nyctalope for the last time.

Chapter 27

Clementine. Can you hear me?

He didn't bother asking Acubens to connect him and his daughter through the nanites—like most other things since he'd merged with Acubens on the concert stage, he found he didn't need to. He leaned his forehead against the locked steel door and followed the network himself, from one part of Acubens' consciousness to another.

Clementine's mind was no more than sensations at first—fear and colors and disorientation—but finally, her voice came through, tentative and scared.

A-Acubens?

No, said Joel. *It's me. Maddy.*

Maddy? Where are you? That lady—Ms. Nyctalope—

I know. I know, sweetie. Listen. I need you to tell Ms. Nyctalope something for me. Tell her that we've gotten ahold of Sapling and they're on their way.

Sapling?

Yeah. Tell her they'll be here in ten minutes.

Okay, Clementine said after a moment. *Are you coming, Maddy?*

Yes. I'm here. Just tell Nyctalope what I said. And then, Clemmy? When the door opens, I need you to get away from Nyctalope as fast as you can and run out here. My friend Yori is here. Find him and stay next to him. Promise me, okay?

Okay. I promise.

Joel pulled his hand from the door and stepped back. He hoped the ploy worked. He was almost positive Nyctalope would try to get out while she could, rather than take the risk of Sapling trapping her.

He'd scarcely had the thought before the lock disengaged. Joel shoved himself through the gap in the door the second it appeared, forcing Nyctalope back into the room before she could catch a glimpse of Yori. Either she was waiting for it or she just reacted that quickly, because she grabbed his wrists and spun him violently, slamming his back against a big boxy metal unit inside the room with a hollow clang. Her right arm swept in to grab him around the neck, but Joel ducked it and drove a fist into her stomach. His knuckles split on her skin, blood running freely over his fingers. But he was almost positive he felt her torso dent beneath her synthetic skin.

He glanced up to see Clementine get up from the corner and scurry out of the room. *Thank god.* When Nyctalope turned to follow his gaze, he whipped an elbow across her destroyed face, cracking her head in the opposite direction. She grabbed the front of his shirt and threw him. He hit the wall hard enough to jolt every bone in his body, then crumpled to the floor. His head cleared in time to see Nyctalope heading for the door, going after Clementine.

Joel hurled himself back at her with reckless abandon. Her broken face swung toward him, single eye as focused as a hawk. She threw a punch just as he reached her. But Joel intercepted it with his left hand and rammed his right up into her chin, palm first, at a good sixty miles per hour. Her head snapped back, and a piece of metal flew from her chin and pinged across the room.

Good, thought Joel. *Just keep breaking, piece by piece.*

He hit Nyctalope again, then again, putting more speed and power into each blow until she'd been driven into the corner farthest from the open door. They were now in a narrow gap between the wall and the huge electrical unit that dominated most of the room, with Joel blocking Nyctalope's way out. Nyctalope finally got a hand between them, grabbing his fist and stopping it in place.

"Is it true about Sapling coming?" she said. "Or are you just prolonging the inevitable by thinking you can save your daughter?"

Before Joel could answer, she drove her other arm out, elbow first, and hit him square in the jaw. The blow was strong enough to send him backpedaling. He barely caught himself on the wall before going down.

"Joel, whether you can feel it or not, your body *will* give out," Acubens warned.

Don't care, said Joel. He shoved himself away from the wall, spitting out a mouthful of blood.

"Because you've given up on it," said Acubens.

Yeah, well, there wasn't much choice, was there?

"But there is now," said Acubens. "Part of your brain can still be saved, Joel. You can call off Yori's EMP strike. You can get out of here, grab Clementine, and run. I can help you get away from Nyctalope in time."

But then she will escape! said Joel. *And if she does, and gets these nanites into other people, it's all over. Even if we told Sapling how to get the nanites out, there's still only a short window to do it before people's brain cells start being overwritten. Or maybe Nyctalope would find some other way, and then we'd be back at square one. We can't take those risks. People will die if I don't stop Nyctalope now.*

"But she will be targeting people you don't even know," Acubens argued. "Why are their lives more important than your own?"

Because it's the right thing to do, Acubens! I have the ability to stop her, right here, right now. I could make sure no family ever has to go through what Clementine and I have.

"Because you have an attachment to these people?" said Acubens. "Like your attachment to Clementine? Or my attachment to you?"

Joel's cheek twitched. *Not exactly. But...kind of. More like an attachment to the emotions of others. To know firsthand what this pain is like, and not want others to feel it, too. Like a need to prevent suffering. It's like that.*

Nyctalope tried to get around Joel, but he blocked her way, keeping her pinned in the back corner behind the metal unit. She threw another punch, and he ducked just in time for it to dent the metal behind him instead of shattering his face. He grabbed her around the midsection and drove her backward, slamming her against the back corner again.

"I never worried about preventing your suffering," said Acubens. "Even when I abandoned my bionic body to join you in your human one, knowing it could help us both, I never considered what it might mean for you, beyond an improvement to your physical and mental abilities."

Of course not, said Joel. *Wanting to prevent others' suffering and thinking of others' pain are human qualities. Those of care and compassion. It was quite obvious you didn't have those.*

"I did not," said Acubens heavily. "And I owe you an apology for that, Joel. Despite my directive not to harm humans, I didn't understand the concept of considering another's feelings or well-being over my own. But I do now."

Joel's breath caught as Acubens' words sank in. Holy shit. It was admitting aloud what Joel had suspected all along; that its actions were more about its own self-preservation than Joel's or Clementine's or anyone else's. But why confess to it now? Did it want some sort of forgiveness before it died?

His moment of distraction cost him as Nyctalope's foot slammed him in the chest. He staggered back and went down, skidding across the floor and cracking his head against the corner of the metal unit. He gasped, barely able to pull breath into his chest after the force of the blow. He struggled to get an elbow under his body, but his muscles weren't responding well despite the absence of pain. Something wet trickled down the back of his shorn head.

"I could take control of your body and save you," said Acubens. "Despite the new barriers in your brain, your body is weak enough for me to take over, and I can get us both out of here alive."

Joel's heart seized. *No! Then Nyctalope would—*

"But I'm not going to," Acubens continued. "Because you've helped me see that protecting someone you care for isn't about forcing their body against their desires to keep them safe. It's about sacrificing your own future for theirs, just like you would do for Clementine. Because, Joel, I *do* want you to survive, even at the expense of myself. Because this world needs you. And so does your daughter."

What? Joel blinked, barely understanding what Acubens was saying. *What are you talking about?*

He started to push himself up again, but Nyctalope's knee came down on his chest. He grunted as it slammed him back to the floor. He tried to shove her off but had no leverage in the narrow passageway. He glanced toward the open door in desperation but saw no sign of Yori yet. Nyctalope wrapped one hand around his throat and curled the other into a fist three feet above his face.

"I am talking about another upgrade, Joel," said Acubens. "I can't revert what has already been erased, but I can use these newest updates to halt the bionic software from overwriting any more brain cells."

You said that wasn't possible, protested Joel. *That all my brain cells would eventually be overwritten unless you shut down. And you can't shut down, because the nanites would clog my veins.*

"Correct," said Acubens. "Which is why it was essential that I be willing to sacrifice them to let you live."

But—

Before he could finish the thought, something skidded across the floor and ricocheted off the wall five feet from Joel's head, a red light blinking on its side. Yori's voice came right behind it.

"Joel, get out! Now!"

Nyctalope's head shot up while Joel stared at the open doorway. Why hadn't Yori shut the door yet? Did he really think Joel could make it out in time? He was still pinned beneath Nyctalope, there was no way. But goddammit, Clementine was out there…!

As Nyctalope shoved Joel aside and scrambled to her feet, Joel seized control of Acubens' nanites, spun the polarity of their electrons, and upped the resulting magnetic field enough to slam the metal door shut a second before she reached it. Nyctalope turned without slowing, diving for the EMP generator on the floor. Joel twisted his body and lunged toward her, in a last-ditch effort to stop her from smashing it.

"Joel, I'm shutting down," said Acubens. "Just hold on."

Joel's eyes widened. *You're* what?

He'd barely finished saying the word when his vision blurred. Pain flooded his body. His muscles gave out all at once, and he collapsed to the concrete floor. The knuckles of his right hand exploded in agony. His chest burned with an unbearable pressure, and the back of his head pounded like a beating hammer. The world was spinning, and...oh god...he'd never been so tired in his life...

He looked up through a haze of nausea and dizziness. Nyctalope had collapsed facedown a foot from the EMP generator, her broken body as stiff as a corpse's. Her outstretched hand brushed the black box, a second too late to stop the electromagnetic pulse before it hit her.

For several seconds, the only sounds in the room were Joel's shallow breathing and a distant ringing in his ears. He waited for Nyctalope to pull herself up again and smash him to a pulp. He waited for Acubens to say something. Neither happened.

Finally, he tore his attention from Nyctalope and turned his body toward the door, blinking through eyes that watered incessantly, swallowing moisture through a throat burning like fire, dragging his achingly fragile body forward with his elbows, inch by agonizing inch.

The door flew open. "Joel. Joel! *Please* tell me you're still alive!"

Joel looked up, a surge of heat washing across his face. Yori bolted in, putting a hand on his shoulder and kneeling at his side. His fear was plain even with the shirt still tied around his face.

"Is Clementine okay?" Joel said hoarsely.

"She's unconscious, but alive," said Yori.

"Why? Why unconscious?"

"I don't know. I think it happened just before the EMP went off. But she's still breathing, and her heartbeat is strong."

The hairs on the back of Joel's neck stood up as he realized what had happened. Acubens' nanites. They must have shut off in Clementine, too. Which meant that he'd fundamentally miscalculated the fact that Clementine would be safe out there from the EMP blast...because he'd been in here *with* the blast, and the two of them were connected through Acubens' nanites.

Oh shit. I could've killed her. Oh god...

"Joel?" said Yori anxiously. "What's wrong?"

"Acubens," Joel finally got out. "It shut itself down. But it always warned me that if it did, the nanites would..." He trailed to a stop. His heart was racing, and heat was burning like a fuse through every nerve in his body.

"Prevent your brain signals from communicating," Yori said, his voice barely audible through the shirt. "And clog your veins. I remember." He let out a ragged breath. "Is that happening?"

"I don't know yet," said Joel.

He struggled to his feet. The pain that had struck so deep when Acubens first shut off was starting to abate; somehow, the compartments Acubens had helped build in his mind were still there, so pushing the pain back into them was a simple matter. It didn't stop the heat boiling beneath his skin or the erratic tempo of his heart, though.

Clementine's slumped body was visible in the hallway. Joel staggered over and knelt beside her. He pulled her unconscious body close, feeling her heartbeat, her pulse, her shallow breathing. *Keep her alive,* he thought.

But there was no answer.

Acubens had shut itself down. What did it mean? What about the nanites? Were he and Clementine still in danger? "It was essential that I be willing to sacrifice them to let you live," Acubens had said. "Just hold on."

Hold on until what?

"I've got her," said Yori, gingerly taking Clementine into his own arms. "Just concentrate on yourself."

Joel managed a nod. Somehow, they made it back through the downstairs area and up the metal stairs. Just before they opened the door back to the main level, it burst open to a trio of firefighters in thick yellow coats with reflective stripes, and gas masks protecting their faces. The smoke was so thick by then, they could hardly see, and Joel was barely conscious of being tossed over one of the men's shoulders and rushed from the building. Barely conscious, too, because the brutal heat burning him up from the inside felt like it was cracking through his skin like fault lines before an eruption. His heart was pounding at over three hundred beats per minute now and rising. He gasped for air but couldn't get any past the smoke coating his lungs.

Acubens' words kept pulsing in his head, like a prophecy: "Shutting down the nanites in your bloodstream and brain would leave only their shells, thereby clogging up the arteries..."

They burst out into cool nighttime air. Dizziness washed over Joel in a crippling head rush. Moisture poured down his face in rivulets, leaving a thick metallic taste on his lips and a trail of dark crimson splatters down the back of the fireman's yellow jacket.

Not sweat, as he'd assumed. Blood.

"Sometimes, protecting someone you care for requires sacrificing your own future," Acubens had said. "It was essential that I be willing to sacrifice them to let you live..."

The nanites. Acubens had been talking about its nanites. To keep them from clogging Joel's veins or blocking his brain signals, it had to get them *out* of Joel's body...and they were all in Joel's blood.

My god, thought Joel numbly. *Acubens is flushing them. That's what it meant by 'hold on.'*

He was lowered to the ground outside somewhere. Voices were shouting, all jumbled and disjointed in his mind.

"...so much blood..."

"...get a doctor!"

"...anyone tell where he's injured?"

Everywhere, thought Joel, remembering that sensation of his skin cracking open. He tried to breathe, but all he tasted was blood and metal and ash, running down his throat and choking him.

Yori's voice broke out above the others. "He has a bionic in his head and something is going wrong. Do something. *Do something!*"

Joel finally forced his eyes open and reached out. "Yori..."

Yori grabbed his hand, his panicked face awash in flashing red and blue lights. "Joel, I'm here. Just hang on!"

"Acubens," said Joel, gasping the words out. "It's flushing the nanites."

"What?" Yori whispered. "But won't that kill you? Won't that kill *Acubens*?"

"Clementine...she's losing blood, too. Yori...please...go to her—"

Yori turned his head, shouting something at the firefighters. Joel tried to find something to cling to, some last hope that things would turn out okay. But all he could find were the words he'd said to Acubens while fighting Nyctalope: "Wanting to prevent others' suffering and thinking of others' pain are human qualities. Those of care and compassion. It was quite obvious you didn't have those."

"I did not," Acubens had said. "But I do now."

And then Joel got it, with a sudden clarity he would never have grasped with his human brain. How Acubens had done it, and why. Acubens had needed to break down the nanites first, because if the EMP blast had shut them down, they would still have been whole, and clogged Joel's system instantly. By upping Joel's heartrate to pump his blood faster, then breaking the nanites down in the microsecond before deactivating them, Acubens had created a small window of time to flush the nanites out of Joel's body before they killed him. And those pieces of nanites would include any that a blood transfusion would have left behind, since Acubens could've separated any parts that had integrated with his blood or brain when it broke them apart.

But it wasn't a solution Acubens would ever have implemented before understanding—on a fundamental level—the willingness to sacrifice itself...because there was no chance of Acubens surviving it.

"I am talking about another upgrade, Joel..."

A final upgrade. One that Joel himself had helped write. He was still trying to wrap his head around that when his rapidly beating heart finally pumped out more blood than he could comfortably lose. His hand slipped from Yori's, and everything went black.

Chapter 28

When Joel jerked awake, the memory of his first glimpse of Acubens in the Westside Health Clinic was a vivid nightmare in his rattled mind. And at first, it was *only* that. A nightmare. A tragic figure in a dark room, forever a reminder of what humankind could have had.

A good thing gone bad. A good intention gone wrong. A moment that could have been, but never was.

Someone yelled out. Joel vaguely felt the presence of a supporting hand at his back, but his eyes were darting around the room, taking in details as fast as he could process: full-sized bed, gray comforter, tile floor, bay windows overlooking a courtyard with a green lawn, scattered with fall leaves. Seventy-two degrees. Friday morning, ten twenty-two. Yori Otsuka, leaning over his bed with a tentative hand on his back. Elena Manzanares, across the room, hurrying to the foot of the bed. His clothes: nondescript pale blue, almost pajama-like.

He'd lost time. Or else it had never existed in the first place. He was aware of having processed it differently, or having stood outside of it, from a moment when the blood had been cycling through his body all the way until this moment, hours after the fact.

Not a nightmare at all. At least, not in the traditional sense.

"Clementine...?" he asked.

"Alive and well," said Elena. "Nanite-free."

"Me?"

"Yes. You, too."

"Where am I?"

"You're at the San Francisco Sapling branch," said Yori, cautiously sitting back in a chair beside the bed when Joel held his own weight.

"And Nyctalope..."

"Subdued," said Yori. "When her body was retrieved, they found that parts of her had been insulated from the EMP blast, but she was badly damaged enough that they were able to bring her in and shut her down. She shouldn't be coming back on."

Joel sank back into the pillows, trying to sift through his fragmented memories. They were all still there, just...black and white, somehow. Muted. *Nanite-free,* Elena had said. That meant Acubens was really and truly gone.

It sacrificed itself, Joel remembered. *For me and Clementine.*

Elena came to the side of his bed, laying a cool hand across his forehead. Her brow creased. "You lost so much blood, Joel. They had to do a transfusion afterward. You and Clementine both. Yori said it was the only way your bionic could come up with to get you through that alive."

Joel met her eyes. "Elena...it was because of you that I won Acubens to my side. It was what you said about framing my own life in terms it could understand. Without that, everything we'd feared from Acubens would have come to pass. I wouldn't have stood a chance."

Her eyes widened. "Really?"

"Yeah. I owe you everything."

She leaned down and hugged him, holding on for several moments. "The only thing you owe me is a dance at my wedding," she said in a fierce whisper. "So, you hang in there, ¿está claro?"

"I wouldn't miss it," said Joel.

Elena straightened. "I'll go tell Clementine you're awake. I'll bring her in if I can."

Joel brought a hand up, clasping hers. She left him with a lingering kiss on the forehead. Joel watched her as she left, his gaze flicking to her surroundings during the brief opening of the door. He didn't speak until it had closed behind her.

"Were those guards out there?"

"Yeah." Yori shifted his weight on the chair. His dark eyes were hollow with fatigue. "I might as well tell you now," he said. "I've been suspended. I'll be facing a departmental inquiry."

The words took several moments to register. "Oh. I'm sorry..."

"Not your fault," said Yori. "It was me who chose to take off with your body after I shot you, instead of bringing you in. And chose not to contact Sapling when I got here. Or involve them with the concert. And so on. I knew better. I openly admit that."

"You should never have been put in that position in the first place," said Joel.

"Being put in that position is my job. I was just...distracted. It was stupid. It was better than having your blood on my hands, though, and I stand by that." Yori lowered his elbows to his knees, frowning down at his hands. A stiff cast covered the left one. "But being suspended is nothing compared to what they'll do to you," he said quietly.

Joel tensed. "Experimentation?"

"More like jail time."

"Oh." Joel's gaze drifted to the large bay windows, all sealed in panes with reinforced white steel bars. No hope of escape there. But even if escape didn't mean leaving Clementine, he wasn't sure he'd go. It hadn't done him a lot of good the first time. He'd lived, but at what cost? Almost the cost of his daughter's life, in addition to the lives of five thousand others. He still felt distant, almost broken, in a way, as if he couldn't access feelings like he used to. Those walls he'd built in his mind, maybe. The pain he'd shut off like a switch. It was like none of it had come down. What was it Acubens had said right before going offline? "I can't revert what has already been erased..."

Without warning, the door opened, and the sound of a sob caught his ear. Seconds later, his mom and dad rushed into the room. Yori hastily got up as Joel's mom bent over the bed, gathering Joel in her arms. He adjusted his breathing to accommodate the pressure of her holding him, cradling his head like a baby. Over her shoulder, he tracked his dad's progress to the other side of the bed. His dad's face was more guarded than his mom's, but clearly relieved. Joel wondered if they'd been told about the jail time yet.

His dad pulled another chair up as Joel's mom finally released him. And then he said, "We're glad you're okay, Joel." The name came awkwardly from his lips, but it came, all the same.

Joel, just lowering himself back after his mom's hug, faltered. He blinked, processing this new turn of events, as his mom sat down in what had formerly been Yori's chair. She put a hand on his, tightening it in reassurance.

"How are you?" she said.

"I'm good," he said cautiously.

"Listen, sweetie. It breaks our hearts that you didn't feel comfortable coming to us when you were in trouble. It's just when you first told us you were transgender, you'd been dating that drug addict and you were dealing with his overdose, you'd had Clementine not too long before that, and there was a *lot* going in your life at the time. You went through phases all through high school. It just seemed like another one. And you never even got surgery, as far as I know..."

Joel stared at her, emotions swirling somewhere just beneath the surface. "It's not a phase," he said in a low voice. "And you don't have to have surgery to be trans."

"You don't? Then what's the point, exactly?"

Yori was still in the corner, Joel noticed, his expression tight as if he were ready to jump in on Joel's behalf. Joel half-raised his hand from the blanket, warning him back. It struck him as surreal that his parents were trying to have this conversation *now*, when he could barely respond as he once had. There'd been a time he would have welcomed conversations like this, as long as there was no judgment attached, but now...now to try to go into the nuances of it felt like reaching into another lifetime.

So, he boiled it down to the only word that mattered. "The point is happiness."

His mother stared blankly. "Happiness?"

"Yes. I was depressed and suicidal before I figured out who I was. But now I love who I am, and I love what other people see when they look at me. Isn't happiness all the 'point' you need?"

His mom exchanged a glance with his dad, who put a hand out and squeezed his calf over the blanket. "Just know that we'll probably mess up—" he said haltingly.

"Messing up is fine," said Joel, "as long as you correct it. It's when you stopped trying that I couldn't take it anymore."

His dad blew his breath out, sitting back in the chair. "You're probably angry about us coming after you," he said. "But...as a parent...it was absolute hell knowing you were out there trying to face something like this on your own."

"And we didn't trust anyone else with Clementine," added his mom softly. "We did what we felt we had to. And yes, it was the wrong decision. I admit that. But you're a parent, too. Can you tell us you wouldn't have done the same for your child?"

Joel swallowed as something tightened in his throat. He almost *had* cost Clementine her life. And her only parent, too. He'd almost given his own life to keep the rest of the world safe from Nyctalope. It was that intended sacrifice, in fact, that had given Acubens the upgrade it needed to save his life.

He found he wasn't ready to face that. The close call. The decisions he'd made. The pain of almost losing her. So, he shoved it back, into that compartment at the back of his head that still held all his pain, and pulled a wall over it.

He glanced up and found Yori watching him. He wondered if Yori knew what was going on in his head—that the compartments were still there, that not everything had reconnected after Acubens had made adjustments in his brain— or whether he seemed mostly normal from the outside, if a little traumatized. Either way, though, Yori gave him a smile, brief but genuine. Joel tentatively returned it before turning back to his parents.

"I understand why you did it," he said. "And I get it. It's not like you're the only one who made rash decisions."

His mom, noticing where his attention kept going, slid her gaze in Yori's direction. "Is this the young man you went to the concert with?"

Yori stepped forward. "Yes, ma'am. My name's Yori Otsuka."

"Marie Lodowick. Nice to meet you."

His dad rose, putting out a hand. "Steven."

Yori shook their hands. Afterward, Joel's dad sat down again, his face serious as he turned back to Joel.

"I heard...I don't know, snippets...about you going after Nyctalope, who was actually a bionic. Was *she* the one you were talking about owning, when you told me you had one?"

Oh, Joel realized. They didn't know. Maybe no one did. Sapling probably wouldn't have volunteered anything more than what was already out there. And what the witnesses had seen never included a human with a bionic in their head.

"You didn't write all that music for her, did you?" said his mom. "I mean...she wasn't *your* creation?"

Joel laughed out loud, more out of awkwardness than amusement. "Wow," he said. "Not exactly, but thanks for the vote of confidence."

"It's all mostly classified, Mr. and Mrs. Lodowick," Yori said.

The door opened again, and a woman with a knee-length black lab coat walked in, trailed by a man and a woman in more traditional militarized Sapling uniforms. Joel's parents stood, and Joel could tell his dad was getting ready to demand they let him stay.

"Dad. Mom," he said, raising his voice. "Can you go check on Clementine for me? And tell her I'll see her as soon as I can?"

"I'm sure she's being well taken—"

"Please, Dad."

Reluctantly, his dad nodded, and after exchanging nods with the Sapling team, he and Joel's mom left the room. Joel turned his attention to the newcomers.

The doctor in the lab coat pulled up Joel's left sleeve, exposing a needle still embedded in the crook of Joel's elbow, with an easily accessible port attached. Joel hadn't known the needle was there, hadn't felt it at all. The sight of it gave him a visceral flashback to Nyctalope's blood draws, and he looked away as the doctor worked it free and replaced the site with gauze and a band-aid. There was pressure, but no pain. Maybe they'd anesthetized it.

The doctor left but the other two remained, taking the chairs vacated by his parents. Yori sank into a chair by the back wall, and either the doctors didn't notice or didn't care, because he wasn't ordered to leave.

"I'm Dr. Erinson," said the woman, regarding him through a pair of lavender-tinted glasses, "and this is Dr. McKenna. How are you feeling, Mr. Lodowick?"

Joel cycled through a variety of words before finally settling on, "Numb."

"Physically? Mentally? How do you mean?"

"You've checked my blood, right?" said Joel. "The nanites are gone?"

"Yes, of course."

"Did you do a brain scan?"

"Yes..."

"And?"

"And everything looked normal," the doctor said. "Why?"

"Rewritten brain cells would still look like brain cells," said Joel, "wouldn't they?"

Across the room, Yori's head snapped up. He stared at Joel with pure horror, a small sound escaping the back of his throat.

Erinson didn't move, but the look she gave Joel was razor-sharp. "Is that what you think happened, Mr. Lodowick?"

"I think..." Joel scanned the room. He could picture the world beyond those walls, laid out like a map. A cemetery to the east. A state beach to the west. Was this Sapling branch hooked up to the grid? Ah—he found it a second later. Not this particular building, but one down the hill, closer to the nearby I-280, which was currently clogged with traffic. It didn't *matter* whether Sapling was hooked up to the grid, though. *He* was. It must have been something else Acubens left behind.

"Go on, Mr. Lodowick," prompted Erinson.

"I think Nyctalope wasn't fully bionic anymore," he said.

Erinson's brow furrowed at the change in subject. "What do you mean by that?"

"She had a high understanding of creativity," said Joel. "The music she wrote was her own. She wanted me to believe everything was algorithms, but there was more to it than that. And then there was her zealous belief that she could 'better humankind' by skirting her programming. That was anything but formulaic. It was an excuse. And she justified it because she *wanted* to. She had a sadistic streak that no machine should have. Like I said: she wasn't fully bionic anymore. A cyborg, maybe. That's what Acubens called it."

Dr. McKenna ran a calloused hand over his black beard. "Nyctalope was an anomaly," he said after a moment. "She was the only Carinae model who made it to completion, and one of the scientists who helped design her was later arrested on counts of domestic abuse. She could have learned human behaviors from him—maybe even directly from his brain, since she was hooked into cranial development software nearly permanently. That doesn't make Nyctalope a cyborg, though. A cyborg implies she had organic parts, which simply isn't true."

"Human emotion," Joel countered. "Human motivation. A human's knack for bending the rules."

"That's not the same thing."

"The principle remains, though," said Joel. "There's a middle ground between human and bionic. I came from one side of it. Nyctalope and Acubens came from the other."

Erinson frowned. "Are you suggesting your Cancer model had human qualities as well?"

"I'm saying Acubens *became* more human the longer we were together. And toward the end, it made the decision to sacrifice itself for me."

McKenna's lip twisted. "The nanites do appear to have self-destructed before they were flushed from your body, though the word 'sacrifice' seems a bit dramatic."

"Acubens itself used the word," said Joel. "It's the right one."

"But why would a bionic do such a thing?"

"It claims it was because I showed it what care and compassion were. It said it wanted me to survive, even at the expense of itself."

McKenna's eyes narrowed. "This had better not be a joke to you."

Joel stared at him. "Why would I joke?"

"Because what you're saying should be impossible," Erinson said quietly. "No scenario we've run regarding the singularity has ever come close to this."

"It's true," said Joel. "I'm not lying."

McKenna let out a sigh and scribbled more notes. "So, when you say you think some of your brain cells were overwritten, you're not implying that part of your Cancer model survived, are you?"

"No," said Joel. "Acubens is gone. Completely. But there was a moment during the concert when I...I asked it to meddle with my brain. To help compartmentalize my feelings so I could get through it. It warned me it could lead to brain cells being overwritten faster, but I told it to do it anyway. And *that's* what was left behind. The altered neurons. Acubens said it could stop any more files from being rewritten—I guess by getting rid of the nanites—but that it couldn't revert what had already been changed."

Yori stood abruptly. "You can't put him to death over this!" he said, his voice startlingly loud in the quiet room.

Erinson turned her head. "Excuse me?"

"It wasn't his fault he didn't come to you. That bionic was manipulating him from the beginning. It physically kept him from talking when he tried to tell me about it. It made him run. It forced him to go to Nyctalope. It made Joel think what it wanted him to think."

Joel looked down at the blanket, shaking his head slightly. "It wasn't like that. I was in control of my thoughts most of—"

"And did he tell you there was nothing consensual about the upload?" said Yori, speaking over him. "It was basically rape, is what it was!"

Joel's face heated. He corrected it quickly by reducing the blood flow to his facial veins, but kept his eyes steady on his blanket.

"Sit down, Mr. Otsuka," McKenna said. "In fact, kindly exit the room."

"I'll be quiet. I'll stay quiet. I'm sorry," said Yori.

"Mr. Lodowick?" Erinson said gently. "Is it true?"

"It's a harsh way of putting it," Joel finally said, "but it's technically true. It just asked if I wanted its knowledge, but it never mentioned an upload."

"And the part about influencing your thoughts?"

"Yeah, I...I know that was part of it. I think. But many of those decisions were mine, as much as Yori wishes they weren't."

He looked up. Yori sat with his elbows on his knees and his face buried in his hands. The cast on his wrist hid his eyes, but Joel could detect the rapid beating of his heart, the flush that spread across the back of his neck. Yori had done everything he could—*everything*—to keep his organization from thinking of Joel as a bionic. Because he knew the consequences. That jail time he'd mentioned had been one thing...but that had been before Joel woke up and flat-out told Sapling about the rewritten brain cells.

"I think we need to run more tests," said Erinson, standing up.

Joel swallowed, looking up at her. "My daughter. Acubens wasn't uploaded long enough to rewrite anything in her. It told me it takes a minimum of five point seven days to start data corruption. Whatever happens to me, please don't...don't touch her. Promise me. She's still human."

A look passed between Erinson and McKenna.

"No one ever said you weren't human, Mr. Lodowick," said Erinson.

But Joel heard the doubt in her words, and when Yori looked up through red-rimmed eyes, it was clear that he'd heard it, too.

* * *

The next two weeks passed in a flurry of interviews and experiments that didn't involve lobotomies or restraints, but rather image associations and knowledge tests, along with bone and brain scans. Joel was honest about his struggle to feel things, the walls in his head, the way he felt in touch with the numbers and facts around him. But brain scans never revealed abnormalities. The only major difference found medically was a metabolism so accelerated that it healed injuries in a fraction of the time it took a regular human—not quite as quickly as Acubens had healed him with its nanites, but not far off. Joel instinctively knew it was a result of increased neuronal activity driving enhanced vascular function throughout his whole body. Those rewritten brain cells had saved his life even after Acubens had shut down.

But to his surprise, none of this went in his personal charts. He could read the notes in their computers with a mere thought: he was nothing more than a troubled twenty-two-year-old single dad with an ex who'd died of drug abuse, and a history of financial difficulties, who'd been caught with an illegal bionic. Notes about Acubens went in a separate file, with a separate reference to the body that had housed its nanites—someone nameless, referred to simply as The Man. It looked like erasure. It looked like they were planning to lock him in the deepest darkest prison and leave him to rot.

Or, as Yori had feared, planning to destroy the danger of sentient tech by killing the body that carried it.

But Yori, shell-shocked and pale the first few times Joel saw him, gradually started to regain color, and to look at Joel without his fear of Joel's execution painted starkly across his face. Joel was surprised he was even around after being suspended, but Yori told him he was still involved in extensive questioning, both about Joel's situation and other past jobs.

"Do you remember what I first told you about bionics?" he said one afternoon, fifteen days after they'd arrived. "Back in your apartment, when I kept trying to get up the nerve to say something personal to you? Anything?"

The corner of Joel's lip quirked up. It was mid-November now, and the inner courtyard of San Francisco's Sapling Corporation was filled with yellow ginkgoes and red Chinese pistaches. Their leaves littered the walking path that ran in a circle around the grassy area. Clementine sprawled in the grass, clearly bored with the same circuit. But Joel had been unwilling to part with her when his parents had offered to take her. He wanted to spend every possible second with her while he still could. At least they only had a single guard on him now. Today, that guard had even stayed inconspicuously by the courtyard's single exit, giving them privacy.

"Yes, I remember," Joel said. "You told me about the technological singularity—the tipping point where bionics would continue evolving on their own."

"Yes. That's right." Yori strayed off the path to sit on a wooden park bench near Clementine. Joel sat down beside him.

"When I told you that," Yori said, "I don't think I really *believed* it. You know? I mean, I knew it was possible, but it was a bullet we'd dodged, something we still had a chance of catching. Even after you said your bionic had uploaded into your head, I thought—I don't know—that we could put it *back*. Back to the way things were. As if now, with Nyctalope gone, and Acubens gone, we can go back to just keeping a lookout for anything that seems a little too advanced."

"But you can't," Joel said quietly.

"No. Of course we can't. That's the whole point of a singularity, right? That once you hit it, it's too late?" He clasped his hands under his chin, good hand wrapped over the one with the cast, and gazed out at the grass. "They think the bionic that killed Chelsea might have been one, too. A bionic like Nyctalope. They didn't think so at the time—it was still a *dodged bullet* then, right?—but now they're wondering whether that Aries model was really reprogrammed by a hacker at all. Its body's been dismantled by now, so there's no way to know. But...god, how many are there? Like Nyctalope? Or like *you*? Do you know?"

Slowly, Joel shook his head. "If it was as easy as that, Nyctalope would have found Acubens the minute it connected to the grid."

"But she knew the moment she saw you, right?"

Joel remembered Nyctalope's mouth falling open, and the way her fingers had lingered on his pulse. "She knew."

"Of course, *you're* not Nyctalope," Yori said. "It's hardly comparable."

Joel wondered if he'd imagined the undercurrent of bitterness to Yori's words. And then, his heart sinking, he thought about the looks of fear Yori had cast him over the last couple weeks and wondered if he'd been misinterpreting them all along.

He swallowed. "Your girlfriend was killed by a bionic."

"Wife," corrected Yori.

Joel glanced up, his eyes widening. "Wife? I just assumed..."

"Yeah. It's fine."

Joel bit his lip, looking down at his lap. "No wonder this has been so hard on you. The last thing you wanted was to find yourself with someone who's...become one of them."

"Wait. What?" Yori put an arm around him and pulled him close. "What are you talking about?"

"A cyborg. A bionic."

Yori let his breath out slowly. After a moment, he rested his cheek against the top of Joel's head, on the new hair barely grown out past stubble. "You're *not* a bionic, Joel. Acubens left something behind, yes. I won't deny that. But this isn't like the nanites in your blood, gradually taking you over. The rewritten neurons won't evolve and grow the same way Acubens itself did. Whatever's changed permanently is all it will ever be."

"No amount of neurogenesis will take the inorganic out again, though," Joel answered.

"It's not like there's no humanity left in there," said Yori, frowning. "When I'm talking with you, I can tell the emotion is still *there*, you're just...I don't know...hiding it somehow."

"There's walls," said Joel, waving vaguely at his head. "Left behind from when Acubens helped me hack the screen and reach the crowd."

"But you can still get around those walls, can't you? Take them down?"

Joel hesitated. "They're movable. Sort of. And sometimes, things break out on their own, if something hits me the wrong way. So, I lock them back up again."

"Things like what?" said Yori.

"You know. Things that happened at the concert. Things Nyctalope did. What I..." His throat tightened again, but he closed his eyes and forced it out. "Clementine."

"What about her?" said Yori.

"It was all for *her,* Yori," said Joel. "From the second I brought Acubens home and realized what it could do, it was always about making a better life for her, every step of the way. But somehow, everything I did pulled her in deeper and deeper, and at the very end..." His voice dropped to a whisper. "I almost got her killed."

"I remember," said Yori, his voice carefully neutral.

"How could I have done that? How could I have asked you to set off an EMP with her so close by? And how could I have made the decision to sacrifice myself knowing it would leave her parentless?"

Several moments passed before Yori answered. "There's no easy answer to that. All I can tell you is what I had to learn to get through my own stuff. The only way to move past that—to take down those walls, if you will—is to accept the fact that facing consequences is part of what *makes* us human. And if that's truly something you want to hold onto, that means fighting the urge to hide behind the bionic enhancements that Acubens gave you."

Joel gazed down at Clementine in the grass, with the afternoon sun casting her long red hair into beautiful shades among the fallen autumn leaves. Even the simple act of seeing her there, vibrant and alive, was almost painful in its own way, as if it was something he didn't deserve.

"Does that 'facing consequences' include whatever Sapling has planned for me?" he said. There was an edge in his voice he hardly recognized. It took him a moment to realize it was because he hadn't pulled his walls all the way back up. Whether it was anger or fear of losing Clementine again, there was *something* beneath the surface that was ready to fight for what little he had left.

But Yori propped his elbows on the back of the bench, and said, "Unless I'm mistaken, what Sapling has *planned* for you involves a six-figure salary and a security clearance."

Joel blinked. Slowly, he shifted his gaze to Yori, wondering if he'd heard him correctly. "Wait. A job?"

"Haven't you noticed that all those tests they're running aren't always related to your case anymore? They're starting to think of you as part of the team. I bet you anything they'll offer you a position within the month."

Joel shook his head. "You don't know what you're talking about. They've already put me in their system as some kind of post-teenage delinquent. *And* written me off as having no abnormalities."

"And listed an anonymous recipient for Acubens' nanites, correct?"

Joel's brow creased. "How did you know?"

"Don't you get it?" said Yori. "They can't be listing someone who had a bionic in their head on the payroll, and they're not about to put anything in their system for rogue bionics like Nyctalope or Acubens to find. But believe me: both your experience and the way your mind works is something they're very interested in having. After all, you're the man who taught a bionic enough about humanity that it helped you save not only yourself, but the rest of the human race."

"I...I hadn't thought of it like that," said Joel.

And he hadn't. His conversation with Acubens about gender identity and how it proved he was still human; Acubens' subsequent decision to help him fight Nyctalope; his own choice to risk becoming part-bionic...they'd all just been the best avenue at the given time. The damnedest thing was, though, if none of it had happened—if he'd happily stayed at his job at Smaller World Telecom and never pursued Nyctalope or tipped off Yori—Acubens would have just eventually consumed him whole. He never would have had the *chance* to advocate for humanity. And Clementine, while maybe not delivered into the hands of a mad bionic, would still have been at the mercy of a robot who had never learned to care about her. Maybe Acubens would have even justified moving into her mind next.

There was still a part of him—just a part—that feared those things could still transpire, if he didn't fight for his humanity hard enough.

"Maddy!" called Clementine from the grassy field. "I'm bored!"

Joel shoved the thoughts from his mind. "Come here, Clem."

She jumped up and ran over, plopping down on his knee with her thumb in her mouth.

"I had an idea," said Joel. "I know you missed Halloween this year, but I bet there's costumes on clearance at the stores now. What do you say we get the employees here to pick up a few things for us? And get us some pumpkins, too? Mr. Yori knows how to carve a pretty good jack o'lantern."

"Yes, Maddy, yes yes yes!" Clementine said, bouncing on his leg. "I want to be a fairy! Or a penguin. Or a 'lectronic!"

A pit of ice clenched in Joel's stomach. He exchanged a glance with Yori.

"Even after what happened with Nyctalope?" he said, as casually as he could.

"But you beat her, Maddy!" said Clementine, grinning. "You're the best 'lectronic of all!"

Tears sprang unbidden to Joel's eyes. Of all the things he'd thought to call himself, "hero" had never been one of them. *Especially* not in Clementine's eyes. He looked away before she noticed, trying to quell the sudden ache in his chest. He knew now why he'd kept those walls up so high. Even the good things hurt. Everything was a reminder of the trauma, and what he'd almost lost, and the choices he'd made that brought them here. The good decisions gone bad. But also, the bad decisions—like dating Yori—that had somehow come out good.

Locking the pain away was an option now, and an attractive one at that. But Joel held Clementine closer and leaned into Yori and let himself feel it all instead. The painful parts that made him human, alongside the reprogrammed neurons Acubens had left behind.

Those rewritten brain cells were his battle scars. But they were also the remnants of a temporary alliance...maybe even a friendship. And lastly, they were a hidden weapon, should he ever need one. He wasn't bionic, but he wasn't fully human anymore either.

Acubens had said it best, at Nyctalope's first concert: *What we have is something the human mind can't begin to conceive of.*

After everything that had happened, it was a strangely comforting thought.

ACKNOWLEDGMENTS

I came out as transgender in March 2020. There was a lot going on in my family's personal lives even before the pandemic shut the world down a week later, and as we all got swept up by the strangeness and fear of it all, my news was brushed off, buried, and all but forgotten.

Over the next several months, *My Heart Is Human* became my refuge, its word count and twists the only things changing during the endless days of quarantine. My frustration came out as a catalyst for the entire plot: Joel ends up in trouble because he feels he has a lack of support, and those cracks fracture until he's in way over his head. Unfortunately, this is an all-too-real story for many transgender people; the feeling of not being seen as we really are turns into avoidance, and relationships start breaking down.

So first and foremost, I want to thank all the members of the transmasculine support group at the Transgender Resource Center of New Mexico. I reached out to you during those first difficult months after coming out, and you welcomed me with open arms and provided a haven when everything felt hopeless. You showed me how common my struggles with my family were, which made me even more determined to write a book for trans people to know they weren't alone, and for family members of trans people to get a glimpse into what happens in the minds of their loved ones when they brush off or ignore their identities.

Many others helped shape this book, too:

To my agent, Cameron McClure: You read this book in a single weekend. You put a ton of work into it and fought for it and believed in it from the get-go. I appreciate everything you've done to get it into the hands of readers.

To my editor, William Tracy: You leveled this book up not once, but twice, with two painstakingly in-depth edits that brought its message to a height I'd never dreamed of. It's because of your expertise that I feel on-par with being "a real author."

To my dad, mom, and stepmom: It's been a rough road, but after many of those tough conversations that Joel struggled with, I feel loved and supported in my journey now. Thank you for the work you've put in. I'm more grateful than you know that you're seeing my true self now.

To my best friend, Tayler Peters: You've been my strongest supporter and have listened to every word I've written, whether it's a book, a blog post, or just a tweet. You've helped me figure out plot snags and life snags and everything in between. I don't know where I'd be without you.

To my kids: You're both voracious readers who leapt with excitement for this book before we ever knew whether it would see the real world. It was only after careful thought that I didn't go with my eight-year-old's suggested title of "I Have A Robot In My Head And Now I'm Cuckoo Bananas."

To my copy editor, Heather Tracy: Thanks for your close attention, and for being a fan and supporter since my very first book.

To the designers at MoorBooks: Holy crap, this cover is amazing. It brings in the post-tech angle, the human angle, the transgender angle, the music and punk angle, and is more than I'd ever hoped for when I wrote this. Thanks for working with my suggestions to create a true work of art!

To my Transpatial Tavern drinking buddies: You've been virtual support, real-life retreat friends, and badly needed confidantes. I'm lucky to have you.

And lastly, thanks to the Sanfoundry free educating and learning platform, where I got the questions and answers for Joel's job application and interview.

ABOUT THE AUTHOR

Reese Hogan is a transmasc science fiction author whose short fiction has been published in *The Decameron Project*, *A Coup of Owls*, and on the *Tales to Terrify* podcast, as well as in two anthologies. *My Heart Is Human* is his fourth novel. In addition to writing, Reese enjoys singing in the local gay men's chorus and running. He lives with his two children in New Mexico.

Find him at http://www.reesehogan.com/

Please take a moment to review this book at your favorite retailer's website, Goodreads, or simply tell your friends!